Choose your Lane to love!

Readers love *Fish Out of Water* by AMY LANE

"...*Fish Out of Water* is a bit of a different turn for author Amy Lane, but one that I really enjoyed."

—Joyfully Jay

"*Fish Out of Water* delivers an intense plot as well as a sizzling relationship between Ellery and Jackson."

—Gay Book Reviews

"...I will promise you this, you WILL be left with one hell of a book hangover."

—Rainbow Gold Book Reviews

"*Fish Out of Water*... really captured my attention and kept it. This book is gritty and urban. It's suspenseful and I found myself gasping more than a few times."

—Diverse Reader

By Amy Lane

Behind the Curtain
Beneath the Stain
Bewitched by Bella's Brother
Bolt-hole
Bonfires
Christmas with Danny Fit
Clear Water
Do-over
Food for Thought
Gambling Men
Going Up
Grand Adventures (Dreamspinner Anthology)
Hammer & Air
If I Must
Immortal
It's Not Shakespeare
Left on St. Truth-be-Well
The Locker Room
Mourning Heaven
Phonebook
Puppy, Car, and Snow
Racing for the Sun
Raising the Stakes
Shiny!
Shirt
Sidecar
A Solid Core of Alpha
Tales of the Curious Cookbook (Multiple Author Anthology)
Three Fates (Multiple Author Anthology)
Truth in the Dark
Turkey in the Snow
Under the Rushes
Wishing on a Blue Star (Dreamspinner Anthology)

CANDY MAN
Candy Man • Bitter Taffy
Lollipop • Tart and Sweet

DREAMSPUN DESIRES
THE MANNIES
#25 – The Virgin Manny
#37 – Manny Get Your Guy

FISH OUT OF WATER
Fish Out of Water • Red Fish, Dead Fish

KEEPING PROMISE ROCK
Keeping Promise Rock
Making Promises
Living Promises • Forever Promised

JOHNNIES
Chase in Shadow • Dex in Blue
Ethan in Gold • Black John
Super Sock Man

GRANBY KNITTING
The Winter Courtship Rituals of Fur-Bearing Critters
How to Raise an Honest Rabbit
Knitter in His Natural Habitat
Blackbird Knitting in a Bunny's Lair

TALKER
Talker • Talker's Redemption
Talker's Graduation

WINTER BALL
Winter Ball • Summer Lessons

ANTHOLOGIES
The Granby Knitting Menagerie
The Talker Collection

Published by Harmony Ink Press
BITTER MOON SAGA
Triane's Son Rising
Triane's Son Learning
Triane's Son Fighting
Triane's Son Reigning

Published by Dreamspinner Press
www.dreamspinnerpress.com

RED FISH, DEAD FISH

Amy Lane

Published by
DREAMSPINNER PRESS

5032 Capital Circle SW, Suite 2, PMB# 279, Tallahassee, FL 32305-7886 USA
www.dreamspinnerpress.com

ISBN: 978-1-63533-763-1
Digital ISBN: 978-1-63533-764-8
Library of Congress Control Number: 2017904700
Published August 2017
v. 1.0

Printed in the United States of America
∞
This paper meets the requirements of
ANSI/NISO Z39.48-1992 (Permanence of Paper).

Mate, Mary, kids, Kim, Amelia, and Karen—
how is it you all are there when I need you?

Acknowledgments

KIM FIELDING and Karen Rose—thank you both so much for your knowledge and your willingness to help me refine my skills in this subgenre that I've long admired and have finally dared to write.

Prologue: Belly Up

"ELLERY, HAND me my phone," Jackson mumbled. "It's ringing."

"You're not back at work yet," Ellery slurred. "You have two more weeks."

Jackson rolled over on top of him and then yelped as he reached unwisely for the phone Ellery had strategically put on his own end table. For a moment, Ellery was covered with tense, warm man, and then he shoved Jackson off.

"I'll get it!" he snapped, officially awake. "Jesus, what in the—"

"It's Mack's ringtone," Jackson defended. "I told him what we were looking for."

Ellery tried not to roll his eyes. Mack. This was the same Mack who had helped Jackson out when Jackson had wrecked the car *unofficially* helping Ellery with an investigation.

At the time, Ellery had been so happy to get Jackson back in one bruised piece—and on a plane to somewhere he could rest without incident—that he hadn't questioned this Mack's existence. Once he found out that Mack Flanders had been Jackson's bedmate a few years ago, he'd been irritated but unsurprised.

Now that Mack was calling them in the whore of dawn's sweaty crack, Ellery wanted to kick him in the balls.

Except….

"Cottage Park, near the outbuilding. Yeah, I got it. There's a way to get in there, right? I'm not climbing the fucking fence. Of course there's cops and crime scene tape. That's not what I'm asking." The voice on the other end spoke patiently, and some of Jackson's defensiveness seeped away. "Okay. Thanks, Mack. Owe you another one. No, sorry—told you. Not paying favors that way anymore, but it's nice of you to ask."

"God in heaven," Ellery muttered.

"Yeah, okay. I'll be there in half an hour."

"We'll be there." Ellery rolled out of bed and headed for the shower. Thirty seconds to run some soap under his pits and pack a suit for court later that day. He could do it.

"Crap," he could hear Jackson say as he closed the shower door. "*We'll* be there. Thanks."

Five seconds later, Jackson stepped into the shower with him and grabbed his own shower gel from the corner of the tub. They'd had some nice times in there together—particularly when Jackson was still healing from his gunshot wound and his shattered scapula and needed Ellery's help.

They'd had a few after that too, but not today.

"Body?" Ellery asked, not really needing confirmation.

"Yeah." Jackson scrubbed his pits with care but not vigor—moving was still painful and probably would be for a little while. He'd gotten out of the hospital less than six weeks earlier. By all rights he should still be chilling in the fall sunshine, maybe swimming in the pool at the gym—but not Jackson.

Ellery had needed to haul him to San Diego to give himself time to recover.

It was even more infuriating that he was right today. There really was no time to rest.

"Our kind?"

Jackson shook the water from his dark blond hair and squinted at Ellery through eyes as green as bottle glass. "We have a kind of dead body? Most couples just go with favorite song."

Ellery soaped his hair efficiently. "You know what I mean."

Jackson grabbed the shampoo. "Yeah."

Jackson, the private investigator at Ellery's defense firm, had gotten shot helping Ellery bring down a ring of corrupt cops. They'd put the ringleaders in prison—but one of the underlings had gotten away.

Turned out he was the one the police should have been chasing all along.

"Young," Jackson said, ticking off items on the list. "This one's Hispanic. Male, but slender. Recent involvement with drugs. Maybe a week of turning tricks."

"Dirty pretty," Ellery confirmed grimly. They had been Scott Bridger's words, actually, one of the men they'd brought down, to describe the kind of person who had disappeared on his partner's watch. Gender hadn't mattered, nor race. Just a little bit of street dirt and some physical beauty.

Tim Owens liked to take the "dirty pretty" ones and make them not so pretty anymore.

"Mack says there's something new about this one," Jackson said, stepping in front of him to rinse his hair.

Ellery wasn't sure why he did it, except it was not yet four in the morning and he and Jackson were naked together, and that wasn't something he'd learned to take for granted yet.

He wrapped his arms around Jackson's shoulders and kissed his neck, softly, gently, with just enough tongue and teeth to make Jackson regret they weren't making love this morning but going to work instead.

Jackson tensed for a moment, probably caught off guard, but then he relaxed into Ellery's arms and leaned his head back.

"What?" he asked suspiciously.

Well, Ellery had been known to be an autocratic bastard—that was probably warranted.

"Just…." Ellery couldn't find words. Or he could find words, but neither of them had said the words yet, and you just didn't spring those words on a guy whose entire life had been an act of insufficient self-protection.

With a sinuous movement, Jackson turned his head and caught Ellery's mouth, something he couldn't have done a month ago, something that felt huge and necessary now.

"Don't worry about me, Counselor," Jackson said cheekily, pulling away. "But the cuddle was downright friendly."

Well, sure. Friendly. Just two friendly lovers getting out of bed extra early to go catch a serial killer. Nothing strange about that *at all.*

"Just be careful," Ellery said, trying not to sound bitchy or officious and failing. "He's got your cell phone. You know that, right?"

"Well, he had it for a couple of hours before it got deactivated," Jackson said. "And yeah—fuck me for owning an Android with the shitty security. Thank you so much for the iPhone, Ellery. Now I am safe from serial killers everywhere."

The snark in his voice was the only thing that kept Ellery from conking him over the head and tying him to the bed in a completely nonkinky way.

MACK WAS still at the scene when they got there—but not for long. Ellery had just enough time to register that the state trooper was older than he'd thought—maybe in his forties—and not particularly handsome. He stood around five six, with a small face that showed signs of childhood malnourishment and acne. He sat comfortably in his skin now, his thinning blond hair cut close to his head and his smile warm and friendly as he shook hands with Jackson.

Ellery abruptly forgave him for sleeping with Jackson in the past—he wasn't a cover model, he was a human being, and that seemed to be the kind of person Jackson was the most attracted to.

Which gave Ellery hope for himself, because it meant Jackson saw something in him besides the shark he'd honed for so long.

Mack greeted Ellery pleasantly, ushered them both into the crime scene, and left unobtrusively. Jackson gave him a salute as he got into his vehicle—he'd put himself out for them. This wasn't even his beat. Jackson would—Ellery had no doubt he would—find a way to return the favor.

Twenty minutes later, they stood in the corner of Cottage Park under the emerging sunshine. Jackson wore faded jeans and a hooded sweatshirt, because by October, mornings were getting a little chilly.

Ellery wore slacks and a polo shirt and was grateful.

This little corner of the park had a stream that usually passed through. But the body had been thrown into a bottleneck of the stream, and the entire corner was a swampy, bloody, rotting mess.

Walking into court with that ick on his pant cuffs wasn't going to win any cases.

Which is what Ellery kept thinking to avoid the thought of *the body in the water.*

"The knife work is new," Jackson said, voice cool. Ellery knew he wasn't unaffected—in a moment of candor, he'd once confessed to bringing Tic Tacs to the morgue for a reason. But he managed to sound composed and ordinary in the face of….

Oh my God.

Ellery fisted his hands in his pockets and tried not to throw up.

"He knew what he was doing," Jackson said softly, standing well back from the frantic CSIs who were working the case. "He wanted to play with him."

Ellery actually felt Jackson's shudder through their touching shoulders.

"Was he raped?" Jackson asked the tech. The CSI officer wearing a white hazmat bunny suit was a familiar face these days—she'd caught a few other cases Jackson and Ellery had investigated. Now she crouched in a bloody puddle, taking samples from the clothes, from the water, from the surrounding area. She was African American, with a bold nose and a strong jaw—strikingly beautiful with just a trace of girlish flirt in her eyes when she smiled at Jackson.

Awesome. Another conquest.

But there was no flirting at all now when she looked up and nodded soberly.

"He's got DNA all over him," she said, a soft Southern accent in her voice. "We've seen this pattern before, but not the knife work."

No, all of Owens's other victims had been beaten and assaulted. This one had been beaten as well, his face almost unrecognizable. His pants had been cut cleanly down the back, and the blood leaking from that quarter of the body was unmistakable. So were the scores along the back, like someone had been bored and doodling with a knifepoint in flesh, probably while, *oh my God*, in the act.

"Somebody got bored during sex," Jackson said grimly. "What a douche."

Ellery nodded. Douchebag. It was a funny word. And so less frightening than monster.

"I know we have other bodies like this," Jackson said lowly to the tech—Roberta, if Ellery remembered aright. "Have you matched the DNA?"

"We've matched it to itself," she confirmed. "Since you first asked me to keep track of these, this is our third body. They've all got the same DNA on them—we just don't have anyone to match it with in the computers."

Jackson frowned. "Did you take samples when you searched Owens's place?"

She gave him a classic *What kind of miracle worker do you think I am?* look. "We didn't take samples from Owens's apartment—we didn't even know he was a suspect here."

Jackson let out a little growl. "He's still not," he admitted. "But goddammit, he should be."

Roberta nodded, and Ellery's respect for her grew when her hand hovered for a moment over the back of the neck. The gesture was human and curiously tender. She saw a person here, not a piece of meat. She would do her job—but her job was, ultimately, to get justice for the human being who'd been discarded like so much garbage.

Whether the police recognized it or not, that was Jackson and Ellery's job as well.

"Rivers? Jesus—can't Ellery keep you in a crate or something?"

Jackson growled, and Ellery rolled his eyes. "Down, boy," he muttered. "He's just baiting you."

Golden-haired, blue-eyed, with a cheerleader nose and a superhero jaw, Sean Kryzynski was aiming to be a very young detective, and—at one point—had been aiming to be in Ellery's bed. Given that Ellery hadn't had that many offers, he'd been flattered.

Given that Kryzynski had propositioned Ellery when Jackson was being hauled away on a gurney, he was pretty much over Kryzynski before he even opened his mouth. But Kryzynski didn't see it that way, and judging by Jackson's growls, reformed tomcats didn't like to share.

Kryzynski popped his gum and winked. "Don't worry, Rivers. I can't take what's not on the table—whoa!"

Ellery had to stand in front of him and shove him backward.

"There is a *boy* here at our feet!" Jackson snarled. "And yeah, he was a little bit dirty—but our perp takes the ones on the cusp, see? The ones who could be saved. So this was a kid, and he needs us now when we weren't there for him when he was alive." The fight went out of him, and he glowered over Ellery's shoulder. "Try being an actual cop, a good guy! Not the guy looking to get out of his blues."

Ellery caught his breath. A vulnerable expression crossed Jackson's face. He'd said more than he meant to, shown more than he'd planned.

"We need to do something," Jackson said, looking at Ellery with pleading in his eyes. "Why is nobody listening to us?"

After Jackson had been shot—and Bridger and Chisolm, the guys behind the shooting, had been arrested—law enforcement had declared their jobs done. They conveniently overlooked the fact that Tim Owens had probably been the triggerman behind Jackson's shooting and clapped themselves on the back.

"Because every case he had, every person he arrested—ever—will be tainted," Ellery said patiently. They knew this. Neither of them was naïve.

Jackson shook his head. "I think it's time to tell the boss," he said after a moment.

Ellery regarded him with surprise. "Contact an authority figure? Jackson, are you well?"

"Ha-ha." With an irritated one-armed shrug, Jackson broke away from him and prowled around the cops, looking for things forensics had possibly missed while staying out of their way.

Kryzynski walked up to Ellery looking surprisingly contrite. "Look, Ellery… I hope you know we take murder seriously here. It's just…." He shrugged in apology. "Street people. They die a lot, you know?"

Ellery turned a flat-eyed gaze toward him. "Really fucking sensitive. Do they always die covered in the same guy's ejaculate?"

Kryzynski recoiled. "They do what?"

"Maybe *you* should talk to your forensics crew. Roberta there has some shit to teach you." Ellery took a step toward where Jackson wandered, wanting to do something—touch his hand, reassure him, *something.* But Jackson's past was… complicated.

Ellery tried his best to keep things simple. Ellery, friend. The rest of the world? Could fuck off.

That didn't work when Jackson felt pressured or closed in. Dogs did well in crates, but cats, not so much. If Jackson didn't have space, Ellery firmly believed he'd scratch at the walls that confined him until he bled to death.

Kryzynski put a hand on his arm. "I'll talk to my lieutenant," he said softly. "If the same person did all this, we should be investigating. He's right—this is awful."

Ellery nodded. "It is. And it's escalating. If we're right, Owens did this once in a while under Bridger—maybe every three, every four months. Since Bridger went away, this is the third body in two months."

"Were they all found in Arden-Arcade?" Kryzynski asked. "Because that's sort of hard to hide."

The Arden-Arcade area was actually pretty nice—lots of parks with dark corners to hide bodies, but it wasn't exactly a hotspot for street people. A little farther north, to Watt Avenue, and the hunting grounds were richer. Follow Watt down past the freeway and it was beating up stoned fish in a broken concrete barrel.

Reluctantly Ellery shared some information. "Ask Roberta, but we're pretty sure this is the secondary crime scene—a body dump. He and Bridger used to work District Three—midtown. We've been looking over old cases. Six of them are looking like our guy, and they've been found on both sides of the freeway, mostly in places like this." Weekends, after work, they'd looked through morgue records and police reports practically since Jackson had gotten out of the hospital.

Today had been a breakthrough, because today they'd hit a forensics officer who knew Jackson and would share. And also because today, with Kryzynski, they'd managed to catch somebody's attention.

"Got your own murder board?" Kryzynski cracked.

Ellery gazed at him, the same level look his mother used to employ to get him to admit he hadn't done his homework.

"Uh, yeah." Golden Boy looked away uncomfortably. "Why should you have a murder board when we should be doing our job? Hear you."

"I am so very glad," Ellery said, smiling. From the corner of his eye, he saw Jackson walking to the playground that stood at the highest point in the park. The playground itself used recycled tires as a thick safety mat under the toys, but it was surrounded by lush grass and soft earth. Jackson was heading for the swings. "Now if you will excuse me—"

"Wait!" Kryzynski looked embarrassed when Ellery turned back around. "How… uh, I mean, how is he? You know when that sort of hospital time happens on the job you have to talk to six shrinks and a shaman to get back on duty. How's he doing?"

How was he? "He's fine." Sure he was. "Wiseass is still a wiseass. He's like a cat—nine lives."

Kryzynski grunted. "That bad?"

Ellery closed his eyes, thinking about the car Jackson had wrecked overdoing it too soon and the way he worked, daily, to prove that he could *too* pull his own weight in the firm, in Ellery's house.

Ellery's life.

He kept talking about moving to the duplex when it was finished in two months.

Ellery figured he had until mid-December to convince Jackson that there were no shadows in the corners of Ellery's house, no scary monsters, no hidden emotional traps.

"If I liked easy, I would have done corporate law," Ellery said, hoping his mother never heard him.

His mother the corporate lawyer could skin a fish as it swam and eat it raw as she smiled at you. People who thought cast-iron balls were tough had never met Taylor Cramer when she had her hair coifed and her no-nonsense low-heeled pumps ready to roll.

But Kryzynski bled true-blue. As far as he was concerned, criminal law was the only kind that counted.

"Well, you know, if shit gets too hard…." He smiled prettily.

"I'd like a copy of your report on my desk." Personal time over. "And with your permission, we'll ask Roberta for her report as well."

Kryzynski backpedaled, looking confused. "Who in the hell is Roberta?"

"Your forensics officer," Ellery said smugly. "You really should work on your people skills."

And with that he turned to get Jackson, who had gone from rocking moodily on the swing to working up quite a head of steam.

Jackson saw him coming and hollered, "Stay there!"

And then, when the swing was at its highest arc, he jumped.

Ellery's heart caught in his throat as he watched Jackson arch his body impossibly, like one of those kids at the skateboard parks who did stupid shit for kicks. He flew high, then, *oh my God*, tucked his knees to his chest and flipped.

He extended his arms and would probably have done a creditable roll in the thick grass and spongy ground of the field, but his shoulder gave, collapsed, and he went tumbling down the hill.

Ellery had to dodge out of his way or end up in the free-for-all sprawl Jackson was heading for—and unlike Jackson, if Ellery did that sort of thing, he'd end up with broken bones or worse.

Jackson ended his roll, coming to a stop on his back, arms flung out on either side. He had his eyes closed, like he was trying to figure out if he was in pain or not, and if so, how bad.

Ellery could have answered him.

Jackson Rivers had been in pain since the day he was born.

But he'd go to his grave saying he didn't feel a thing.

"You going to live?" Ellery asked, keeping the panic out of his voice.

"Did you see that, ma? I went *high*!"

"How's your shoulder, asshole? Do we need the brace again?"

Jackson took a deep breath and winced. "Goddammit."

"Yeah. Here—let me give you a hand up. I've got the spare in the back."

"Fine."

Jackson took his offered hand but stopped short as Ellery pulled him up. They stood facing each other for a moment, Jackson's expression hauntingly naked.

"Talk to who you have to," he said soberly. "The DA, our bosses. This isn't a pride thing. These kids…." He looked away, probably remembering he'd been two good friends and their mom away from ending up just like these street kids, these young, troubled, beautiful kids who would never live to see if they could turn themselves around.

"Yeah," Ellery said softly. "Yeah." He leaned forward then, just barely grazing Jackson's temple with his lips.

Jackson didn't flinch, didn't recoil or pull away. He just gave Ellery a flirty wink and a grin, like that was his payment for affection.

Ellery let him get away with that, and together they trudged to the car.

TWO HOURS later, Ellery briefed Carlyle Langdon, second chair of Pfeist, Langdon, Harrelson & Cooper, about the work he and Jackson had been doing.

"I thought Rivers was on medical leave?" Langdon said, looking sleek and regal, a silver fox in an amazing gray pinstripe.

"We've been working the case together, sir. To keep him from going stir-crazy."

Would Langdon care about Ellery and Jackson? Probably not. Did Ellery want the whole world knowing his personal life? Definitely, absolutely not.

Langdon smiled sunnily. "You're a good friend, and I'll sound out the DA's office to see if I can get a nibble. But you know how this goes, Ellery…."

Ellery gave a sigh. "Leave the investigation to the pros," he muttered. Except the pros were usually drowning in legit bad guys, or bureaucracy, or sometimes their own incompetence and/or corruption.

And sometimes people just needed an outside eye to show them where the monsters were.

Ellery and Jackson had done their bit to get rid of the corruption, and neither of them suffered incompetence well. It was the other stuff they were having problems with, and the horrible, godawful fact of the matter was…

More people were going to have to die before somebody besides Kryzynski looked up and saw the monster.

An hour later, after Ellery's *own* frustrating call with Arizona Brooks, his contact with the ADA's office, he wanted to throw the whole of law enforcement in the hole to get eaten.

"Arizona, we've got an MO, we've got a profile—if you'll give us a profiler—and we've got DNA—"

"But we don't have it matching a suspect," Arizona said patiently. Arizona—buzz-cut, gruff Arizona, who was the only woman Ellery had ever seen wear a white power suit to court and make it work—was never this patient.

"Are you getting pressure to ignore this?" he asked point-blank.

"Like you wouldn't believe," she said grimly. "Everybody here thinks the Bridger/Chisolm thing is all gone bye-bye now, and the triggerman on your boy's house just doesn't matter."

Ellery growled. "I will inundate your office," he threatened. "I will send you every scrap of evidence we have, twice, in triplicate, until somebody has to claw their way up from the bottom of the paperwork graveyard just to call the cops and authorize the investigation."

She sighed. "That was a beautiful threat, Ellery. But until you have the name of the perp, we're just going to buy some flippers and a snorkel and keep swimming."

"We *have* the name of the perp!" Ellery snarled. Oh dear Lord, he was becoming feral, like Jackson. Awesome. "Tim Owens!"

"Well, prove it," she said patiently.

Patiently.

"I *will* keep you apprized," he told her spitefully. "And someday, someday soon, when he kills again, or maybe twice, we'll find a break in the case. And then we won't go to the fucking DA or the police department or the sheriff. We'll go to the *press*, and you can have the whole almighty world asking you why you didn't do a damned thing."

"And we'll deal with that when it happens."

She sounded smug, smug and superior, like ignoring dead kids put her on the moral high ground.

Ellery hung up on her.

Jackson, tapping desultorily at the small table in the corner of Ellery's plain beige-carpeted office, jerked upright.

He'd probably been that close to dozing.

"How'd that go?" He yawned and stretched carefully.

"Like ass. How's the shoulder?"

Jackson gave a one-armed shrug. "You know—the wound that wouldn't go away."

"Well, it needs to. You're still not okayed for work, and it's time for you to go home."

Jackson held up his hands in front of him, puppy-dog style. "Oh, come on, Ellery. Please let me stay!"

Ellery shook his head, feeling like his mother. "Home. Nap. Run. You heard the doctor."

"Three miles," Jackson said, his voice assuming a terrifying determination. "And a full range of motion."

"Amen," Ellery said brusquely. But Jackson looked so dispirited. "We'll keep looking," he said. "Don't worry, Jackson. You know, this summer, having that all fall out in two days, that was an anomaly—"

"Like us?" Jackson asked, so seriously Ellery's chest ached.

"We would have happened," he promised. He had to believe it. "The circumstances—they helped. But we would have happened. This other thing? This is just going to have to rely on the resources we have. They're not great. But we're not giving up."

Jackson managed a bleak smile. Then he straightened his back and raised his eyebrows. "So, Counselor, since you don't have to be back until court at two, how about a quickie when you take me home?"

Pure bravado, propositioned because Jackson didn't want to be left alone with his own thoughts.

Well, Ellery would take what he could get.

Fish on the Run

Six weeks later

NOW THAT Jackson was back at work, Ellery *finally* set up Jackson's new phone to charge on the expensive mahogany end table next to the bed.

He was mostly healed—hadn't worn the brace in four weeks after his foolhardy attempt at gymnastics in the playground. Getting the phone was a simple matter of rolling just enough to grab it off the table, which he tried not to take for granted. The bed was pretty big, but he clung to the edges even in sleep, in spite of Ellery's frequent attempts to pull him to the middle bodily, so it wasn't even a *big* roll. More like a yawn and a stretch and a reach.

"Mike?" Jackson's neighbor, the guy who rented the other half of Jackson's duplex, was also his friend. As such, calling at four in the morning was not something he did often.

"Jackson, man, I didn't want to bother you, but those assholes are here again."

Jackson sat up in bed abruptly, not even bothering to cringe at the pain in his shoulder. "You're sure?"

"I think they're asleep right now, but the dog's been barking, and the outside trash can is full of chemicals and shit. Industrial drain cleaner, cold medicine—someone's going to start baking any second, and it's not cookies."

Oh hell. "Call the cops," Jackson muttered, keeping his voice low enough that he didn't disturb Ellery. "I'll be there in ten minutes."

"You should tell him about this," Mike cautioned, because dammit, the guy knew what Jackson was doing, and Ellery wouldn't like it.

"My place, my problem."

The place had gotten shot up when Jackson did. It *still* was not up to code—and shouldn't have been livable, even a little. But for the last week these yo-yos had been trying to move in and use the place as a little nest of illegal chemical entrepreneurship, through a combination of squatters' rights and avoiding Mike like the plague.

Mike didn't have a problem waving his .45 around or walking his German shepherd, Albert, back and forth across the driveway for an hour every night, so he did have some fear factors keeping them at bay.

It didn't hurt that his girlfriend, Jade—Jackson's ex and his forever friend—was afraid of no man and only one woman. The first time she'd seen these guys trying to take over the vacant half of the duplex, she'd chased them off with a baseball bat.

The last time, she'd clotheslined one of them as he'd ridden past the house on his bicycle, taunting her about catching up. According to Mike, the guy had stayed down for a good ten minutes, gagging and twitching, before he'd pulled in enough air to get back up and wobble away.

The fact that they were back indicated two things—one was a high degree of stupidity.

The other was an active agenda they refused to give up.

"Jackson," Mike growled. "The police alone are going to try to kill you."

Jackson hung up.

"Who wazzat?" Ellery mumbled, reaching behind him for Jackson's hip. Ellery spent most of the night snuggled up against Jackson's back, waiting, it seemed, for the nightmares to jerk him out of a sound sleep.

Just having him there, breath echoing in the foreign darkness of his vast and stately hardwood-appointed room, was enough, sometimes, to keep Jackson grounded. He would wake up with a gasp and feel it, the warmth at his back, the random touch of an ankle or a hairy shin, sometimes even that absent hand on his hip, and the dream would tatter like a cobweb and float into the night.

Sometimes Jackson bolted upright, screaming, and Ellery would have to tackle him bodily, shoving him against the mattress and holding him while he came apart. The dreams were a grim reminder that you didn't live the life Jackson had without some scars.

The scars on Jackson's body, his torso, his back, his chest, his shoulder, stood like twisted markers to the real horror show in Jackson's head, and the monsters did so love to come out and play at night.

Jackson didn't trust anyone who promised to help keep the monsters back.

"My alarm," Jackson whispered roughly. "I'm going running."

He found his running shorts and sweats in the clean pile of his clothes on top of Ellery's elegant mahogany dresser and pulled them on, hoping Ellery wasn't, right then, squinting at his clock.

"It's four in the morning?" Ellery sat up in bed, and Jackson had a chance to sneak a wistful little peek at the only person to actually keep him for longer than three months since he'd gone steady with Jade back in high school.

Ellery was worth looking at, his brown eyes squinting blearily in the chilly dark, his hair—usually gelled back—falling softly across his forehead. He had a surprisingly wide chest with enough dark, silky hair in the middle for Jackson to feel like he was groping a man and not a Ken doll when they were (shudder) making love. There was something… something about him. Something strong and compelling. He had a long bony jaw and a sharp nose. There must have been some magic to those features, because as far as Jackson could remember, he was the only lover *ever* to use the specific term "making love," as opposed to basic, human animal sex.

Jackson resented him for it most days, right up until Ellery touched him as they were sleeping or kissed his cheek when he got home or even petted Jackson's beatass tomcat, Billy Bob. That quickly the resentment faded, melted away, became vapor—often steam.

But Jackson couldn't lose his edge—not this morning. "I'm going the extra mile," he said dryly. Then, with reluctant steps, he neared the edge of the bed and gave Ellery an awkward kiss on the temple. "Go to sleep," he ordered. "I'll be back in a couple of hours. We can go in to work together."

"Sure," Ellery mumbled. "I'll drop you at home during lunch."

He turned on his side and cuddled deep into the generous comforter, while Billy Bob—the tattered, three-legged, snaggletoothed, blue-eyed Siamese traitor—curled up in the hollow behind his neck. Ellery didn't hear Jackson's huff of exasperation, but then he didn't need to.

Jackson was ready for full-time duty—he *was.* The running wasn't bullshit. He was up to three miles a day and would be back to five to ten miles in the next month or so. But no, Pfeist, Langdon, Harrelson & Cooper was taking the *doctor's* suggestion that Jackson be kept on part-time duty for another four weeks.

If Jackson hadn't taken it upon himself to protect his damned shot-to-shit house, he might have killed the best domestic living situation he'd ever had out of sheer frustration.

He put on his running shoes and an old SCPD sweatshirt, grabbed his phone and his keys, and was—

"Whaddya need yer keys for?" Ellery slurred.

"Driving to the river to run the trail," Jackson lied and slid out of the bedroom. He'd gotten as far as the front door when his phone rang again.

By the time he'd finished piloting his brand-new—and comfortably crumpled—Honda SUV through the darkened streets of the American River Drive suburb and hung a left on J Street, his breathing had returned to normal.

By the time he'd turned right on Elvas and followed the curve of the river around its gentle dogleg, his mind was focused exclusively on the thing he was planning to do when he got to his duplex and started kicking ass.

He passed the house, swung a uie, and parked the car, going the wrong way, in front. It was easy to spot the pink-and-black premium bicycle parked on the front porch—a sign for an open druggie mart if he'd ever seen one. Sure enough, trudging up the sidewalk of the shabby but not dangerous neighborhood was an individual out of a profiler's textbook.

Sand-brown hair matted around his filthy face, his clothes were tattered, and his tennis shoes were brand-new and cheap. He turned up Jackson's driveway and looked furtively left and right, letting out a little start when he saw Jackson stalking up the clean concrete.

"Not here," Jackson growled. "Cops are on their way."

The addict slunk toward the road, looking at the bicycle wistfully, but Jackson glared, scaring him away for the moment.

Jackson's fury flooded back, and if it hadn't been his own damned house—and a new damned door—he would have kicked that fucker in. His house. *His house.* He'd bought this place, claimed it as his own. It hadn't been a palace, not like Ellery's place, but it had been homey. He'd had pictures on the walls and furniture that didn't break you, and his goddamned cat. The salvageable stuff was at Ellery's now, but there wasn't much of it.

All Jackson had was the living space, currently being refurbished and spackled and painted, presumably so Jackson could go back and live there with the newly laid hardwood floors and the bright white-painted walls. Wasn't much—the thought of being alone there ran razor wire from his groin to his throat—but it was his, dammit.

He wasn't letting anyone crap it up, especially when it wasn't even finished yet.

He got to the top of the porch and squatted by the bicycle, then used the screwdriver on his key chain to pop the chain off the gear and render their one getaway vehicle useless.

Then he put his hand on the doorknob, an ugly, angry satisfaction welling up in his gut as he turned it.

"Heya, fellas—gonna try to sell me some smack?"

He'd have to classify their response as a no.

Cold Fish

FOUR THIRTY in the morning was a positively filthy hour to get up. Ellery's drive, shivery in the November cold, didn't improve his opinion of mornings any. He managed to hit every light between American River Drive and Elvas, and by the time he pulled up to Jackson's duplex, his fury was enough to keep him warm.

Running.

Jackson said he was going fucking running.

Oh yeah, up at fuck-you a.m., Ellery, going running, back soon.

Ass. *Hole.*

Ellery welcomed the anger, using it to shore up his bones and his spine for the shitfest the next few weeks were going to be. He wondered if he could place bets on how many times Jackson was going to try to break up with him before they were done.

He'd put down money on the breakup not happening, but that didn't mean the game wasn't going to be an absolute *joy.*

He pulled past Jackson's CR-V, whipped his Lexus around in a circle, parked nose to nose with the damned wrong-way Honda, and leaped out of the car in time to see a kid—bronze skin tinged gray, glossy hair pulled back in a blue-black ponytail down to his waist—run out Jackson's front door and pick up the bike on the porch. He hopped on the bike at the bottom, stood on the pedal, and flipped over.

Ellery heard the crack of his head on the concrete like an overripe watermelon, and recoiled, nauseated. At that moment, a midsized, white-haired redneck with the spryness of a lemur jumped out from behind the black pickup truck in the driveway and held a gun in ponytail-kid's face.

"Freeze, asshole. Don't fucking move."

The kid groaned and rolled to his side, vomiting on the concrete in spite of Mike's warning, and Ellery tried not to hold his hand to his chest like an old-time movie heroine.

"Jesus, Mike, what in the—"

Mike didn't move his eyes from the kid/bicycle combo on the ground. "This little asshole's been trying to cook drugs for the past week.

Whenever they can sneak in past me and Jade, they set up shop. Gotcha now, punk. Fuckin' cops are on the way, aren't they. Uh-huh, you can go bleed your brain *in prison*, asshole!"

The kid retched again and twitched, and Mike gave a positively evil laugh.

"Little fucker—did you see him, Ellery? Flipping the bike like that? Fucking *beautiful.* I wish I had it on camera."

A giant crash echoed through the doorway of the house, followed by a roar of outrage that could have only come from Jackson. Sirens began to wail in the background. Oh Jesus, this poor delinquent barfing on the driveway was the one that got away.

Another crash, another roar, and what sounded like a yelp of genuine pain.

Mike and Ellery exchanged glances. "You'd better get in—"

"I need to get in there."

He saw the spin of the cherry lights in his peripheral vision as he opened the door, but by the time those guys got out of their cars, it could be too late.

He stood in the doorway, squinting in the sparse light. A body flew by him from his left—the kitchen—bounced off the wall, and then stumbled backward into the guest room. Ellery pressed himself against the wall as Jackson charged past, hitting his bad shoulder on the doorframe and emitting an enraged bellow as he threw himself bodily into the guest room in pursuit.

Ellery stepped into the house and left the door open, then peered into the guest room in time to see Jackson slam his opponent into the built-in shelf along the back wall. The victim, er, housebreaker scrambled to stand, and Jackson caught him by the shirt and slammed him into the shelf again, heedless of the crack of shattered wood.

"Please!" the guy begged, and Jackson wound his good arm back and clocked him in the face. His head slammed against the wall, his eyes fluttered shut, and he crumpled to the ground.

"Please?" Jackson kicked him in the ribs, and he curled instinctively onto his side. "You're gonna beg me, motherfucker?" *Kick.* "You wanna beg a guy, maybe *next* time drop the goddamned knife!"

And as he was pulling his leg back to kick again, he twisted his torso, and Ellery saw the four-inch switchblade embedded in his recently healed shoulder.

"Goddammit, Jackson!"

Jackson checked the swing and hopped on one foot. "Ellery?" He blinked his thick-lashed brilliant green eyes once, slowly, and then—in an expression Ellery was beginning to associate with Jackson being in extreme pain—several times in succession, his full mouth parted slightly.

"Yes?" Ellery crossed his arms, holding on to his rage and his fear in equal measures.

"What are you doing here?"

"Toe-Tag called me. He wanted me to remind you to bring some form of identification when you go in to the morgue today."

Jackson's jaw went slack, as if he was trying to place this information in the world as he knew it. "The morgue?" he asked carefully, his concentration fully on the groaning man on the ground. The guy's blond hair hung in his face, lank and greasy. Like his friend in the driveway, he wore an oversized black jersey with big white numbers. This kid's said fourteen, and Ellery would bet the other kid's did too. Nothing like a uniform—and co-opting a gang from LA.

"Yeah, Jackson. I know about the morgue. And when I found out about the morgue, I called and you didn't answer. And then you want to know who called me?"

Jackson staggered back like it had just occurred to him that the knife stuck in his shoulder hurt like hell. "Mike?"

"You wish. Sean Kryzynski. The cop who's about to come storming in. He said that he'd gotten a call that there were squatters trying to come live at your address and wanted to know if it was true before he brought people over."

"He didn't take Mike's word for it?" Jackson scowled—and Ellery didn't blame him.

"He didn't take Jade's. Apparently she called while Mike camped out there with his gun and waited for them to come out again."

Jackson shoved himself back against the adjacent wall, his knees buckling.

"What assholes," he muttered. "Jade's a reliable witness."

"And some of the cops are still racists with long memories." Jade had screamed bloody murder at a bunch of cops in this very house—while Jackson had been triaged in the hallway. The cops had deserved it; Jade hadn't. "It's a good thing Kryzynski's one of the good guys—"

"Who wants in your pants."

Oh God—he was going to sit down. "Here," Ellery said, coming to support him. "You don't want to do that, Jackson. Look."

Jackson squinted in the barely graying light and noticed the small plastic objects with the potentially lethal metal ends. They had apparently all been thrown in one corner of the guest room and scattered by the recent violence.

"Needles," he said dully. Then he stood up, shook Ellery off and stalked to the guy moaning on the carpet, then leveled another kick to his ribs. "You got *needles* all over my house, motherfucker?"

The guy sobbed. "Stop… stop… please. We won't make it through jail. We'll get shanked. Just let me piss blood and die."

"*Augh*!" Jackson screamed from the pit of his stomach. "You sniveling assfuckers! Do you have any idea how long it's going to take to clean this shithole up again? *Jesus fuck!*"

"Stand down, sir!"

Ellery couldn't help the icy sheet of fear that coated him at the sound of drawn weapons. Jackson simply glared over his good shoulder and raised a slow hand to the shoulder leaking blood down his elbow. "So nice of you douchebags to show up."

The young uniform standing in the door grunted and adjusted the aim of his service pistol to the guy lying on the ground.

"You couldn't leave this to the professionals, could you, Rivers?"

"The professionals got nothin' on a talented amateur." Jackson smirked, but Ellery heard it—the slur of pain and the loopiness of adrenaline and blood loss in his voice.

Young Officer Kryzynski moved into the room, holstering his weapon before sinking gingerly onto one knee on a needle-free patch of carpet so he could cuff the kid on the ground, the muscles in his shoulders and back flexing as he did so.

"You guys can go make your statement while I read him his rights." Kryzynski dismissed them, keeping his attention rightly on the suspect.

"You be sure to do that." Jackson pushed off the wall he'd let bear his weight as Kryzynski moved. "And when you're processing him, make sure the courts know Ellery's representing him. He's a pro bono case at Pfeist, Langdon, Harrelson & Cooper."

Ellery grunted. "Because why?"

Jackson turned away from the mess on the floor, and Kryzynski's partner moved in past them, holstering his weapon as he went.

"Because these wahoos are working for somebody else, and while Captain America is trying to find this dick in a hole in the ground, I'd like to find out who the big fish is so his minnows can stop breaking into my house."

Ellery saw Kryzynski's outraged look at the both of them and ignored it, following Jackson into the hallway, where he paused to survey the damage.

"There's needles in the sink," he muttered under his breath. "And a big old pan of not-meth that will kill you on the floor. Baggies of heroin all over the counter, some of them burst open. I can't… I don't even want to see the rest of it." He looked up and met Ellery's eyes. "It's going to take another month to even be livable again. I can move into a hotel if you don't want me to stay."

Ellery mentally counted "one." The first time Jackson would try to break up with him.

"I want you to stay," he said, not even taking a deep breath. "I'll let you know if that changes."

Jackson nodded and looked despairingly around the recently remodeled house. "The good news is, none of the appliances had been replaced, and the air-conditioning unit is still on order. Mostly we just need a hazmat crew." He went to scrub his face with his hands and let out a whine like a kicked puppy.

"There's probably an ambulance outside, Jackson. Would you like them to take the knife out of your shoulder?" Ellery showed all his teeth, but it wasn't a smile.

Jackson eyed him warily. "That would be peachy," he admitted and then grimaced and—oh God!—yanked it out himself, staring at the blade intently, looking for something. The blood ran fresh and red, and Ellery *needed* a deep breath this time. "The wound is burning," he said frankly. "I think there was some sort of drug on it."

Ellery took another fortifying breath and wondered if it wasn't psychosomatic. Jackson had a justifiable fear of street drugs. "Well, we'll just have to get that all taken care of," he said brightly. He wrapped his arm around Jackson's waist and willed the stubborn jackass to actually give him a little bit of weight.

"You have a stick up your ass," Jackson pronounced as they cleared the doorway. The first ambulance—there were three by now—was scraping the kid up off the concrete and divorcing him from the bike wreckage. Jackson took it all in and chuckled. "You see that?"

"Yes, I see that." The memory of the kid's head hitting the concrete wasn't going to leave him soon.

"I did that."

"You weren't anywhere near him!"

"I popped the chain off the gears," Jackson bragged. "Did he go over good? Did he endo?"

"It was spectacular. You would have loved it." At this point, any news for Jackson was good news, he figured.

"Jackson!" They both looked up and saw Jade, comfortable and rumpled in a tattered chenille bathrobe, hustling over the cold driveway in bare feet. "Jackson, are you okay?"

"Fine, not a problem, don't touch. It's icky." Jackson angled his shoulder away from Jade and toward Ellery, and Ellery grimaced at the amount of blood. Jackson never seemed to notice bleeding—but Ellery did.

"Hey, over here!" Ellery signaled one of the ambulance drivers conferring with some of the policemen waiting for Kryzynski and his partner to come out, and unfortunately got the attention of both the paramedic *and* the police officer.

"Oh God," Jackson muttered—but he stumbled. "Why?"

"Give the nice officer the knife," Ellery ordered. "He's got a stab wound in his shoulder," he said to the paramedic. "There were drugs all over the house. You may need to test the blade or the wound for some of them before you do more than give him antibiotics."

Jackson groaned. "Oh God—not even a Vicodin!"

"We'll get one of the CSIs over here with a kit," the paramedic told him, leading him toward the ambulance. The officer, Campbell by his name tag, stood in their way.

"Just a minute, Rivers—you're not getting away without questioning—"

"You want to question someone, question me," Jade snapped. Campbell turned toward her, and Jackson got led toward the ambulance. Ellery stayed to make sure nobody gave Jade crap. Three months ago, not his problem. Now she was the closest thing to family Jackson would ever have, and he wasn't leaving her at the mercy of this asshole.

"What relation are you to—"

"I live on the other side of the duplex. Those guys have been breaking in and using the place for a week. If Mike and I catch 'em, we drive 'em off, but Jackson owns the duplex, and he was not going to deal with that bullshit today."

Campbell—a perfectly average fortyish man with an unfortunate chin, unremarkable cheekbones, and graying brown hair—narrowed his eyes at her and scowled.

"So what was he going to do about it?"

"He ejected intruders from his property." Ellery crossed his arms and eyed the guy with distaste. "Which sounds absolutely fine in court. Trust me."

Campbell eyed him back. "And you are…."

"Ellery Cramer, an attorney for Pfeist, Langdon, Harrelson, and Cooper," he said, not offering a card. For one thing, he was still wearing his pajama bottoms under his sweatshirt. His wallet was in the car. He'd driven over in leather moccasins, for Christ's sake. For another, the guy pissed him off, and he felt like any professional courtesy was a betrayal of Jackson.

"And you're here because…."

"I feel like it. Mr. Rivers was alerted by his friend and tenant, Mike Chambers, and he arrived here with the intention of evicting intruders on his property—"

"Why was the house standing empty?"

"It's being renovated after a drive-by shooting. Where have *you* been?"

Ellery was glad Jade said it. Personally, he'd be happy not to mention that day ever again for as long as he lived. He'd be even happier if Jackson only ever returned here to visit Mike and Jade and the other tenant he rented the duplex out to as soon as he agreed to make his move in with Ellery permanent.

An event that remained a pipe dream, but Ellery refused to give it up.

"So, does this house get a lot of action?" the officer sneered, and Jade was surprisingly ready for him.

"A vacant house is an open invite to drug dealers and meth labs, and you know it," Jade told him squarely. "It's a national epidemic. Most of the time, it starts with mattresses and people moving in claiming squatters' rights. That didn't happen here. They tried, but the minute the mattresses hit the ground, Mike towed them off."

"Did you report it?" Campbell asked, typing something into his tablet.

"Do I look stupid? Wait, scratch that. You're too stupid to know smart when you see it. Yes, we reported it, because we didn't do anything wrong."

Campbell scowled and kept typing—probably looking up Jade and Mike's reports.

"I didn't know about that," Ellery said softly to Jade while the policeman was busy.

"Jackson didn't want to bother you with his bullshit," Jade told him quietly. "We…." She looked over to where he was being tended to by a hapless paramedic. "We didn't agree with it," she said after a moment, meeting his eyes. "But, you know…."

"You knew him first." Ellery got it. He'd gotten it three months ago when Jade's brother had been falsely accused and Jackson had asked him in on the case. Jackson Rivers had a short and finite list of people he trusted in a pinch—Jade, her brother Kaden, Kaden's wife, Rhonda, and Mike, his neighbor—that was pretty much it. Ellery was getting there, but Jackson wouldn't burden him with this. Not when he felt like he could take care of it himself.

Fucker.

"Yeah," Jade said, shoulders slumping as she wiped sleep out of her eyes. "I'm sorry, Ellery. You've been there for him. He owed you better."

Ellery looked over to Jackson again—and caught Jackson looking at *him*, face crumpled with unhappiness and guilt.

"He did," Ellery said softly. "But this is small potatoes."

"To what?" She sounded upset, and he didn't blame her, but at that moment Campbell finished whatever business he had on the tablet and addressed them both.

"Okay—your story checks out. You, ma'am, and your boyfriend have made multiple calls to the police. Can you tell me why this is the first time we've shown up here?"

"Because Jackson Rivers's name is on the mortgage," Jade snapped. "And you fuckers have been trying to kill him for years."

Campbell recoiled. "That's hardly fair—"

"Who do you think shot the place up?" she demanded. "The guy's partner's in jail—it was a big ol' thing in the press. Don't tell me you didn't know!"

Campbell's mouth opened slightly, and he stuttered. "I just transferred in from the Bay Area, Ms. Cameron," he said. "There is stuff here I didn't know."

"Then ask me." Sean Kryzynski sauntered up to them. Ellery had seen him and his partner putting Jackson's victim, er, assailant, in the back of their unit.

"Or me," Ellery muttered, not looking at the young police officer.

"Is there anything else I need to know?"

"My firm—Pfeist, Langdon, Harrelson, and Cooper—is representing one of the perpetrators," Ellery said, rolling his eyes. No, he didn't want to help the vicious little scumbag. Yes, if this was a crime ring, he wanted to get the head guy so Jackson didn't feel compelled to come here and do this again.

"Only one?" Campbell and Kryzynski asked, surprised.

"These guys apparently work for a bigger operation," Ellery said. "He's hoping a decent lawyer will make a decent deal, and we can get whoever it is out of this neighborhood."

Kryzynski and Campbell looked at each other—one of those mind-reading sort of glances that good colleagues had. "So, a sting operation? Like, something you'd need help with?"

Ellery felt his mouth purse up sardonically and couldn't make it stop. "Did we get a nice promotion after the Chisholm case?" he asked sweetly.

Kryzynski nodded. "You betcha—as soon as Abrams retires next month, I'm out of blues and wearing a cheap suit. I sure would like in on whatever you've got."

"Ditto," Campbell chimed in. Then he shrugged sheepishly. "I'm a little long in the tooth, but I sure would like to move up too."

Ellery grimaced. "Not that I don't applaud ambition"—because Lord knows he had his share—"but your promotions are not my priority right now."

"We get it," Kryzynski said quietly, and Ellery met his eyes for the first time.

"Really?" He didn't actually believe they did.

"You just care that we have his back."

Oh. "Bingo. Now, do you need anything else? I need to talk to Ms. Cameron for a moment."

"I said I was sorry," she muttered, but both of them were watching Jackson, leaning his head against the side of the ambulance while the paramedic cleaned him up.

"And I said I wasn't mad." He wasn't. Jackson's family had looked after him for a long time before Ellery showed up. Being Jackson's primary support person was going to take time.

"Then what?"

"Is there any way you could take his car to work? I'll take you back home. I really need to talk to him on the drive."

Jade's expressive brown eyes widened. "Do I need to know what about?"

And Ellery told her about the morgue.

"Oh…." She sucked air in through her teeth and shoved her hair back, pulling it away from her face in a cloth band. When Ellery had first met her, she'd worn it in microbraids, dyed bright magenta. The contrast against her rich burnt-sugar skin had been striking. She'd since had the braids taken out, and it was now in soft waves around her shoulders with magenta streaks from her temples. Ellery had never given thought to how women wore their hair, but having known Jade for the last three months, he wished he could find the words to tell her that the magenta was perfect in either incarnation.

He'd never met a more vibrant woman.

And now, even when she was pissed off and rumpled, he was grateful to her. She was, if nothing else, practical, and her desire to see Jackson in a good place was only slightly less imperative than Ellery's own.

"When?" she asked after she'd thought for a moment.

"Toe-Tag said the body came in at 1:00 a.m. He called Jackson when he was on his way over here." Ellery assumed. He remembered Jackson's kiss on the temple—an unlikely gesture but welcome—and then Jackson had left. Toby "Toe-Tag" Tagliare had called Ellery about five minutes later.

"How's he going to do the ID?" she asked, still gnawing on her lush lower lip.

"Toby offered pictures, but Jackson said in person."

Jade growled. "Jesus. Talk about a person who can do more harm dead than alive."

Ellery let out a frustrated breath, and they watched Jackson slump dispiritedly against the ambulance while the paramedic finished taping up his shoulder and cutting off his sleeve. He used his good hand to shove his dark blond hair out of his eyes, and he leveled a quiet, reassuring smile their way, winking when he caught Ellery's eye.

And that quickly, Ellery was up for the fight.

"I'll go get his keys."

When Ellery walked up, the paramedic—a squat man with a broad ruddy face and thinning brown hair—was giving Jackson instructions as though Jackson was listening.

"Now, I gave you tape and gauze there, but given how much damage I can see was done recently, you're going to want to go in for X-rays and an ultrasound to make sure all that good work didn't just get ripped to shreds."

"Groovy," Jackson said, tugging at his blue SCPD sweatshirt sadly. Worn and faded, Ellery imagined you could only get one of those attending the academy—one of the few good reminders of Jackson's short time on the force.

"I'll make sure he goes," Ellery said, and the paramedic looked at him gratefully.

"Good. I ran a quick reaction test on the wound. Mr. Rivers here said it burned, but I didn't get any drug reaction from the blood on the shirt near the wound. Hopefully when you pulled the knife out, you washed away some of the bad shit. You should never do that again, by the way. Next time you'll probably bleed out. Do you remember your last tetanus shot?"

"Three months ago," Ellery said quickly.

Jackson scowled. "How in the world do you know that?"

"Because you got it shortly after surgery, and it was in your right arm, and you bitched about it for hours." Ellery's icy control was slipping. He could hear the anger roiling in his voice.

"Sorry," Jackson muttered. "I'm just a big old pain in the ass. You should dump—"

"Don't finish that sentence. I draw the line at two passive-aggressive breakup attempts before breakfast."

"I'm not trying to break up with you," Jackson shot back, annoyed.

"No, you're expecting me to break up with you. Can we just say it's not happening and move to the big old fucking fight we're going to have in the car on the way home?" The flush of Ellery's anger warmed him in the chilly November dawn.

Jackson looked at him sideways. "We're going to have a—"

The paramedic handed Ellery a series of fliers he'd pulled from the door. "Mr. Rivers declined to be taken to the hospital, and he's already signed the AMA—"

"I'll take him to the hospital," Ellery said shortly. "And make sure he's treated appropriately."

The man smiled, obviously relieved. "Good, because I'm worried about what might have been on the knife. If he said it was burning, that's a bad thing."

"There were enough drugs in there to fund a coup," Ellery told him, trying not to let his own skin crawl. "My lungs are burning just thinking about that."

"Yeah—these places get pretty nasty. Do you know if they'd been cooking in there?"

"They tried," Jackson said with a snort. "I saw the pan. It was like they looked up SparkNotes for how to cook meth. They were missing some of the details that would have made it anything other than crystalized drain cleaner."

The medic rolled his eyes. "If you cook it, someone will try to shove it up their nose. Just as good you shut this place down."

"This place," Jackson said, voice bleak, "used to be my home."

Ellery couldn't help it. He put his hand on Jackson's good shoulder and squeezed. "We won't leave it like this," he promised. He didn't promise Jackson would move back in—he couldn't. That's not what he wanted to happen, and he wasn't going to make it easy.

But Jackson must have heard a promise he liked, because he briefly covered Ellery's hand with his own and squeezed.

"So, if I'm promising to take him to the hospital, can he leave?"

"Yes, sir. If you can, get him there early. Here—how about I'll make the appointment myself." He picked up a tablet and began to tap in information. "Davis Med Center?"

"Yeah."

"Good, you're set. Doctor Creedy. Eight thirty." The medic ripped off an appointment reminder and thrust it into Ellery's hand.

"Thanks." With a courteous head bob, Ellery offered Jackson his hand and pulled him up from the back of the ambulance.

After giving his own mumbled thanks, Jackson followed him toward their cars, still parked nose to nose.

"Give me your keys," Ellery said. Jackson pulled them out of his pocket and handed them over, no questions, because, see? There was *trust.* "Hey, Jade!" Ellery called. Mike had moved over to talk to Kryzynski, and Jade stood there, hand absently at the small of his back. She looked up from the conversation, and Ellery tossed the keys over the heads of the cops and right into her hand.

"What in the *fuck*?" Jackson jostled Ellery with his elbow—and hurt his shoulder at the same time. "*Dammit!*"

"She's bringing the CR-V to work," Ellery snapped, unperturbed.

"But I've got something to do at the hospital after my appointment, and you've got to—"

"I can defend your scumbag from the toilet with my iPhone," Ellery said crudely and hated himself a little because Jackson's smirk made him feel better. *Damn* this impossible man.

"Is that what takes you so long? I thought you were getting rid of—"

"Yeah, yeah—the stick up my ass. I know what you have to do at the hospital, Jackson. Now get in the damned car."

He opened the door and shooed Jackson in, slamming the door when he was belting up. He thought it was a sign of profound trust that he didn't do the seat belt himself.

He'd started the car and done his own seat belt before Jackson asked quietly, "How did you know?"

"Check your phone. Toe-Tag tried to call you about two minutes after you left."

"I turned my phone off," he said reluctantly.

Oh, I just bet you did. "Why on earth would you do that?" Ellery asked sweetly. *C'mon, Jackson… let's talk real.*

"I wasn't thinking," Jackson said with visible reluctance. "I just wanted to… to get those fuckers out of my house."

Ellery grunted. "Were you ever going to tell me?" he asked, the bitterness hurting his throat. "Or were you just going to drive to the morgue and make the ID yourself?" Jackson didn't actually have to go to the morgue. He could have looked at pictures. Toby told Ellery he'd originally offered to send a policeman to his house with stills.

"There's no reason you had to get sucked into this," Jackson said. He leaned his head heavily against the window, but he sounded strong and resolved.

Ellery planned to show him what strong and resolved really looked like.

"Jackson, she's your mother—"

"My mother was Toni Cameron—"

"Okay—so she was your progenitor, who had legal custody of you for sixteen miserable fucking years! Maybe you even wanted her dead. I don't blame you!"

"I didn't want her dead," Jackson said, but he sounded surprised, so Ellery wondered if he'd ever dreamed about it when he'd been younger.

Ellery would have killed her himself if it had been legal. Fuck moral—ridding the world of Celia Rivers was a goddamned benefit to society.

"Then you're going to have something to grieve," Ellery said, trying not to be too gentle. Probably failing.

"Fuck that. Not fucking grieving. Not pulling you into the fucking sludge pit of my family. Dammit, Ellery, can't you just let me do this alone?"

Ellery thought about it. "It would be easier," he conceded. Then he started the car and backed it up before shifting gears and driving. "But no," he said decisively. "No. You're going to make my life fucking miserable for the next few days—or weeks. Whatever. But no. Would you like Starbucks?"

"God, yes. And one of those chorizo egg sandwiches? And a croissant? And one of those toffeedoodle cookies?"

Ellery looked at him sideways and wondered if his eyes were dilated. "And a blood test for meth?"

"That shit in the pan wasn't meth," Jackson said disdainfully. "No, this has nothing to do with getting high from a switchblade wound and everything to do with adrenaline dump." Ellery heard him swallow, and he stuck out his hand for them both to study at the light.

It shook slightly.

Ellery let out a breath and turned toward Arden. "Nearest Starbucks, coming up."

The car idled at the drive-through before Ellery could speak again. "Why?"

"Hunh?"

And there was Ellery's least favorite word in Jackson's vocabulary. "Why wouldn't you tell me? About any of it? The squatters, your mom. Why?"

He didn't answer for a long moment. His answer bruised Ellery's heart.

"It would be nice," he said idly.

"What would?"

"Having something to bring to this relationship."

Two months earlier, Jackson had delayed his full recovery by putting his car in the way of a drunk driver. He'd been on stakeout without Ellery's knowledge, getting information to discredit the prosecution's key witness.

Mission accomplished—the guy couldn't have possibly seen their defendant committing a crime when he was one shot away from alcohol poisoning—but to prove that, Jackson had needed two weeks of recovery, most of it on a beach in San Diego.

Only one of it in good enough shape to take advantage of resting on a beach in San Diego.

It had been a gift, of sorts. Like a cat leaving a dead mole or a rabbit on your porch. Jackson had left his brand-new car in the shop and his body bruised and battered and said, "Here, look what I did! A gift for you!"

Ellery had tried to take it in the spirit in which it had been intended—but he'd spent his own two weeks counting Jackson's bruises, sick to his stomach.

"You've got you," he said now.

"Your mother bought me a car."

"Which you promptly wrecked—yes, to help me. It's why I paid for—"

"You keep paying for shit."

"If you move in, you can pay part of the mortgage." He froze. Oh God. What had he just said? To Jackson. Right now?

Jackson's bitter laugh assured him that his fuckup was complete. "I can't afford even a tenth of your mortgage. If I get a renter in the half a crack house I own—"

"Heroin."

"Illegal narcotics house, I can maybe pay a third. And I'm just enough of a selfish bastard to think about doing that to you, you know? But now Celia's tits up and you're all, 'Oh my God, Jackson, let's have a purge of your negative feelings!'"

"I never said that."

"And I'm like, 'I'll bet other guys, healthy guys who don't wake up in a cold sweat once a month—'"

"It's twice a week, baby—"

"*See*? Normal guys don't do that. What on God's green earth makes you think I can deal with this… this dead-junkie-mother bullshit when I can't even sleep through the goddamned night?"

"Hi, welcome to Starbucks. Can I take your order, please?"

I'd like two Xanax a day and a shrink, please?

But Starbucks probably couldn't provide that, so Ellery just gave them his order, plus Jackson's insane amount of food, before moving up in the interminable line.

"Decaf might help," he muttered after a moment.

"What?"

"Decaf. I just ordered you a Venti quad-shot latte. Do you think maybe you'd sleep better if you went to chai tea?"

Jackson's chuckle warmed him inside and out. "If I ever go for chai tea, we're probably at the Starbucks in hell, 'cause—"

"You'd have to be dead first. I get it."

Ellery kept his foot on the brake and moved his hand off the wheel to brush his thumb against the corner of Jackson's smiling mouth. "I like you alive," he said softly. "I have money. I don't know the value of it. I don't care. You, not having to sleep alone—*that* I care about. Please… please stay in my home with me while you figure this out. Please don't feel obligated or in debt or anything fucking noble like that. Just… just stay."

Jackson sighed and caught his hand—and kissed his knuckles. "I'm not going to grieve," he said gruffly.

"I've got no problem with that."

"I want to spend *hours* of the firm's time tracking down the assholes who *pay* the assholes who broke into my house."

"Sounds like fun!" Because truthfully, it did. Ellery would have done it on his vacation just to watch Jackson bully, slither, and snark his way through a case.

"And you're going to have to let me spend hours of my own time tracking down the stupid cockroach who murdered the junkie in the morgue."

"Your mother was *murdered*?" Ellery's voice cracked obscenely on the word as he let the car jerk to a halt in front of the window. "I thought she OD'd!"

"Twenty-two ninety-seven, please," the clerk chirped.

"And you're going to have to let me pay for breakfast," Jackson finished savagely.

"Sure." Ellery's smile held more than a hint of angry evil. "All you have to do is pull your wallet out of your sweats."

Jackson made a sound that drew a sympathy yelp from the poor girl in the Starbucks window, and Ellery paid for breakfast.

Tastes of Fish

JACKSON ALMOST regretted eating that breakfast.

He and Ellery went home with the plan of staying just long enough for the two of them to shower and change, Jackson in jeans and a T-shirt and hoodie, Ellery in his habitual suit. Jackson spent a brief moment while Ellery was getting dressed petting his cat, accepting Billy Bob's affection without strings and qualms—and wishing like hell he could do that with Ellery Cramer.

It seemed so cush, right? Nice digs, nice—well, *good*—guy. Ellery was still a stubborn asshole who couldn't take no for an answer, but Jackson was starting to lo—like that about the guy.

But it made him uneasy to get so comfortable. Nearly ten years of his life had passed without a long-term relationship of any kind, besides his family, of course. Jade, and he'd loved Jade, but even being lovers since they were in high school hadn't made him feel about Jade the way he felt about….

Oh God.

How could he drag Ellery into this?

"You ready?"

Jackson looked up from Billy Bob. "Okay, but first—your tie."

Ellery made a face and turned to look in the mirror. "What about it?"

Jackson stood and stroked a finger down the fine silk. "Are you really going to wear this in to work?"

Ellery grinned, obviously pleased. The tie had a design of tiny Siamese cats lined up in little rows. From a distance, they looked like cream-colored diamonds against a dark blue background. "You complained about the picture ones," he said, obviously pleased.

Jackson bit his lip, that strange shyness that accosted him sometimes in Ellery's presence returning. "They were nice, but this is more your style."

Ellery shrugged, and they were both suddenly in a layer of time between. On the bottom was Jackson in his ruined home, kicking the shit out of the two drug dealers. On the top, waiting for them, was the shitshow at the morgue.

In between was this strange feeling of safety, of intimacy, and Jackson wanted to curl up and nap in this sunshine moment, secure that this, at least, wouldn't leap out and eat him.

Carefully, using his good hand, he cupped Ellery's long jaw, leaned in, and tasted him.

Ellery opened for him, sensual, happy, and Jackson made the kiss deep and strong—but not urgent. They had no time for what Jackson really wanted to do, and he needed his blood panel to come back, and any analysis of the substance on the blade.

He was already enough of a liability to Ellery as it was.

On that note he pulled back, taking a step away, only to be pulled back into the kiss, but this time Ellery led.

Aggressively.

Jackson backed up, surprised, as Ellery crowded him against the bed, helping him lie down just carefully enough to not jounce his sore and swollen shoulder.

And proceeded to kiss Jackson senseless.

"Counselor—" Jackson tried when Ellery came up for air, but Ellery wasn't listening. He was pulling off his tie and unbuttoning his slacks.

"Shut up," Ellery muttered gruffly. "And take off your jeans."

Jackson gasped, hard to the point of pain at the one command as he didn't think he could be. He gaped for a moment, and that's all it took for the slacks and shirt to be draped over the end table and for Ellery to be on him, ripping at the fly of his jeans and shoving them down with his briefs.

"Ellery—*augh*!" Ellery's mouth, hard and merciless on Jackson's cock, ramped him up another 120 mph. Jackson knotted his fingers in Ellery's slicked-back hair and tugged, trying to back him off, trying to pull his world back into safe, back into— "Nungh…."

Ellery's spit-slickened finger, manicured smooth, made a quick foray into Jackson's asshole, and Jackson shook with need. Another one, stretching, scissoring, and that thing Jackson hadn't known he craved hit his gut like a cannonball, leaving an endless, needing void behind.

"Why?" he managed, even as he hauled at one of his thighs to spread himself wider, welcoming.

Begging.

Ellery let go of him, moving his warmth to scramble for the end table and the bottle of dwindling lubricant inside. Their third bottle, because as soon as Jackson had recovered enough to run, sex had been *on*.

The cool of the slick against his sphincter made him hiss in pleasure, and before he'd drawn his next breath, Ellery's cock battered at his peace.

"Why?" he panted as Ellery filled him, stretched him, made him terrifyingly whole.

Ellery closed his eyes and shook his head, the lawyer for once out of words. He finished his thrust, bit his lip, and opened his eyes again, locking Jackson in place with his murderous intensity.

"Just stay there," he grated. "Don't fucking move."

Jackson sucked at following orders. He let go of his leg and grabbed his own cock, squeezing hard, running a firm stroke from balls to head. His focus turned inward as he lost himself in the invasive joy of being mastered, taken, forced to open and enjoy someone else's attention.

So many lovers—and only Ellery took him this way. Dorky, prissy, uptight Ellery, who could make Jackson lose his inhibitions.

His mind.

His heart.

That last thought hurt—and Jackson never minded a bite of pain when he was coming.

He cried out, spurting hot and dirty on his hand, and Ellery's angry "I'm coming!" wasn't far behind. Ellery's hips stuttered, and what had been a hard and fast fuck turned into mindless rutting. He froze, whole body caught in that indignant time warp of orgasm, and the heat of Ellery's seed inside Jackson's body warmed him, filled that void again.

Jackson gave a soft cry and spurted one final time just as Ellery collapsed, mindful of the bandage on his shoulder.

When Jackson could hear over his own heartbeat, he asked it again. "Why?"

Ellery took a couple of deep breaths before falling to the side, resting his head—almost by habit—on the uninjured part of Jackson's chest. "I'm tired of you kissing me good-bye," he said at last. He'd obviously not fucked the irritability out of his system.

Jackson gave a half laugh and palmed the back of Ellery's head possessively. "Just to check, is there a secret password I need to know so you'll know I'm not going to take 'You can't break up with me' for an answer?"

Ellery scowled at him, and then a strange expression, one Jackson remembered seeing a lot when he'd been in the hospital, crossed his face.

"If I come home and the cat's gone," he said softly. "Then I'll know you mean it."

Jackson turned his head to the side and noticed that the cat—unimpressed by the shenanigans on other parts of the bed—had curled up on Jackson's pillow and was licking where his balls used to be.

"You two deserve each other," he grunted, but he kept his hand fisted in Ellery's hair and pulled his head back gently, but still with some control.

Ellery raised his face—oh, sober and earnest with a knife-edged nose and velvet brown eyes—and Jackson took his mouth again, plundering and stealing, taking what Ellery had already taken, allowing himself to need.

Ellery made a little hum in his throat, and Jackson released him. They both had things to do. It was time to start their day.

But Ellery stopped and ran tender fingertips over Jackson's cheekbones, his forehead, his eyelids. "I deserve you," he whispered. "The good and the bad. Don't take that away from me."

Jackson closed his eyes and felt. Felt the sweat cooling from his body, felt the spend dripping between his cheeks and down his thighs, drying on his stomach.

Felt the fragile balance of how strong he wanted to be and how brittle his iron really was, crackling along his bones.

"Please."

Augh. Ellery only begged when Jackson was taking him apart in bed.

"Okay," Jackson said gruffly. "I'll stay—at least until my place is clean again and we've got those guys wrapped up. And…." Oh, this sounded corny. "Even if I move back into my place, uh… you and me, Chinese Food Fridays, Mac and Cheese Mondays, these things can still happen. You know that, right?"

Ellery just looked at him for a moment, like he was figuring something out in his head. Finally he nodded. "Yeah, Jackson—they can still happen. You and me can still happen. But it's a lot easier for them to happen if you're living here."

Jackson opened his mouth to argue and then shut it. There was nothing he could say—no amount of "Your place is too nice for me," or "My cat would wreck your carpet," or even "I need room to stretch" that wouldn't be a lie.

Yeah, he'd been forced here because he'd been recovering from surgery and his own place had gotten shot up, but he *liked* it here. He genuinely enjoyed Ellery's company, even when they weren't fighting or fucking or running together in the morning or working a case together.

He was having enough trouble maintaining the pretense of being okay today. He couldn't compound it by lying about not liking it there.

"I'm selfish," he said after a moment. Ellery just looked at him, brown-eyed gaze unwavering. "It's just so… so easy-good to stay."

"Sometimes stuff is easy to do because it's right, Jackson. You ever think of that?"

Jackson wrinkled his nose. "You've met me, right?"

Every decision in his life to do the right thing had been the hard decision. Ellery knew that. He rolled off the bed and started pulling on his boxers and his suit, not even bothering to clean up.

Jackson would have to live with the knowledge of their sex on Ellery's skin for the rest of the day.

"Yeah, yeah, I've met you." Ellery yanked his boxers up savagely. "I've *fucked* you." And there went his slacks. "I've lived with you." His dress shirt—it took a while to do the buttons. "I should have known better. By all means, let's make this relationship as challenging as possible. Let the games begin." He finished the buttons, grabbed his tie, and stomped off to the bathroom, presumably to fix his hair.

Jackson pushed himself up off the bed painfully and started to pull on his own clothes.

Well, the cat was still here and so was Jackson. Ellery should be happy for that win.

AN HOUR later, Dr. Creedy—older, tiny, no-bullshit, with a tiny careworn face—stared at Jackson's chart and poked at his shoulder wound with patent disapproval.

"Your tox screen says there were no traces of heroin on the knife, Mr. Rivers. If there was any at all, it should probably be out of your system by this point, but you shouldn't drive." She frowned. "Did you drive here?"

"No," Jackson said briefly.

"Good. You may want someone there when you sleep—in case your dreams are especially intense tonight."

"Got one of those," Jackson said, thinking he should probably warn Ellery. It was only fair.

"You've had a tetanus shot, and… and Jesus, son, do you think you can let yourself heal before you take another shot to that shoulder?" Surprised, she peered in horrified fascination at the network of scars and tender skin.

"Well, I *am* working part-time," Jackson told him, because she seemed like a nice lady and possibly needed a break today.

"Did this happen on the job?"

Jackson held out his good hand. "Yes, no… it's a gray area. It happened on my property, but, well, about two hours after I leave your office, it's going to become my job."

Dr. Creedy raised ginger eyebrows. "Sounds like a good way to visit your doctor. A lot."

"My last visit lasted a month," Jackson told him, pained. The one before that had lasted a year.

"You're a young man," Dr. Creedy said, eyebrows going up higher. "Don't you have anything to live for?"

Unbidden, Ellery's face as he'd nailed Jackson to the bed popped behind Jackson's eyes—and stayed there for a couple of moments, followed, finally, by Billy Bob licking his privates, which was followed very quickly by Kaden and Rhonda Cameron, their kids, and Jade and Mike.

"Hunh."

Dr. Creedy probed at his shoulder with gentle fingers. "Is that a yes or a no?"

"Ouch!" Because that spot right there was tender.

"Okay—shoulder first. Your EMT did as good as he could with a butterfly bandage, but I'm going to shove a stint in there and irrigate the crap out of that, and then stitch it closed with a shunt to drain it."

Jackson wrinkled his nose. "That's sexy."

Creedy scowled at him. "No, it's not. In fact, it will send most women screaming from your bed for at least a week until the shunt comes out."

"What about men?"

Those graceful ginger eyebrows really did look like flying birds. "Sometimes gross things impress men. It's a crapshoot. My point is, if you would like people in your bed, maybe try not to have things sticking out of your body that don't belong there."

Ellery would probably take it as a challenge.

"Ten-four, ma'am. I'll keep it in mind."

An *extremely* uncomfortable half an hour later, he was hurrying to the morgue, Ellery trying to keep up at his side. Ellery's dress shoes rang sharply on the tile, and Jackson's tennies just sort of squeaked pathetically. Aces.

"What'd the doctor say?"

"She said my shoulder is hella gross and you should probably not want to sleep with me."

Ellery stopped in the hallway, outraged. "The hell she did!"

"Well, she should have, because it is," Jackson grunted. He didn't want to think about the little plastic tube draining crap into the gauze taped to his skin. Everybody had their phobias. Spending over a year in the hospital hadn't changed the way Jackson saw needles and draining shunts, and the extra time he'd spent this year hadn't either.

"Wait—Jackson, what did she do?"

Jackson shuddered. "Put a shunt in. I need to change the dressing periodically." And then, because it was true, "She said it would have gotten really infected if you hadn't made me come in, so, you know. Thanks for being a big nagging baby who didn't want me to die."

"And some guys hold out for flowers," Ellery muttered. "Jackson, slow down."

"I told Toe-Tag we'd be there—"

"Fifteen minutes ago. I texted him while I was waiting for you. He gets it. Now slow—hell." They came to the elevator and stopped to wait. Ellery was panting a little, and Jackson had a head rush. Yeah, he'd pretty much rocketed out of the room as soon as the doctor said he could go. "Jackson, do you really want to run into the morgue like this? Seriously, ten minutes of internal prep—"

"It's not as though I liked this person," Jackson said through gritted teeth. "You said it yourself. If it wasn't this, it would have been an OD or hit by a car 'cause she was high or fallen into the river or—"

"You've thought about this a lot," Ellery said quietly as the doors opened.

"It's like having this… this *thing* sticking out of my body." Jackson stepped into the elevator with his hands clenched, angry at the cold sweat that stuck his T-shirt clammily to his skin. "It's necessary, but that doesn't mean I have to like it."

"Your mother?"

"*She wasn't my mother*!"

"Your… your personal Easy-Bake Oven, then. You just compared her to a drainage shunt."

"Skanky cunt, drainage shunt—"

"*Jackson*!"

"I can't do this now," Jackson snarled, meeting his eyes and begging him, *begging* him to see that Celia Rivers didn't get a regular grieving process. "I can't get all… all soft. All… introspective. I'm not going to see the meaning of life when I see her corpse, Ellery."

"Then why look? Most people do this with pictures. You know that, right?"

Jackson took a deep breath, and the elevator doors opened to the basement. Like a switch, he could smell it—cold and rot and shit and meat.

The morgue.

"Murder, Ellery." He blinked slowly and squared his shoulders. He had things to do today. He had to interview the little shits who'd broken into his house and cooked not-meth over a propane stove in his kitchen. He had to start an investigation for their boss, find the key players. Inform the police. Perhaps launch an investigation or tip-off for an arrest.

And he had to find out how Celia Rivers had been killed and look into that death like he poked, prodded, and nosed his way into everything else.

"You're not here to grieve." Ellery spoke through clenched teeth. "You're here to kick some ass."

"It's all I got," Jackson told him.

Ellery shook his head, muttering "No it's not," but at that moment they rounded the corner and took a right into the medical office that fronted the morgue.

"Mr. Rivers?" The assistant forensic pathologist was a surprisingly young man, broad as a barn, with a sweet-cheeked face and aw-shucks-ma'am blue eyes and blond hair.

"Josh? I mean, Dr. Black?" Jackson felt a massive twitch of twisted reality as he stepped forward to shake the hand of the young internist who had worked on him when he'd been in the hospital proper eight years earlier. "You're working down here now?"

Josh Black shrugged uncomfortably. "Well, I've always gotten along better with the dead than the living. You know that."

Jackson smiled nostalgically. "What on earth did you say?"

"I have no idea." He shook his head with emphasis. "There was an old lady in a coma, and I told a dead cat joke to a pretty nurse, and suddenly there was screaming and hysteria, and the next thing I know

I'm being sued for threatening to kill this woman's cat. I didn't even know her cat! Anyway—the hospital sort of stashed me here."

In a day full of fraught emotions, Jackson felt an unlikely smile fighting to take over his face. "Well, you and Toby should get along great."

Josh nodded. "I love him. His wife cooks for me. I think she's trying to set me up with their oldest son. I don't have the heart to tell her I'm straight. She cooks *really well.*"

Jackson laughed a little and was about to ask to be brought into the morgue proper when Josh drew nearer and spoke conspiratorially. "Look, there's a homicide detective in there—just so you're not blindsided. This body you're looking at, Toby was just supposed to put it on the bus for the coroner's office and the autopsy, but he sort of commandeered it, and the coroner bitched to the cops and the cops sent—"

"Mr. Rivers?"

Jackson turned and saw what might have been his type before Ellery. Tall, in half boots with wedge heels, legs in black slacks for miles, she was the kind of ice-blonde goddess he simultaneously wanted and wanted the hell away from. Women like that were stronger than he was—cool, incisive, substantial. Most of the time, he didn't have time for a relationship.

Until Ellery came along with the masculine brand of cool strength, and Jackson had been melted in the crucible that was the two of them and somehow reformed.

So he was not on the prowl when the woman strode up and shook his hand, but he was impressed.

"Detective…?" He gave her firm grip back and let his gaze flick down her red silk blouse under her black blazer, to the badge she wore at her belt.

"Dakin. Tess Dakin. It's nice to meet a department legend."

Jackson heard Ellery's suppressed snort, and he glanced sideways so they could exchange a brief eye roll. Yeah. They were very aware of what the department thought of Jackson.

"It's nice to meet a stellar actress," he said dryly. "Is there anything I can do for you? We have an appointment with Toe-T—Dr. Tagliare."

She nodded, her wing of chin-length blonde hair barely moving. "I am aware. We were just speaking, actually. Do you have any idea why Dr. Tagliare would think this case would pertain to you? Either of you?" She smiled at Ellery, the wattage dropping just a tad. "I'm sorry. I'm Detective Dakin, and you're—"

"Ellery Cramer, defense attorney for Pfeist, Langdon, Harrelson, and Cooper." He stuck his hand out and dared her with his eyes not to shake. "Pleased to meet you."

Her eyebrows went up as she took his hand. "Why on earth would you bring your defense attorney here, Mr. Rivers? I find that very interesting."

"He's here as a friend," Jackson said, already sick of this shit. "I had a doctor's appointment anyway, and driving's not on my list of things to do." He pointed to his shoulder, where the blood draining from his wound had already seeped through the gauze—and his gray sweatshirt.

Tess's blonde eyebrows winged right up past her hairline.

"Rough morning, Mr. Rivers?"

Jackson shrugged. Not as bad as the morning he woke up when he was ten and discovered Celia had told the guy she'd gotten coke from the night before that he could feel her son up as he slept as payment. Jackson had elbowed the guy in the throat. He'd gone down, blue, and they'd had to call an ambulance before he choked out and died on their apartment floor. In the resultant mess, Celia had told the cops that Jackson had just attacked the guy, no reason whatsoever, and he'd spent two nights in young offenders detention before Kaden's mother had shown up to bail him out.

"Some nights are worse than others," Jackson admitted grimly. "Can we go make the ID now?"

Tess Dakin clenched her jaw. "Normally I'd say no. Most IDs are made through photos. There's really no need to see the body. I believe you know that already. But this body was found under some… special circumstances."

Oh God. "Special?" He and Ellery exchanged glances again. "Would you care to elaborate?"

Tess smiled perkily and looked around. "Where are we, Mr. Rivers?"

"The hospital morgue?"

"Why aren't we at the coroner's office?"

Jackson blinked and took a deep breath. "Because the decedent presented as alive enough to call an ambulance?"

"That's right. And when we moved *this* body, there was a body underneath it. One that had been there about a week."

"Who?" Jackson asked, hoping, God, it was nobody he'd known.

"A junkie, one who hadn't been in the life long, we don't think. Still pretty—a mixed-race girl—blonde, just a little bit of wear on her."

"Dirty pretty," Ellery said grimly. "Is there an ID?"

"No, sir—the body is at the coroner's office now, and I do believe they're running tests."

"Mixed-race, blonde—green eyes?" Ellery muttered to himself. He pulled out his phone and started pushing buttons, and Jackson watched him, wondering what was going through his head. Ellery was smart, damned smart, and he forgot nothing.

Something had piqued his interest.

"Do you think the two bodies might be related?" Jackson asked, a familiar sick feeling in his stomach.

"Well, you tell us. Dr. Tagliare still hasn't told me why he wanted you in for the ID. The logical reason would be that it has to do with a case you're working on, but he wouldn't confirm that. Can you tell me why you were called in?"

"Can you tell me why you're so suspicious?" Jackson retorted. "How do you know I'm not a family member, getting a special favor from a friend?"

Tess Dakin snorted—an unlikely sound, at odds with her ice-queen appearance. "You're an ex-cop, a private investigator. The department may not like you, but you've got a reputation as a ladies' man. This wasn't a lady, by any stretch of the imagination. I'm guessing she was an informant you told Toe-Tag to keep an eye open for, but he's not spilling the beans."

Jackson laughed humorlessly. "Any other reason you're here being a presumptive bitch and a pain in my ass?"

Dakin's eyes narrowed. "Now that wasn't nice. Here I am, making nice conversation, trying to establish common ground—"

"Sucking up to me in all the wrong ways," Jackson told her, not even knowing where to start. "Was there anything else that caught your attention?"

Tess ground her teeth grimly. "There was, but I want to wait until you see the body before I comment."

So she could watch his reaction, screen him, gauge his tells. Unless you were stone cold and a sociopath to boot, looking at grisly death very often provoked a reaction, even if you were ready for it.

Jackson thought he was ready for it. He'd been ready for it for years.

Josh escorted the two of them into the back, where Toby "Toe-Tag" Tagliare bent over a body bag on a stainless steel table. Toe-Tag—a sweet-faced, round little hobbit of a man—dealt with death and despair and sadness all day, and smiled and lived to invite the living to his house for dinner in the evenings. He'd been a good friend to Jackson over the years, and Jackson was grateful to him for his gentle smile now.

"Jackson," he said, turning around carefully so Jackson couldn't see the face of the person on the slab. That told Jackson all he needed to know.

"Toby." Jackson jerked his chin toward the body. "Shouldn't I—"

"I can identify her for you," Toby said, casting an unfriendly look at Dakin. "You wouldn't remember, but I was actually on the floor when Jade and Kaden kicked her out of the hospital."

Jackson frowned. "I don't remember—"

Toby scowled. "She was trying to get your death benefits, Jackson. You weren't out of the woods yet, but you were still breathing."

Ellery made a sound like a Great Dane getting gut-punched.

"Fucking Celia." Jackson let out a deep breath of disgust. "Is there any other reason you're not letting me see the body?"

"It's… disturbing." Toby sighed. "You sure you're up for this? You look like hell."

Jackson looked at Ellery and drawled, "I would have said I looked like shit. He's being nice."

"And I would have said you looked like ass—*hole.* Jackson, c'mon. Let's just go—"

"To the office to get that little fucker off so we can bleed him dry," Jackson said darkly. "I'm not going home."

"Fine," Ellery said, his voice taut. "But do we have to—"

Jackson wanted nothing more than to turn and let Ellery hold him. In his whole life, he couldn't remember wanting another human being's arms around him more—not even the morning after Toni Cameron had gotten him out of juvie.

He took three steps and gently hip checked Toby out of the way.

"Gross," he said with feeling. "What in the holy fucking hell?" His body felt thin and bloodless, brittle, transparent sugar candy, ready to shatter and dissolve.

"The coroner will need to confirm cause of death," Toby said softly. "There were no signs of struggle, in spite of the trauma. He's going to need to do a thorough autopsy and tox screen. If I had to guess, I'd say she was drugged or already dead when it happened."

It.

It happened.

"Do you know what was used?" Jackson asked. "The weapon?"

"Something big—he'd need rib spreaders, and the cut to her abdomen looks as though it was done with one long blade."

"Jackson?" Ellery said, his voice thin. "Did her killer—"

"Rip out her heart and put it in her… stomach?" Jackson had trouble even looking at it. He'd seen bodies here. He'd seen some awful goddamned stuff. But this took the cake for weirdness, no two ways about it.

"Her womb," Toe-Tag said softly. "It's in her womb."

Jackson swallowed convulsively, closed his eyes, and pretended that when he opened them, he was going to be looking at an oil painting.

It worked. He didn't throw up. "Tell me about the bodies," he said. "Where were they placed?"

"Why would you ask that?" Dakin's voice grew sharp with interest. "What does that have to do with it?"

"I won't know until you tell me, will I?" Jackson very carefully cataloged details, as coolly and impersonally as though he was looking at a grocery list. Lips blue, face gray, thin, dyed blonde hair lank around the head. Collarbones prominent—she, the victim, would rather do drugs than eat, always had. "There's a tattoo missing," he said before he could make himself demand an answer. "The skin was lifted off."

"Yeah, we don't know where that went," Toby said.

"You obviously know this person," Dakin said, and thank God her voice was anything but gentle. "May I ask how?"

"Where was she found?" Jackson asked harshly.

"Arcade Creek, in a thicket of blackberry bushes near the golf course," Dakin said. "There was a tarp set up. She doesn't have a scratch on her."

"Did the other victim?"

"Decomp too advanced to tell."

"Where were they in relation?" Jackson asked, thinking… thinking….

"She was lying right on top of the other victim. There was a shallow grave, uncovered, and the victim at the coroner's office was on the bottom. This one—her blood was still running, by the way—was on the top."

Jackson felt Ellery's hand in the small of his back and used it to ground himself. "Who found them?"

"A…." Dakin leafed through her book. "A jogger. A regular, actually—he goes by this spot every night, same time. Saw bloodied pieces of cloth leading to—"

"From," Jackson said. It was obvious. "From—someone meant for you to find her."

"Yes." Dakin closed her book. "That's what we believe."

"Not the first one."

"No."

"This one, on top of her."

"Yes, probably."

"It means something…." Something poetic. Something metaphorical. Her heart in her womb—that was a laugh. Celia's heart had always been in the party. The things that came from her womb—Jackson, the sister he'd never met—those things were disposable.

He was disposable.

"Jackson, you're going to pass out," Ellery said from a long way away. "Or throw up. I'd be fine with either one, but you're the guy who wants to go kick ass."

He nodded. "Yeah. Well. Don't see this every day."

"Mr. Rivers—how do you know this victim?"

"She was…." *Not my mother not my mother not my mother*. "We're related by blood," he said at last. "She was too young to flush me."

"Oh God—Jackson—" Ellery shoved at him, actively trying to get him to turn back around.

He was shaking, trying to remember something—anything good about the slab of mutilated meat on the table, anything that would connect him, make him feel human again.

"She used to sing Dolly Parton songs," he said, not sure if he remembered that or hoped it had been true. "When I was a baby."

Had there been a time she hadn't gotten high? There must have been. He hadn't dealt with any symptoms of fetal drug or alcohol poisoning. Maybe, when he'd been a baby, she'd actually had hope.

"Jackson—*now*!"

Jackson didn't have a memory of being herded through the morgue and back into the office, but somehow it happened. Toe-Tag was there with a bottle of water, which he took gratefully.

"You've got a good memory," Jackson said, drinking deep. "That was eight years ago you saw her."

"It was an… interesting puzzle," Toby said, sounding bitter.

Jackson managed to focus on his friend's happy, lined face. "Her? Me?"

"Where you came from. Then I found out you grew up with Jade and Kaden—and it wasn't a puzzle anymore."

Ellery snorted.

"Yeah, well, your job is harder than mine," Toby said dryly.

Jackson managed a smile at that. Ellery's job was impossible. The whole world knew it but Ellery.

"You knew?" Dakin accused. "Dr. Tagliare? You knew who this person was and you didn't tell—"

"Jackson deserved first shot," Toby said staunchly. "You want to write me up for it? Arrest me? Fire me for violating procedure? I dare you."

"It would have been good to know," she muttered. "There's obviously bad blood between them. How do you know having him here doesn't impede the investigation?"

"How do you know I'm not going to investigate it myself?" Jackson asked. He still had spots dancing in front of his eyes. "I have resources, contacts—"

"What did the other body have to do with it?"

"Jennifer," Ellery muttered. "Jennifer Ricci."

"What?" Dakin turned stunned eyes toward him, but Jackson let out a humorless laugh.

"That was, what—two weeks ago?"

"Yeah." Ellery held up his phone, showcasing the mugshot of a young woman, pretty, high, who had just been arrested for possession and solicitation in Discovery Park. She had blonde hair worn in dreadlocks with tiny curls around her ears and temples, a poignant china doll face much like Celia's had been in her younger years, and skin colored a delicate brown. "This is Jennifer Ricci, a former client of mine. She was arrested two weeks ago, and the firm assigned her to me. At first I assumed she was pro bono, but then I found out someone was paying her bills."

"Do you know who?"

Ellery shrugged. "Doesn't matter. I did my best. She was let off as a first-timer with community service. Is this your other victim?"

Toby took the phone from him and looked at it carefully. "It's hard to make an ID off this," he admitted, handing the phone to Dakin. "But it could be."

"If nothing else, this gives us a place to start," Dakin conceded. "What do you know about her?"

Ellery shrugged, his hand warm against Jackson's sweat-soaked sweatshirt. God. He'd soaked through his sweatshirt. He wished Ellery would stop touching him. He must be foul.

"I know she was—her words—'Just out for a good time.' She liked to laugh. Her giggle was pretty fucking obnoxious, really, but nothing she should have died for."

"Parents? Contacts?"

"It's in the docket," Ellery said. "Give me your card. I'll have the firm check you out and send you the info."

Those eyebrows arched again, precise as scalpels. "You don't trust me?"

"Nope. You're not telling us everything." Oh, bless Ellery. He was sharper today, could read her better. Jackson was having a hard time just counting his own breaths.

"Neither are you," she pointed out dryly.

"Me?" Ellery smiled with all his pointy teeth, and Jackson was suddenly uncomfortably reminded of Ellery's mother. Scariest woman on the planet—but by God, she'd flown across the country when she'd thought her son was in danger, hadn't she. "We've been trying to talk to the police for months. I'm all for telling you everything. I'll turn the whole works over. We might even have phone calls and slumber parties. I'll braid your hair. I just need a few minutes to run you down and see who you are and why you want this case so bad. And to figure out if we should trust you."

"We?" Her eyes flicked from Ellery to Jackson.

"We," Jackson said strongly. No matter how he and Ellery ended up as lovers, in this they needed to be united. He had the feeling the stakes were too damned high for them to play solo. "I'm an investigator at his firm. We're a team."

"Interesting," Dakin said, her eyes growing cooler by the minute. "So, as a team, do you have any idea who might have done this? Who would want to kill these women in this way?"

"Was the other victim mutilated the same way?" Jackson asked, his stomach rebelling.

"No," Toby said. "But we're pretty sure she was sexually traumatized—and there were knife wounds on the back."

Jackson's brain went blank. Ellery had to ask, "Was Celia Rivers sexually assaulted?"

Toby's reply was a quick and merciful "No. Whatever else happened to her, that wasn't it."

"Thank God," Ellery muttered. Probably because he knew Jackson's brain might explode.

"I can't think." It could have been the most honest thing he'd said all day.

"And we're running late," Ellery said smoothly. "Jackson?"

"Coming."

Ellery reached out and took the card Dakin was offering, and Jackson all but ran to the elevator. He found himself holding his breath after the doors closed, his chest tight with the need for freedom. When he got into the open air, a crisp, bright blue November day greeted him, and he had to take three deep breaths before he believed he was out in it.

And freezing.

"Your sweatshirt is sopping," Ellery said grimly.

"I've got a spare in the backseat," Jackson said absently. It had become habit to bring a small change of clothes when they were commuting together. It made Ellery nervous when he saw Jackson's clothes getting battered or scuffed in the course of Jackson's regular day.

"Jackson, are you sure I can't take you—"

"No," Jackson grated. He couldn't go back to Ellery's house. Not now. He sort of loved Ellery's home—the grace, the dignity, the pretty things. Why would he want to contaminate it with everything inside him right now? "We've got work to do."

"Okay, fine." Ellery slid into the driver's seat and waited for Jackson to change into a T-shirt and hoodie not saturated with sweat and blood. Jackson regarded him unhappily from outside the car for a moment as he stood, bare-chested, bandaged, under the cool autumn sun.

Ellery's eyes were narrowed in either irritation or concentration, and his square, bony jaw shifted as he thought. He alternated between squeezing the steering wheel and thumping the flat of his hand against his thigh. He was gnawing on a problem—probably Celia or the druggies or what to do with Jackson's house. His brain, always turning, his words, always shuffling and reshuffling, trying to find the exact thing to say.

He'd faced down Dakin without blinking, had read Jackson's mind—as much as Jackson had been able to think—without skipping a beat.

He'd throw himself between Jackson and danger in a heartbeat, without a vest, thinking his words alone would protect him.

Jackson's throat swelled, and his chest, and for a moment he wondered if his whole body would just seize up, lungs frozen, heart stuck in place, unable to get past this moment when he was forcing himself not to grieve, not to care, not to *need*.

Ellery looked up at him and blinked slowly, incuriously, as though Jackson stood out in the chilly fall morning shirtless and puzzled all the time.

Jackson swallowed past the lump in his throat, and time started again. He dressed quickly, shivering, and jumped into the car. Ellery had pumped the heater up, and he welcomed the warm air on his face, closing his eyes for a moment to get his bearings.

Ellery sighed. "Do you think?"

Owens.

And Jennifer Ricci, the girl under Celia's body, fit his profile to a *T*.

"We haven't heard from him in six weeks," Ellery said, but not like that meant he was dead or anything. "Not since Jason Rivera. Do you think he's been…."

"Biding his time? Doing his homework?" Jackson's blood went cold. "Watching us?"

Ellery took a deep breath and grunted. "I think we should talk to Mike and Jade. Like, now. While we're driving. And I think we should warn Kaden. I know he doesn't live in Sacramento anymore, but he's isolated, and it's a day trip from here. I'll talk to the marshals' service and ask if we can put a detail on both of them. Anyone else you—"

"I've slept with half the city, Ellery." Jackson's voice crackled. "But no. If he went after Celia, he's not going for the fish I've thrown back. He's looking for the big fish, the ones that'll…." *Hurt me.* "Why not you?"

"I beg your pardon?" Ellery was laughing, which actually cheered Jackson a bit. It meant he wasn't scared.

"You're the one who arrested Bill Chisholm. You're the one he took a potshot at after Bridger was arrested. Why didn't he come after you?"

"Who says this isn't him coming after me." Ellery smirked as he said it, and Jackson found himself spinning his wheels.

"What do you mean?"

The smirk twisted. "Look at yourself, Jackson. You're a wreck. You don't know whether to rage, cry, or throw a bloody party. If Owens wanted to hurt me, all he had to do was tie you into fucking knots."

Jackson let out a keening noise. "You're right," he mumbled. "I should go. I should move out. I should take my cat and find a hotel—"

"And that's three," Ellery sighed. "No, you're not going to do that, and do you know why?"

"My cat loves you more than he loves me and he will shit on all the things?"

Ellery's eyes flickered to him and then back to traffic down Stockton Boulevard. "That's sweet you think your cat loves anybody as much as he loves you. No. Because once you're out of my life, he's coming after me. Think about it, Jackson. Me, all alone in the house, you not there to protect me—I'd be naked."

Transparent. And effective.

"You're not naked with anybody but me," Jackson muttered and then realized what he'd said—*done*. "I could have a protective detail set. Your buddy Kryzynski would be happy to do it."

"You really want that?" Ellery baited. "Pretty young Kryzynski, watching me at night. Would that make you happy?"

"Augh!" Jackson kicked the floorboard. "You are the dumbest smart person I know. Take the protective detail. Ditch the asshole who's a fucking liability."

"You have to leave me first, Jackson," Ellery said calmly. "Go to my house, pack up all your stuff, take the cat, and don't forget to say good-bye. You'd feel like a real asshole if you didn't say good-bye."

Jackson leaned his head back against the seat and let out a breath. "I'm not trying to be an asshole," he admitted. "Tim Owens killed my mother, Ellery. And he did it horribly, like he was trying to make a point. And he buried her on top of a girl *you* defended."

"Another point," Ellery acknowledged.

"I'm… I'm so damned scared right now, I'd probably blow Kryzynski myself if he'd just watch my cat."

"Not happening," Ellery warned. "But I do think we need to talk to Jade and Mike. And we need to get to the firm—Jade told me the arraignment for your scumbag is this afternoon."

"Okay. So, talk to everyone I know and warn them. When this scumbag is released, I try to follow him. If I lose him, I go back, talk to the scumbag in the hospital—"

"The one we're not defending?"

"That's the one. He might get pissed the other guy's getting a fancy lawyer and roll."

Ellery laughed, low and evil. "Nicely played for a guy with a knife in his arm."

Jackson's lips twitched. "I try not to make it easy for them."

"Well done. So when he wakes up, we maybe interview the second scumbag—"

"Scumbag on a bicycle."

"Scumbag on a bicycle, and see where that takes us. I'll research the crap out of Jennifer Ricci's docket, look into anything that can help us there. As soon as the county does the notification, you can interview friends and family, and we can see if there are any connections between her and Celia—"

"I wonder if she's pregnant," Jackson said, the idea surprising even him.

"*What?*" Well, yeah—'twas a horrifying thing.

"He put Celia's heart in her womb—but her heart never *was* in her womb. Celia was like, you know, what Jennifer would become if she'd kept going. Party girl."

Ellery digested that for a moment. "So, like a progression. The pretty dirty party girl and what she'd become if she had a baby."

"Yeah." Jackson nodded, thinking about that poetry he'd seen. "Like… he *saved* her from her future."

"Hunh."

Ellery only made that sound when Jackson had surprised him. "What?"

"Nothing. Nothing at all. Now call Mike, and we can talk to Jade at the office."

On any other day, Jackson would have pressed him. Would have made him spill what "Hunh" meant.

But not today.

Radio Silence

JACKSON DIALED Jade's number, and Ellery ran the call through the car's speaker system, wishing the whole time that he was taking the car down US 50 to Power Inn so he could take Jackson home.

His home.

Yeah, he was an autocratic bastard. He knew it. He'd gotten Jackson's damned cat fixed when Jackson was still touch and go in the hospital that summer. A lot of people hated him for that, but Ellery didn't give a damn.

He loved the damned cat too.

He wanted Jackson to live with him, in his house, where he was safe. And not just from the Tim Owenses of this world.

God, watching him try to keep it together had been one of the hardest things Ellery had ever done. Ellery's whole body screamed to touch him, to comfort him.

Simple things—human comfort, human emotions.

Jackson had no idea how to deal. The woman on the slab they'd just left behind had drank, snorted, and injected Jackson's entire childhood and almost any hope he could have had for emotional normalcy.

The man who'd been left behind had a sense of decency and honor—most of it imparted by Jade and Kaden's mother, and then by Jade, Kaden, and Kaden's wife, Rhonda. Ellery would readily concede that.

But he also had the emotional stability of a freaked-out tomcat with a newly amputated leg getting accustomed to a new home.

Yeah, sure Jackson could function as an adult—could hold a job, maintain a home, take care of his adopted family. But could he function as a lover?

Three months of baby steps—and damn Celia Rivers for dying anyway, because who knew what this was going to do to Jackson's hard-earned peace?

If she wasn't already dead, Ellery might have killed her himself. No, he had no sentimentality—not toward her. Ellery's own mother was a terrifying, overbearing helicopter parent with insanely inflated expectations. Ellery was not going to wax rhapsodic over the woman who had tried—almost since birth—to destroy the only man Ellery was probably capable of loving.

"Yeah, Mike—is Jade already at work?"

Ellery tuned in to hear the conversation.

"Yeah, Jackson—she drove your car, in case you need it. I'm doing cleanup on the yard, and I called the same company who came out and spackled the bullet holes. I figured they'd know what to do with all the needles."

Jackson groaned. "Augh! Dammit, Mike, I'm sorry. If I'd been living there—"

"Jesus, kid—the place is still unlivable. The only room that *was* clean was the guest room, and you know—"

"We have to clean the guest room," Jackson mumbled. "Yeah, I know. Can I ask a huge favor of you?"

"Yeah, sure."

"Go buy a fuckton of locks and latches and lock the place up. Sure, they'll break the lock, but if we replace it every time it happens—"

"Sends a clear message," Mike agreed. "They got sneaky on us. I think the window in the garage, otherwise—"

"Albert would have gotten them. Yeah, I get it."

Albert was Mike's German shepherd, an animal that sounded fierce as hell over the fence but who was really a big snuggling carpet in real life.

"So I'll reimburse you," Jackson said, ignoring Mike's "Pfft…." in return. "But look, Mike, I've got something serious here, and I want your suggestions for what to do."

"Is this about…"—even over the phone, Ellery could hear him floundering—"your trip to the morgue?" In his mind, Ellery could see Mike, weathered forty-fiveish face wrinkling in distaste, front teeth showing as he raised his upper lip and ran his hand through his prematurely white hair. "'Cause… I mean, any other woman, I'd tell you I was sorry, but I'm just glad I didn't kill her myself."

Jackson laughed shortly, but the sound held no humor. "I think Ellery would trip you and walk over your back for a chance to do the same thing. No, this is actually scarier than Celia. Mike, we haven't told the police about this, and we're not going to unless we can get some solid proof. But we think maybe Celia's death might have something to do with… you know. That shit that went down in August."

"I'm sorry?"

Ellery had never thought of Mike as old before, but his voice suddenly went thin and quavery. Uncertain.

"We arrested the people in the corruption ring. You know that. But one of the guys—the guy who got away. Bridger's muscle. Ellery and I… we've been sort of investigating him on our own." Ellery had taken the evidence to the state more than once since Jason Rivera's death, but it was all too thin. No fingerprints, no DNA to match their samples against, just a bunch of "dirty pretty" young people whose lifestyle may have killed them anyway.

"Wait—you've told me about this—Owens."

"You told Mike?" Ellery burst out.

"Because Mike's gonna call the press?" Jackson shot back. "Besides, he's the one who shot up my house. Mike had the right to know. Anyway, yeah, Mike. Owens. We…. Celia wasn't… didn't OD. Her death was…."

"Ritualistic and symbolic, and her body was found on top of Owens's favorite type of victim," Ellery finished, because Jackson was looking so many places at once he was going to get carsick. "And we're thinking he might be targeting Jackson."

"Or you," Jackson said bleakly.

"Naw, probably Jackson," Mike said over the speaker. "Kid, I love you, but you're like… like all the things this guy would want to mess with, right down to being really pretty and hella fucked-up. And an ex-cop, and an IA rat, and all comfy with your sex and—"

"I get it, Mike." The dryness in Jackson's voice almost shriveled Ellery's skin. "Let's go with hella fucked-up. I'm his target, and I put Ellery in danger just sitting in the goddamned car."

"Ellery, if you let him get out of the goddamned car, I'll hunt you down and skin you myself. Kid, hold yourself together, okay?"

"How can you call me 'kid' and then date Jade, who is *exactly my age*!" Oh good—contentiousness. For the first time in his life, Ellery wished he were his mother. His mother could deal with this. His mother could make Jackson settle down, scream, cry, beat something up, and *see reason*.

"Because Jade's full-grown, Jackson. You still need training up. It's like your adult got fucktarded when you were in the hospital, and it just got another kick in the nuts. Now, shut up. I need to tell you something."

Ellery made a mental note to buy Mike something really expensive and manly for Christmas. Like a tractor or truck nuts or a tool system made of adamantium. Yeah, his language would have gotten him kicked out of Liberals-R-Us, but his psychology was right-the-fuck *on*.

"Fucktarded?" Jackson repeated blankly.

"Yeah, it's probably a bad word. Now shut up and listen." Mike's voice sank a little. "Jackson, your mother—I saw her not too long ago."

Ellery slowed to turn left off Alhambra, heading toward their law offices on Seventh, and tried hard not to stand on the brakes and kill them both.

"I'm sorry?" Jackson asked, voice shredded and breathy.

"No, kid, I am." Shame. That was the note in Mike's voice. Aces. "I saw her—about a week back. She was… well, you know. She was always unpleasant and usually high. But she seemed higher than usual and more… well, I've never seen her frightened. She was like you that way—didn't have the sense God gave a turnip to just up and fucking run. But she was scared. She wanted to know where you were, wanted to talk to you. Said… wait… what was it? Someone had the screws to Billy, whoever that was."

"Her pimp/dealer," Jackson said hollowly. Elliot's stomach churned because Jackson would even *know* that. "Not a bad guy, really. Used to give me granola bars when I was a kid so I'd stay out of his hair."

Ellery breathed really slowly through his nose and tried to pay attention to his driving.

"But she wanted you, and she wanted money. I… I didn't talk to her. Jade did, and then Jade screamed for me to bring my gun, and Celia took off, and that was the end of the conversation."

Jackson grunted. "I'll just bet."

"I'm sorry. We should have told you, but—"

"No." Jackson's swallow rang through the car. "You… you were trying to get rid of her—"

"We didn't want her around you. She's—she *was*—like toenail fungus. Ugly and hard to get rid of and just easier on you not to see her. She fucked you up inside every time."

On second thought, there was no gift big enough for Mike. Maybe a house. Maybe buy Jackson's duplex from Jackson and just give it, carte blanche, to Mike. These were hard truths—terrible, painful truths. From Ellery they'd sound petty and self-serving.

From Mike they sounded like a friend who worried.

"Did you get a sense of who had the screws to Billy?" Jackson asked.

"No. Wait! Hold on, hold on…." Mike's voice sounded like he was rummaging through something. "She gave me a card, of all things. I… I should have thrown it away, but, you know—"

People kept cards. It was almost reflex. The damned things got shoved to the back of the wallet and thrown away later. Jackson, in fact, was one of the most meticulous people Ellery had ever met when it came to taking information on a card and putting it into his phone. He was almost compulsive about it, and Ellery wondered now if that came down to never knowing who would give him food when he was little. Knowing who to talk to was the difference between eating and not getting beaten when Jackson was a kid.

"Here!" Mike's triumph rang over the phone. "Okay, I'll keep it so you can see it later, but right now, it's got the name 'Billy'—like you said—and here." He read off the number clearly. "And it's got a… well, she wrote 'Please, Jacky' underneath." Mike sighed. "I'm sorry, Jackson."

"Not a worry," Jackson said, voice neutral. Yeah, he might be upset about it, but Ellery knew Jackson's priorities. Mike and Jade had trumped Celia when she'd been alive. He wasn't going to change that now.

"No, I mean, I would have driven her off, but I should have told you."

"That's not my worry." His voice was so flat it sent chills up Ellery's spine. "My worry is if Owens comes after you and Jade. He's dangerous, Mike—and smart. And he likes hurting people. We've been looking for months, and we haven't found him."

"Well, it seems like he got bored of you looking, doesn't it," Mike said grimly. "What a sweetheart. Do you have a description?"

"Five eight, brown and brown, medium build, medium nose, has been known to use prosthetics to alter his appearance—for years at a time."

Mike sucked air in through his teeth; the sound was unmistakable. "This fucker ain't screwin' around," he said softly. "Jacky, do you think he'll come after Jade?"

"We can put you two into protective custody," Jackson promised—rashly in Ellery's opinion, because dammit, they didn't have enough evidence to get that sort of backup. Then Mike answered, and Ellery got it.

"In a rat's eye," Mike muttered. "For one thing, they wouldn't take my dog. He's pining away for your damned tomcat enough as it is. For another, who's gonna watch your goddamned house, Jackson? Nobody. It'll just be open here, and those drug people will make it their bitch. They'll whore her out to meth-heads and shit, and we'll have to gut her to live in her again. I just got this place to where it didn't feel like a cracker box, dammit!"

Jackson grunted. "I'll see if I can get some guys to drive by the place. They should be on the lookout as it is because of the drug activity. Just… you know. Owens was a cop for five years. Don't let anyone in the house you don't know personally."

"I like that Kryzynski guy," Mike said, brightening considerably. "Maybe he can help us out."

"Fucking *aces*," Jackson snarled.

"If he's watching Mike and Jade he won't be crawling up your ass like an ugly bug," Ellery said quietly, thinking it would make things better.

"It's not my ass he wants to crawl up, but fine."

Mike heard everything, of course. "He's got the hots for Ellery? That's *amazing*! Ellery, he's too young for you."

"Chronologically or emotionally?" Yes, he knew it would get a nasty side-eye from Jackson.

"Nice one." Mike chuckled, but they could hear him sober up quick. "Jade and I won't take any chances, and we sure would appreciate whatever supervision you can give us. But it's getting cold enough to keep Albert in the house at night, and you had that alarm system installed in August, so that's a relief."

"You did what?" Ellery asked, surprised.

"I was paranoid," Jackson responded without shame. "Sue me."

Ellery pulled into the outside parking lot by the river and parked far away from one of the trees dropping soaked yellow leaves on everything. "I'd rather not. Mike, I'm going to send you Officer Kryzynski's number. Call him if your dog has so much as a gas bubble, or a workman starts working next door that you don't recognize."

"Will do, chief," Mike agreed. Then, "You guys going to tell Jade about this? She might take it more serious from you two than she does from me."

"You fuss over her," Jackson said, smiling just a tiny bit. "I know she knows how to fight."

"Yeah, well, as proud as I am of her, I'd just as soon she not have to remember."

Jackson let out a sigh. "More than fair, Mike. I'll do what I can."

"Take care of you, kid. What did the doctor say about your shoulder?"

Jackson groaned. "He put in a tube, Mike."

"Aw—I'm sorry. Well, don't do anything stupid, and do what he says and maybe it'll come out before you absolutely positively have to yank it out yourself."

"Thanks, man. Talk to you later."

Jackson hung up just as Ellery killed the ignition.

"Ouch," Ellery said, thinking about Jackson's shoulder.

"It's the least of our problems." Jackson looked moodily out the window to the tree-lined levee. "When do we need to check on our scumbags?"

Ellery consulted his phone. "I have a conference at the jail with the one waiting for his bail hearing. You're coming with?"

"'Course—when?"

"Few hours."

"Okay. I'm going to have Crystal run down the phone number Mike gave me. If it's a landline, I'll pay a visit—"

"And if it's not?"

Jackson was getting good at the one-shouldered shrug. Well, he'd been in bandages and slings for a couple of months. "We'll see who's paying the bills. I'll also ask Toe-Tag to run a dead body search for any fortyish drug dealers named Billy."

Who used to feed little kids granola bars. Ellery wasn't going to eat for *days*, his stomach was so upset.

He sighed now, though. He could see where Jackson was going with this. "Meet me at the jail in two hours and forty-five minutes. Take the car if you need to leave." He held out the car keys even though the jail was within walking distance, but Jackson didn't take them. Ellery had given Jackson the keys before.

"If Jade brought my car, I'll get the key from her."

"Just…." Ellery closed his hand over Jackson's, trapping the keys between their palms. Jackson's hand felt clammy and uncomfortable, and his eyes were still a little bit dilated and shocky. "Come see me before you go anywhere. I mean it. If I've got time, I'll go with you."

"I'm fine," he lied. To Ellery's face, he lied.

"Sure. But I'm asking you to do this anyway, because that thing we just saw? That was horri-fucking-fying. I don't want to think about you tooling around the city and into that bullshit all by yourself." *Here it comes. What are we up to, five times?* But Jackson surprised him.

"You're afraid for the car," he said, with a pale ghost of his usual fuck-me grin. "You can admit it. Me and cars—you think my luck's run out."

"That's right, Jackson. It's the car." He'd had to have his own engine replaced that summer, because the drive-by that had taken Jackson out—the one perpetrated by Tim Owens, the guy who was probably responsible for the butchery they'd just witnessed—had shot up Ellery's beloved sedan.

If Ellery knew how to work a grenade launcher, he'd blow the damned thing up himself if it would keep Jackson out of the investigation and forced to look into his own head.

"I knew it." Jackson winked and pulled the keys out from Ellery's grasp, sliding out of the car. "You go through one little car—"

"Three," Ellery argued, getting out of the car and grabbing his suit jacket from the back. Early November and a rare, stunning fall in the Sacramento area meant it would be a comfortable seventy or so degrees. Ellery felt almost naked without a lightweight trench coat, but he would have felt overheated with it.

"Three?"

Ellery slid on his jacket and shut the car door. "Three," he repeated, counting on his fingers. "The Toyota, in the first drive-by."

"Owens," Jackson said with a grunt.

"The first CR-V in the second drive-by."

"Owens!"

"And the second CR-V in a car accident you engineered to keep a drunk witness from driving."

"Emile Whatsis—"

"No, that one was all you." Ellery snorted in disgust. "I don't even blame the guy who got convicted. You were being stubborn."

"Did you win the case?"

Well, yes, because without that witness the prosecution's testimony fell apart, and who could trust a witness who would get into a car falling-down drunk?

"That," Ellery said with dignity, "is beside the point."

"What's the point?"

By this time they were walking companionably across the street, like any two colleagues who had carpooled. Neither of them had said anything about their relationship going public. The law community was pretty conservative on the whole. Heterosexual couples didn't routinely give public displays of affection, and Ellery was more comfortable holding hands or bussing Jackson's cheek when they were in their street clothes, in their home neighborhoods.

In this moment, though, Ellery wished he could hold Jackson's hand or put his palm in the small of Jackson's back.

"The point is, I'd rather have you destroy cars than yourself, but try not to make a habit of either."

Jackson turned a pale, drawn face toward him—and winked. "You worry too much," he said winsomely, and then had the gall to chuckle as Ellery sputtered his way into their law office.

Pfeist, Langdon, Harrelson & Cooper was located handily on Eighth Street between the courthouse and the jail, a couple of blocks down. The outside was a squat concrete building like much of the area around the park, but once inside and on the fourth floor, the elevator opened to a pleasing, modern office space with shiny chrome accents in the leather furniture and warm wood paneling, as well as cream-colored carpet.

Ellery had always loved the offices because they looked—to him—exactly like a successful lawyer's working space, but now, as Jackson sauntered in next to him, his everyday game face on, he had to wonder. Jackson lived much more simply than this. Ellery's house still weirded him out. Did this place ever make him uncomfortable?

"Mr. Rivers!" Unlike Mr. Pfeist, who was a broad man who favored bow ties and looked like he ate bugs for breakfast, Carlyle Langdon smiled surprisingly often. "Here, come visit me in my office!"

His office was large—but not intimidatingly so. He liked fresh-cut flowers in crystal vases and small, bright paintings peppered about on his cream-colored walls. He also liked deep, plush, buttery-soft leather furniture. Ellery sank into the chair across from his desk with happiness. His head was starting to hurt. It had been that kind of a morning.

Langdon offered him a mint from the bowl on the desk, and Ellery accepted. He turned the bowl toward Jackson, but Jackson—leaning casually against the wall by the door—shook his head politely no.

Pleasantries done, Langdon got straight to the matter at hand. "I understand you and Mr. Cramer requested a pro bono case?"

Ellery opened his mouth to throw himself on the mercy of his bosses, but Jackson beat him to it with either a really convincing lie or a really astute line of reasoning.

"The guys got busted in a vacant house selling smack—and trying to cook meth. Thing is, they're both too stupid to either cook *or* run a business. I'm thinking that if we get one turned loose and follow him around, we can find the bigger fish."

"And then defend him for money?" Langdon asked hopefully. "Because this firm really does like to make money."

Ellery bristled, but again, Jackson spoke up with that surprising charm. "Oh, come on now, Mr. Langdon. All that publicity we got in the Bridger/Chisholm case didn't generate a *little* bit of extra income? Just a smidge? You know, enough to cover the two hours, tops, Ellery here is going to need to free up Bozo Number Two so I can track him down?"

Langdon laughed heartily, because *of course* the case had generated good publicity. *Great* publicity—and Ellery knew for a fact that at least four big-time clients had signed on to pay Pfeist, Harrelson, Langdon & Cooper a big fat standing retainer afterward. Ellery had gotten two of those guys, and he'd had to turn two of the others over to other associates, mostly because they were scumbags, although Ellery didn't always get to pick and choose whom he worked for.

"I think we can spare Ellery here for that." He smiled at Ellery, who smiled and nodded back, feeling like a fraud because he would have taken the time anyway. And then he remembered that they really *did* need to take some time.

"That's not going to be the biggest thing, sir." Ellery sobered and moved in, trying to pull Jackson into a close conference. Jackson remained slouched against the wall, arms folded in front of him. The mental fetal position—who could blame him? Ellery carried on. "You may recall the research we've been doing on Tim Owens."

"You've made some discoveries there?" Langdon's eyes were a pale shade of blue, and Ellery almost hated to fill him in. He looked as innocent as a baby.

But fill him in he did, while Jackson leaned back against the wood paneling like none of this affected him or even ruffled his cool.

"You're certain this is Owens?" Langdon asked after a moment.

"The victim was very carefully chosen." Ellery darted a glance at Jackson, who managed to look bored. "It was a clear message, and we have reason to believe that people who were close to Mr. Rivers or myself during the investigation might be targeted."

Langdon frowned. "So we should ask for another marshals' detail for the Camerons and some officers for our paralegal?"

Ellery blinked. "If possible, yes."

"You didn't think of asking?" Langdon looked concerned, and Ellery couldn't blame him.

"I thought of asking, sir, but I'll be honest—I didn't think we'd get it."

Langdon's lazy smile was uncomfortably perceptive. "I think Mr. Rivers is rubbing off on you, Ellery. Remember, we're the law part of 'law and order.' We get to expect the system to help us."

Ellery nodded, feeling numb. When had he stopped believing that?

Maybe it was when he'd looked up Jackson's past and put together what had been done to him—how Jackson had trusted the system, and the people in it had betrayed him.

"Well, I'm grateful," Ellery said, his throat dry. His head pounded too. He felt disloyal and weak, because Jackson had pretty much refused all but the bare minimum of painkillers. "Anything else you can think of?"

Langdon looked over at Jackson. "Do you have the Jones case info, or Carruthers? I can give you a few more days—"

"Not a problem," Jackson said, uncoiling from his lean against the wall with feline grace. "I actually had that info for you yesterday—here." He pulled out his phone and started tapping. "I've got two witnesses on video claiming Jones was coaching his daughter's soccer team when the files were pulled from his computer. Somebody at work had to have done it, and I'm forwarding you a big file from the security guard, who has Jones leaving out the front door—with his electronic ID—about two hours prior. I also have a list of the employees still in the building. You'll see I highlighted the guy with the gambling debts in Jones's department, but don't discount his boss, because she's on something. Coulda been caffeine, but coulda been something else. I ran her financials, and there's a lot of commercial debt, but that could be covering something else too. So you've got two good suspects if you want me to go after them and enough evidence to clear your client completely before the investigation wrecks his life. Let me know how you want to—"

"I meet with the ADA today. After I get Jones off, I'll turn over the evidence on the other two. We'll let them do the heavy lifting."

Jackson nodded. "Sir." Simple word—but it told Ellery volumes about how much he'd like to see the case through. Well, that wasn't his job. He knew it, Langdon knew it, everybody accepted it. "Now, about Carruthers…."

Langdon raised his eyebrows. "Yes?"

"Well, I have some wits with grudges who would be happy to discredit the state's case, and if you want to go that way, I can turn that over."

Langdon's mouth twisted—half wry humor, half exasperation. "But—"

"Carruthers is guilty. He sold out his brother to the mob, his brother said no, and they killed him. They had *Carruthers* kill him, which is worse. I know he's got a lot of money, and your case is your problem, but you gotta know the cops are gonna bring it all back to the truth. The guy did it. Hates himself. Wants to die for it. Would rather take an ice pick through the brain than elude prison and is just going through the motions for his wife—but he did it."

The wry twist went away, and Langdon sighed. "Thank you, Mr. Rivers. Ellery. That'll be all."

Jackson nodded and massaged the back of his neck. "Yes, sir." He turned toward the door, and Langdon cleared his throat.

"Rivers?"

"Sir?"

"Don't ever stop speaking your conscience. We might not follow up on it—sometimes we can't. But we get very adept at looking for the big win here. It's good to be reminded that law and order doesn't always equal justice."

Jackson flashed a quiet smile that didn't quite reach his eyes. "You do your best, sir. We all do."

And then he was out the door.

Ellery was at his heels, but Langdon stopped him.

"Who was she?"

"Sir?" It should have been completely out of context, but Ellery knew. He'd evaded this question during their entire interview.

"The female victim connected to you and Rivers. Who is she?"

"Who?"

"The second victim. You told me about Jennifer Ricci, and we'll look into who paid for her defense. But you said two victims, and then you evaded like a seasoned class A defense attorney, which makes me think you're not getting paid enough. But Rivers is gone—if he's who you were protecting."

"His mother."

Langdon was so surprised he stood up. "His—?"

"Well, sort of his mother. Like, you know how Spartans used to throw their children into pits with vipers and see if they could survive?"

"I'm not sure that's how the legend goes—"

"The Spartans were better parents. So were the vipers. And given the way the body was mutilated, Owens knew it."

Langdon sucked air through his teeth. "That's… that's horrifying. Do the police know the connection?"

"Yes, but since the department was unwilling to hunt for Owens in the first place, we didn't want to share what we had until we had a stronger case."

"Thinking like a prosecutor?" Langdon smiled, which was encouraging, but Ellery couldn't even smile about this.

"When Bridger was first arrested, he said he'd been working with Owens and that there was something not right about the guy. Think about that—a man who beat a girl to death, a girl he'd known, thought there was something 'not right' about Tim Owens. And then we discovered that Tim Owens had no past or human connections beyond the military. And this is scary shit, right? But the police drop it, and the DA lets them—"

"They were afraid of how much evidence would be tainted if more than Bridger and Chisolm were indicted," Langdon explained—as though Ellery didn't already know this.

"Yes, I know, and I don't care. Because since Rivera, we've gone backward, and we've got a folder keeping track of likely victims—men and women of all races."

"Young?"

"Late teens, early twenties, new to the street life, attractive. He likes blonds, both genders, doesn't care if it's dyed. They must be lookers—high cheekbones, delicate jawlines, wide-set eyes. Usually beaten, more recently knifed, and there's usually some sexual component to the death."

"God." To Langdon's credit, he sounded legitimately revolted, and Ellery felt marginally better.

"He's a monster, sir. We've got nineteen—twenty if you count Jennifer Ricci." He let out a long breath. "Twenty-one if you count Celia Rivers."

Langdon grunted. "Do you have any more evidence since the Rivera boy?"

Ellery let out a frustrated breath. "Now, see, all of that evidence has been sent to the lab, and we have the last three murders with matching DNA on them. But…."

But Jackson had pulled a miracle to get Bridger ID'd in three days. Then he'd been shot. Ellery had used the evidence, of course, to put Scott Bridger away and nail the coffin over Chisolm, the guy Bridger had worked for, but that was Jackson's favor. The rest of their investigation wasn't sanctioned by the police department, wasn't even sanctioned by the law firm, although Ellery kept them apprised.

It took a long time to get back nonpriority DNA evidence.

"This is heating up," Langdon said thoughtfully. "I need you to send me the case codes, and I'll light a fire under them myself. This guy is active. He's not slowing down. If we can hook all of these murders together, we have a case and we can get manpower."

"Thank God." Ellery thought of all the work he and Jackson had done, late at night over Ellery's kitchen table, looking through unsolved deaths, finding ones that fit the profile, putting together their case.

This was the kind of help that came at the end of that rainbow, and he'd never been so grateful.

"So, we've got Rivers's family under surveillance. We've got the DNA tests hopefully coming through in the next few days. Can you think of anything else?"

"Well, Jackson and I tried to see where Owens came from. Bridger knew him from the service, but we can't pin him down on a unit or even a rank. Sir—nobody can."

Langdon's eyes opened wide. "Define 'nobody.'"

"Well, we tracked down his CO when he was overseas, and the guy he has listed died when he was there, and there's something hinky about that death." Ellery frowned—friendly fire, the dossier had said. But he'd been killed with a service-issue pistol at close range. Who had been friendly enough to fire a gun from twenty feet away?

"You suspect this guy?" Langdon looked concerned.

"Well, no—but only because given what we've seen, we think he served under that guy much earlier. Let's just say that the file the DOJ sent us was like two pieces of a five-hundred-piece jigsaw puzzle."

"A lot of black ink?"

"If that much of *my* life was redacted, my mother would install a camera in my collarbone."

Langdon laughed, but it came out strained. "Okay—have you thought about contacting people who were *supposed* to be in that unit?"

Ellery nodded. "Yes, sir. That was next on our to-do list."

"Carry on, then." But Langdon paused in the middle of his grand gesture.

"Mr. Langdon?"

"I don't like to pry…." The tone was apologetic, but those pale blue eyes were hard in their resolve.

"About…?" But he knew where this was going. Three months of Jackson actually living at his house, one month of the two of them coming in together—and leaving together too. They didn't work with idiots.

"You two. Your outside relationship isn't going to affect the job you do here, is it?"

Ellery grimaced. "That depends on what you mean," he said honestly. "If my girlfriend or wife had just experienced a death in the family, it would be expected that I take some time off to help her grieve."

Langdon nodded. "True."

"He's not going to take time off voluntarily. But that doesn't mean our job is just going to cruise along without a hitch, right?" Ellery heard Jackson's voice in his head when he said that—the part of Jackson that could reason through life and people with curt, clean lines and an easy logic and grace.

"Also true," Langdon conceded.

"And it's not unreasonable to expect that the people in his life will take time off from work to help him."

"But you don't know when or for how long." Arched gray eyebrows really *could* inspire terror. Now Ellery knew.

"Yes, sir."

Langdon shrugged. "You've both got a big stack of laurels to rest on. What can I say? And there's always simple human decency to let a man grieve on his own terms. And at this point, nobody else is investigating the Owens case. Someone needs to. Continue on."

Ellery nodded. "Thank you, sir."

"Go get 'em. And…." For the first time, he looked uncomfortable. "Do what you can to take care of Rivers. I… he seems pretty damned tough, and we all know about his past. But… he's not… this? It's going to shake anybody up."

"Yeah."

Langdon nodded him out, and Ellery left the room. Jackson stood over the counter in the reception area, tapping on his laptop with more efficiency than enthusiasm. He paused for a moment and scanned what he was working on. After biting his lip with one slightly crooked tooth, he went back to fix whatever didn't work.

Ellery couldn't help staring at him from the hallway. He seemed so natural, so purposeful, and Ellery wondered if their entire morning had been in his imagination.

Then Jade bumped his shoulder with her own.

"How is he?"

Horrible question. "Emotionally crippled, angry, terrified, and absolutely sure that if he tells us all he's fine, he's going to be, by God, fine. Any suggestions?"

"Beat him over the head with a club, tie him to his bed, and don't let him up until he deals with it," she said, like that was a real possibility.

Ellery looked at her sideways, reluctant to address the thing neither of them spoke about but they both disliked knowing.

"Did that ever work for you?"

Jade snorted. "Are we married? Expecting children? Living the sweet little happy life we both wanted after watching my brother? No. Because I never had the heart to beat him over the head, that's why." Some of the defensiveness eased out of her posture, but that didn't leave her looking any less upright and professional in a black pantsuit. Because Ellery knew her, he could see the same signs of worry—tightness around the eyes, swollen, chewed-on lower lip, sagging, exhausted shoulders—that he could feel in himself.

"I'm not going to do it," Ellery protested. "For one thing, he's still got a tube in his shoulder."

Jade hissed. "He hates that."

"Yeah, I've been told. I just mean… I don't know. I told our boss he could function. How deluded am I?"

She cast him a droll look and laughed—but not as if she found anything particularly funny. "Green men would be an improvement. You really *are* going to have to sit on him to get him to deal with whatever you two saw this morning."

She kept her gaze steady, her kohl-rimmed eyes not giving an inch.

Oh. "This morning—you really want to know?"

"What did you guys see? Seriously—he's still shock white."

Ellery told her, and she shuddered visibly.

"Okay. So the boss man knows there's a bad guy, and you two are in his sights. And we got cops watching me and Mike and marshals watching Kaden. And who's watching you and Jackson again?"

Yeah. "Me and Jackson?"

"And he looks pretty lively for a man in an emotional coma."

Ellery grunted. "Well, you find the restraints and the thing to clock him over the head, and I'll be right there in front of him so he has no idea it was us."

"Yeah—I don't know if he'd forgive us for that."

Jackson finished sending his e-mail and glanced up around the room again, his expression unguarded. In that moment he looked bleak and hurt and young.

His gaze hit Ellery and Jade then, and his lower lip firmed and eyes narrowed, leaving older, wiser, cockier Jackson in place of the lost child they'd glimpsed.

Jade's sigh rippled through the room.

"When my mom died, he was going undercover with a wire while partnered with Hanover."

Ellery sucked in air, because that time in Jackson's life, when he'd trusted nobody, had left claw marks in his soul.

"We can't let him do this alone," Jade continued. "Not this time." She bumped Ellery's shoulder. "Call me if you need anything." She took a few steps forward, calling, "No, Jackson, you're not putting that thing away without the case, dammit. It'll collect dust. No, I don't care if you're planning to do work tonight, because one, it's a lie, and two, it's like an open invitation for somebody to put their coffee on that shelf when they don't put their coffee anywhere else in the world. Why don't you have an office?"

Jackson frowned. "Why would I have an office?"

"So you can keep your computer there. And a change of clothes."

"I keep my clothes in my car. And I've been in Ellery's office since I got back from leave. I'm not even in your hair."

"It's about having your own space, dumbass. Make them give you an office."

"I don't get this thing you're saying about an office. It's not making any sense."

Jade's growl echoed through the reception area, and the two other paralegals working at their desks both grimaced and hunched their shoulders in fear.

Ellery didn't blame them.

"You ask these nice people for an office, asshole. You act like you ain't grown." With a bustle and a hip check, she shoved Jackson out of her space in front of the standing counter and moved her chair back into position in front of the desk that sat behind it. In short order, Jackson's laptop—in the case—was set respectfully on top of the counter.

"Now take that with you."

"Fine," he mumbled, taking the computer and heading toward Ellery's office without even a look to see if Ellery was coming with him. "If I live to next week, I'll ask for an office."

Ellery's blood ran cold.

"Why would you even say that?"

Jackson shrugged. "I don't know. I guess that's why I never asked for an office in the first place. I just assumed I wouldn't be here long enough to need one."

"Today," Ellery said darkly. "Ask for one today."

"I was kidding."

"You didn't sound kidding. Snap out of it."

Jackson rolled his eyes.

"Like a fucking teenager," Ellery growled. "Can you be an adult for long enough to admit you are not okay?"

"When are you getting our housebreaker out?" Jackson asked, taking a right down the hall and heading for Ellery's office. Ellery had commandeered a good chair to go with the small side table. He privately had to admit he didn't mind that Jackson didn't have a space of his own—but he didn't like that Jackson saw his entire life as a short-term operation.

"Two hours." Ellery looked at his phone. "Two and a half. I've got some paperwork to do before then, and I need to look up Owens's unit—"

"I can do that. You do your real work. And I've got to run down Billy too. I'll make phone calls from here, then follow our guy out of court after you get him let off."

Ellery grimaced. "You do have faith in me, don't you? The cops have this guy dead to rights."

Jackson's wolfish grin made him look almost like the man Ellery loved. "Claim brutality. God knows, I was pretty fuckin' brutal."

"Well, he got some licks in," Ellery said, trying to disapprove. It was hard to be an asshole about this. Yes, it wasn't sound medical practice, and no, Ellery would rather not see Jackson hurt.

But the part of him that would rush into a fight and ask questions later? Ellery had to admire that. He absolutely didn't have any of that in himself.

"You jealous 'cause you didn't get in yours?"

Ah, prurient humor.

"Me? Jealous of that guy you beat into the carpet? Hell no. I'm only jealous of people who've been in your pants."

Jackson's low—definitely dirty—laugh echoed through the modest-sized room.

"That's half of Sacramento," he admitted freely.

"It makes me cranky. Do me a favor and behave."

"Yeah, I'll behave shopping for a ball gag for you while I'm doing my job. You like that idea?"

Ellery considered it briefly. "If I don't get to talk during sex, I think it has to go."

"Handcuffs it is." Jackson raised his eyebrows a couple of times and then settled down to work. His voice lowered to the murmur of professionally cadenced phone calls, and Ellery got to the work at his own desk, so solidly entrenched in what he was doing that when he got a pop of recognition from his data, he actually had to catch his breath.

"Jackson—"

"Hey, I got something!"

They both looked up from their computers, Jackson across the room at his little table, Ellery at his desk.

"You first," Jackson said soberly. "We're going to court in an hour. This we're going to need."

"Okay, our scumbags are Robert Corona and Larry Sherwood. Ol' Bob here is the one in the hospital in what they hope is a healing coma, and Larry is the one who stuck the knife in your shoulder. Both of them were low-level delinquents through school, but in their senior year they sort of cleaned up their act. I'm not sure how. Anyway, that was a year ago, and they've managed to stay out of prison since."

"Good for them!"

"Yeah. Anyway, I don't have a parent contact for either of them. I'm assuming that ship has sailed. But when Larry did two months in juvenile detention for theft, a Claudine Levine—"

Jackson snickered.

"Yes, it rhymes. Anyway, she has a son their age, Jael—"

"Jail?"

Ellery grimaced—yeah, that was an unfortunately chosen name. "Jay-ell, I think is how you pronounce it. Anyway, he too was in juvenile detention around the same time."

Jackson raised his eyebrows. "Hunh."

Sometimes that word didn't suck. "Indeed."

"This woman—this Claudine Levine—might have some knowledge about where these boys have been hanging out."

Ellery nodded. "She might."

"Good. Text me her stats. I'll keep that in mind while I'm trailing darling Larry. Now for you. You remember Davis?"

"The nice policeman who brought you home after you wrecked your car—"

"Helping you!" Jackson pointed out, showing animation for the first time since he'd sat down.

"You got hurt," Ellery pointed out. Again.

"You can't stop that from happening." And oh God, he sounded gentle. "And don't forget—he helped us find Jason Rivera, and he's still helping you, so behave. Davis was a Marine, and he had a buddy, Corporal Lee Burton, who got recruited, he thinks, to some sort of shadow op. You know, nth level shit, super training, that kind of thing."

"And…?" Although that name—Lee Burton—was tickling his lizard brain. Not like the man had been important, but he'd been a footnote somewhere.

"Well, Burton told Davis a story before he got recruited, and Davis looked it up to see if it was true. Apparently Burton was outside of Afghanistan when the base camp got attacked. He was stuck in a bunker with a bunch of green recruits and a sergeant when the sergeant got up and left him in charge. Said he was worried about a guy—the guy's unit didn't have his back."

Ellery's eyebrows shot up. "I'm sorry?"

"Yeah. Scary, right? Anyway—shelling stopped, and the sergeant was wounded by shrapnel. He'd been found in the auto bay with his friend—Private Sonny Daye, if that name rings a bell. He was promoted to corporal at the end of his tour."

Ellery gasped, remembering where he'd seen Burton's name before. It had been in the list of contacts for one Corporal Sonny Daye, in San Diego.

Ellery and Jackson had gone to San Diego less than two months earlier, after Jackson had crashed the car. The purpose of the trip was for Jackson to recover, but Ellery had tacked on an interview, just so Jackson wouldn't feel like Ellery had pulled up stakes and put everything on hold for him. Ellery had—but that hadn't mattered.

What mattered was that in the course of investigating a defendant's alibi, they had discovered a couple of unsolved murders and the catalyst for two low-level mob branches wiping each other the hell out of existence.

At the core of the tornado had been one Ace Atchison and his terrifying shadow, Sonny Daye. Mechanics, garage owners, ex-street racers, lovers.

And neither of them had enough evidence on them for Ellery to even call the police—but Jackson's instincts and a few well-chosen details had told the whole story, and Ellery didn't doubt his take even a little.

"Really?" he heard himself asking from far away.

"Really," Jackson confirmed. "And inside the auto bay were two casualties—a little girl from one of the refugee encampments near the base and one Master Sergeant Galway, who by all accounts was a real motherfucker."

"How were they killed?" This sounded so bad—they had let Atchison and Daye *go*.

"Not the way you're thinking. The girl had been killed by falling debris—there was no doubt about that. And apparently she'd grabbed Atchison's weapon and had been aiming it at Galway's face when the shell hit. Gun went off, Galway died, Atchison took shrapnel, Daye was conscious to give testimony. The girl had been defending herself and Daye from Galway, it seems, because he kept threatening to throw her outside the auto bay."

Ellery's eyes widened. "He what?"

"Well, regulations said she shouldn't be there. Apparently he thought the middle of a shelling was a good time to enforce that. Anyway, Burton thought the whole thing sounded funny. Fishy funny. So he did some checking on Galway. Turns out the guy had not just one, but *three* guys off themselves under his command."

"So they kept him in command?" Ellery knew his voice dripped judgment, but… but….

"The thing about corruption," Jackson explained patiently, "is that it has inertia. You know this. People higher up can know there's something fishy going on, but all the effort they have to expend catching that fish seems like it would just be better spent harpooning the whales outside the system. Now you and me, we know that's not true—but when you're a little higher up on the food chain…." Jackson let his hands finish that sentence for him.

"So," Ellery said slowly, "Burton figured Galway was a bad guy. He probably threatened Ace—"

"Sonny," Jackson said flatly. "You didn't talk to him. I did. Galway threatened Sonny, Ace pulled his weapon—and maybe even pulled the trigger—but shrapnel hit, things got cloudy, and they blamed it on the dead girl because—"

"Who'd want to believe a private and a sergeant, and who'd want to open that can of worms anyway."

"Exactly." Jackson shrugged while Ellery's gut roiled. After all this time working with Jackson, it still hurt Ellery in inexplicable ways when he realized how many more people needed defending than the world had champions to defend them.

"So this has to do with our psycho how?" Ellery pulled him back on track.

"Well, Burton wasn't just name-dropping to Davis. He was getting Davis to do some digging for him. Because three suicides? Someone's got to notice that. So Davis did some digging, and he realized that the guys were assigned to the auto bay—they weren't your usual guys. A lot of these guys had some sort of blotch on their record before they got sent. Insubordination, whatever. This was after DADT, but some of them were suspected of being gay—in the closet or out—and some of them were just… meat. Vulnerable. Afraid."

"So why would you take guys who were already afraid…."

"And put them on the front lines with a sadist who likes to fuck with people?"

"Yes?" Because duh!

Jackson leaned forward, resting his forearms on his knees and his weight on his forearms. "See, that's what Davis and Burton were trying to figure out. And he discovered that this Galway guy, he wasn't just regular Army. He actually ran a special unit in the States, one of those psych operations where they test soldiers in extreme conditions. It's not on any of the books—"

"So we take your buddy's word for it that this place exists?" Ellery asked dryly.

Jackson actually laughed, like a caught-out schoolboy. "Well, I'll give you that—it sounds like a Jason Bourne movie. But here's the thing.

Davis said Galway was a plant. His job was to see if extreme conditioning could create better soldiers. So, battlefield conditions sort of thing—"

"That's horrible!" Ellery couldn't even fathom it. "That's the US government—"

"Who gave LSD to soldiers in the sixties and shot radiation up their noses in the fifties and has a couple of thousand reports of sexual misconduct *every year*. See—they've got a track record that's a conspiracy theorist's wet dream, and you know it. But in this case, I think Galway's job was to browbeat people into better performances as a soldier—"

"But we know that shit doesn't work!" Because who did not take beginning psych?

"Well, you and me do, but remember, the psych community is hard to change and the military even harder. There are still reality shows out there that like to present people in extreme conditions and then tout the immediate results as a positive thing. This is that same idea. Let's do something spectacular and amoral in behavior management and see if it works. But you're missing the point here—"

"Which would be absolute horror?"

"Which would be *Owens*, dammit!"

Ellery blinked. "Owens?"

"Yes. The guy served under Galway for a good six months, before Daye and Atchison, actually. Galway made a request and had him stationed stateside—a little-known training camp in the wilds of Nevada, from whence Galway himself hailed."

"Oh God—training?"

"Yup. And about six months after he was transferred there, he was discharged—honorably—but remember, he'd served under Galway—"

"A sadist," Ellery reiterated.

"And whoever was worse than Galway, whom Galway reported to."

"So… this guy was *trained* in covert serial killing?" Ellery hated that he could even consider this.

"Well, yes. Think about it. How long was Hanover in operation?"

Ellery shuddered. Hanover had been the corrupt cop that Jackson had almost died trying to build a case against. "Sources say five or six years before you came along."

Jackson nodded. "Right? And Hanover cherry-picked me—sponsored me through the academy, asked for me to be his partner. Like you said when we first met, I could have been dirty so easy."

"No you couldn't!" Ellery hated it when Jackson said things like this.

"Well, *I* couldn't have been," he conceded bitterly, "but someone with my background. It was an easy assumption to make. Anyway, Hanover is in operation, and he gets taken out by Bridger and Chisholm. And Chisholm is in a position of power and rising. So someone—someone in charge of DOJ funding—thinks 'Hey—can we put someone on the case of how this crooked lawyer is getting funded?'"

"And they assign Owens." On the one hand, it made as much sense as that DEA sting agents had tried to run a couple of years earlier, when suddenly all sorts of grown men thought they were in a remake of *Miami Vice* and tried to act like Colin Farrell.

On the other….

"So what good does this do us?" Ellery asked. "We have some sort of shadow government conspiracy and a serial killer trained by the Army. What good does it do us?"

Jackson grinned, almost like he'd forgotten who Owens's last victim had been. "Well, I can give you one thing. That profile-changing makeup that's been bothering us?"

"Yes?" Oh, Ellery hoped he knew where this was going.

Jackson opened his laptop and turned it around so Ellery could see. "We know what he looks like without it."

It slipped out before Ellery could censor himself. "Oh Jesus, he's cute!"

"Oh dear God." Jackson rolled his eyes.

"I mean, big hazel eyes, nice jaw, little bow-stung mouth. He looks like the boy next door."

"If the boy next door was a trained soldier and a certified mind-fucker who has probably killed more than twenty people as a hobby!" Jackson protested.

"No, seriously—he looks like one of those… you know, Backstreet Boys?"

Jackson's eyes widened like he'd said something really heinous. "When we were ten, sure, he'd look like a Backstreet Boy. Now he looks like that Zayn kid who left One Direction, but with less stubble because it's his enlistment photo. Now add ten years to that, and a few more kills, but still—"

"Pretty," Ellery finished, still boggled.

"Yeah." Jackson shrugged. "Pretty." His mouth thinned. "Dirty pretty."

"Oooh…."

They both paused. “Once we turn this over to the police, they’ll get a profiler in here,” Ellery said after a moment. “But if I had to guess, this guy doesn’t really….”

“Like himself.” Jackson’s turn to finish the sentence. “Yeah. Explains the victim choice, the beatings. Maybe even the sexual component. Pure sadism—gets him off, punishes him for doing it. All the same shit.”

“We really need to get the cops in here,” Ellery breathed. “Jackson—this isn’t us thinking we know something they don’t anymore.”

“Yeah. I know. It’s personal. He’s trying to get our attention. It’s like he’s been killing himself off for months, going ‘Hey guys, lookit me. I’m a bad guy!’ But we didn’t catch on quick enough.”

“Okay. So, that’s the rest of our day. You follow Larry when he leaves the courthouse, and as soon as I spring him, I light a fire under Langdon and we turn this over to the police and hopefully the FBI.”

Jackson stood and stretched—and it was a testament to how tired and sore he was at this point that it was the first time he’d done it in an hour. Usually he moved, paced, executed a sort of tense, coiled roaming around Ellery’s office.

He grunted, raising his arms to chest level and pressing in front of him while he lunged slowly forward, and Ellery fought back his umpteenth urge to tell him to go home.

“What about Dakin?” he asked, moving his hands behind his back and switching out his legs. “Think we should bring her in?”

“Only if she can not hit on you,” Ellery growled, not proud of it.

Jackson let out a short rasp of laughter. “That woman wants less to do with *fucking* me and more to do with arresting me. God, Ellery—that was not the kind of heat I’d go after even if—”

He stopped and glared.

“Someday you’re going to finish that sentence,” Ellery told him savagely, hitting Print on his computer and getting out his briefcase.

“Even if we weren’t together,” Jackson said, like he had pincers to his toes. “Even if I wasn’t living with someone and monogamously involved. See? I can say it out loud, and I could even say it to someone else. Just not—”

“Yeah.” Ellery deflated. “I know. Not then. Not now. I’m sorry. You’re just… you’re scaring me.” He put the papers in a folder, marked the top of the folder carefully, and put it in the case.

Jackson had the nerve to look at Ellery like he didn't understand. "I'm fine, and you have better things to do. I'm going to see if Jade brought the car here like you asked her to, or if she drove it home like you wanted her to because she read your mind. If it's here, I can follow the kid in my CR-V because it doesn't stand out quite like yours does, and you can drive home."

Ellery scowled. "Wait—you think this is going to take that long?"

Jackson laughed, and he sounded almost joyful. "I forgot. I haven't really gone on stakeout much since we've been together. God, you never know when you'll hit your rack, you know? Anyway, see? That way you're not stuck without a car."

And with that he turned away like Ellery had never expressed concern and like he was going to always be okay.

Ellery jumped out of his chair to stop him from leaving just like that—because he felt it, in his gut, a helpless terror he wondered if Jackson lived with every day of his life. He would forever remember that moment with deep loathing and terrible venom—but even at his bitterest, he could never think of a single way to make the next twenty-four hours go differently.

And that would hurt even more.

Fish Gone Walkabout

JACKSON LOOKED at the text from Ellery and decided on one more loop around the block behind the courthouse. What could checking out the odd concrete sculptures that dominated the lunch area one more time hurt?

Jade had come through with the car and agreed to let Ellery bring her home, so that was nice. If Jackson had to hunker down in a vehicle and dredge through some of the worst neighborhoods in the city, he wanted to do it in a car he wasn't afraid of.

Not that the Lexus would *do* anything, turn on him or anything, but Ellery had been right. With Jackson's luck these days, he didn't want to be responsible for Ellery's baby getting hurt.

Jackson felt guilty enough for all the bad shit he brought to Ellery's life as it was.

He should be walking down the steps right now. Jackson checked his buzzing phone. *Stringy blond hair, a polo shirt, and my emergency client tie.*

Jackson chuckled. Ellery, he didn't miss a trick—including trying to make the client look more presentable for the court appearance.

And in this case, old Larry had needed all the help he could get.

At the moment he was trotting down the steps, glaring at Ellery over his shoulder. Ellery shouted something—probably when his next court date was—and Larry made a rude yet vague gesture over his shoulder.

So he didn't want the free time or legal advice of Pfeist, Langdon, Harrelson & Cooper, which was a real shame. Jackson doubted another lawyer could have gotten the kid off a charge like breaking and entering plus assault with nearly the efficacy of Ellery Cramer.

Well, Jackson really didn't care about his next arrest. What he *really* wanted to see was what had spawned this baby drug dealer into the overwhelming current of distribution and production.

He had the feeling it wasn't burning ambition or even basic street savvy.

Larry Sherwood got closer, and Jackson recognized the punk kid with the switchblade immediately. The same couldn't be said for Larry, who didn't seem to know Jackson from a hole in the ground.

Yeah, well, the little asshole probably thought everybody over thirty was a square.

Jackson had expected the kid to go trekking for the nearest bus stop, which was less than half a block away. Instead, Larry prowled the sidewalk like a panther, stopping twenty feet away and coming back to pace the next ten feet without even looking inside Jackson's double-parked CR-V.

Just when Jackson was about to drive around the block one more time to make sure he didn't get made, a beat-up Chevy Impala in sort of an optimistic light brown puttered up to the sidewalk, ignoring the No Parking signs just like Jackson was.

Looking relieved—and very young—Mr. Sherwood opened the door. Another kid got out—same age, but this one with a brown buzz cut and a lot of black-line cartoons inked on his skin. Larry jumped in the backseat, the newcomer hopped into the passenger side and slammed the door shut, and Jackson was on the tail.

If Jackson ever had a grandmother, he would have accused the person behind the wheel of the Impala of driving just like her.

Slow at the stop, whup, whup, whup, are we turning right? Oh yes. We're turning left. And whoa, a big, loud, ugly, drifting left-hand turn, and down we go down J Street.

Excellent.

This could take us anywhere, right?

Well, no, not anywhere. A right down Alhambra and a left down Broadway and Jackson recognized the Pocket Area. And then another right down Twenty-Fourth and past the hospital and right on Second.

Jackson made that final right and looked around, puzzled. The Impala was quickly disappearing, going up one of the few deep driveways that led around to the personal residences.

Jackson wanted to sputter—and he definitely wanted to snark at Ellery.

This was a nice street—snug little houses, slightly larger buildings that held multiple single-family places. The sidewalks were well-kept but aged concrete, and the houses were thick stucco with charming porches and loads of plants, not to mention nicely planted gardens in both the front and the backyards.

It wasn't just a nice suburban neighborhood, it was a pricey *urban* one, and Jackson had no idea what he was doing there.

Nevertheless, he parked back from the quaint little stucco house that the Impala had pulled into and settled in to see what he could see.

One of the first things he saw was a pretty woman, late thirties, blonde, probably blue-eyed, wearing tight little capri pants and a cardigan sweater set as she swapped out the festive flag on the front porch.

Jackson frowned.

The original flag had been sort of a generic Thanksgiving flag, with pretty orange and yellow leaves and a school of some sort.

This one was brighter, bolder, in green and black and purple, of hard plastic Halloween candy.

Was Halloween coming? No, actually. Two weeks ago he and Ellery had handed out full-sized candy bars and sticker books to kids wearing expensive—and often expensively engineered—homemade costumes. No Party City knockoffs for kids on American River Drive. Jackson had been boggled.

Now he looked at the flag and frowned, his suspicions hitting him hard.

Candy—an age-old metaphor, right?

He settled back into the seat, pushing against it strategically so he could stretch and get counterpressure, working the aches out of his bruised body and trying to get rid of that last moment with Ellery before they left the office.

Ellery's hand on his wrist, warm and strong, and Jackson spinning to find him intimately close.

"Be careful with yourself, Jackson. Please."

Jackson tried to pull his mouth up at the corners, make his response carefree and irresponsible, and to not give Ellery any more worry than he'd already had today.

"Yeah, 'course. I'm like Billy Bob—I land on my feet."

Ellery's eyes burned. "I saw that cat fall off the back of the couch and land on his back just last week. He's fine—you won't be. Promise me."

Face, chest, eyes—hell, sphincter!—all tightened, along with Jackson's stomach. He couldn't. He couldn't promise. There was nothing in him, no substance, no resolve, no sense of self to make that promise.

"I'm not good at.... You should just...."

Ellery's mouth crashing down on his shocked him out of his emptiness and into fire. Demanding fingers in his hair tugged to pain, and Ellery's tongue took angry possession of his mouth. Jackson mmphed, *pressed back against the closed door, his shoulder screaming in agony, but not nearly as loudly as his body howled for Ellery's touch.*

If Jade hadn't pounded on the door, telling them they were going to be late, Jackson would have sunk to his knees just to have Ellery's cock in his mouth, Ellery's come coursing down his throat, Ellery inside him again that day, filling the emptiness and void.

Ellery pulled back from the kiss and rested his forehead against Jackson's. "You know your way home," he rasped. "Come home to me when you're done."

Jackson nodded, agonized.

Even the nod was a promise, and he shouldn't promise anything.

Couldn't Ellery see he came from a place where his promises were cheap chemicals and sticky ashes?

But Ellery was glaring at him, pissed off and worried and not about to let Jackson out of there without a promise.

Jackson needed to get out of there.

Needed *to get out of there.*

He couldn't breathe in that office, surrounded by the ghosts of criminals and the complicated, corrosive task of sifting the fact from the fiction, the real from the fake, the guilty from the maybe this person gets one more shot at life.

"Promise," Ellery snarled, up in his face, forcing Jackson back until he banged his head on the door.

"Promise," Jackson wheezed, hating himself. He had to try now. Had to go back to Ellery's beautiful house with Jackson's ugly-assed tomcat and his shitty wardrobe pressed and hung up in a section of a walk-in closet bigger than the apartment he grew up in.

"I'll hold you to that." Ellery backed up, and Jackson opened the door, avoiding Jade's pissed-off face so he could dodge out.

Ellery's fingers brushed the small of his back as he followed, the touch burning like an ember in a smoke-clogged dark.

Jackson could still feel it now, reminding him, none too subtly, that he *had* promised, and he might feel like his whole life boiled down to the mutilation of a corpse on a slab, but hell, even Celia had once possessed a heart to disfigure.

Jackson had at least that much to put into a promise.

Oh, hello!

The kid on the bicycle—eighteen, nineteen—startled Jackson out of his turmoil. Larry Sherwood's age, stouter, standing on his kickback brake as he skidded into the driveway with the new candy flag, the kid looked as normal as any other junior-college-ditching junior millennial. He grew his hair long, kept his scraggly beard trimmed short, and wore cargo shorts in November.

He dismounted the bike and walked it toward the small outbuilding—a garage? A toolshed?—that the Impala had parked in front of. As he neared the building, his slumped shoulders straightened, and he perked up a little, right when Larry Sherwood stepped out.

He and Larry did the shake-hands thing—clasp, clasp, fist bump, chest bump, flame out, chill—and then the kid with all the black-line tattoos stepped out, and the ritual was repeated. When they were done, Larry and Line Tattoo looked behind them with their arms extended. Jackson couldn't see exactly what they were gesturing at, but as he watched, both kids started pulling rolled-up newspapers—the new kind that paperboys rolled themselves—from a container of some kind behind them and putting them in the basket on the front of the boy's bike.

Line Tattoo held up two different newspapers, and even from where Jackson was sitting, he could see the thick bright-red rubber band of one and the almost invisible green band of the other. He gestured with the bright-pink rubber band and thrust it in an apron for the boy, then waved the other one around and shoved it in the basket.

Jackson raised his eyebrows, thinking of the thousands of times he stepped over little local newspaper bundles on any given street.

If there wasn't some care involved here, this could be the worst drug distribution idea *ever*.

He watched some more as the boys finished loading up the basket and then put the apron on the bike rider with the "special" rubber-banded bundles inside.

Hunh.

Jackson very casually got out of the car and walked up the sidewalk of the house next to him—apparently unoccupied for the moment, as he'd scoped it out. He got up to the door and knocked, angling just enough to watch the bike kid push off and start his route.

He threw the bundles with the small rubber bands while Jackson watched. Jackson watched him turn right at the corner and walked to the end of his porch, then back through the tiny alleyway between the houses, cursing when he saw the neighborhood featured eight-foot wooden fences.

Yeah, he could vault one or two—but six houses' worth?

No. Instead he sprinted back to his car and took off, following the trail of badly thrown newspapers like bread crumbs.

He caught up with the bicycle two blocks over, passing the kid just as he pulled up a driveway and hopped off the thing, leaning it against the porch and in plain sight while he trotted up the steps.

The guy who came out at the boy's bold knock didn't look any different from any other suburban dad. A hooded sweatshirt, tattered jeans, gray in the short-cut mess of his hair and his rumpled beard.

But even from the car, Jackson could see the tremble in his hand as he reached for the newspaper.

This guy was jonesing, and the kid took a wad of cash from him that would probably pay for every newspaper on the route.

Interesting.

Jackson pulled away from the curb before either of them noticed he'd been watching.

Okay, then. That was interesting. Not the strangest thing Jackson had seen, but interesting. Because Larry, Robert, and Jael—probably the guy with the line tattoos who had been in the car that picked Larry up—were running a very handy distribution operation here. It looked complete. They had probably rolled up the product in the newspapers, and the red rubber bands were the product, specially sold, and the green bands were the everyday tree pulp that decorated every driveway in America.

But that explanation left some big questions.

Why would they ditch the sweet little setup here to break into Jackson's house across town? And what were they selling? It wasn't the toxic not-meth that had stunk up Jackson's one working appliance, because if it was, that nice-looking fatherly guy would be a wild-eyed dead man by now.

And where did the mom in the little capris come from? And the heroin?

Inquiring minds needed to know.

This time Jackson came in from the other side of the road and parked about three houses down.

He pulled out a couple of candy bars he'd snagged from the vending machines in the courthouse while he'd waited for Ellery to get Larry Sherwood off for *stabbing him in the shoulder* and began to munch, a corner at a time.

Ah, endorphins. Couldn't beat chocolate for them—and Jackson didn't want to.

Of course, chocolate was the same color as Ellery's eyes, and that gave Jackson some uncomfortable moments of contemplation as he sat and watched the house.

What was he going to do about Ellery?

As though conjured by the thought, his phone buzzed.

Got some intel on Owens—can you talk?

Jackson hit Call. "Talk to me."

"I got a conference with his CO tomorrow morning. Will you be there?"

Jackson squinted. Oh hey. Someone was coming to visit. A young couple, their clothes just a little shy of clean, with a little girl wearing a pink backpack, all turned down the driveway, went up to the porch, and knocked on the door.

The adults were twitchy as hell, feet and hands tapping randomly on the porch or the porch railing. The little girl looked bored and depressed.

She stood, staring out from the porch with her hands holding tight to the backpack, and studied the neighborhood with desperate interest while tuning out the twitching adults.

Jackson needed a Xanax and a shrink appointment just looking at her. It was one in the afternoon on a weekday, and he wondered if she'd even gone to school, backpack or no. Had these adults in her life pulled her out so she could stand here on a stranger's porch? Were these her parents? Her babysitters? The aunt nobody talks about?

Where was the girl going to go when these people got their candy?

The candy in Jackson's mouth turned to ashes as he remembered being that kid on the porch.

Someone should do better for her.

"That depends," he said, thinking about that kid, and about this case, and about the other things on his plate. "I've got some leads on our delinquents, but I haven't had a chance to call about Billy the granola-bar-dealing drug daddy, and *definitely* haven't had a chance to track Owens from that second lead. If I'm still out and about tomorrow morning, I may have to miss it."

"You couldn't even take my damned car, could you?"

"Oh, the bitterness. Ellery, I'm in a decent neighborhood right now, but your car would still stand out. I couldn't even leave it and expect the hubcaps to still be in place, so maybe just say 'Thank you, Jackson, for taking that one thing off my plate!'"

"Maybe I don't want that thing off my plate. Maybe I like things on my plate—"

"Meth cookies," Jackson muttered. "Do you want meth cookies on your plate?"

"Hell no. What are you talking about?"

"Hush."

Jackson pulled out his field glasses and watched interestedly as the door opened and Capri-pants Cardigan Mom poked her head out. She smiled chirpily and handed the other mom—a sallow-faced woman with a sullen expression and flyaway brown hair that looked like it hadn't even visited with a comb in the last month—a small packet.

The little girl, her hair at least in braids, looked up at the woman and waved shyly. In return, the woman pulled out one of those single-serving packages of cookies from her apron pocket. The kid smiled, two teeth missing like they did at this age, took the package and ripped into it with a single-mindedness that told Jackson she'd probably missed lunch too and maybe hadn't had the extra-special "I'm so glad we're not dead" meal he and Ellery had shoved down their maws.

"Jackson?" Ellery asked tentatively.

"I've got an address for you," Jackson said, keeping his voice down out of sheer paranoia. "But don't send the cops for another hour. Me and Mrs. Meth Cleaver here have to have ourselves a conversation."

"She's got a cleaver?" Ellery's voice cracked.

"No, she doesn't have a cleaver. It's a television reference. You know, that thing we watch sometimes at night when we don't have work to do?"

"But not tonight," Ellery said sullenly.

"No, not tonight. Here, I'm texting the address. Now I need this family to leave and… oh shit."

"Oh shit what?"

"We've got bored college student looking to score. Jesus, this little drug setup in the suburbs is a sweet deal. Who knew?"

The happy drug family left, miserable little girl looking behind her with a forlorn hope, like maybe if she was good enough she could stay with the woman who gave her cookies.

Jackson was a heartbeat away from being the star felon in an Amber Alert just to get her out of there.

But hey, the college student had his cookies now—and real cookies too. The suburban mom in the tight capris had handed them over with a smile and a pat on the shoulder, chatting animatedly like she knew this kid.

How would that conversation go?

"Oh, so you're gearing up for finals and need a way to stay up? Sure, got the meth for that! And then the heroin for the comedown. Don't use too much. You know this is for grown-ups, right? Of course you do, sweetheart. Your mother would be proud. Here you go, and some cookies too—don't drink too much on the weekends!"

Jackson's stomach churned.

Because the worst part of that was it was *still* more attention than his own mother gave *him*.

Oh God. He was going to throw up his candy bar.

Don't think about it. Don't think about it. Don't think about it.

He'd gotten good at compartmentalization. He'd spent three months wearing a wire in a nest of dirty cops, for sweet chrissake! He could do this. He and Ellery were working on making a case so the cops could go after Owens. He could get the lowdown on these scumbags so he could get them out of his neighborhood—and out of his house!

Duplex.

Rental property.

Whatever.

Mike could probably turn that place into a mansion. He and Jade could get married and have beautiful spoiled foul-mouthed brilliant babies.

And where would Jackson live?

Did it matter?

"Jackson, are you still there?"

Ellery's voice, with that clipped, stuck-up back-East intonation, snapped him to attention.

"Yeah—sorry. Waiting for the college student to leave so I can go talk to drug-dealing mom."

"You're going to *talk* to her?"

When had he decided to do that?

"Yeah. She's…. Ellery, she's giving out cookies."

"Meth cookies?" Baffled.

"No, cookies to the customers. Like little packages of Oreos. She… she fed the kid with the addicted parents. Patted the college student's cheek. Who *is* this woman?"

"Claudine Levine?"

Oh yeah. "Right? I'd forgotten. She has a name. And her kid. Jail."

"Jay-el. If you tell a drug-dealing mom that she named her kid Jail, she's going to hurt you."

Jackson's laugh was cut short by the violent tap of metal on his window. The ugly butt end of a knife descended again with unnecessary force, and Jackson threw himself sideways as the glass shattered.

"*Jackson*!" Ellery screamed.

"Yeah, gimme a sec!" he shouted back, scrambling across the seats to the passenger side, where young Line Tattoo stood with a gun. Without pausing, Jackson shoved the door open into Line Tattoo's stomach and he doubled over, fumbling the gun as Jackson scrambled out.

Jackson caught the gun in middrop, because it was apparently that kind of fuckin' day.

Ugh. His right arm, though. The weight of it tore at his shoulder, and he swore but held it steady, one-armed, pointed at Line Tattoo's head while he fumbled at his side for the Taser he'd tucked into his belt before going hunting.

A piercing scream stopped him, and he put both hands back on the gun to keep it steady.

"Don't hurt him! Don't hurt him! He's my son!"

Jackson spared a glance for Claudine Levine, hustling from her front porch in the black capri pants and cardigan twinset, complete with a little apron over her front.

She probably smelled like cookies.

"Stay right there, kid," Jackson snapped. In the background, buzzing like a bee, Ellery was losing his mind over Jackson's phone. Jackson felt bad about that, but he was a little busy here. "Larry!"

"What!" Oh, there you go, Larry Sherwood, standing like an idiot next to Jackson's driver's side door.

"Drop the knife. Right now."

"Or what are you gonna do—shoot Jael?"

"You think I can't shoot you both, Larry? Do you really want to try to stab me again? Look how well that turned out."

"Oh my God—it *is* you!"

Heh-heh—Jackson sort of wished he could look at Larry's face. That could be fun. That could be the most fun he would have this month.

Ellery's body, hard, demanding, inside Jackson, rendering him pliable, mute, and needy....

With hard effort, Jackson kept the gun leveled and tried an appeal to reason.

"Claudine, you're the grown-up here. You need to call your dogs off, and we need to talk."

"Give me one good reason—"

"The guy squealing on the cell phone has your address, and he just called the cops. They may not like me much, but they know me, and they'll listen when I tell them about the two kinds of newspapers, the paper route, the drugs. Ingenious, by the way. I mean, I've got a few questions—"

"Why should I tell you sh… shit?"

Claudine had a flowered hot-pad glove on her hand, and she tucked it under her arm defensively while she tried to pretend she said words like "shit."

"Because Larry here already used his 'get out of stupid free' card. Did he tell you that? You don't just stab people in a home invasion and walk out unless you got connections. Larry, did you tell her who your connection was?"

"You stabbed someone?" Startled, Claudine looked at the boy, who had edged his way to their side of the car. Jackson had to give him credit—either for loyalty or stupidity—because he didn't run.

"He said he owned the place," Larry said sullenly. "And then he started beating the hell out of us."

"I own the place," Jackson said with relish. "And you weren't supposed to be there."

"What happened to Robert?" Claudine asked, her voice throbbing with concern. "Nobody would tell Larry."

"He's in the hospital—"

"You *animal*—"

"Lady, it was not my fault that kid jumped on a broken bicycle and flipped it. He's got a hell of a concussion, maybe a cracked skull, but he's going to live. Now can you tell me what he was doing there?"

"*Jael!*"

It was a near thing.

While Jackson was paying attention to Claudine, Jael took the opportunity to scramble to his feet and rush Jackson like an amateur. On any other day, Jackson would have just kicked him back to the ground, but his shoulder was killing him, and the gun was drooping.

His first instinct was to yank the gun back level, and his finger slipped on the trigger.

The gun went off in a deafening bang, and the sidewalk behind Jael exploded as a pothole opened up in the middle.

For a moment everybody stared at the splinters of concrete, small chunks of cement-covered gravel rocking as they landed. Claudine screamed and burst into tears. With a splatter and the smell of ammonia, Jael lost control of his bladder, and it streamed over his shoes.

Jackson tried to still the trip-hammer of his heart.

"My name is Jackson Rivers. I am a private investigator for Pf—the law firm that got Larry here out of jail on his own recognizance for stabbing me this morning. He was breaking into my house and trying—emphasis on *trying*—to cook meth."

He took a deep breath. "There was heroin all over my home. I spent—" His voice cracked, and he reined it in again. The kid was not dead. The kid was standing next to his sobbing mother, looking desperately embarrassed. Jackson did not shoot anybody. That was the thing.

"I spent the better part of my life working my *ass* off to *not* be the guy with heroin all over his kitchen. Can you tell me why that happened?"

His arms and shoulders were shaking. Jesus, guns got heavy when you weren't in the mood. He straightened slowly, pointing the gun at the ground in classic at-rest pose.

"Claudine, why are you making your son and his friends deal meth out of your garage?"

Claudine patted her son's shoulder, tears leaking out of her squeezed-shut eyes. "Heroin," she said quietly. "We're dealing heroin out of my garage. But Billy, our supplier, he… he went to ground over a week ago. This is our last batch, and people…." Her voice broke. "People get mean, right? And I don't know how to make heroin. We just get the packages, and we distribute them like this 'cause Jael and Robbie had a paper route, and we figured they could keep that and, you know, use it and—"

Oh God. She was all over the place.

Jackson took a deep breath. "Claudine, *why* are you getting your son and his friends to deal *heroin* out of your garage?"

She opened her eyes and begged him with them. Her makeup stayed perfect, but her nose had swollen, and she looked like she needed a tissue and a glass of wine.

"Because my husband killed himself to get out of debt, and we were going to lose the house."

Jackson sighed.

"Of course." He swallowed then. Ellery had stopped shouting over the phone, and Jackson figured that telling his lov—his frie—his boyfri—his *colleague* that he wasn't dead would be the considerate thing to do. "Claudine, Larry's going to drop the knife—" He glared, and the weapon made a dull thud and a clink as the haft hit the ground first and then the blade hit the cement. "—and now I'm going to get my phone. The gun is loaded. My shoulder hurts because Larry there stuck a switchblade in it, so yes, making me raise the gun is going to be a risk."

He glared at them all again. This time Larry wet his pants, the stain spreading across the black denim like a plague map.

"Don't. Make. Me. Do. It."

They all nodded soberly, and Jackson put the gun in his good hand and twisted his shoulder behind him. Something tore and something bled and he swore.

Claudine gave a little moan and buried her face against her grown son's side, and Jackson managed to pick up his cell phone.

"I'm alive."

"Good. I'm going to kill you myself." Ellery's voice shook.

"No jury in the land would convict you," Jackson assured him. "But it's not worth the trial expense. I take it you called the cops?"

"Are you injured?"

He'd bled through the gauze. He could feel it.

"No more than usual. How long until they get here?"

Claudine burst into a fresh round of sobbing.

"Well, given that I told them shots fired, you should be hearing sirens about now."

Jackson let out a sigh. "How would you like to defend Ms. Levine and her band of merry pranksters—"

"Pro bono?"

Jackson looked over her shoulder at the house and the pricey neighborhood. "No. I think she's going to sell her house."

She sank to the ground, rocking back and forth, and her son and his friend joined her. Jackson gave a grunt and sat in the passenger seat of his car, avoiding the broken glass on the seat.

"Great. I'll do it. The partners will be thrilled. *Now* will you come in?"

"Nope." Jackson had ibuprofen and water in his glove compartment. Just as soon as he could shake Ellery off this interminable phone call, he was going to get him some of that.

"What are you going to do *now*?"

"Her supplier's name was Billy—and he seems to have fallen off the map. Does that sound like anyone you know?"

"Oh God. Jackson, calling that number is an epically bad idea."

"Two cases, one granola-bar-toting asshole—"

"He might be dead!" Ellery said rashly.

Oh Jesus. "You're having someone watch the house, right? While you're there without me? You're not going there alone—right? I mean, you can sleep on Mike and Jade's couch, but you can't go home—"

"Langdon will give me a detail, Jackson—just, why can't you come home yourself?"

"'Cause I've got shit to do. Now keep me briefed on Owens, and don't go home by yourself!"

Jackson hit End Call and shoved the phone into his pocket, where it buzzed furiously. Well, let it.

"Claudine, Mommy dearest, I need your attention. Can you chill out long enough for me to connect the dots here?"

Claudine Levine had big blue eyes and a tiny Audrey Hepburn nose, as well as blonde hair in a little ponytail. Her son held her like a precious thing, and Jackson's heart twisted as he heard sirens wailing in the background.

"Yes?" she sniffled, wiping her nose on the sleeve of her sweater.

"So let me get this straight. Your husband died—"

"Blew his brains out," Jael said, the hostility in his voice evident.

Aces.

"And you found him." Jackson had to say it. "I'm sorry for that—it wasn't fair. So your dad dies, and you lose your shit for a little. You go to juvie, and you meet up with Larry and Robert and your buddy on the bicycle—"

"Thad," Jael said helpfully and then assumed a classic *doh* expression when Larry smacked him in the arm.

"Wow. Thad, Jai—Jay-*el*, Larry, and Robert. All you need is a water cooler. Scary. Anyway, Larry and Robert have effectively alienated their families—"

"Their mothers were both messes," Claudine confirmed, patting Larry's knee. "And they'd been good to Jay in juvenile detention."

"Saved my life," Jael said softly. Larry inclined his head, and Jackson hated the world all over again.

"Great. So who suggested selling drugs?"

"Me and Bobby," Larry said, like Jael's quiet worship had given him strength. "We were in for possession, but we were already distributing. My mom knew Billy since I was in diapers. I knew how to call him up and set up a buy. Mrs. L. was, you know, letting us crash on her couch, feeding us. Treating us right. But she was worried that her husband's insurance wouldn't come, and they had to sell the minivan and buy the POS and stuff. So Bobby and me, we said we knew a way to make a lot of money really fast."

"Me and Thad had a paper route before I got in trouble," Jael said quietly. "Thad, he's known me his whole life. He wanted to help out."

Jackson grunted, and the cop cars rounded the corner, five of them, sirens blazing. He stood, weapon in hand, safety on, held by the trigger guard so the muzzle pointed up, and waited patiently.

"So, my house…?"

"Billy disappeared," Claudine said, her voice crumbling. "And we were running out of product. And people had already threatened me and Jael. So I looked up how to make meth online. It's bad for you." She nodded earnestly at Jackson. "And so we thought we'd do it in vacant houses. I…." She grimaced at Larry. "I guess Larry couldn't tell you still lived there."

"It's been under repair," Jackson said. "But it's part of a duplex—"

"Dammit, Larry!"

"Sorry, Mrs. L. It was on my bus route, and it looked okay to me!"

"Well, not if there were people right next door!"

"Yeah. Sorry. We were running out of time. That's why there was product in the kitchen. We were cutting and measuring the last bit."

"And using," Jackson said as the SPD came screeching to a halt. Larry looked away, and Claudine gasped. "Well, jail will clean you out—"

"Jail?" All three of them had the nerve to look surprised.

"Yes, you'll still serve time!" Jesus, what did they expect? Being white and cute did not a soccer mom/drug lord excuse! "And you've earned it. But maybe we can keep the boys out of hard time, Claudine—if you pony up and own most of it."

"My fault," she whispered, leaning her head on her son's shoulder. "All my fault."

Well, yes, a little, he thought, comparing her to the other women he'd known. Not *his* mom, of course, who was worse, but… but Rhonda or Jade. Kaden's wife was too damned smart to need to sell drugs to keep her house. Jade would kick Mike in the balls for even suggesting it.

Jade and Kaden's mom, Toni, would have done exactly what she *had* done. Work her ass off, make her own clothes, and keep her son and daughter and their worthless damned friend fed, warm, and with a roof over their heads until they got big enough to do their own damned raising.

Claudine Levine didn't deserve the name *mother* next to Toni Cameron.

But she wasn't a monster either.

Jackson had grown up with one of those, right? He'd recognize the breed.

"So I can keep you from doing hard time. I need you guys to do two things for me as you're getting processed."

Claudine looked at him with trust in her eyes.

"The first thing is remember the name of this law firm. Pfeist, Langdon, Harrelson, and Cooper."

"Pfeist, Langdon, Harrelson, and Cooper," she repeated dutifully.

"Freeze!" the cops called out, and Jackson turned and rolled his eyes at the point man.

"I'm a PI for Pfeist, Langdon, Harrelson, and—"

"We know who you are. Put the weapon down slowly."

Jackson breathed out some of the tension that had been holding his body captive and squatted very slowly so he could set the weapon—bargain basement .38, if he knew his guns—on the ground in front of him.

"What's the other thing?" Claudine asked, voice shaking.

"Give me the last place you guys saw Billy the drug dealer."

"Crack house out in Meadowview," Larry replied promptly. "Billy's place, actually." He looked down. "You know them old neighborhoods, where everyone's got foreclosure signs up and nobody gives a shit where you squat? Place was the size of a shoebox, you know? But he had girls in the bedrooms and people weighin' product on the table. Like a business." Larry brightened, his scrawny, big-nosed face looking pathetic and young. "Sorta like when we were, you know, doin' business in the garage, Mrs. L."

Claudine Levine looked up and smiled through her wobbly lips and tears, and at that point the police came swooping in to cuff everybody and read them their rights. Claudine and the boys seemed to pull themselves together while they were being cuffed and processed, and Jackson stood patiently, hands over his head while his shoulder squealed like a pig in protest, until the lead officer came to talk to him.

"Rivers?"

Thirty-fiveish, sandy-brown hair, hazel eyes, a square jaw with a bold nose. Not bad-looking—Jackson would admit it.

"Officer Pierpont?" Jackson checked the badge on his chest. "Wait—Eric Pierpont? You know Mack Davis over at Highway Patrol?"

Oh thank God.

"Yes, sir, I do. You may put your arms down if you please. I just want to chat."

Jackson let out a groan of relief as he lowered his arms and gave a brief thanks that—when the SPD could have made his life a living hell, like they had so many other times when he was working a case—in *this* instance, he happened to know one of the good guys.

"So, can you tell us what went on here?" Pierpont indicated the nice little house with his chin.

"Yes, sir, I can—if you can make sure my firm is contacted when those three are out of processing. You've got one more kid out there—stocky, white, brown and brown, first name's Thad, and he's got one of those kid faces that looks like he's gonna be mouth-breathing his entire life."

"My sister's kid," Pierpont said, catching on immediately. "Big red lips—girls or boys go nuts after these kids. I don't get it myself."

Jackson let out a chuckle. "Well, thank God, or you'd be in the wrong line of work."

Pierpont winked at him lazily. "Naw, I get to meet strong-jawed faces with green eyes and sort of a pout on this job. That's a perk."

Jackson's eyebrows about hit his hairline. "Uh, taken," he said, suddenly grateful for the reflex. For a moment his old days came flooding back, when he could take Pierpont around the corner in a lull in the investigation and nail him to the wall, getting rid of frustration, puzzlement, and raw physical exertion in one blind act.

But Pierpont would not shit his pants on the other end of the phone when he heard a gunshot, and Jackson, as strung out as he felt on emotion, on anger, on… *(pain)*… on whatever—he couldn't leave Ellery hanging.

Not with sex and not with knowing he wasn't dead.

Apparently he had a line. Now he knew.

"That there's a shame. I thought I was going to get a crack at a legend." Pierpont flashed an appealing smile, and Jackson wondered how many people had actually heard of him from his man-slut days.

"Davis talks too much," he mumbled. Yeah, he and Mack had done the wild thing once. Mack had even been close to doing it again, but Jackson had shied away.

As far as anybody knew, Ellery was the only relationship he'd had besides Jade that lasted more than twice.

"Well, he had a thing. But speaking of, let's get back to business. This place doesn't look like a hotbed of drug activity, Mr. Rivers, except for the bullet in the sidewalk—" He frowned at the wound in the concrete, and Jackson grimaced.

"That's my fault. That Larry kid rushed me—little asshole."

Pierpont wrinkled his nose. "And you didn't shoot him?"

Ugh. Jackson scowled. "No, I'm not going to shoot him. He weighs ninety-eight pounds soaking wet, and I spent the morning beating the crap out of him legally. It would be like shooting a puppy for shitting on your floor."

"Point taken. Now, why were you holding a gun on a kid so he could rush you?"

Jackson was suddenly glad he wasn't single. Ellery would have managed to say that without sounding like an asshole. And even if he had sounded like an asshole, Jackson would have forgiven him.

"Can you take the fact that they smashed my window in and held a gun—"

"That was his gun?" Oh God—now he was impressed.

"Yes, the gun was Jael's, the knife was Larry's, and the drugs belong to everybody. Do you want to see?"

Pierpont looked at the huddling family and let out a low whistle. "Sure."

"Then follow me."

Jackson trekked up the driveway, the kind with the double strip of cement and a strip of lawn between it, growing soft and mossy in the damp of the fall. The yard was raised to the level of the house, and the side walls that held in the earth and lush lawn were made of the same discolored old concrete with the big shiny rocks in it that made up the sidewalks. Someone had mowed the lawn and trimmed the flowers—and even put a fresh coat of paint on the white wooden porch. The stucco was brown, but dark and sturdy brown, and a slurry of wind chimes danced in the faint autumn breeze.

The place, in short, was everything Jackson had ever dreamed of in a house when he'd been a kid.

He was glad they were heading for the garage—*glad* the garage was where they did their business. The thought of the inside of a place like this—with china hutches and dusted tchotchkes and pictures of Jail from the time he was a tadpole all vying for space in a room with pretty wallpaper—used as a background for drug paraphernalia made Jackson want to throw up.

Drugs were meant for dingy apartments full of smoke and dust, with rotting food on the counter, and a dirty mattress with some blankets in the corner for the pet who refused to run away.

"So I'm not sure what's in the house," Jackson confessed, trying not to admit his heart was threading a steeplechase as they walked. "I'm going to assume you'll find something, and what's here, in plain sight, should get you a warrant nice and legal."

The box of newspapers was still there—neatly divided.

"Oh look, the Wednesday ad flier," Pierpont snarked. "Whatever shall we do?"

Jackson was over it. He grabbed a paper with a red band and rolled it off, wincing when the rubber snapped back and bruised his fingertips. Yeah. *That* fucking day. Then he unfolded the paper and slid the two dime bags into his palm.

He handed Pierpont one of them, held between his thumb and forefinger, and palmed the other one neatly, sliding it into the pocket of his jeans. Pierpont was too focused on the evidence in front of his eyes to see the evidence Jackson had just stolen.

"All the newspapers?" he asked blankly.

"No. Just the ones with the fat red *expensive* rubber bands." Jackson gestured to the bins—three of them, big green plastic ones, labeled with street names and divided between the two different color-coded rolls of newspaper. Two of the bins were mostly tiny green rubber bands, and the third was almost all big fat red ones—and took note of the street names, unsurprised.

College students. Some of them were just dying to piss away their lives.

"Do we know who the kid was delivering to?"

Oh. "I think the kid on the bike—Thad? He had a notebook in his hand, probably to keep track of the original deliveries to begin with. If you want to make this a big fat sting, go for it." Jackson shrugged, suddenly tired when this was the smallest part of his day.

"What are you even doing here?" Pierpont asked as he was getting out his radio. "I mean—how did you even know about this?"

"They ran out of heroin and were using abandoned buildings to cook meth. Guess whose house is still being fucking repaired." The injustice burned. *Damn* Claudine Levine anyway, for thinking her kids were more important and more special than everyone else's kids.

Pierpont's soft red mouth fell open, and Jackson wondered if he'd looked like an eternal mouth breather as a kid. "That was *you* this morning? I heard the owner got stabbed!"

Jackson looked at his shoulder, unsurprised to see some pink seeping through the sweatshirt. "Greatly exaggerated." He sighed. "How much of my statement are you going to need?"

"Can you hang out in your car a while? I'll be by to make it official right after I get the DEA in here and get your happy heroin family down for booking."

"Don't forget to look out for Thad," Jackson muttered, and then, because this guy seemed a little gun-happy, "He is *not* armed and *not* dangerous. Try not to shoot him if he turns to ride his bike away. Hear me?"

"Yeah, yeah—I'll treat him like a helpless fuzzy bunny. I hear you."

Well, yeah. Wearily, Jackson turned back to his car, promising the buzzing in his pocket that he'd get to it in a second.

"Oh for fuck's sake!" The upholstery—the stain-resistant velour kind—was covered with broken glass. With a grunt, he reached around the back for a towel and his gym bag. First he dumped out the gym bag. Then, carefully, using the towel over his fingers, he began brushing the little glass pebbles into the pocket of the bag. Well, it was an old bag anyway, wasn't it? Fuck. No. It was new. The bag was new. Because his old bag had been in the old car that'd been shot up when Kaden was falsely arrested.

Well, shit.

With a snarl, he kept brushing the glass into the bag, then cleared it from the floor mats, then got it out of the center console. He finished and put the bag on the floor of the passenger seat and looked around for progress.

The DEA hadn't arrived yet, the happy heroin family were all cuffed and sitting, numb and dazed, each in his or her own cop car, and the police not guarding the dangerous drug dealers had begun marking the entire house off with crime scene tape so when the forensics team arrived they had a clean scene.

Jackson grunted and pulled out his phone. They had until the end of this phone conversation to come question him. Otherwise he was the fuck out of here.

He had the head of the snake to cut off.

In the Wrong Bowl

ELLERY'S PHONE rang, and he almost fumbled it in the middle of his conversation with Langdon.

"Are you okay?" he hissed.

He looked apologetically at his boss, who waved him outside into the hallway, while he listened with desperate care for the slightest hitch in Jackson's breathing, the carefulness.

The hum that indicated he might be very close to losing his shit and falling completely apart.

"I told you—I'm fine. I've got a locale for Billy, I've got his number—I'm going to check it out."

"Wait. I'll come with—"

"No." Jackson's voice rang brittle into the phone. "No. You don't get to come with me. You need to stay there and do important things in a suit. I need to go swim through the pond scum. It's a deal."

"Then why did you call?"

"Because you were buzzing my phone. You need to stop that. I'll check in after I visit Billy. It'll be fine."

"Check in? Why can't you *come home*?"

"'Cause gotta go. Bye!"

Ellery had to fight not to throw his damned phone. He kicked the wall instead, and Langdon stuck his distinguished head out of his office. "Is anything wrong?"

"Your PI is a stubborn, intractable, irritating fucker with no sense of self-preservation and the ability to find trouble just opening a ketchup bottle."

"Sounds like he needs a keeper," Langdon said, voice mild. "I thought you were volunteering for the job."

"He slipped his leash. Do you know what happens to cats who run away? Do you?"

"They end up in the shel—"

"They get hit by trucks. They turn into road waffles. Assholes shoot them with pellet guns. They get attacked by dogs. But do they think about that when they take off? No. They just think 'Hey, I want to see what's behind this trash can!' and then they fall in and get hurt or killed or covered in crap." Ellery fought the urge to slide down the wall and hold his phone to his head, *willing* Jackson to get back on the line, admit he'd had a fucking day already and needed to come in, and maybe, actually see sense.

"Sometimes they find their way home." Langdon's voice was so gentle Ellery had to look up to see if he was being mocked.

"Sure," he said without conviction. "About the military—"

"Do you really want to pursue this investigation now?" Crap. He looked concerned, but Ellery had been around long enough to know a question like that, in this stage of the game, could roughly be translated to "We can replace you with someone sane in a hot minute."

He worked hard to school his features so he could give his boss a green smile.

"I'm fine, sir. Jackson is working this same case from a different angle. In fact, although I'm not exactly happy about how he's doing it, this lead he's following sort of serves a double role."

Langdon raised his silver eyebrows. He apparently believed in minimalist self-expression.

Ellery told him about the card with Billy's number on it and how the drug dealers he was about to defend had been buying from the same guy. Langdon's reaction was… well, Ellery's, actually.

"So why doesn't he just give the location and the number to the police?"

"That is exactly what I'd like to know," Ellery snarled. "Why does he have to go see this guy for himself?"

Jade walked around the corner at that moment, but apparently she'd been standing around the corner long enough to have heard everything.

"Billy the drug dealer?" she clarified, eyebrows raised.

"That's the one."

"He's gone missing too?"

"Yes."

"Well, he hung with Jackson's mom a lot—pimped her out, got her drugs. He was sort of the closest thing Jackson had to a male role model, really, until he and my brother started hanging out. Maybe, you know, he wants to see Daddy?"

"I'm going to throw up," Ellery muttered.

"You and Rivers knew each other in school?" Langdon asked with polite curiosity.

Ellery and Jade locked gazes, and she laughed bitterly. "He's like my other twin," she said, her voice dry as dust. Then she sobered. "Seriously—he means a lot to my family. Ellery, I called my brother. He's leaving as soon as Rhonda gets home from—"

"No." Ellery's heart stalled in his chest. "Jade, you can't. We've got marshals going up there to watch his family. You can't take Kaden away from them."

Jackson wouldn't want it. Not even a little.

But that didn't mean Jade was excited about leaving their boy in the cold.

"Look, Cramer, you cannot tell me that he doesn't need his family around him. Do you understand that? My brother has been the one person on the planet who could keep that man safe, sane, and stable since they were in the fifth grade, and now he's…." She shook her head and glared at him. "I thought you could keep him under control. How could you let him out into the world when he's got all—" She made vague gestures around her chest with scarlet-tipped nails. "—all of… *this* going on?"

"Have you ever known *anyone* who could tell him what to do?" Ellery demanded. "It's like telling a cat to sit and stay. Has that ever worked?"

Jade *hmph*ed and turned away, making that same shake-the-ass-and-kick-the-sand motion with her hips that Jackson did.

"Jade!" Ellery snapped, and she barely deigned to look over her shoulder at him. "Please—I can call Kaden too, but he'll listen to you. We just want him safe. You get that, right? Jackson almost killed himself to keep your brother safe this summer. Why would he want anything different now?"

"You being right is all that's wrong with the fuckin' world." She sniffed and stalked off, while Ellery let out a breath of fear and leaned against the wall.

"Well handled," Langdon said with a little awe.

"I hope so. I think I just sweated through my shirt." The thought of Kaden Cameron driving from the relative safety of his small town in the foothills down to the mess Jackson was swimming in right now was enough to send rivers of perspiration running under his arms. Jackson would kill him if anything happened to Kaden.

Or worse.

"Do you have a new one in your office?" Langdon asked, sounding serious.

"Yes, sir."

"Good. Because I've got you a contact at the recruiter's office. He's a good guy. My son was thinking about joining up, but Sergeant Buchannan steered him to the Marines instead, after two years in junior college. He didn't have to do that. Barrett was a good find for a recruiter, but Buchannan was looking out for him."

Ellery nodded. He had a conference with Captain Karl Lacey the next day—maybe. They'd tracked down Owens's CO during his last reported stint in the Army, and the guy had agreed to fly out from somewhere in Vegas the next morning.

Which actually made Ellery suspicious. His query to Langdon of "Why is he coming to us?" was met with "I have no idea. Why don't you ask him?"

But Ellery had wanted to ask somebody else.

And Langdon had come through.

"Thank you," he said now. But he was thinking *Oh thank God. I have something to do.* "I have an appointment in fifteen minutes, but I can go do that interview afterward."

Langdon nodded. "Take Jade with you."

"I'm sorry?" Ellery tried not to sputter. Heinous waste of manpower, sending their most experienced paralegal to go ask some questions in the field.

"Look." Langdon uncharacteristically fiddled with the end of his tie. "Ellery—the two of you are doing a good job of being professional and not freaking out. Well, sort of. I just think you'll worry less about him if you can actually complain about how much he's worrying you."

Oh. "How do you know we won't kill each other?" Because he and Jade had reached a rapport in recent days, but—obviously—she was not ever going to be simple, easy company.

"Because if you did, you'd never see Jackson again."

Ellery's stomach cramped hard. "Thanks. Thanks a hell of a lot."

Langdon laughed heartily, probably because he couldn't see the sweat that sprang up on Ellery's back again. "He's going to be fine. Tell me how the interview goes!"

Langdon went back into his office, leaving Ellery to lean his head against the wall, careful not to displace the framed watercolor of the capitol building as he did so.

"He is not going to be fine," he muttered. "He's never been *fine*. He was *functional*. But I let him walk out of here barely even that. I should have bribed the damned doctor to sedate him until he saw sense."

"Are you talking to yourself?" Jade had rounded the corner again, looking meaningfully at Langdon's office door.

"Yes," Ellery said shortly. "I am talking to myself because…." He *thunk*ed his head backward again.

"You should have bribed the doctor to sedate Jackson until he saw sense," Jade said wearily. Apparently her earlier irritation was forgotten. Holy cats, the woman was as mercurial as… Jackson.

"Yeah." He closed his eyes and swallowed. "It seemed like such a good idea. He'd follow the guys. He'd tell the cops where to look. But there was a shot, and he was talking crazy, and now he's going on to the next thing…."

"And the next thing and the next thing," Jade confirmed. "Yeah. Like how he dealt when he got out of the hospital. The first time. Banged everything that moved and some things that didn't, I'm sure."

He let out a humorless laugh. "That's gross."

"Hey, some people you bring home and they just lay there. It's weird. We've all gotten some of those, right?"

Ellery shrugged, remembering the guy who had made Ellery rock back and forth while on his knees. "Yeah."

"But it's different if you care for someone, if you want to see them happy. Then you have to move and make it real. Even if you're just moving out of the way."

He looked at her in earnest then, saw her usually scowling face set into the lines of a tired woman, weary with worrying. "Did you move out of his way?" he asked, not sure how that breakup had happened, only that it *had* happened a very short time before Ellery had arrived on the scene.

"Yeah." She nodded. "We weren't going anywhere, so maybe I moved out of mine too."

He was not aware how badly he needed comfort until he felt her tentative fumble with his hand.

"I was sort of glad, finally, that he had you," she said, like they weren't holding hands like children. "But… this thing with his mom—Ellery, this is going to fuck him up so bad."

"Yeah."

They didn't say anything for a moment. Then Ellery squeezed her hand and let go. "You and me, interviewing an Army recruiter to get some background on the guy who might have fucked up Owens. Game?"

"'Course," she said.

"I'll take you home afterward, maybe. Maybe Jackson will be there." He didn't believe it. Not if they hadn't heard from him first.

"Maybe he'll be at your house," she said, like she was trying to believe it too. "We'll see."

STAFF SERGEANT Buchannan looked like he'd been born a father—or at least a big brother. Or maybe even a shop teacher. In his midfifties, with iron-gray hair in his buzz cut, he had the sort of broad, patient face and no-nonsense manner that a good nurturer might have, someone who believed in baseball, Mom, and apple pie.

Or he'd looked that pure when they'd walked in and introduced themselves.

The man had pulled them to his desk, offered them snacks and coffee, and served it on little napkins.

Once Ellery started asking questions about Galway, though, he suddenly turned into everybody's favorite bookie uncle who only brought Christmas gifts when the long shot came home—but jeepers, mister, they were some good gifts!

"Look, Staff Sergeant," Ellery said at last, keeping a rein on his temper. "I'm not saying you've done any wrong—"

"I never said you—"

"I'm just asking some basic questions about this guy we're going to meet tomorrow. Captain Karl Lacey is coming up from Nevada—and he's on duty—but I can't find where he'd be stationed. Now, he was in charge of a couple of people we're interested in—Master Sergeant Galway—"

"He's not stationed here," Buchannan said briefly.

"I am aware. He was stationed outside of Pakistan and in charge of the auto bay, apparently a decent soldier—"

Buchannan snorted. "Sure."

Ellery and Jade both regarded him steadily. "You could explain that?" Jade said with extreme politeness after a frozen moment.

"Augh!" Buchannan lost his poise completely and stood up. "I can't—I just really—"

Ellery used to be a by-the-book interrogator. Everything on record, every advantage given.

But he and Jackson had worked together for three months, and Jackson had a different set of rules than Ellery did. There was no doubt about it.

Sometimes Ellery just liked those rules better.

"Staff Sergeant?" he said, smiling prettily. Buchannan leaned backward. Dammit—Jackson was so much better at this. "Look." He dropped the flirting—he did it poorly. "None of this is on record, you understand? None of this will be used to build our case."

"Ellery!" Jade hissed.

"No. Seriously—this guy is doing his job. He's giving us the time of day. We don't want to arrest you, or start a scandal, or hurt your career. But Tim Owens—Corporal Tim Owens—is suspected of killing street people for over two years. He was posing as a police officer—"

"Not posing," Jade corrected quietly.

"Crap. Yeah. He went through academy, had a social security number, but he used his position to… well, be a sadistic bastard. Do you understand me?"

"More than you probably know," Buchannan said quietly. "Why are *you* here and not somebody from the ADA or the police department?"

"We're building a case," Ellery admitted. "This summer, my… our PI stumbled on a ring of dirty cops led by a guy at the capitol. It wasn't pretty. But one of the things that came out in the trial is that this guy's buddy was…." He had no words for the abomination he'd seen that morning.

"A fucking psychopath," Buchannan snarled. "Yeah. I know. Well, not *this* psychopath—but…."

He took a deep breath.

"Off record. No recording, no signing shit. No names. I am two *months* away from retirement. You understand me? My wife has been planning our trip around the world for thirty-five years."

Ellery nodded. "I can understand that."

"Okay—so here's the thing. It's all… spots. None of it is a whole story, but if you read enough books, you can connect the spots—"

"Dots," Jade corrected.

"Measles—I don't give a crap. You can connect the dots. So I'll tell you what I know and see if you get the same picture, deal?"

Ellery nodded, excitement building in the pit of his stomach. He and Jackson had put together a pretty spectacular picture themselves. He wanted to see if Buchannan had some details they'd missed.

"Okay, so about four years ago, a kid comes into my office. I was stationed down in Barstow, right? Because God, what else is there to do when you graduate but join the military. But this kid doesn't wander in from a school. He looks like he's been on the street for a month, and the way he acted, he looked like he'd spent the first part of his life locked in a box, right?"

Ellery nodded. "I hear you."

"So I tell him he can't sign up without… everything. Social security number, birth certificate, proof of graduation—the works. And he looks like he's going to cry. And he says he'll do *anything* to get into the Army. Well, I felt bad for him—but not that bad. Besides not swinging that way, you can get into a shitload of trouble falsifying documents. So I give him some money for clothes and a hotel room to clean up and some suggestions for shelters or places to work, and the kid disappears. I wouldn't have thought anything about him, except, about two months later, I'm promoted in charge of my district, and I'm looking through names of new recruits—and I see his."

"You recognized it?" Ellery asked, impressed.

"The kid's name—or at least the name he was claiming was his—is Sonny Daye. You don't forget that name."

Ellery sucked in a breath, hearing Jackson's voice in his head just as clear as, well, a sunny day.

"No, sir, you don't," he said, taking a quick swig of coffee. Wow. Way better than the coffee at the law firm—who knew? "So, young Sonny Daye is now a private in the military. What happens now?"

"Well, see—I want to know who recruited him, because whoever it was, he had to have taken that thing Sonny put on the table that I wasn't buying. I didn't want to make waves, but…." He shrugged.

"You wanted to maybe steer this guy somewhere else?" Ellery said delicately, because that's what Jackson said about how bureaucracy worked, right? It was *hard* to get rid of the crooked or the incompetent. One of the reasons people like Scott Bridger or Patrick Hanover could abuse the system for so long was that the DA's office was terrified of getting rid of them. Once they got rid of a cop, everything that cop had done was suspect. It wasn't just plucking a poisoned flower. It was digging deep into the bedrock of things and uprooting an entire tree.

The same would hold for the military. It would be easier—and possibly more efficient—for Buchannan to steer the scumbag to a position where he (or she) held no authority over young men in his (or her) command and couldn't abuse underlings the way Sonny Daye had begged to be abused.

"Exactly." Buchannan nodded, but he still didn't look comfortable. Well, he'd looked the other way—this shouldn't *be* comfortable. "Anyway, the guy who'd inducted Private Daye was actually not a bad guy. As far as I could see, this was his one transgression, and that kid had been so desperate, I was thinking it might have been a kindness. So I tracked where Daye had gone to see what became of him. And he'd been put in the auto bay—which was fine, because as far as I know, a way with cars was the one honest thing he'd put on his entrance forms—but then I ran into a little problem."

"And that would be?" Ellery asked delicately.

"I think you know very well what it would be." Buchannan's eyes narrowed suspiciously. "You even said his name."

"Galway." Ellery's balls actually tingled, knowing how close they were to something.

"That guy's a real motherfucker. So I see his record—kids are offing themselves on his watch, and I shoot off an e-mail to the CO over there. He's cagey, hostile, like he knows something's hinky. But instead of telling me he's going to investigate it, he gives me the number to the 'Department of Behavioral Engineering'—if you can believe that shit."

Ellery blinked. "I really can't. Is there such a thing in the Army?"

"Not in any manual I've ever seen. So I call this department for the hell of it, and I am put directly, do not stop at the secretary, do not pause at Private Runaround, directly linked to Captain Karl Lacey, and he is reading me the riot act about getting in the way of an official US Army protocol here—but it wasn't one I'd ever heard of before. The fact was, I'd come to the end of the line. Captain Lacey outranked me, and this was a kid on the other side of the world that I could not help from here."

Ellery nodded, unable to get mad at him. From the confines of his job, he'd done his best. "What did you think when you heard Galway was dead?"

"Galway's *dead*?"

"Apparently he didn't know."

Ellery cast Jade a quick look, and she shrugged. Well, it was only stating a truth.

"Yes, sir. Galway died in an incident outside of Pakistan. He was…." Ellery shifted uncomfortably. This sounded just so implausible. "Our sources say that Daye was watching a little girl, and Galway wanted to throw her out of the camp in the middle of shelling. She stole Staff Sergeant Jasper Atchison's gun from his belt and shot Galway right before the auto bay was hit."

Buchannan's eyebrows hit his hairline. "Really?"

Yeah, Ellery felt exactly that way about the story.

"Corporal Daye was in the auto bay at the time. He gave testimony, since Atchison was still in surgery because he'd been hit by shrapnel."

"Really?" Buchannan asked again.

"Sir, I only know what my PI's source told him." Ellery had actually met the sergeant—and Corporal Daye himself—but he wasn't sure this was the time to reveal that.

"Has it occurred to you that Corporal Daye could have shot Galway?"

"Or Sergeant Atchison, since he was there at the time. Yes, an alternative explanation has occurred to me. The question is, why has it occurred to *you*?"

"Because Galway was… was becoming a liability. I mean, maybe it was a coincidence, maybe it wasn't. But if I was sniffing around Galway, and if he was a part of this 'Department of Behavioral Design' or whatever bullshit, maybe someone wanted him dead?"

"Or maybe he died and they didn't give that much of a shit." Jade sniffed, and Ellery gazed at her thoughtfully.

"I've met Daye and Atchison," he admitted after a pause. "Jackson and I interviewed them for something unrelated in October—"

"San Diego?" Jade asked, a soft smile on her full lips. "That's probably the only time he's ever been on a plane. You know that, right?"

Yes. Jackson had admitted as much to Ellery as the plane took off, and he'd watched the fields underneath the jet become a big brown-and-green puzzle.

"He was like a little kid," Ellery murmured, before pulling himself with an effort to the confused recruiter. "They were… well, they weren't innocent as children. But Jackson said they were like rattlesnakes. Completely harmless unless you stepped on one of them, and then watch the hell out."

Buchannan nodded. "Okay. So, given that the story is crap, who's thinking that maybe Galway was a problem someone wanted to sweep under the rug?"

Yes—all three of them nodded.

"So," Ellery said, hoping Buchannan was the kind of ally they really, really needed at this point, "who thinks that Tim Owens might have been the same sort of problem?"

Buchannan raised his graying eyebrows, and Ellery was suddenly struck by how innocent—in his own way—Buchannan really was. Yes, he'd been suspicious, but he hadn't raised hell. All his actions were still guided by sort of an implicit faith in the system. Buchannan was a small fish who believed that somebody, somewhere, *must* know of a person with the brass and the resources to fix this problem.

Except this problem had been nagging at Master Sergeant Buchannan for nearly four years now, and he'd just discovered it was so much worse than he'd imagined.

Perhaps—just perhaps—he was *exactly* the sort of ally they needed.

"I have honestly never heard of Owens," Buchannan admitted. "But I can ask some questions. I served over there for eight years. I still know some folks."

"Thank you," Ellery said softly. "That's… that's so appreciated."

Buchannan looked away. "I know I have no right to ask, but about Corporal Daye—"

"Atchison was cleared of all charges. That incident we investigated… well, we're pretty sure he and Sonny weren't guilty of killing anybody. Not that I don't think they *could*—just that I don't think they *have*. Or," he amended, remembering the rabbity, feral way Sonny Daye had glared at him and Jackson as Ace had kept up a redneck patter to distract them, "nothing on our radar right now."

Buchannan nodded, like he got that. "Okay. Good to hear."

"My PI was going to call them up, maybe, and ask them about Owens, but we could just as well leave that nest of rattlesnakes undisturbed if…." He waited for Buchannan to fill in the blank.

"If I can get my sources to come through."

"Excellent," Ellery said with meaning. "Now, I only have one more question to ask you, and then we can get out of your hair and let you get home for the evening."

"My wife will be appreciative." Buchannan winked, and Ellery thought he seemed like a genuinely good guy. God, he didn't meet many of those in his business.

"Captain Karl Lacey—I'm meeting with him tomorrow. Now, given that I don't know where he's coming from, I don't know what department he's in charge of, and I just ended up with him on a plane when I said Tim Owens's name, is there anything you can tell me?"

Buchannan's eyes had gone wide—and his face pale. "Lacey's a snake. Not a sweetheart snake like a rattlesnake, who warns you and nurtures its young and has moments of compassion. No—Lacey's like a coral snake. He's good-looking, makes things sound great to the brass, but…." Buchannan glanced around the office like suddenly *now* he was worried about being overheard.

"Remember when I said I'd been out in Afghanistan for eight years?"

Ellery nodded.

"I almost got sent out again. This post? This is a promotion. I almost got another promotion that put me back in the desert, less than twenty-four hours after I got off the phone with that guy. I do not know whose boots he's licking, but I can tell you right now, he must be doing a damned good job."

"Well, fantastic," Jade said, dusting her hands off with purpose. "I'll just sit back and let Ellery talk during that meeting. Good with you, Cramer?"

And suddenly the little bit of headway, the strategic plan of attack, the camaraderie he'd just built with Jade—it all fell away.

"Jackson was supposed to make tomorrow's meeting," he said softly.

Jade's shoulders slumped. "Well. Maybe he will."

"What time is your meeting with Lacey?" Buchannan asked, ignoring their byplay.

"Right before lunch," Ellery said. He eyed Jade speculatively. "Would you like to pick him up under the guise of being the company go-to guy?"

Jade's smile was wide, bright, and pure evil. "You betcha," she said, nodding without hesitation. "I might even give myself a raise for being indispensable."

"You'd be good for it." He turned back to Buchannan and stood, then extended his hand, gratified when Buchannan shook with him, his grip firm and reassuring.

Ellery would take what he could get at this moment.

When he and Jade walked out of the recruiter's office, the sun had been down for nearly forty-five minutes, and a damp cold was sneaking into Ellery's bones. He checked his phone out of reflex and saw the usual messages. He scrolled through them with unnecessary haste, almost chucking the phone across the parking lot when he didn't see the number he was looking for.

"He didn't call me either," Jade muttered glumly, and Ellery managed an encouraging smile.

"Well, there's always this evening. Here, I'll take you home."

Jade sighed—and given what her strength could usually yield, it was good to have her on their side.

"Come inside for dinner," she ordered. "Mike is cooking chicken something. It'll be good."

Ellery half laughed. "Chicken something? Is that a cordon bleu dish?"

Three months ago she would have ripped his face off for being a spoiled rich boy, but now she maybe got that he was kidding.

"Yup. Mike's chicken something. It'll be in all the cookbooks next year—but it never comes out the same way twice."

THE DUPLEX looked sad at night without the lights on in Jackson's side. The front of his part of the structure was covered in yellow crime scene tape, as was half the driveway and Jackson's side of the yard.

Ellery parked in front of the house, looked at the place, and swallowed. It wasn't a bad building—working-class, certainly, and there were houses and duplexes along that street that were in better and worse condition. But Jackson had painted *his* home a cheery blue with white trim, and his yard was well-tended sod. He'd planted a tree—the purple kind, with the little plums—in the corner of the yard a couple of years earlier, and it was getting big enough to shade the guest room on his side.

It wasn't sad or lonely—at least not when it was fully occupied—and it wasn't a place to be rescued from. It had been, in fact, a thing Jackson had been most proud of.

He'd brought people there—bedmates, mostly, and friends. If his behavior toward Ellery when they'd simply been work partners was any guide, he'd offered them food or beer, a shower, and a place to sleep, even if it was the couch or the guest bed sometimes.

Ellery felt a stab of shame. Yeah, sure, he wanted Jackson to come to his house and move in. Ellery's was bigger, it was nicer, it cost more—but what had Ellery done to earn that house?

Jackson had put his whole heart into making himself a home. It hadn't been spectacular, but it had been safe. He'd had a friend next door that he'd turned into family. He may not have had a partner there, but he'd felt secure enough to bring lovers there to fight off the darkness that swamped his soul at night.

It would cost Ellery nothing but a bit of snobbishness, of material pride, to ask if they could both move into the duplex instead.

Ellery would do that. He'd move his suits out of the walk-in closet and put up with the teeny shower just to be able to hold Jackson at night when the dreams got scary and no amount of strength or courage or good memories could keep them away.

"He should move in with you permanently," Jade said, surprising him. They'd both been standing there staring at the dark face of Jackson's duplex like he'd suddenly turn on the lights and walk out.

"I could move in here," he said humbly, and Jade's snort was actually a relief.

"Oh my God, why? He's got some shitty furniture in the garage and some clothes that didn't make the cut—"

Ellery frowned. "Wait—were they winter clothes? I think he's been wearing the same two pairs of jeans and sweatshirts since it started getting colder."

Jade groaned and tilted her head back at the stars. They were close enough to the river there that a few were actually peeping out through the light pollution. "God! You forget, you know? He's just so… so strong. Even when he was in the hospital—both goddamned times. If he was breathing, he was going to be okay. You just don't think a thing like this is going to…."

They both looked at that dark half of the house, then waved slightly at the police car parked on the street in front. The officers looked a little bored but mostly alert, and Ellery was glad they were there.

"Why hasn't he called?" she asked. They'd both called him on the way over—nothing, not even a recording.

Suddenly Ellery had a thought. "Hey—I bought his phone."

She rolled her eyes. "Well la-de-fuckin' *da*."

"Don't be shitty. I bought his phone. I set it up. I have insurance. Jade—it'll take some calls and, well, some lying, but I think I can have them track it."

"Oh!" Jade let out a half laugh. "Well come on in, smart guy. I'll serve you chicken something, and you track down Jackson."

It wasn't that easy.

Well, *dinner* was that easy. Dinner was chicken left in the Crock-Pot with a big jar of salsa. On a tortilla with some lettuce and some sour cream, it was really delicious.

Ellery ate it while he called his phone provider and asked them to track down the iPhone he'd bought three months ago.

"It was for a business associate," he lied smoothly. "And it seems to have gone missing. It might have sensitive data on it. If it's just in his briefcase or something"—Jade snorted—"I don't want to deactivate it."

"Well, sir, your associate must have had a mishap, because that particular phone seems to be offline."

"I'm sorry?" Ellery said, dinner at Mike's plain wooden table turning to ashes in his mouth. "Explain how he could have deactivated it?"

"Well, usually being offline like this means the SIM card was taken out and the phone itself destroyed."

"So, like, deactivated." His chest couldn't move. He couldn't breathe. He couldn't think.

"That's what I said."

Jade snatched the phone from his hand. "Where was it last? Do you have any idea?"

"According to our records, it was east of Freeport Boulevard."

"Okay, thank you. We'll tell our associate he needs to start shopping for another goddamned phone."

Jade hit End Call and handed the phone to Ellery.

He tried not to let it slip out of his suddenly sweaty fingers.

"Jade?" he said, keeping his voice as even as he could. "Has the family Jackson got arrested for drug dealing been processed yet?"

Jade frowned. "No—we have a bail hearing for them tomorrow. Why?"

"I can't remember if I put their file in my briefcase or not. I need to…." Deep breath. Deep fucking breath. "I need to talk to the arresting officer to see if he can maybe check that area out for us. It would be… unfortunate if we panicked because Jackson dropped his phone—"

"And ripped out his SIM card and drove over it with a truck," Mike said grimly. "You look like death, Ellery. I'm gonna put on some coffee. Jade, can you find that name?"

But Jade was still standing at the table, looking down at Ellery, her chin trembling as she did what Ellery was trying to do and keep it together.

"Both of you!" Mike snapped. "Stop acting like he's dead. He's shook-up. He's not suicidal. He's not an idiot. Now start looking for him. I don't know a goddamned thing about files or cops or any of that shit, and I certainly don't know a damned thing about Freeport Boulevard!"

"Meadowview," Jade said, shrugging. "Lots of repo'd houses, lots of vacant land behind the housing tracts. Crime's up, education is down, and there's not a lot of places for people to work if they don't have a car."

"Worse than Del Paso Heights?" Ellery asked.

"It's bigger," she said frankly. "It's a bigger stretch of really fucked-up and bad. But, you know. Jackson knows how to survive fucked-up and bad, right?"

Ellery nodded. So many reasons. So many. For Jackson's phone not to be functioning and for Jackson not to be home at—he looked at the clock above Mike's stove—eight o'clock at night.

"Shit," he muttered. "I should have asked when it got deactivated. I wasn't thinking."

"Yeah, well, neither was I." She looked up with some relief at Mike, who was puttering around with the coffeemaker. "Once again, Mike was the only one with his brain on. Good job, honey."

Mike beamed at her, quiet worship, and Ellery got absurdly close to tears.

"Go get the file," he said, wiping under his eye with his third finger. "Let's see if we can send somebody out there to check for him."

"Good," Jade agreed. "Because sitting here pretending it's all okay was driving me batshit."

BY NINE o'clock, Ellery had talked to one Eric Pierpont, and the news was not heartening.

"Jackson? Yeah, sure. He seemed okay when I saw him. A little, you know, wired, but then someone had smashed his window in with a knife hilt, and he'd spent about ten minutes holding a gun on those drug dealers until the police got there."

"More like five," Ellery said, not liking the hyperbole. "I was the idiot on the other end of the phone."

"Oh," Pierpont said, like this explained a lot. "Well, he's very loyal. You should know that. I told him I was interested, and he said he was taken straight off. Some guys would have tried to play, you know?"

Ellery grunted. "Yeah. I know. But where did he go afterward? Do you know?"

"Well, he asked the kid about someone out in Meadowview, and the kid gave him a description of the house before we took him away. He was trying to find a drug dealer, I think. Someone named Bobby or—"

"Billy." Okay. Good. So that had been the same plan Ellery knew about, and there'd been a reason behind it. Ellery could deal with a reason. "We sort of know why he was going there—but he should have been back by now. Can you think of anything else?"

Pierpont made some unspecific sounds over the phone. "Uh… look, your guy didn't have… you know, a problem, did he?"

Uh-oh. "Define problem."

"Well, he showed me how the drug business worked—the drug packets were folded up in the papers. It was pretty clever. But the paper he showed me had one packet, and as we were doing the inventory, we noticed that all other papers had two. At first I thought 'Oh well, drug dealers—not always the brightest bulbs in the pack,' right? But you calling up, and him wanting to go to Meadowview to find another dealer…."

"Two and two does not make five," Ellery said flatly. "Jackson won't even take painkillers most of the time. He's got a full bottle of oxy from when he came home from the hospital, and he was *shot*."

Jade was listening on speakerphone. "And he hates needles," she threw in for good measure. It was true—too much time being hurt. Just the thought of the shunt in his shoulder had made him nauseous.

"Okay. Well, would there be another reason for him to sneak a dime bag of heroin?"

"No," Jade said flatly. "Must have been coincidence."

Ellery analyzed her expression—but he bided his time. To Pierpont he said, "I know you're off shift right now—"

"No, not a problem. I've got a buddy on patrol near there. I'll have her check it out."

"Good, thank you." He swallowed, thinking about this nice, cheerful officer hitting on Jackson and taking no for an answer. Thought of him taking Ellery and Jade's word for it that Jackson hadn't stolen drugs from a crime scene—and about the last time he'd seen Jackson at a crime scene he had nothing to do with, and how the police hadn't been nearly so friendly. "Sincerely," he added. "Thank you."

"I'm a friend of Mack Davis. He's always told me Rivers is a good guy. I didn't see anything today to change that. Cops can be assholes—I try not to be."

Ellery let out a steady breath. "Mission accomplished. Call me if you hear anything, okay?"

"Will do. I, uh, hope we only hear good news."

Ellery squeezed his eyes shut. "Me too." His voice was way huskier than he would have liked.

They rang off, and Ellery looked at the bottom of his empty coffee cup. "I've got to go," he said. "What if he, you know. Went ho—back to my place. What if he's there and I'm not there?"

"Good idea," Jade said gruffly. "Just, you know. Tell us if you hear any news."

Ellery looked her in the eye. "What were you thinking when you heard about the drugs? You don't think he's going to use them, but you had something in mind."

Jade fidgeted, looking over his shoulder for Mike. "You're going to have to fill in the blank all on your own, buttercup. This is your ghetto—" Mike stopped and swore. "I'm sorry." And then, as though by rote, "That was culturally insensitive of me, and I am desperately trying not to be the cracker you first thought I was when we met."

Jade laughed and scrubbed her fingers through the waves of hair at her nape. "I hate this 'do," she muttered. "I mean, it looks good, but braids were always the fuck outta the way, you know?"

She was tired, and the accents of her college education fell away, leaving her with the same cadence Jackson spoke in when he wasn't paying attention. Something about this little pocket of the universe trapped a mix of your basic Southern accent, street Spanish, and, God help them all, surfer lingo in the language of the natives. Ellery had noticed that it went beyond socio- or even economic groups. It was like the area was one big melting pot.

Well, it was.

"I know," Mike said kindly. He moved from his spot by the coffeemaker, around the table, so he could massage her shoulders. "It's your hair, hon. However you want it. You know I think you're beautiful."

She looked over her shoulder at him and smiled shyly. "Okay—you need to not say 'cracker' when you give the speech. You're not that guy. You can say 'uneducated.' That's closer, okay?"

Mike nodded, and Ellery had to wonder how many rough patches they'd ridden to get to the spot where they had the language to deal with race and region and cultural sensitivity without rubbing each other raw.

Maybe the world could take note.

"I'll say anything you want." He bent and kissed the top of her head. "But you should probably answer Ellery's question so he can drive home and worry about Jackson."

"And feed his cat," Ellery acknowledged.

Jade grimaced. "He's talking to a drug dealer, Ellery. I mean, we both know he doesn't use, but he could use it as ID—hey, is this your product? He could use it as a bribe for a junkie—give me your dealer and I'll give you a fix now for free—"

"That's not very bright of them."

"They're *junkies*, Ellery. They've killed a lot of brain cells getting to that point. Anyway—I think he took it for one of the above. He was going to walk into a drug dealer's den, and he figured it would come in handy. The cops never logged it. Pierpont didn't see him palm it—"

"I take it he's done that before," Ellery said dryly.

Jade raised her eyebrows. "For a while, in the sixth grade, he'd bring me and Kaden candy bars. Took us a couple of months, 'cause we were kids and kids are stupid, but we realized he'd been stealing them from one of the five liquor stores on our block. We told him to quit it or we'd have to tell Mom, and he stopped, but he must have been good, 'cause he never got caught."

Ellery's heart twisted. He nodded and stood, keeping his face averted. "I'll just see myself out—"

Jade threw herself into his arms and hugged him tight. "Mike will walk you out," she said. "There's still cops outside, remember? It's not safe."

He had no choice but to hug her back, surprised at how comforted he felt by her soft, solid body and her warmth. She wore something exotic-smelling in her hair, and that comforted him too.

"He'll...." He couldn't finish that thought.

"He'll come home," she told him.

In the end what got him to his car and through a simple handshake with Mike was faith in her word.

He got home and was greeted by Billy Bob, bitching at him piteously. Jackson—who had been working only part-time for the last two months—was not home.

Ellery usually waited until he'd undressed to pick the cat up. He spent enough time with the lint roller on his slacks as it was. But today he walked through the door and scooped the damned cat into his arms, careful of the mostly healed missing leg but needing the warm animal smell and the reminder of Jackson more than he needed a clean suit.

"Heya, buddy. How you doing?"

Billy Bob swore at him. At least Ellery assumed it was swearing, because Jackson wouldn't even own an animal that couldn't say "Fuck you, bub. I'm hungry, lonely, and pissed!" in whatever tongue it favored.

"Yeah, I miss him too."

More swearing, followed by the cat unexpectedly touching noses with him and scent-marking him with a little free drool thrown in. Ellery let him finish and then carried the cat to the bedroom bath so he could wipe his face off.

"That was sweet," he muttered, spitting fur. "Maybe don't love me so mu—"

The cat did it again, and Ellery let him, trying really hard to keep his lips closed. Finally he just sank down to the bed, slacks and all, and cuddled the cat, since Billy Bob wasn't going anywhere. After a moment he pulled out his phone with the intention of calling Pierpont and riding his ass for news he obviously didn't have yet.

Instead he found himself on the phone with his mother.

"Ellery! So nice to hear from you. At twelve o'clock at night."

Ellery pictured Taylor Cramer as she'd been around midnight all through his childhood. During the day she wore impeccably tailored suits with sensibly heeled pumps and, always, hose.

At night she changed into pajama pants—something soft and tasteful. His father got her a new pair for Chanukah and for her birthday, every year, with a T-shirt to match. She'd be wearing one now and a pair of fluffy, angel-soft slippers, with a blanket or shawl Ellery's sister had crocheted her recently. Rebecca had started the craft in high school, and although their mother had been bemused by all the expenditures on yarn, she'd been grateful for every gift. (Rebecca had once told Ellery that she would, just once, like to crochet for their mother in a color other than black, camel, cream, ecru, or white—but she picked interesting patterns and luxury fibers to keep herself from getting bored.)

"Hi, Mother. I was just…." Oh God. His mother didn't do sentiment. She did legal sharkery, but tonight Ellery needed comfort, and he felt like a foolish child for even picking up the phone in the first place. Billy Bob meowed plaintively, and Ellery fondled his ears, trying to think of something to say.

"How's Jackson?" Taylor said into the silence. "Has he resigned himself to being a part of the family yet?"

Ellery let out a sharp bark of unhappiness. "I would have to say that's a big no."

"Oh, Ellery—are you having problems? I'd ask if you two had broken up, but I hear the cat in the background. One thing I know about your young man is that he's not going anywhere without that cat."

Except he did. "He's having a tough time right now," Ellery said gruffly. "There's…." *Too many things to count.*

"Ellery, spit it out. I'm starting to worry."

Crap—he really had to get it together. "His house got vandalized, his mother died, and he's disappeared."

His mother's gasp of breath on the other end of the line was oddly reassuring. It meant he wasn't alone in being worried.

"Oh, Ellery—what have you done to find him?"

God—*Mom*! "I tracked his phone—it's been destroyed. I called the police to look for him in the place he was last, and they're doing that. He's only been off the grid for a couple of hours—"

"How did you let him go?" The censure—and the horror—in her voice was also reassuring.

It meant he wasn't alone.

The story of their morning poured out, from Jackson's oddly disturbing good-bye kiss to the fight in the house, the trip to the morgue, oh-God-*Owens*, and Jackson's insistence on continuing the investigation like it was any other day.

"Oh," she said softly when he was done. "You didn't really let him go, then. He ran away."

"No," Ellery protested automatically, trying to be sure. "If he'd really run away, he would have taken his cat."

"That's not what I meant—not that he was going for good, Ellery, but… you know. Like the cat. If he hears a scary noise, he'll run away."

Billy Bob drooled on his lap and marked the shoulder of his suit again.

"Not this cat. This cat will jump on its head."

"In perfect health," she conceded. "Honey, he was hurting—"

"Mom, she was a monster—"

"Are you sure?"

"Of course—do I have to tell you about his childhood? Because…." It felt private, but he would, if only to convince her that Jackson was not the grieving son she thought he should be.

"Ellery, when you were nine you threatened to run away because we refused to get you a puppy. Do you remember that?"

"No." Of course he remembered.

"You wrote up a brief detailing why I would be convicted as the worst mother in the entire world if I didn't get you a puppy. I kept that brief. It was flawless. I was planning to show it to Jackson when you two visit over Thanksgiving."

And that was another twist of the knife.

"Is there a reason you're bringing this up?"

"Ellery, do you love me?"

"Of course." There was no question. Yes, his mother was insufferable, meddling, controlling, perfectionistic, and irritating as fuck. But he had never, not once, doubted her love.

"Jackson's mother may have been a horrible mother—I'm not going to ask for details, but I do trust you, you know. But even if she was a monster, and he doesn't have one damned good memory of her, he knows what a good mother should have been. You told me, right? His friend, Jade? Her mother had a hand in his raising. Am I right?"

"Yes," Ellery said, remembering how Jade and his mother had clashed—many times—in Jackson's hospital room.

"Well, if the mother was anywhere near as bright and resourceful as the daughter—not to mention protective—then Jackson knows what a good mother should be. Do you think he doesn't mourn *that*? His mother's death means that this idea of her, as awful as it is, is final. She will *never* be that mother he'd always hoped for. Do you understand?"

Ellery closed his eyes. "Dolly Parton," he said, remembering Jackson's blurry rambling over the mutilated body of his mother. "She used to sing

Dolly Parton songs. And…." He'd seen this over the summer, right before Jackson had been shot.

I thought you were out of that, Jacky.

"She worried about him. Wasn't going to do anything about it, but, you know—worried."

"So maybe just enough to give him some hope. Cruel hope, really, but hope."

"Yeah."

"I think you're right to be worried, Ellery," she said after a quiet moment when even the house seemed to breathe. "I don't think he would have run away for good. But when he comes back, I think he's going to need some room before he talks about it. It may take years before he admits he's hurt and sad. You got to give me a brief and tell me all the reasons I failed as a mother, and then we got to compromise and you got a fish tank when your grades proved satisfactory, and I got my annual Mother's Day chocolate with a minimum of resentment."

"Jackson got to throw his clothes in a trash bag and move to his best friend's apartment when he turned sixteen," Ellery finished.

"Charming." Her breath came out in a rush.

"It was the high point," he told her bitterly.

"Are you worried?"

"That he's not home? Did I not just call you out of the blue when you're in your pajamas?"

"Don't bite my head off, Ellery!"

He took a deep breath and lay back on the bed, figuring his suit was toast. Billy Bob was comfy on his chest anyway, and this conversation with his mother in the dark of his house was as much reassurance as he was going to get.

"I'm sorry, Mother. I didn't mean it that way."

"Well, for what it's worth, neither did I. I meant…." The pause was uncharacteristic of her in the extreme. "Are you worried that he's too damaged to stay?"

Oh. Ellery rubbed noses with Jackson's cat, taking in the tattered ears, the broken tooth, the deep trenches in the fur on his face and shoulders from hard-fought battles.

And don't forget the bald stump of his back leg, where the fur hadn't grown back out.

"There's no such thing as too damaged." He tilted his head back and resigned himself to puncture wounds in his shirt.

"Then as long as he comes back to you, I think he'll be fine," she said, and for the first time maybe ever in his life, he realized his mother was bluffing. Her voice was too smooth, too sweet, and oh my God—

"You're worried too," he said, the knot in his stomach exploding all over again.

"Of course I am," she said softly. "He's not home, Ellery, and he needs you. I know you think I'm the worst mother in the world, but I like this young man, and you love him. Of course," she repeated, her voice dropping to the tones of hurt, "he needs to come home."

"Thanks, Mom," he said, voice thick. "I actually needed to hear that."

"Well, anything to help, honey," she replied sweetly, and he heard the recrimination there. Not warm and cuddly, his mother. He wondered if she ever regretted that. Thinking about her, in her soft pajamas, with a lush shawl around her shoulders as she exercised her razor-sharp mind, he wondered at the process that had forced her to hide that part of herself, even from her children.

"Mom, you know you're not the worst mother in the world, right?"

"Well not compared to *Jackson's*!"

He managed a bark of laughter. "Not compared to any mother. You're actually pretty amazing as a mother. Just, you know, sort of a mature child's mother."

Her chuckle warmed him. "Thanks, Ellery."

"Love you, Mom."

"I love you too. Tell me when your young man gets home. I'm worried too."

"Will do."

He rang off and set his phone on the bed. Then, very gently, he detached Billy Bob from his shirt and set him on the bed next to his phone. The damned cat liked to curl up around them when they were warm. Ellery had actually bought him a small teddy bear with a heatable ceramic core. Jackson had been horrified at first, because his cat was a tough asshole who needed no coddling.

But that hadn't stopped him from heating the core in the microwave at night so the cat, too, had a warm body to snuggle up with when they all went to bed.

"I'll feed you now and get you the bear when I get out of the shower," he promised, feeling a little stupid about talking to the cat but hating the silence even more. Jackson liked music and television and using the exercise equipment and talking about random shit in the kitchen while one of them cooked.

He liked movement.

And bitching at Ellery about stupid things he really wouldn't change.

And protecting the vulnerable.

And taking over Ellery's body like a demon possessor who always gave it back with even more soul than he'd had at the beginning.

"Augh!" He stomped to the kitchen to feed the cat before undressing and jumping in the shower.

He wasn't in much of a better mood when he got out, but he put on his warmest flannel pajamas, made himself a cup of tea while heating up the teddy bear, and settled down to bed with the tea beside him while he read over briefs for the cases he'd been working on *before* this horrible fucked-up day.

At midnight Pierpont called.

A white Honda CR-V with the plates removed, a gym bag full of broken glass, and tiny hand-rolled pieces of trash bouncing around the backseat had been found wrecked in a gully outside a suburb in Meadowview. There was no blood at the scene. It looked as though the car had been pushed off the road and allowed to tumble into a ditch.

The destroyed phone was discovered inside.

Pierpont's contact had instituted a search for a white male, early thirties, wearing jeans and a gray hooded CSUS sweatshirt. He was injured and on foot, possibly disoriented, in the area of Meadowview.

Ellery hung up, his mind a blank, his heart numb.

He thought about calling Jade but couldn't. It was cowardly, but she would have the same night he was about to if he did.

He fought back a rush of helpless, angry tears and buried his hand in Billy Bob's fur. "Oh, buddy. Where is he?"

Billy Bob meowed in answer, letting go of the cuddle bear to nose Jackson's vacant pillow.

Okay, God. If you're out there, you need to be listening. I'm Ellery, I'm a nonpracticing Jew, and I tell people at parties I'm agnostic. This makes me a big fat fraud and a liar, because I will go to temple every Saturday for a year if only he comes back to me in—mostly—one piece.

God didn't go "Shazam!" and throw a sleeping Jackson next to him on the bed, but Ellery felt irrationally better.

Thanks, God. I'll do my part too. I promise.

A part of him wondered if Jackson would think he was crazy if he started going to temple. Then he figured if he and Jackson were going to be a permanent thing, Jackson should get used to him appealing to a higher power.

God knew, one of them needed to communicate with the big guy if they were both going to survive.

Fish Caught

IT WAS too goddamned cold to drive without a window.

By the time Jackson got to the freeway, his teeth were chattering and he could barely concentrate, even with the heater on full.

This is stupid. I should at least get the window repaired before I check this out.

After he'd pumped that kid, Larry, for more information on Billy's house, he'd called the number his mo—Celia had left Mike, and the phone hadn't picked up. He'd called Crystal, their computer wizard at work, and had her track down the owner of the phone—Billy Culkin—and look up his address.

She didn't have an address, but she did have a "last known location," which was in Meadowview. Jackson took that as a win and then asked her not to tell Ellery he'd called.

"I thought you and Ellery were tight?" she'd asked, and he could hear the concern in spite of the air whooshing through the open window.

"Yeah, he's just sort of worrying about me right now. I don't want to freak him out, okay?"

"Jackson, I can hardly hear you! If you're on speaker, could you close your window!"

"No!" he'd shouted back. "My window got shattered!" When he'd slammed the door, he had heard the rest of the glass pebbles swooshing inside the hollow between metal and pressboard, sounding oddly enough like rain.

"Then come back and fix it!" she'd hollered. "This is bullshit!"

"I can't hear you, Crystal!" he lied. "I'm signing off! Thanks for the info! Bye!"

It was a relief to click End Call. Sweet girl, but she was worrying too much.

His mind kept a pleasant blank as he merged from Highway 80 east to the interchange, and then to 99 South. If it wasn't for the fact that he couldn't feel his fingers by the time he got off Florin Road, he would have enjoyed the ride.

As it was, by the time he made his way to the southeasternmost part of the development, he was seriously thinking of pulling off for some coffee or soup or something before he got to his destination.

Except it was frickin' *Meadowview*, and there was very little in the way of fast food or Starbucks when you were exploring what had been designed to be a sweet little prosperous suburb.

There were a lot of foreclosures in Meadowview, particularly since the crash in the early 2000s.

Some of the houses had been standing vacant for nearly five years, sometimes back to back. Holding companies tried to keep squatters out, some with varying degrees of success, but Barrington Road backed up against vacant land. A house that stood empty for more than a few weeks was subject to squatters, with nobody to drive them out.

Jackson had asked Crystal to check Zillow—the houses along Barrington had been empty for between three and five years.

The address Jackson cruised by didn't look vacant.

The For Sale sign leaned drunkenly against the tree in the front yard, and grass grew up between the cracks in the sidewalk—but not that high, considering how rainy this November had been. The yard was patchy and fungus-like—but there were tattered curtains in the dingy window, and someone had kept the weeds cleared on the side yards. The garage door had been graffitied up, but it had also been spray-painted white again.

Whoever lived there must have enjoyed spray-painting, because the old and battered blue Corolla out front sported two gray fenders airbrushed the same way.

Jackson tooled by once, looking lost, and then wandered down the side street before stopping at a dead end with a cattle guard.

Hunh.

Jackson pulled a U-turn and went down a block, then took that street to the next cross street.

This one ended at another dead end with another cattle gate.

The property behind the housing tract could have been prime development land—but it hadn't been developed, and any of the clearing and leveling that various contracted companies had done was now growing a lush green crop of grass. If the lot had remained level, someone could probably make some money mowing it for hay in the fall, but as it was, the entire lot was damned lumpy under the greenery.

Jackson grimaced. It probably needed to be cleared out again anyway. Trash abounded, and he hated to think of the quality of trash. You'd need a damned hazmat suit and super-spiffy lead-lined gloves to come out of that place without disease or some sort of blood poisoning.

There was a thicket of oleander lining the back fence that separated the housing tract from the field, its roots scattered with soda cups, dime bags, and used condoms. Jackson gave it a wide berth on his way in.

The sun was at the horizon as he slunk along behind the six-foot plank fence, counting houses, and he pulled his phone out of his pocket, frowning through the twilight. Jade and Ellery had been texting him all day, and he took a moment to lean back against the fence and read.

Jackson, please text me if you can, I'm worried about you.

Jackson, please don't bother with Billy's place today—I'll go with you tomorrow.

Jackson, please, just come back. We're eating dinner at Jade's after this next interview.

Dammit—would it hurt you to answer your phone?

By the way, if you don't come home, your cat will grieve until he dies of a broken heart, so you need to be careful, whatever you're doing. You understand that, right?

Those were from Ellery.

Kaden is two seconds away from running out here and grabbing your stupid scrawny worthless ass, throwing it into his trunk, and driving you to some godless shithole in the foothills where they don't even have Dish, so you'd better stop being captain cowboy wonderpants and get your stupid self back here and deal with it.

Oh, and by the way, that stupid yuppie you're sleeping with who's got the stick up his ass is completely losing his shit over you. I hope you're happy, because I've had to be nice to him all day, and I'm starting to like him better than I ever liked you.

You're a stupid asshole. Get your shit home and man up. She was a horrible person and you're fucking not, and if she's gonna hurt you this much, I'm glad that rank bitch is dead.

Please, Jackson—just come home.

And there was Jade. But wait—the fun wasn't over.

Kid, you're scaring the people who love you. I see what you're doing here—could you maybe do it where your people can see you?

And Mike. And wait….

We could move into the duplex if you want. It doesn't have to be my place.

He stared at the text, absurdly moved. Oh, Ellery.

No, your place is fine. Backspace, backspace, backspace. *I like your house.* Backspace, backspace, backspace. *You shouldn't miss me when I go.* He stared at it for a moment, finger hovering on Send. A sound from the house on the other side of the fence startled him, and he deleted that message too.

He had better things to do.

He turned and peered through the slats of the fence, grateful the house in front of him had its lights on. If his count was right, he was where he was supposed to be. Time to suck it up, stop wishing he was home and could take a Vicodin, and climb over the damn fence.

It was worse than he'd anticipated. He dropped to the ground on the other side with a muffled whimper and tried not to throw up. Oh shit. Shit. He had to stand and force himself to breathe past the spots in front of his eyes. Oh god*dammit.* His shoulder throbbed, and the new gush of blood through the gauze stuck his sweatshirt clammily to his skin.

He clung to the shadows of the fence, hoping nobody inside heard him but not betting on it. Oh hell. He squinted through the lowering dark at the side yards, wondering if there were fences or locks between him and the front yard, because… oh God.

He couldn't scale the fence again.

Maybe he should call Ellery now and ask him to send a patrol car?

Off in the distance, maybe four blocks away, he heard shots and screams, and he caught his breath.

Waited.

Waited.

Waited.

Let out his breath in a big rush and realized nobody was coming from four blocks away. Nobody was coming here.

He was as he had always been—all by himself.

He stayed to the side of the fence, in the dark, creeping soundlessly through the long November green grass until he was even with the corner of the house. Ahead of him was a walkway, maybe four feet across, between the house and the fence. A gate, slightly shorter than the fence itself, sat at the end, barely illuminated by the streetlamp on the sidewalk. He saw no lock in the latch. Okay—good to know. Given nothing noxious lurked in the shadows he *couldn't* see, freedom lay thataway.

To his left was the stucco corner of what had once been a small and serviceable tract home. The tan stucco was chipping and faded, and the paint at the gutters peeled and cracked. Nobody had loved this house in a long time, but it was still sound and whole, maybe.

Depended what was on the inside.

Jackson had just turned his body so he could creep forward and peer inside through the sliding glass door when a shadow cast from the inside fell against the concrete.

Oh shit oh shit oh shit oh shit.

The back door slid open, then the screen slid closed, and the house farted. Or that's what it seemed like when a noxious burst of overheated air wafted into the chilly November night.

Oh my God, kill me now!

The smell of cooking chemicals, human feces and vomit, burnt hair, and—worst of all—fried chicken rolled from the bowels of hell into the surrounds.

Jackson fought everything in him not to fall to his knees and retch. He'd seen enough bodies at the morgue, and even more at the coroner's office. He knew the smell of human decay, and sure enough, that's what moved like a great sluggish undercurrent in the putrescent bouquet that overwhelmed his senses now.

Hold it together. Hold it together.

Okay—there was a dead body in there. Jackson would stake his reputation on it. He had some proof to offer the police. They could call Tess Dakin, and she could put on her hip-waders, and Jackson could go whining back to Ellery and tell him maybe he *shouldn't* have gone haring off into the wild blue without backup.

Jackson remembered this smell—minus the dead body. He'd lived through this smell before. One more second breathing the smell of his childhood and he'd be a mewling baby in the corner of the yard, and his ability to help a damned soul would be blown out of his mind by the trip to memory lane he'd been putting off all day.

He waited, not breathing, until the footsteps moved away from the back before venturing through the darkened pathway to the gate.

He tripped on the body halfway mashed into the crawl space and almost wet his pants when it moaned.

"Jesus!" he hissed, pulled out his phone, and turned on the lighting app. "Oh… dear God…."

The man—probably—moaned again through broken teeth and vomit crusted on the side of his mouth. Under the matted hair, layers of grime, and the emaciation of the starving junkie, Jackson detected—barely—a glimmer of familiarity.

"Billy?" he whispered. "God—is that you?"

"Where'd Celia go?" he mumbled. "Bitch… sent her for help."

"Yeah, well, you helped her so good she's dead," Jackson said bitterly. To his horror, Billy started to cry.

"Celia… baby… come back for me…."

Oh hell. The last thing he wanted was to feel bad for Celia's *dealer*. But maybe you couldn't interact with someone for years and years without a little bit of a bond.

"Kk, Billy," he muttered. "I'll go get help." He pulled away from the filth and the smell then, hating himself for being too revolted to care much for the human being under it.

"Help," Billy muttered pathetically. "Good kid. Feed ya anytime."

He had. Mostly to get Jackson out of his and Celia's hair when they were conducting business, but he could have used his fists instead. Could have screamed epithets, threatened with the big bowie knife he always carried—could have done lots of shitty things.

But he hadn't. He'd given Jackson food instead, when Celia more than likely forgot.

Didn't make him father of the year. Didn't even make him a decent human being. But he still deserved better than dying in a pile of rags.

Just like even Celia didn't deserve to get carved up like a slaughtered deer when she was still alive.

Yeah, Toe-Tag had been careful not to elaborate—Jackson had understood. If she'd presented as alive enough to end up at the hospital, her blood had still been flowing when she'd been found.

She'd been alive when she'd been gutted—and Jackson wouldn't wish that on an enemy, much less… much less….

He took a deep breath of stench and heaved to his feet, thinking escape, safety, calling the police and an ambulance and calling this fucking day at five thirty, the end, Ellery you fucking win.

The body at his back stopped him—as did the arm across his throat.

"Jackson? You came!" The voice sounded younger and higher than Jackson had imagined it—not the voice of a serial killer, but the voice of a fourteen-year-old chess geek.

"Well," Jackson graveled, barely able to catch that breath, "you issued such a nice invitation."

A low, filthy laugh tickled his ear, and then a tongue, sloppy and foul, licked him.

He jerked hard enough to see stars when his windpipe made contact with the killer's forearm.

"I did, didn't I?" Owens—it had to be Owens—whispered into the hollow of his ear. "I wanted you to come to me so bad…."

At their feet, Billy whispered "Help…." to the indifferent elements.

"Oh yes, I'll help." The iron grip at Jackson's sore shoulder disappeared, and Owens fumbled for something at his belt. Jackson fell to the ground and attempted to roll away, but Owens stood on his shoulder and, while Jackson watched, threw his knife directly into Billy's throat.

Billy's body twitched a couple of times as he breathed his last, but Jackson waited until his eyes closed tightly and then relaxed before he looked away.

"He wasn't bad for a junkie," Owens said conversationally, squatting to haul Jackson up by the arm. Jackson gave a squawk to wake the dead, because his shoulder had one too many insults to be powered through, and Owens stopped what he was doing.

Jackson doubled over, spots dancing before his eyes, and he barely noticed when Owens pulled the knife out of Billy's throat and held it, still dripping, in front of Jackson's face.

"Now I know you're going to want to run away again," Owens said, almost playfully. "Can we just agree that I don't want to hurt you, but I will?"

"I don't know how much incentive that is," Jackson panted, straightening out his body when all his ass thought he could do was crouch and gibber. "I have to admit, I was going already. Not my kind of jam."

Owens laughed and ran a thumb down the side of Jackson's face with the bowie knife still clenched in his fist, scraping blood off on Jackson's shirt.

"I thank you for your candor," he said, almost courtly-like. "Here." He reached into his pocket with his free hand and pulled out a… oh God. Oh God. A pressure syringe, needle capped, full of a pale liquid barely visible in the gleam from the soda lamp as Owens stood.

"No," Jackson whispered, taking a step back from the knife, from the heroin, from all of it.

"Oh, come on now. Don't tell me you've never tried it!" Owen's laugh assumed so much between them—and it rang shrilly with a brain that had obviously cooked a cell or a thousand of them using something very like that deadly little bottle.

"Not once," Jackson replied. *I can make it. I can turn and I can run and I can make it.*

"That's too bad." Owens took a step forward, a cobra advancing on a small prey animal, but Jackson couldn't help his retreat. "I thought you were so… pretty. Violent and pretty. Saw your picture in the paper—I was glad you lived."

Even the shadows couldn't hide the twist in his leer.

"That's kind," Jackson muttered. One more step. "It's nice when people are rooting for you." He'd seen his mother smoke, snort, and shoot up for his entire childhood.

The needles had been the worst. They'd lain about the apartment, wherever she'd dropped them. He'd preferred the coke mirrors, actually, but she kept those up on counters, probably as a throwback to the days when she cared if he lived or died.

Owens flicked the syringe lovingly. "I could make you so dirty," he purred.

Jackson bolted.

One step… two steps… the gate was almost there… three steps….

But he hadn't eaten in twelve hours, and he'd been bleeding all day. He'd gotten less than five hours of sleep the night before, and his day had been… his day had been—

He felt the hand yanking on his hood first, lifting him off his feet, and then a strong arm around his chest as the syringe sank into his neck.

And things got ripply and swimmy and purple after that.

And filled with the worst dreams.

ONCE UPON a time, an informant he was hitting up confessed that he'd just dropped acid.

"So, uh, how's that working for you?" Jackson had asked.

"I was in a real good place when I took it," the guy confessed woozily. "That makes the trip go smooth as silk. You're in a shitty place, the trip's no good."

When the heroin hit his bloodstream, he was in a really fucking shitty place.

When he came to, he was propped against a wall in a filthy living room, legs sprawled in front of him, his throat sore from what felt like screaming.

Tim Owens was standing above him, masturbating.

Jackson had just enough of himself left to close his eyes and his mouth and turn his head as ejaculate splattered on him. He used his sleeve to wipe himself off and looked around in the glare of one dim light.

There were people in here.

Some were lying, still as death, their breathing barely enough to sustain them. Some were sitting against walls, knees drawn up against their chests, in various stages of drug use.

A few were shaking out withdrawals.

And a few—like the guy across from Jackson with the swollen tongue and bulging filmy eyes—were actually dead.

Owens fell heavily to his knees next to Jackson and licked his cheek. Jackson's limbs—which had not been his own for however long he'd lost time—strained to pop him one.

But Jackson wasn't alert enough to win that fight. He needed to save his strength until he could try. He held still, kept his eyes at half-mast while he tried to orient himself.

"That was lovely," Owens muttered. "Can't get off with any of these assholes—all too dirty, you see?"

Must not flinch from dead body in front of me. Must not vomit.

"I mean, I could keep you stoned for ages and just use you however. I had to get the first one off kind of quickly," he confessed, as though a little embarrassed. "Jackson, you've got to understand—I've been waiting for you for so long."

Jackson let out a whimper on purpose. A reaction.

"Yeah, I know. I should have been going after your boyfriend—he's the brains of the operation. But he's besotted with you. Anyone could see it. And you were just so…." He licked Jackson's chin and the crease of his neck. "Delicious. Better to go after you, dirty up all your fucking pretty. And you have to admit, running into your mother's dealer—that was special. I got all the drugs. I got to give away all the drugs. Just look at this place. It's a testament to unholy greed and addiction. Ain't it grand?"

I need to get him off me.

"Someone'll see my car," he slurred, only partly on purpose, but it had the desired effect.

"Right you are," Owens told him. His hand in Jackson's pocket brought back the stunning nausea of the crashing hit, and Jackson shuddered hard and tried to stay limp. "Oh, you're coming down a little." He kissed Jackson's cheek and grabbed his crotch. "Don't worry, pretty-pretty. I'll come back and dose you up again."

"No," Jackson protested—a real protest, one he couldn't stop making. "Head's all swimmy."

"Yeah." A tender kiss on the cheek. "That's the idea, pretty. Keep you all dirty, use you. You're not as young as my usual toys, but you're feistier. They never threaten me with discovery, for one. Why, Jackson, I think you're *hoping* for the police to show up—and we all know how you hate the police."

"Fuckers," Jackson slurred, and Owens chuckled.

"Oh hey—" He stopped, rummaged through the front pocket of Jackson's hoodie, and came up with Jackson's phone. "Look! Something else to get rid of."

He pushed himself to his feet and zipped up his fly. "Juice always does it to me," he admitted, like this made him special. "Every single time."

Jackson's cock ached in his jeans—a side effect he'd read about, but God, he could have done without the real thing. But that didn't mean he couldn't use it. "Mm horny," he mumbled.

"Oh, you hang on, Jackson. You and me are gonna *play*."

Jackson kept his eyes unfocused in the direction of his dead friend with the black tongue. "Play," he whimpered.

Owens caught him by the chin and turned his face so they were nose to nose. Like Ellery had noted, he was beautiful, even strung out. Bridger had said the guy used when he was on the force, but apparently Billy's place had been the proverbial candy store. Dirty spoons and bottles of water were everywhere among the human detritus. He must have just opened the place up as a smorgasbord for whoever popped in looking to buy from Billy. Well, that heroin in Jackson's pocket was looking pretty superfluous now. There were dime bags stacked up on the kitchen counter, overflowing, just ready for the taking.

With any luck, Jackson would remember to throw that thing in his pocket away before he got stopped and searched.

Dumbest idea he'd ever had.

But first he had to look like he was too stoned to move, which wasn't hard. He was barely clear enough to know why he should move in the first place.

It had something to do with Owens's jizz on his face and why he shouldn't throw up.

But Owens was up, footsteps thudding across the filthy carpet, and Jackson waited. Waited. The door closed, and he waited. Some more.

In the distance, he thought he heard his car revving, and that was his cue.

He lurched forward, almost into the dead guy, and fell back on his ass. No, no, no, no—out. Out of here.

He had to push himself up on the wall. He stumbled into the coffee table, piled high with paraphernalia and drugs and, oh God, three buckets of what had once been fried chicken, a thing Jackson would never again eat in his life. One of them tilted over and littered the carpet with moldy bones as Jackson gave up on subtlety and just concentrated on barreling out of there.

He fumbled with the lock on the sliding glass door, leaving it open as he stumbled out.

And almost wept when the cold night air washed over him.

He wanted to fall to his knees and get sick and cry—but he couldn't. Because Owens was out there, and he'd take Jackson *back inside that house*. He'd drug him and violate him, and eventually Jackson would be a gibbering skeleton, stuffed in a hole, waiting for a knife in his throat.

He'd be lying in his own refuse on a squelching carpet, black tongue extended, and Ellery would see him that way, and that would be the last memory he'd have of Jackson.

Jackson had to fucking move.

He didn't go left, even though he knew that way. Left was too close to the fence, and Owens had to pass the fence when he was done doing whatever with the car. And Jackson's phone.

God!

Okay, down the darkened corridor next to the house, and his eyes blurred at the gate latch at the end. Was there a lock? Was it short? Could Jackson scale it?

There was a reason Jackson couldn't scale another fence, right?

He'd have to remember the reason.

But first… oh God… past the shadows, the shadows that held hands and matted hair and dying scarecrows, and to the fence, and oh, sweet God, into the light!

The light!

Owens could find him in the light.

The fence opened, so easy it was magic, and Jackson crossed the street, feeling like a duck in a target shoot, staggering but keeping to his feet. On the other side of this next house, around the sidewalk, the streetlight was broken.

Ah, shadows.

Jackson hugged the shadows.

He meandered, lurched, lollygagged, and staggered from one block to the next, to the next, to the next. He heard shots and screams, crashes and fights, but he avoided every open garage, every approaching car, until he saw it, under a streetlamp, with a vacant lot behind it.

Glowing like a jewel.

A bus stop.

He was so grateful he sank to his knees and vomited stomach acid on some stranger's lawn.

THE BUS driver almost didn't let him on. Jackson managed to produce a tattered five from his wallet—which Owens had left alone, thank God—and to trade it in for a ticket and a transfer. He'd made it to Franklin Boulevard, which was, by his estimation, about a three-mile meander from Owens's little slice of hell, and he would have been impressed with himself if he'd had anything left.

Even if this bus didn't get him where he needed, there was bound to be a liquor store that would give Jackson some cash and some change so he could get across town.

And right now he was dizzy and still nauseated from the comedown, and he would have sold his soul for a bottle of water.

He had to settle for sinking onto the bus cushion and resting his aching head against the pole.

And comfort himself with the fact that he was still swimming from his first drug high, and he didn't have the slightest fucking urge to do that shit again.

HE MANAGED to stay awake on that bus, but after the transfer, on the next bus, the one that went from Florin Mall to Stockton Boulevard, he fell asleep, dozing uneasily, dreams filled with being stuck in that room forever and ever while the whole world rocked like the bus. People came and went, looking at him without looking. He could feel their disgust as soon as his smell hit them.

He heard someone say "Fucking junkie."

Everybody chanting "Fucking junkie!"

His mother laughing at him, cackling, because he was a fucking junkie, just like her.

He woke up with a start, blinking from the toxic running lights around the hostile and indifferent faces, peering into the darkness for a landmark, anything to tell him where in the fuck he was.

Oh, great. K Street—somewhere past the transfer that would have taken him to Power Inn, to Ellery.

Shit.

He blinked against the strobing greenish light of the inside of the bus, trying desperately to orient himself. A bus… he hadn't ridden on a bus since… since… he and Jade, Kaden, and Rhonda, getting to Natomas to watch a movie. They went once a month, taking a bus down Grand, across to Northgate, up to the Regal.

But he couldn't do that anymore—Ellery wouldn't be caught dead on a bus.

He pulled himself abruptly to reality, got off the bus at J Street, and took the one going north. He got off near Elvas, sick of the smell of his own vomit.

He was a mile from his duplex.

Funny, how in the empty honesty left by hunger and high, he couldn't make himself call it home. Not anymore.

It would have been so easy to alert the police watching Jade and Mike, to tell them he'd been abducted and assaulted and needed help.

But he didn't want to talk to any of those people. He didn't want to deal with the police. He didn't even want to deal with Jade. He wanted to go ho—go get his cat and check in to a hotel and get the fuck out of Ellery Cramer's life.

But first he needed… *needed* to get out of these fucking clothes.

He couldn't walk into Ellery's house like this, covered in vomit and a serial killer's semen. He couldn't talk to Jade or Mike like this. His entire life felt like a violation right now. He'd been violated and soiled, and he soiled the people he loved just by breathing near them.

He walked two blocks out of his way so he could come around the duplex on the dark side and sneak into his garage window, left open by the crime scene cleanup company on Mike's request.

Neither of them liked the chemical smell that lingered.

His shoulder gave a throb as he clambered over the windowsill, and he figured the last of the heroin was wearing out of his bloodstream. He hoped he could let himself out of the side door, or he was gonna be stuck here. He stumbled on his own feet and caught himself on the couch, which was pushed into the back by the tool shelves.

Forever.

He needed to move, do what he came for, and get to Ellery's house or he'd die in his own garage, too tired and disoriented to move.

People would miss him.

God, they'd find him like this—he couldn't let anyone see him like this.

Shit.

Jade and Mike had packed his clothes in boxes, Jade's bold, looping writing declaring the boxes "Decent Jeans," "Holey Sweatshirts," "Future Dust Rags," "Clothes I might let him wear in my house."

Picky woman.

She was cleaning out your house while you were in surgery.

Good woman. Good woman who finally had a good man in her life and didn't deserve to be saddled with Jackson in the name of childhood friendship.

All that bullshit about helping people. Serving the greater good. You're the spawn of a drug-addicted whore. Your father figure just died in a pool of his own filth.

Your mother was ripped open and gutted like a deer.

A sound—an ugly one—echoed in the little garage, and he ruthlessly focused his mind on business.

He stripped off his clothes, grunting softly to himself when his shirt stuck to his shoulder, cemented with layers of dried blood. The gauze came off, and the shunt pulled out with it, and he moaned a little.

It didn't hurt enough.

That morning, when he'd been afraid of something on the blade, the pain had been excruciating.

Now that he knew what real drugs felt like coursing through his system, he recognized the lingering aftereffects of an opiate, muffling the sound of the pain in his neurons, and he welcomed it.

He was shivering with cold as he unpacked some old clean clothes—cold-weather gear, thank God. New underwear, new jeans, a new T-shirt with a goldfish cracker on the front, on its back with little *x*'s for eyes, and a zippered hoodie—it all abraded pleasantly against his skin. New socks and an old, worn pair of sneakers felt even better.

A quick drink—stale and tasting of rubber—from the garage sink helped too. Enough to have a second and a third before his stomach rebelled and threatened to cramp. He rinsed his face in the shockingly cold water, then took a step or two back and made himself finish.

Conscious of evidence, he grabbed a trash bag from the shelf and shoved the sweatshirt/T-shirt combo into it before he rooted around his washer for a laundry marker.

On the back of an old box, he wrote, *Jade—get these to the lab. Owens's DNA is on the sweatshirt near the neck.*

His washer and dryer still worked. He shoved the rest of the clothes into the washer and started the load, so grateful to know his stench was being washed from the fabric that he almost cried.

Then—as quietly as he could—he let himself out of the garage door, making sure it was locked from the inside as he left.

The sun wasn't quite up, but it was maybe thinking about its last ten minutes before it had to yawn, stretch, and scratch its pits. Jackson took advantage of the imperfect light to leave the garbage bag and his little sign on Mike's porch.

The policemen, yawning in their squad car as they tried to stay awake, didn't see him. On the one hand, that should have been scary as fuck, because they were supposed to be looking out for Jade and Mike.

On the other, the damned dog started barking inside the house as he was walking away.

He didn't know he had it in him to sprint.

He made it all the way back to J Street and was closing in on the bridge when the shaking in his limbs forced him to slow down.

And walking slowly, every step an agony of shaking limbs and regret, he asked himself why he didn't just knock on her door.

Not clean.

The drugs were completely gone now, sweated out by that final sprint, and he tried to fight this idea with logic.

None of this was your fault.

Well, except the part where he'd gone to a drug dealer's house at dark, alone, without backup, and gotten caught.

But really, wasn't that part and parcel of the whole Jackson package? Had to be a hero, right? Had to wear a wire—for way too goddamned long. Had to be the one to save Kaden, right? Had to save Ellery and go back in the damned hospital all over again, right?

Do you regret those things?

No. They're the best things I've ever done.

Which just went to prove—a guy like Jackson? The best he could do would be dying for a cause. Go hang out in a cheap hotel and put up a banner. "Come get me!"

Bait. It's what's for dinner.

He had his exit planned in his head by the time he got to Ellery's house. Knew where the duffel bag was, knew exactly which clothes he'd bring. He remembered where the cat carrier was. He'd borrow some Tupperware for Billy's food, and he'd make himself a couple of sandwiches. He could catch a cab somewhere—somewhere he could sit and drink and nobody would find him until Owens came and finished him off.

It all made perfect sense.

The sun was up—blazingly hot in the middle of a chilly morning. His skin burned, and he'd sweated and bled through round two of his clothes. It was past eight in the morning, and he didn't have any doubt Ellery would be gone.

A part of him mourned and wailed for his lover, and he stomped on that part without mercy.

We're leaving.

He let himself into the house, and Billy Bob's greeting almost undid him.

"Oh, Billy Bob my man—what you been doing while I'm gone?"

Apparently not being held or loved or fed or having anybody to talk to, ever—which was a total crock, and Jackson knew it.

Ellery doted on the damned cat. It was disgusting—pathetic, really. Poor guy had never had a cat growing up as a kid?

Well, Jackson hadn't either, but that wasn't the point. The point was Ellery showed the damned cat as much affection as Billy Bob could stand. Sometimes he got petted until he lost his shit and attacked Ellery's hand before taking off. Ellery would laugh and sigh and dress his hand and give him an extra big helping of soft food.

Ellery loved this fucking cat as much as Jackson did.

"You're making shit up, you big freeloader," Jackson murmured, hugging Billy Bob fiercely.

His cat, being awesome, let him, melting into his arms and purring, his drool stream soaking into Jackson's sweatshirt. For a moment he gave himself the luxury of just holding something that loved him without reservation. He didn't have to have any pride around his cat. Cats didn't give a fuck about pride or self-worth. They just wanted some goddamned kibble—that was Jackson's job.

Finally Billy Bob meowed, and Jackson let him go, trying to remember the plan.

He felt a trickle of sweat drip down his back, and he decided he'd shower first, then eat. *Then* he'd pack to leave.

He might have made it out the door—maybe.

He made it to the shower, the water pounding gloriously on his aches, even his damned shoulder, which was starting to scab over now that the shunt was gone. He washed his face, his neck, his cheek, again and again. He soaped his hair repeatedly, and again. He'd given Jade the DNA trace. He could get rid of it, right? He could scrub Owens off his skin, and out of his hair, and off his skin, and again and again and again….

The water ran cold, forcing him out of the shower, his chin and neck and forehead stinging from the skin he'd scrubbed off.

He toweled dry before walking into the bedroom with a towel around his waist, his muscles, lax and boneless from the heat, protesting even walking that far.

The cat was stretched out on Ellery's pillow.

I can't take Billy Bob. Ellery will miss him.

Oh God. That was right. Ellery would miss the damned cat. How could Jackson just disappear Billy Bob from his life? That would be… mean. After all the good things Ellery had done for him, how could Jackson take the damned cat?

But... but I can't leave him here. How could Jackson leave his cat behind?

Jackson sat down on the bed, on Ellery's side, and scratched Billy Bob behind the ears. "You look pretty comfy," he admitted.

The cat drooled and purred. Jackson stretched out on his side, petting him rhythmically. "You do make this look good," Jackson mumbled. He was cold.

With a jerk, he grabbed the other end of the comforter and rolled it around his shoulders. It wouldn't matter, he promised himself. He'd take a few moments, be with his cat. Regroup.

He'd leave in the end. He had to.

He owed Ellery that, didn't he?

Other Things with Scales

ELLERY WOKE up at six in the morning, feeling fruitlessly for the other side of the bed. Panicked, he scrambled for his phone but found no new messages, no news.

He made it to the shower on autopilot and dressed the same way.

Jackson, where are you?

But he had a meeting with Lacey at ten and a crapton of work to do for people who *weren't* the victims of serial killers or soccer-mom drug dealers but deserved help just the same.

Ellery could be just as good at emotional denial as Jackson was when he needed to be.

But it wasn't until Jade knocked on his office door to tell him that Lacey was in the larger conference room that Ellery realized he'd been so sunk into his own misery he'd forgotten to tell Jade about the car.

He grabbed his briefcase to follow her down the hall, saying "I have news" as his door closed behind him.

"He came by my house," she said, her voice shaking.

They both stopped, staring at each other.

"What?"

"You go first," he snarled, because she apparently had proof of life and he didn't.

"He left a garbage bag full of yesterday's clothes on the porch, with a sign that said they needed to be tested for DNA. It was his writing, Ellery. I'd know it anywhere."

"What was on them?"

She shook her head and wiped carefully under her eyes with a magenta-manicured finger. "What wasn't?" she returned thickly. "They were.... God, Ellery, the night he must have had."

Ellery shivered, cold in his bowels.

"Why wouldn't he come in?" he rasped.

"I don't know. I... I mean, he was trying to be quiet. The damned dog didn't even wake up until it was too late, and he starts barking when Mike breaks wind."

Ellery couldn't even laugh. "Police found his car last night, around ten o'clock, in a vacant field. The phone was crunched inside."

"And you didn't tell me!" she cried, actual tears escaping.

"And let you live last night with that knowledge?" he retorted, his stomach cramping. "No—you didn't want to live through that night. Trust me."

"God," she snarled, "you two are so much alike—a couple of goddamned fucking martyrs. When this is over, I need to knee you both in the goddamned ba—"

"Ms. Cameron?"

Carlyle Langdon stuck his head around the corner. "Did you tell Mr. Cram—oh, there you are, Ellery." He smiled tentatively. "Any news?"

"That's what we were just discussing, sir," Jade told him, sounding calm and professional. "Ellery got some disturbing news last night, but we have some proof that he's okay this morning."

"Do you know where he is?" Langdon asked, nothing but curiosity in his voice.

Ellery closed his eyes, the anger and the turmoil and the fear subsiding like a wild surf, leaving scoured sand its wake. "Hopefully at home by now," he said, and Jade bit her lip and nodded.

"Well, as soon as your meeting is over, you should go home and check," Langdon told him, sounding pleased with his generosity.

Ellery nodded grimly. "Sir, I think that would be a most excellent idea."

"But first, Commander Lacey. Jade, you brought him in, didn't you?"

Jade stopped in the middle of taking a deep power breath, probably to calm herself down. "Yes, sir. He was…." She shook her head and fought back a sneer. "Cold-blooded," she said after a moment of warring with herself. "Sergeant Buchannan was right about this guy. He's the kind of snake that gives snakes a bad name."

Ellery nodded grimly, trying to get his head back in the game.

Jackson is alive.

Yeah, there was that.

And he's trying to leave.

Well, fuck *that*.

Ellery had no idea why he wouldn't want to stop and ask Jade and Mike for help, but he had a sick sort of despair in his stomach guessing about it.

What was on his clothes?

What wasn't?

Dammit, Jackson—don't you know I'd forgive you anything?

God—he was usually so good at compartmentalizing. It's what made him efficient in the courtroom—even with a guilty client. He could think objectively about what the client had done and what the law could prove and punish for.

But not now.

Now, standing in front of the conference room door, he had to take a deep breath and close his eyes, picturing a backhoe scraping all his fear, all his worry, all his anger into the other room. The room where Ellery kept the stuff related to his heart. He used to think that room was tiny, cramped, unused—maybe he'd have to throw a box in there now and then.

The night before had taught him different.

The other room was a big fat part of the whole damned house.

And now it was full.

And his kicking-ass room was empty and clean and ready to listen to what Commander Lacey wasn't saying.

He stepped through the door with a professional smile on his face.

"Commander Lacey—so good of you to join us. I'll be honest. I didn't think a simple line of questioning would warrant an entire trip from… where was it?"

"Southern California."

Commander Karl Lacey stood six foot five at the very least and was built like a Sherman tank. Ice-blue eyes analyzed Ellery with the emotion of a computer scan and then skated over Jade as though she didn't exist.

He'd worn his fatigues and not his dress greens on this trip, which told Ellery all he wanted to know about Lacey's respect for defense attorneys as opponents, and his refusal to even look at Jade gave Ellery a pretty good picture of who he was dealing with.

A complete and total asshole.

Ellery could be that guy too.

"Are you sure it's not Nevada? My phone said that was a Nevada area code."

"It's a big desert," Lacey said, without the smile that would have made the remark charming—or even plausible.

"Well, I'm still not sure what could motivate a busy guy like you to get on a plane from Nevada and fly up to Sacramento simply because I dropped a name."

Lacey's gaze turned crafty. "Why, what have you heard?"

Ellery and Jade had a silent eyeball-vibrating conversation as Ellery seated himself one seat away from Lacey and Jade sat to the left of Ellery. Ellery knew that from her position, she could see the guy—could keep an eye on him as it were—and he couldn't look straight at either of them.

Although that was more from evasiveness than from any strategic positioning.

"Look," Ellery said, folding his hands and smiling pleasantly. "All we want is some background on this guy. I understand he was under your command before he shipped out."

"Who told you that?" Lacey's colorless blue eyes suddenly zeroed in on Ellery's face with precision, marking Ellery, cutting him out of the picture with an X-Acto knife, and pinning him somewhere else on Lacey's agenda.

Ellery fought the temptation to shudder.

"My PI has sources." Ellery thought of Buchannan, trying hard to be a decent guy within the restrictions of the military—and the fear that he'd be shipped out when he'd done his tours. "We just need to know if it's true."

"Wait…." Lacey's white-blond brows came together, setting off the sunburned forehead. "Is *she* your PI?"

And like that, he noticed Jade.

"As. If." Jade snorted and crossed her arms, but she didn't break off eye contact with Lacey. They regarded each other like a cobra and a mongoose might, but Ellery couldn't say which one was which.

"Our PI is presently out," Ellery said. He tried not to swallow and look at Jade for comfort. *Other room, other room, other room.* "We're not using this source as evidence. We just really want to know about this man who emerged from the military, got a job as a cop working for a corrupt branch of the force, and who spent his spare time getting hard when he witnessed violence and beating street people to death. If you don't keep detailed files on your personnel, we're sort of hoping for, you know, a list of people who maybe saw him torture and kill small animals or, even better, a CO who perhaps pushed him from angry, resentful young man to serial killing adult—"

"You have no proof of that," Lacey snapped, eyes narrowed.

Ellery smiled, all teeth. "Nothing but theory." *Now.* "But as for the serial killer—I do believe we have some DNA being processed now." *Oh, Jackson—what did you do?* "If this man served under you—"

"You will need to talk to the JAG officer for my statement," Lacey said definitively, standing.

Ellery stayed seated. "So… you flew all the way out here on the drop of a name to invoke your right to JAG counsel?"

"That is my option." Lacey scowled and stared straight ahead, arms folded behind him at parade rest. "You *do* understand the difference between military law and civilian law, don't you?"

"I may have to brush up," Ellery conceded. "Because I definitely don't remember a clause in there that says a military man needs to cover for a serial killer who hasn't served in years." Ellery's eyes went wide—and he wasn't dissembling. "Unless he killed in the service."

Lacey stood absolutely still, and Ellery made another leap. "And you knew about it."

Leap. "And you came here to make sure I didn't!"

He stood too, feeling like he should raise his hands over his head and acknowledge that perfect ten in mental gymnastics he'd just achieved going on no sleep, a little coffee, and a shit-ton of worry.

"This interview is over," Lacey barked before striding from the room.

Ellery and Jade watched him go, and when Ellery checked Jade's expression, he saw the same unpleasant realization he felt in the pit of his stomach.

"That man knew," he murmured. "He *knew* what was being unleashed on the world. I'm thinking he might have even encouraged it."

"Do you think someone gave him a command in some nameless desert hellhole so people in civilized parts of the world wouldn't wake up with their throats slit?"

Ellery shot Jade a look, but she didn't appear to be kidding.

"It's possible." He thought about how Lacey hadn't changed expression during the interview—not even when he was threatening Ellery with the fury of the JAG Corps. His eyes might have narrowed, but he'd maintained a perfect cobra face during the final few moments. "I know *I'll* sleep better when his plane takes off. Are you driving him again?"

Jade looked pleased. "Yup. Which meant he just made that complete dickless exit to wait on the pleasure of a black woman he can't look in the eyes."

Ellery let out a chuckle. "I think you have business in here for at least a half hour," he mused. "Would you like me to bring you some coffee?"

"I'll have Crystal bring it to me," she said before her voice dropped seriously. "Ellery, do you have policemen watching your house like I do?"

Ellery shook his head, kicking himself. "I sent mine home when I left this morning."

"Could you maybe—"

He was already gathering his papers for his briefcase. "I'll text you if he's home," he said softly.

"I'd appreciate it." She turned a troubled face toward him. "You'll tell him, right? That it doesn't matter what happened, as long as he's okay?"

"As many times as it takes," Ellery promised.

"Thanks. Go."

He was out of there in three minutes, barely stopping for his coat, his car keys, and his laptop from his office. He passed Lacey standing by the reception desk on his way out and didn't pause to acknowledge the man's angry demand for his driver.

Ellery fervently hoped Jade lingered over that coffee.

HE SAW the pile of clothes in the hallway to the bedroom and texted Jade and his mother then, which was a good thing.

Once he saw Jackson, folded in the comforter like the naked filling of a quilt burrito, relief swamped him, and he lost nearly five minutes standing in the hallway, one hand against the wall, while he tried to stop his knees from shaking.

Oh God. He was home. He was home and safe.

Ellery started undressing before he was aware he could even stand. He wasn't thinking about sex—not even a little.

He was thinking he could see Jackson shivering under the covers from where he stood, the throes of the dream—whatever new horrors had been added to it—taking him over in the middle of a sunny fall day.

He slid into bed behind Jackson, naked except for his boxers, the fold of the comforter at his back. He wrapped his limbs around Jackson's body and clutched him tight in a convulsive shudder.

"No," Jackson whispered. "Don't touch me. I'm not clean."

Ellery pushed himself up on his elbow and ran fingertips through Jackson's obviously clean hair. "You showered," he said, puzzled. He touched the side of Jackson's cheek, pink and raw from some sort of burn. "Baby, what happened—?"

Jackson made a feeble attempt to roll away, but Ellery stopped him.

"Not clean," Jackson whispered. He pulled his knees up to his middle, and Ellery let out a little gasp of pain. The "burn" covered his forehead, his cheek, his chin, his neck.

"Did you do this?" he asked, stomach knotting.

"You need to let me go," Jackson said simply, staring at the ceiling.

"No," Ellery ground savagely. Deliberately he kissed the scrubbed cheek, holding Jackson's chin in place. "Mine."

"Ellery—"

"*Mine*!" Ellery kissed him hard, fearing that Jackson would do it, would say no again, leaving Ellery with no choice but to walk away. Jackson's mouth opened to his, and a knot somewhere above Ellery's groin opened up and took light and oxygen for the first time since he had woken up the morning before and realized Jackson was gone.

Ellery didn't let up on the kisses, rolling so he was in the vee of Jackson's spread legs. He raised his hands to cup Jackson's cheeks, pulling back to meet his eyes.

"All mine," he enunciated so there was no uncertainty. "You can't go. You're mine. You belong here." His voice wobbled. "Oh God, baby. Where have you been?"

Jackson's eyes grew bright and red rimmed. He turned his face away. "It was sort of a shitty night," he rasped.

"You fucking think?" And Ellery lost it. Mindful of the shoulder—which looked awful, black and swollen from blood under the skin—he buried his face against Jackson's neck and sobbed.

"No… sh…." Jackson comforted *him*, running his hand through Ellery's hair with a tenderness Ellery had never suspected he had. "Don't… it's okay. I'm okay."

Ellery pulled in a ragged breath. "You can't keep asking to go," he mumbled, voice taut with fear. "You belong here."

"I'm…. Ellery, my mother was a junkie. And a whore. And a horrible human being. And…." Jackson's voice broke now. "And I don't know why it hurts that she's gone. Doesn't that make me dirty too?"

"No." He had no more words. Maybe later he could use his mother's wise and well-chosen ones, but not now. Now no was all he had. "No. Not dirty. Whatever happened last night—"

"He shot me full of smack," Jackson confessed.

Ellery kept his face buried against Jackson's neck. "And?"

"And he jacked off on me while I lay there, out of it. I got away when he was wrecking the car."

Ellery let out a humorless laugh, their bodies bare and sweating together under the comforter. This was as naked as he'd ever seen Jackson, and Jackson couldn't look at him, eyes turned away, because it was too naked for Ellery to see.

Ellery didn't care.

"You're really not doing well with Hondas," he said after a moment. "Maybe we should try a Subaru."

Jackson tried to shove up on an elbow. "Is that all you've got to say?" he demanded.

"Do you need a rape counselor?" Ellery asked seriously—because he would.

"I'd rather die," Jackson said with deep venom. "Nobody gets this… this… *crap* inside me. Don't you get that? Why would I want to give it to you? Do you want to hear the rest of my night? The way I threw up in the street and not even junkies would touch me on the bus?"

"*Why* would you want to give it to me?" Ellery rolled to his side, righteously angry. "Because I *asked* for it, God help me. Because it comes with *you.*" Jackson went to roll off the bed, and Ellery stopped him with a grip on his arm. "No, you don't get to run away!"

Jackson stopped and looked faintly embarrassed. "I was going to pee," he confessed humbly. "I'll come back and argue—no worries."

Ellery laughed and let him get off the bed. While he stumbled bare-assed to the bathroom, Ellery straightened out the bed covers. He was just about to slide back in when he heard Jackson's muffled "Goddammit!"

"What?"

He ran to the bathroom and found Jackson with a wad of toilet paper on his nose and his head tilted back as he sat on a towel on the toilet seat. The toilet paper was already dripping crimson.

"What in the hell?"

"Haven't eaten," Jackson mumbled. "Got dehydrated. Happened in the academy all the time."

Ellery grabbed a washcloth and ran cold water on it, squeezed it out, and gave it to Jackson to swap for the saturated toilet paper. "What do you mean you haven't eaten? Since when?"

"Yesterday."

"Yesterday?"

"Starbucks, remember?"

"God*dammit*! Get in bed!"

"What?" Jackson's eyes over the cold washcloth were legitimately surprised.

"Get in bed. I'll go get you ice and food and more ice for your shoulder and some Vicodin and we are going to fucking talk!"

Jackson stared at him, mouth working but no noise coming out. Finally he said, "No Vicodin."

"If you get into bed right now," Ellery snarled, shaking with anger, "I'll think about not taking you back to the doctor."

"The doctor!"

"You're still going, just not today—but that's only if you just shut up about leaving and get into bed right now."

"I don't *want* to leave," Jackson said into the quiet left when he was done issuing orders. "I just—"

"You just think you're doing me a big ol' favor by breaking my fucking heart. I'm over it. Get in bed."

Jackson stood up awkwardly, washcloth folded to catch the most blood. "God, you're bossy."

"Only when you're stupid. Now—"

"Yeah, yeah, I'm getting in bed."

Ellery stomped into the kitchen in his underwear, threw a pot on the stove to heat up soup, and pulled two ice packs from the freezer. He grabbed a package of crackers and another washcloth from the cupboard and stomped back into the bedroom, thinking Jackson would have to do a lot more than get crumbs on the sheets before Ellery let him out of bed again.

He was struggling one-handed into boxer shorts.

"So help me, Jackson—"

"I was naked."

Ellery let out some of his anger. "Yeah. Yeah, I know." Usually nudity wasn't a problem. In fact, he tended to flaunt his body, telling the whole world to fuck off if they didn't like his scars. By God, they were *his scars*.

But not right now.

Ellery set down the crackers and ice packs and moved carefully behind him. "Here—hold the washcloth. I'll get your underwear."

"I'm not helpless." It was almost the tone of a whiny toddler—but Ellery knew better. He kissed the back of Jackson's good shoulder gently after he'd pulled up the boxer shorts.

"You're not. You're never helpless. I just like to take care of you. That's all."

Jackson's head drooped dispiritedly. "I don't know why."

Ellery wrapped his arms around Jackson's middle and rested his cheek on the back of his neck. "I'm going to say something right now that will scare you. Don't freak out and don't respond—"

"Don't do this—"

"No, I'm going to do this. I'm going to say it, and you're just going to let the words sink in. They'll probably bounce off the first time, and maybe even the second or the third. But I don't give up—you know that about me."

"Stubborn fucker." His voice sounded clogged beyond the towel he was holding to his nose.

"Yeah. I am. And I'm going to say the words. Are you ready?" Ellery could feel the fine trembling that emotion and hunger and horror had started in Jackson's body and that hadn't stopped, not once, since Ellery had first crawled into bed with him.

"No."

"Tough. I love you. I've never loved another man like I love you. This thing that just happened to you, it feels like the end of the world. But the man in my arms?" Ellery squeezed him tighter, knowing that even if it hurt, Jackson could take it. "He's still strong. Still good inside. It hasn't stopped how I feel about him. It doesn't change how I feel about *you*."

Jackson's deep breath through his open mouth shook his entire body, and Ellery could feel the fine, hot spatter of tears on his forearms.

He kissed the back of Jackson's neck again. "Get in bed."

Wordlessly Jackson nodded and clambered into bed, pulling the pillows behind his back so he could sit up. Ellery handed him the ice pack for his nose and then wound an Ace bandage around the one on his shoulder. When he was done, he handed Jackson the package of crackers.

Jackson accepted them—but he wouldn't look Ellery in the eyes.

"Eat," Ellery said, satisfied when he moved a cracker from the package to his mouth. "I'll go get your soup."

He came back with the bowl of soup on a towel and a glass of milk. He sat the milk on the end table and crumbled crackers into the chicken soup until it was more paste than soup. He'd seen Jackson do this before and been appalled—until he realized it was a habit from when food was scarce and free crackers could stretch one tin of soup for two days.

Once the soup was fixed, he nudged Jackson aside under the covers and sat at the edge of the bed before pulling up a spoonful and holding it out.

The bleeding had stopped by this time, and Jackson glared, his head turned. "You're not going to feed me—"

"How's your shoulder feel?" Ellery asked sweetly.

Jackson grunted and shrugged—with his good shoulder.

"You have to look at me," Ellery said after a moment.

"You're making me feel like a child again." And he managed to take a bite without meeting Ellery's eyes.

"You were never a child," Ellery told him. "Childhood was a luxury, and you barely had food. And don't bother trying to shrug that off. For one thing, it makes me hurt watching you. But you need to know that I get it. It wasn't my childhood. I wasn't there. But in *my* childhood, we were taken care of. I had mono in my senior year of high school. I stayed home for six weeks on home school, and no, Mom couldn't be there all the time. But one night, when I was so weak I really couldn't lift the damned spoon, she held me up and helped me drink broth from a little kid's sippy cup while she told me about the corporation she was going after for pollution and explained how my father had researched the ingredients of the broth and added vegetables while it was cooking for optimum health."

Jackson smiled faintly and took the next offered bite. "Sounds horrible," he said when he was through.

"I thought it was," Ellery confessed. He offered the next spoonful. "Until now."

Jackson met his eyes and let out the breath that had been holding his back ramrod straight. He took the next bite and looked around the room, reaching out to Billy Bob, who had settled in next to him while Ellery had been busy.

Billy Bob rubbed his whiskers against his fingers and went back to napping.

"I was going to leave," he confessed, looking away again.

"You're expecting me to be surprised." Ellery rolled his eyes. "I've been expecting you to run off since Toby called me."

Jackson gaped at him, and Ellery stuffed his open mouth full of soup.

"Yes. I knew what you were thinking. No, I frequently don't know what you're thinking, but this time you were fucking transparent. Now I wish I'd been able to see that you were thinking about committing suicide by serial killer before I let you go yesterday afternoon, but since that didn't work, I'm going to *hope* you settle down and talk to me before you try to take off again."

"I…."

Ellery held his breath, not sure what he was hoping for from the world's most emotionally constipated thirty-year-old toddler.

"I couldn't take the cat away from you," he said.

Ellery almost dropped his soup. "I'm sorry?"

Jackson glared at him. Then he picked up the last spoonful and fed it to himself. "The fucking cat. You love that damned cat. I couldn't take him away—but I couldn't leave him here, because… you know."

"He's your cat." Ellery's heart was suddenly doing triple time in his chest. Oh God. He'd never owned a cat. What if he'd just assumed it was Jackson's animal and hadn't gotten attached to the cat? What if the cat hadn't liked him—cats were notorious for that. What if the goddamned cat had puked in his shoes every morning, and they'd had one of those sitcom/comic cat/owner's boyfriend relationships, and Jackson had come into this house thinking "Oh, Ellery doesn't like the damned cat. I'll just disappear into the shadows with it and die!"

"Yeah." Jackson nodded. "I couldn't leave him behind."

Ellery set the soup down by the end-table lamp with precise movements before pausing to wipe Jackson's full mouth with the corner of the towel. "Give me the ice pack." He gestured for the pack and the stained towel, and Jackson held them close, glaring.

"Did you not hear that I got popped with a random needle last night?"

"I don't have any open cuts," Ellery snapped. "And the blood is dry. Now hand it over."

Jackson did, still scowling.

By the time Ellery got back from throwing the towel in the hamper and the ice pack back in the freezer, his hands had stopped shaking.

He sat down again by Jackson's side, conscious that neither one of them had said a word for a few moments. Careful of the shoulder, Ellery took Jackson's hand from his lap and twined their fingers together.

"Yes, I love the cat," he said, this time the one to avoid Jackson's eyes. "But I love you more."

Jackson tightened his fingers around Ellery's. "We need to have some uniforms go to that house in Meadowview," he said gruffly. "There were…." His voice failed, and Ellery looked up quickly. "Dead people," he finished. "Junkies. Owens opened the house to Billy's stash—must have been three ODs in there last night alone."

Ellery swallowed. God. "And your mom's dealer?"

Jackson closed his eyes and shuddered, looking away. "He was killed last night."

Jackson saw it—Ellery had no doubts.

"Tell me."

"Why?"

"So when you dream about it tonight, I know what I'm fighting."

"Knife in the throat," Jackson muttered. Then, almost horribly, "He remembered me. Knew my mom. Was glad to see me."

Jesus.

Ellery leaned over and kissed his temple. "You would have saved him if you could."

Jackson nodded, and Ellery kissed him again. "I'm going to go call Kryzynski and Campbell—oh, and Pierpont. They should get a piece of this."

"Good," Jackson said quietly. "I don't want it. I don't want a goddamned bit of it."

"I'll let them know."

He grabbed the soup bowl this time and made his phone calls. Kryzynski, in particular, was grateful.

"Seriously—massive drug bust?"

"And a possible serial killer—God, you really are too young to get old."

"Are you certain former officer Owens is a serial killer? Remember, last time we talked you still didn't have proo—"

"We have his DNA. It's only a matter of time before we encounter a match. There were sexual components to all his crimes. We just didn't have anything to match with. And we have a witness who saw him kill someone. And—" Ellery did a quick send of Owens's military photo. "—we have what he looks like without the prosthetics he wore for two years. Can we at least take him in for questioning and get him off the street?"

"Well, if I see him in a house full of dead people, I'm not going to ask him out! Oh hey…."

"Yeah, he's cute. He's so cute he makes our wit throw up just looking at his picture."

"Who is your wit, anyway?"

"Just find him," Ellery snarled, not wanting to tell the world that just yet. Hoping for a way to not have to tell them *ever*. He'd protect Jackson from all of it—trial, deposition, cross-examination—all of it, if he possibly could.

"Okay, okay! We'll let you know if he's there. What exactly are we looking for at the house, anyway?"

He thought of Jade's reaction to Jackson's clothes. "You'll know it when you smell it," he said grimly. "Don't forget to call Campbell and Pierpont and Pierpont's buddy, Officer…." Crap. He couldn't remember.

"Yeah, yeah—I'll tag all your friends. Trying to suck up to the police force, Cramer?"

Ellery thought of Jackson, alone on the streets. He hadn't said how he'd gotten home, but he obviously hadn't felt comfortable talking to a police officer.

"I need you to have his back," Ellery said, voice hard.

Kryzynski sucked in a breath. "Okay. Yeah. Deal. What's he doing right now?"

"Taking a Vicodin for his shoulder." If Ellery had to shove it down his throat like the cat.

"Ouch—rough night?"

"You have no idea. Ring me when the house is secure."

They signed off, and Ellery brought back some fruit juice and the painkillers, thinking maybe Jackson would be ready for more now.

He was asleep, shivering, in the throes of the dream again.

At three in the afternoon, Ellery left a desk full of work and a raging case in progress and a chance to gloat over the entire police department that yes, they had been right, Owens was a serious problem after all, in favor of sliding in behind his lover and holding him as he shivered and moaned in fear.

But at least he wasn't planning to leave.

Fish Takes a Breath

JACKSON WOKE up after dark, alone in bed, shivering in the thin light from the bedside lamp. Ellery's computer was still open on the end table nearby, but the screen had gone dark. He must have pulled it in to work while Jackson had been out.

He tried to sit up and yelped because God, yes, he really had refucked his shoulder in the last two days.

"Don't move!" Ellery called from the kitchen. "I'm bringing you some ibuprofen for your fever!"

"I do not have a fever!" But he couldn't stop shivering. His shoulder felt hot to the touch.

"And I don't have control issues!" Ellery snapped.

A rusty chuckle escaped Jackson's chest. Ellery organized his shoes by color and type—oxfords or wingtips. He organized his socks by color and type—black dress or white athletic. He organized his suits by color and type—and so on. He'd never seen anyone so neat and so organized.

"Shit."

"Reality setting in yet?"

You said you loved me.

"Sort of." Jackson grunted. "Dammit, I'm going to have to get tested again."

Ellery popped his head in, a glass of juice in one hand and a bottle of painkillers in the other. "We can do that tomorrow morning before we go in to work."

Jackson groaned. "God—what am I going to say about work?"

"You were out on a case," Ellery muttered. "Heroin family is in custody and using our services, and the police are following your lead on the house. What's to do?" He sat down again next to Jackson on the bed. Jackson had time to look at him, the way his eyes softened with worry, how his lower lip had swollen where he'd bitten it.

Jackson had thought he'd never see Ellery again. A chasm of ache opened in his stomach that he could, possibly, have never seen Ellery again.

And then he focused on what Ellery had just said and a whole different relief hit him.

Oh. Oh yeah. The whole entire world didn't know about Jackson's night—just Ellery. Somehow his very pragmatism helped.

"Did you call Tess Dakin?" he asked, and Ellery's patently false look of contrition told him all he wanted to know.

"Oh. Tess. Do you think she'd be interested?"

"No, Ellery—I don't. Maybe we never have to talk to her again, and your buddy Kryzynski could take care of all the police work on this one."

Ellery grunted. "Touché. I called Kryzynski. You can call Ms. Dakin."

And suddenly the jealousy wasn't even funny. Because Ellery had the courage to say the big words, and Jackson's heart was still learning how to swim in that and not drown.

"You, uh…." His chin wobbled, and he willed himself to pull his shit together. "You know—I mean *know* that I wouldn't ever… that you and me, it's different. It's important. It's… I'm not going to sleep with anyone else—" Oh God. Owens's face as he climaxed and shuddered in ecstasy. "On purpose." Oh for fuck's sake. This was hard. Taking Billy Bob and finding a hotel to die in would have been easier.

"Here," Ellery said quietly. "Take this." Jackson took the ibuprofen and the juice without question, knocked the one back with the other, and gave Ellery the glass. He took it and set it on the table and then nudged Jackson to the middle of the bed. When Jackson had scooched over, Ellery slid in next to him and laid his cheek on his chest, wrapping his arms around Jackson's middle.

Jackson stroked the long strands of hair back from his eyes, uncertain of what to do next.

"I'm going to keep saying I love you until it sticks," Ellery said after a moment—apparently talking to Jackson's navel, but that was okay.

"I don't know what to do with that," Jackson told him honestly.

"Someday you'll say it back."

Jackson's heart sped up, and he took a deep breath. Tears threatened, and he didn't think he could do that—not today.

"Not now," Ellery added on a half laugh. "But someday. You'll look at me, and it will just come out. You won't be able to *not* say it."

"How do you know this shit?" God—it should have been the other way around. Jackson was the one who'd grown up on the streets. How did Ellery just seem to know so much more about the world?

"Because I've been not saying it for months, Jackson. I've been looking at you over breakfast or when we get out of the car and thinking 'I love you' and not saying it. But… but you came back to me today, and you knowing it was just that much more important than my pride."

Jackson gasped and rested his cheek on top of Ellery's head. "Yeah," he said. "Yeah."

Not the words. Because he couldn't say them, not now. What were they worth when he was weak and sad and helpless? He'd say them when Ellery knew he didn't need anything from them. That the words had all of Jackson's heart in them. When he was strong enough to love and for it to mean something.

"Anything interesting happen while I was gone?"

Ellery didn't protest the change in subject, instead telling him about his meetings with Buchannan and Lacey—in particular the fact that Lacey seemed more interested in whether or not Owens could be traced back to him than in the fact he'd released a serial killer into the world.

"Is there any way we can subpoena those records?" Jackson asked, unhappy. It was hard enough proving a civilian guilty or innocent. The military had their own legal system, and civilians weren't welcome.

"I was starting the paperwork to make the request," Ellery admitted, "but…."

"What?"

"Remember Victoriana?"

"Oh God." Ace and Sonny. Jackson and Ellery had taken exquisite care to not disturb the two of them. Ellery had even voluntarily lost a case, just so they could pretend the things they suspected about the two garage owner/street racers never had to be looked into.

"Yeah. A subpoena to Lacey would mean Corporal Sonny Daye would have to be looked at, poked at, and subpoenaed."

"Really?" Jackson thought about it. "Can't we just ask for Owens's records—all of them, without redaction? If they say he worked under Galway, then we can subpoena Galway's records, and *then* we can make our way to Lacey."

Ellery grunted and pushed himself up on his elbow. "That's very clever of you. Subtle. I'm impressed."

Jackson managed a smile. "Well, there's a reason you keep me around."

Ellery's eyes grew wide and limpid, and he gasped and licked his lips. Jackson had been reading signals like that his entire life.

"Really?" he asked, surprised.

Ellery looked away. "You probably feel like crap—you're hot and sick and—"

Jackson captured his jaw with his fingers and kissed him.

Ah… ah yes. The sweetness flooded him, Ellery's taste, his eager response. Jackson swept his tongue into Ellery's mouth, probing, stroking, melding the two of them.

Sex had always been easy with them—passionate, incendiary. But Jackson *was* sore and he *was* sick; he would move aggressively, and Ellery would counter with such tenderness Jackson had to retreat, to match him with gentle touches, caresses rather than squeezes or grabs.

Ellery moved the pillows behind him so he could lie flat, and he grunted at the change of position.

"Yeah, it hurts," Ellery muttered. "Because you couldn't just let it heal, could you?"

"Are you going to nag me into orgasm? 'Cause that's fun!"

Ellery laughed shortly and kissed him again as he lay on his back, spanning his hands around Ellery's ribs, his stomach, his narrow, bony hips.

And he was tired and sore—but his body wanted, *craved* beyond the tired, beyond the sore. He licked the salt from Ellery's neck and nipped at his collarbone, and Ellery tilted his head back and gave him full access. His little cries of arousal fed the fire in Jackson's blood, and he struggled with his good hand to shove Ellery's boxers down while he scooted on the bed.

"Stop," Ellery panted, shucking his own boxers. "Stay right… there…."

Ellery scooched up and straddled Jackson's head.

Jackson took a deep breath and smiled, looking up Ellery's body and winking.

"I like this thing," he confessed.

"I'm partial to it myself—ahhh…."

Jackson licked the head, catching his tongue on the edge of the bell and flicking along the tautness of the frenulum. Teasing in its purest form. Ellery clutched the bedframe and rocked unsteadily as Jackson continued.

"Are you just going to play around all night?" Ellery taunted. "Or are you maybe gonna suck my *ahh... yes*!"

Jackson opened his mouth entirely, raised his head, and swallowed Ellery down. Ellery thrust slowly, giving Jackson time to breathe, to adjust, to work his tongue and his throat, and his withdrawal was just as painfully slow.

Again, and Jackson used all his skill, lost in the act of giving that had always made sex a joy for him—but even more so with Ellery.

Ellery seemed to like what he gave just because *he*, Jackson Rivers, gave it.

I love you.

Oh God.

Jackson raised and lowered his head quickly in an attempt to run away from that thought. That Ellery got what he did from their sex because he loved Jackson. That was terrifying—all Jackson could give was sex, right? That's all anyone had asked from him. Ellery was getting *more*? What if Jackson fucked this up!

That whole hallucinogenic night, Jackson had been stumbling for a way home.

A way here.

What if he couldn't stay here? What if Ellery hadn't wanted him?

On instinct, he went into power-blow-job mode—the tenderness, the ache forgotten in the sudden panic of losing this, this *thing* they had between them, this precious connection he'd never had with another human being.

"Easy," Ellery hissed. "Easy… not yet…."

He pulled out of Jackson's mouth and slid down his body, nipping at Jackson's jaw, his ear, his chin. Jackson turned his head, giving him access, but his eyes stayed open and focused inward, on the fear of what he had to lose.

"Hey!" Ellery nipped his earlobe particularly hard. "Where'd you go?"

Jackson closed his eyes and turned back into the kiss. "I'm cold without you." Ellery gasped in surprise, and Jackson took over his mouth again, comfortable here, even with Ellery—oh God—on top.

Ellery pulled away and framed Jackson's face with his hands. "Look at me," he commanded.

Jackson did, feeling vulnerable and naked when he least wanted to be that way in his entire life.

"I love you," Ellery whispered, rolling his eyes when Jackson flinched. "You can't lose me. You can't fuck this up. Just keep being you. We'll make it work."

To his horror, Jackson found himself nodding, desperate to accept comfort. "All last night," he confessed, "running in the shadows, trying to stay awake on the bus. Walking from Jade's—"

"You walked?"

"I just wanted to be home." His throat swelled as he said it, and this time Ellery captured *his* mouth and filled him with warmth from the inside out.

"You're here," Ellery whispered. "Here."

He kissed down Jackson's throat, skipping his chest for once, making his way to Jackson's tender midriff. He bit softly right by Jackson's navel and then kissed his way down, stripping Jackson's boxers off with a few tugs.

Jackson's cock lay, thick and aching, waiting for attention.

Ellery cast him an evil look over Jackson's stomach and took him all the way down his throat in one swallow.

Jackson's hips came off the bed in spite of his shoulder's bark of protest. Ellery pushed up on his elbows and used one hand to press Jackson's abdomen to make him flatten his ass against the mattress.

"If you're going to hurt yourself, I'll stop."

Jackson moaned. "If you stop, I'm gonna be hurting!" he protested. "Could we… maybe…." Ellery licked his crown as he was talking, and Jackson grasped the back of his head and held it in place, thrusting slowly and powerfully into Ellery's waiting mouth.

Ah, so good. So hot and needy. But Jackson wanted more. He wanted Ellery's heat surrounding him, holding him safe, promising Jackson that, even in the bubble of time given to them by sex, he would be warm and loved and protected—

Ah! God!

Loved!

He thrust particularly hard, and Ellery gagged. Jackson took his hand off the back of his head and used it to caress his cheek instead.

Ellery kept sucking, glancing at Jackson again, letting a smile twitch at the corners of his stuffed-full mouth.

More.

"Condom," Jackson gasped, wishing he could reach for one. "We need a condom."

"Augh!" Ellery slid off the bed to root through the end table. He came up with an unopened package he'd been keeping there when Jackson had moved in, as well as the lube they'd been using.

Jackson could see his fingers shaking as he opened the foil packet, and he reached out gently with his good hand.

"That's for me, right?" he said, smiling to ease the tension that had so suddenly sprung up between them.

"I could have lost you," Ellery said gruffly. "I need you inside me. I need—"

Jackson helped him put the condom on, helped him spread the lubricant.

They needed the same things, it seemed.

"Stretch yourself," he ordered gruffly. He usually took his time with that part, made Ellery gibber and cry, but they both knew his window of being able to follow through grew smaller with every breath.

Ellery nodded and straddled him, sliding his lubed fingers behind his back. With a little cry he fell forward, burying his face in Jackson's shoulder and moaning.

"You make the best noises," Jackson whispered. "Make them some more."

"Fuuuck… you…."

Jackson chuckled. "Sit on my cock." The order was unmistakable, and since Ellery had Jackson at his mercy more often than Jackson liked to admit, it gave him a thrill of power when Ellery did just that.

Slowly, rocking back and forth, he lowered himself over Jackson. In little spurts he would bounce up and gasp and sit down again, and sit up and gasp, and slowly, inch by inch, he slid down Jackson's erection until he was flush, his ass pressed up against Jackson's pubis, his face and chest blotchy with arousal.

"Good?" Jackson panted, shaking with the need to move.

"So full…," he whispered.

"You maybe, uh, want to fuck yourself on that thing?"

"Yes!" It came out as a full-throated wail. Ellery rocked forward and back, forward and back, the thrust and pressure around Jackson's cock growing, becoming urgent as well as beautifully, excruciatingly arousing.

"Faster," Jackson urged, resting both hands on Ellery's thighs. "Faster. Harder…."

"Deeper!" Ellery growled, coming down hard.

"Yes!" Jackson held him still as he sat and began to thrust his hips up and down, as fast as he could, endorphins rushing his system and blocking the warning signs from his shoulder.

What shoulder?

Ellery Cramer was riding him, commanding his body with pure will, and Jackson wasn't going to let anything—particularly physical weakness—get in his way.

Together they rushed headlong into Jackson's climax, and as he felt it build in his balls, he gave another order. "Would it kill you to grab that thing?" Ellery's cock was probably getting plenty of stimulation bouncing off his stomach, but Jackson didn't care. He wanted to see Ellery's orgasm wash over him, wanted to see his face go slack with climax, wanted to feel the stripes of come spatter across his chest.

Ellery wrapped his hand around himself and kept bouncing, and Jackson kept thrusting, hard, harder, oh God. Ellery climaxed around him, and Jackson's world was squeezed tight and exploding, coming unglued as red crashed behind his eyes and he pumped into the condom.

Ellery collapsed into the mess on his stomach and chest, breathing like a sprinter after an endurance run.

He lay on Jackson's chest, shaking.

"Hey," Jackson soothed, palming the sweating skin of his shoulders, his neck, his back. "Hey… that was great—"

"You walked home," Ellery muttered.

"What?"

"You *walked home*."

"Didn't we just have sex?"

"Yes." Ellery nodded. "And in the middle of sex, you said you walked home. After a bus ride. And you were alone, and vulnerable and tired and hungry—"

"I lived it, remember?" Jackson started using his good arm to root for the comforter. "Sex—it was glor—"

Ellery covered Jackson's mouth with his own and kissed him hard. He pulled back and glared accusingly. "Baby—why didn't you go for help? You were at *Jade's*—she would have gotten you home!"

"Can we cover up?" He was starting to shiver.

"Sure." Ellery rolled off him and helped him dispose of the condom, then wiped them both off with tissues. Practical to the bone, Ellery, and Jackson appreciated that. But then he pulled the covers over their shoulders and propped himself up, pinning Jackson back against the bed with a furious stare. "I've got lasagna in the oven," he said seriously, "and we can eat dinner in a few minutes. But tell me—"

"I didn't want anyone to see me like that," Jackson muttered. "Not Jade or Mike. Particularly not you. Happy now?"

Ellery traced his face with gentle fingertips. "You don't have to go it alone all the time. You know that, right?"

Jackson sent him what was meant to be a brief look, but the intensity of Ellery's gaze shocked and held him. "I do now," he said, trying unsuccessfully to look away.

Ellery grasped his chin, looked into his soul. "Please—*please*—don't think you have to go it alone. Even if it's not me—you have people. You were right there, Jackson. You could have had Jade call me."

He tried to make it a joke. "Yeah, but I was planning to move out with Billy Bob, remember? Jade would have tried to talk me out of it."

Ellery closed his eyes, and Jackson let out a sigh of relief. "I am going to have nightmares about that for a long time."

"Can we just… you know, enjoy the afterglow now?" Jackson complained, feeling embarrassingly tearful.

Ellery put a cool hand on Jackson's hot forehead. "Yeah—given that we're probably not doing this again until you're better, I'm all for enjoying it."

"I have no idea what you're talking about," Jackson lied. "I think I could go again—right now, in fact." He tried to pump his hips suggestively and ended up yawning instead. "Dammit—I need to get up."

"For why?" Ellery asked grumpily. "Are you going to walk barefoot to the gas station to investigate a candy bar theft?"

"No." Jackson scowled. "I've been sleeping all day. If I don't get up now, my sleep schedule will be all screwed up."

Ellery rolled off him with a bark of laughter. "Fine, cowboy. Get up. Brush your teeth. Hell—get dressed. I'm going to put on my pajamas and make dinner. Go ahead and impress me with your initiative to stay up past ten o'clock tonight. I'm waiting to be dazzled."

"What time is it now?" Another yawn hit, as well as that muzzy-headed wrongness that came with an approaching cold.

"Six."

"You lie!" Dammit—it was like he lost an entire day.

"Only in court." Ellery made good on his threat to put on his pajamas—warm flannel, soft as a kitten's ass. Jackson had actually gotten to sleep a couple of nights by petting those damned pajamas. "When did you get home?"

Jackson tried to remember. "I don't… well, after eight, because you were gone. I must have left Jade's house at six thirty, seven—the sun wasn't quite up. Nine or ten?"

His shoulder felt better after the ibuprofen, but it was still stiff enough for him to cradle his arm by his ribs as he stood up and shuffled through the dresser Ellery had given him when he'd moved in.

"Here," Ellery ordered, coming over to his side of the bed. "Let me."

"I can do it!"

"Shut up and let me do it. You didn't let me help you get home. You didn't let me help you through yesterday. You didn't even let me know you were at the serial killer's house of doom—"

"I was about to text you," Jackson said, embarrassed.

"About to?" Clear disbelief.

"I'd written the text. But then I heard a noise, and I thought I was going to get caught and then I had to climb over a fence."

Ellery shook his head like he was torn between irritation and self-blame. "You know," he said, voice cracking, "I almost wish you'd gone and gotten blown by Officer McDreamy Voice."

"Who?"

"Piers Morgan or whatever—"

"Pierpont?" It wasn't like Ellery to get names wrong—or to figuratively whore Jackson out to random strangers. "Why would you even *say* that?"

Ellery glared at him, eyes red rimmed. "I would have hated you. I would have broken up with you. But at least—at *least* this… this *monster* would not have put hands on you. Would not have fucked with your head. God, Jackson—I know you were raised to make it your last priority, but you have no idea how much I would rather see you safe."

"See," Jackson said, thinking about it carefully—hard to do in a muddled head, "I think, as long as I survived and got back here…." Could he say it? "Home, then I did the best thing, right?"

Ellery closed his eyes tightly. "You… you…."

Jackson didn't recognize giving comfort. But Ellery was shaking and strangely undone. He wrapped his good arm around him and held him tight. "I'm fine. I'm here."

"I want your life to be easier," Ellery confessed against his good shoulder.

Jackson chuckled. "Yours isn't. And it could be."

Ellery shook his head. "I can't argue about it now," he whispered.

"Then what—"

"This is good. Just do this."

Jackson held him until he started to shiver in the shadowed room. Ellery stepped back and wiped under his eyes with his hand, then bent and helped Jackson into his ratty sweats and a T-shirt. He sat Jackson down for a minute while he went to his side of the room and got Jackson a zip-up hoodie instead of a pullover one.

"Thanks," Jackson said gruffly.

"There's a price, you know," Ellery told him. He hadn't turned on a light, and the atmosphere of his vast bedroom—bigger than most of the places Jackson had lived, period—was still unbearably intimate.

"I have to bottom again?" He was only partially joking.

"Sure. Whatever. But we're going to Thanksgiving with my family." Ellery turned and stalked out of the room, and Jackson stood and followed him, stuttering in disbelief.

"You expect me to get on a plane for two hours—"

"Six, Jackson—it's Boston."

"For ten hours so I can live in Lucy Satan's house—"

"My mother's name is Taylor!"

"And meet your happy rich family—"

"Don't forget Jewish if you're going to get all freaked-out about it."

"And have them talk to me and know I'm a white-trash cum-dump!"

Ellery whirled on one foot and slapped his face.

Jackson gaped at him.

"You're the man I love," Ellery said thickly into the silence. "You can call my mother Lucy Satan all you want. I think she likes it. But you be careful when you talk about yourself. And my family doesn't know anything you don't want them to. That's what being repressed white people is all about."

"You slapped me," Jackson muttered, although there hadn't been a lot of sting to it.

"You hurt me," Ellery snarled. "Don't do it again."

Absurdly, Jackson's lower lip began to wobble. God, he was still on such an uneven keel—like walking the safety rail of a ship in a stormy sea. One minute he was gripping the rope and he was pretty sure he was going to make it, and the next…. Ellery was glowering at him with wet eyes, and he felt like *he* was the one who'd smacked *Ellery* out of the blue.

"I never want to hurt you," Jackson confessed. "That was not… not my intention."

Ellery nodded. "I know it's not. Just like I know you'd never cheat on me. And I know you're always trying to make your way home."

Jackson tried a crooked half smile, but Ellery didn't smile back. "I have to get your mother a present," he remembered. "She told me that, in the hospital."

Ellery nodded. "We can go Internet shopping if you want."

"Hunh."

Ellery turned back toward the kitchen. "Clarify."

"I just assumed I'd have to go to the real thing. Macy's or something, where there's silk scarves and smells I'm not really fond of. Internet shopping—that's a good idea."

Ellery chuckled weakly and went to the stove. Jackson was going to follow him to help, but Ellery shook him off. "Sit at the counter and talk to me. Who taught you about Macy's?"

"Jade's mom. She couldn't afford anything there, really, but she would take us shopping and make us pretend we belonged sometimes." He smiled at the memory—he and Kaden and Jade on their best behavior, smiling pleasantly at the salespeople like Toni did, saving their money for an Icee at the food court. "She'd wear the clothes she'd made for work. We'd put on our best clothes, clean up nice, and take the bus to Arden Fair. She and Jade would try on perfume and outfits, and Kaden and me would look at suits and talk about when we'd dress up fine. I figured out later that Toni would go home and buy fabric from the bargain bin and make her and Jade the clothes she saw in the store, if she could. She could sew really nice."

"Not Rhonda?"

He forgot sometimes that Ellery knew they'd all been friends since the fifth grade. "Rhonda's family was, well, better off than us," Jackson said, trying not to squirm in his seat. Economic shame was such an amorphous thing, something that crossed racial boundaries but showed itself in different ways. “Rhonda, you know, wore clothes from Target. Her mom didn’t have to sew her church clothes. I guess Toni’s grandma taught Toni. It’s a good thing, right, but… I don’t know. She used to tell us kids she didn’t want Rhonda’s folks to know we were country. I think it’s because her grandmother was from the South.”

Ellery had pulled the lasagna from the oven while Jackson was talking, and Jackson closed his eyes for a minute and took a deep breath. It smelled warm and homey. He was always surprised when Ellery cooked things. They were always so… so elegant. He knew recipes, even though they subsisted on takeout half the week.

Had Ellery cooked this for him as comfort?

The thought made him squirm too.

“My mom—Lucy Satan—” Ellery gave him a dry—if distracted—smile. “—used to take us to Macy’s to get measured for formal clothes. Bar Mitzvahs, Bat Mitzvahs, formal dinners, plays, occasions. We went once a year. I’d get two suits, and Rebecca would get four dresses. People would come measure us—my tailor was a total pervert. I swear he was feeling me up from the minute I got hair on my balls.”

“Oh my God!” Jackson laughed, horrified.

“Yeah, I got over it. Remember, it was the most action I got until college.”

“Was he cute?” Jackson asked, trying to decide if Ellery was scarred for life or not.

“Very—it was part of the fun. Anyway, we always went out to somewhere *not* formal afterward. Chili’s or Applebee’s or someplace like that. Mother would ask us where we’d want to wear our best clothes *this* year, and we always came up with good stuff. The presidential inauguration, the meeting of the United Nations, a surgeon’s conference for people who helped cure cancer—the sky was the limit.”

While he spoke, Ellery put together the bags of fixings for salad in a glass bowl. He crumpled up the wrappers and threw them in the recycler, before setting the bowl to the side. When that was done, he pulled a loaf of sourdough from the top of the refrigerator and sliced it down the middle. Jackson watched, entranced. Ellery liked to mix real garlic in real butter and then broil the bread until the mixture was melted and the bread was just getting golden brown. It was Jackson's favorite part.

"That's a real nice time," he said, eyes still on the food. "I mean... your mom is scary, but she took care of you guys. She was...." Suddenly—because he was stupid—he figured out that he'd been very gently steered to this conversation right here.

"She was a good mom," he said, his voice breaking.

"And yours wasn't," Ellery said gently. "And you know what you didn't have. But you're still going to miss what you wished you *could* have. You can't tell me you didn't see just enough to wish Celia had been half the mom Toni Cameron was."

Oh hell. "I hate you for this," Jackson muttered thickly, because grief he didn't want suddenly washed up, blocking his throat, blocking his chest.

"Sure," Ellery said, and Jackson couldn't see the expression on his face because his eyes were swimming. Not with the picture of Celia as she'd been in the morgue, or even the last time he'd seen her—asking for money, chain smoking, worn to leather, and, absurdly, worried about him, which he didn't think she could be.

He saw her as she'd been when he was little—before the drugs had taken over, when she sang to him sometimes, when she cooked him spaghetti with butter on food stamp night. She'd had curly blonde hair and blue eyes like an angel and a sweet mouth—Jackson had thought she was beautiful.

He saw her singing about Jolene in a shitty apartment kitchen while she cut up his spaghetti.

He wasn't sure if the memory was real or not—if it had ever happened. But he'd wanted it to happen. He'd wanted *that* mom, and now any chance of *that* mom was gone. Any chance he would go shopping for a silk scarf or perfume for a mother who was proud of him was gone, and he was left mourning the dream of her.

He was left forever with the image from the morgue and the merciless judgment of a monster who knew too much about Jackson, who could paint his dearest dreams in body parts and threaten his sanity with a vial of heroin and a jerkoff that still stung Jackson's skin.

"Oh fuck," he managed before he buried his head in his arms and sobbed.

Ellery set the food aside and came around the counter to rub his back, whispering in his ear that it would be all right. In his entire life, Jackson couldn't remember having that. Not once. Not when Toni Cameron had died, not when he'd been stuck wearing a wire into a snake pit, not even when he'd woken up from a coma and realized the life he'd worked for had swirled down the drain with the blood he'd shed.

But Ellery was there, crying—oh God, *crying* with him—and for once in his life, Jackson was going to have to believe it was true.

It was going to be okay.

The storm passed, and for a breath he was surrounded by Ellery's warmth, his smell, the evergreen body wash he used, and the food smells of butter and garlic. He fought off the urge to bolt in claustrophobia and relaxed into Ellery's body pressed against his.

He wiped under his eyes with his sleeve, scraping along the washcloth-burned side of his face, and sighed. "I've got to go…." He made random gestures to his head-swollen, snot-dripping self, and Ellery dropped a kiss on the top of his head.

"Sure. Go."

He went to brush his teeth—and pull himself together and wash his face and think about kittens and puppies and fucking daisy-burping bunnies because he was tired of emotion. He looked in the mirror after rinsing his face, wincing at the washcloth burns on his forehead, cheek, and neck. He stared into the mirror for a moment, remembering when he'd been a disaster of acne, glad he'd never been able to afford class pictures.

Ellery would never see him like that.

But Ellery had seen him today—lost, sad, sick, and scared. Grieving.

For a moment he tried to juxtapose two images of himself—stoned and terrified, on the floor of hell, looking up into a madman's face, and five minutes ago, sobbing in a good man's arms.

How can he stand to touch me?

But he'd known. And he'd held Jackson anyway.

It was a lot to think about.

Ellery seemed to get that, because when Jackson got back, dinner was on the table and they sat down to eat, talking quietly about the case, about "heroin family," about Ellery's Thanksgiving plans, of which Jackson had been unaware.

"You have the plane tickets and everything?" Stunning.

"Yes." Ellery took a bite of lasagna and closed his eyes, shuddering in happiness. He would run a mile on the treadmill just to have a bite of something bad for him—Jackson knew that about him now. What sort of penance was he doing to have Jackson in his life?

"How can you think that far into the future?" Jackson asked suspiciously.

"Hm… well, I figured next Thanksgiving we could take a pass and go to Cabo or rent a cabin in Tahoe or something that involves lots of sex and some alcohol. But this year we're trying to make a good impression, so I waited for a sale on airfare and—"

"I wasn't asking for a demonstration!" Jackson burst out, torn between laughter and panic. "I was just wondering how… why would you even think… you know. I'd be here?"

Ellery sat back and wiped his mouth, taking the question seriously. "Well, I didn't *know* for certain," he said. "Just like I didn't know for certain if Billy Bob and I were going to get along. But I drew some conclusions based on the evidence on hand and decided it was an acceptable risk to…." He faltered. "To bet my heart that you'd be here."

Jackson's smile could not be contained. "Holy shit, that's romantic. *Ellery!* You covered it in lawyer bullshit, but holy fucking God, you might as well have delivered chocolates and flowers."

He watched, fascinated, as a flush patterned Ellery's face in a perfect crescent, one on either cheek.

"Don't tell my mother," Ellery said softly. "My family doesn't do romance. I think she'd be disappointed."

Jackson bit his lip, feeling like a teenager on his first date. "I think your mother is damned proud of you," he said. "I would be… if, you know, you were part of my family."

"I'd be proud if you became part of my family too," Ellery said, a slight twist to the corner of his mouth his only indication that he had used Jackson's own words to back him into a corner.

"You're pretty impressed with yourself, aren't you?" Jackson asked, but he couldn't be mad. Not after the last two days.

Ellery nodded as though thinking about it, and Jackson wanted to laugh. Little shit. Sure—he thought he was Superlawyer. Well, so did Jackson. What of it?

"I think Mike should come stay with you tomorrow," Ellery said when the moment had faded.

"Why won't I be at work? I mean, those weren't the only two cases on my roster!" Jackson's head felt heavy on his neck, and he'd stayed away from the wine Ellery had served because he was having trouble keeping awake as it was. One night's sleep should make it better, right?

"Because I'm asking you," Ellery said soberly. "I'm asking you nicely—with all the love in my heart. It's Tuesday, Jackson. If I tell Langdon you're out until Monday, he won't bat an eyelash. You can go running every day if you want. You can run searches from home. But please, after the doctor's tomorrow, let that be the end for a few days. You never let yourself—"

"What, slack off?" Helpless. He hated feeling helpless.

"Heal."

Ellery let the word hang between them in the quiet of the dining room. Jackson had just taken a deep breath to answer when Ellery's phone started buzzing urgently on the counter behind him.

Their eyes met and Jackson nodded. Ellery picked up.

Fish in a Waterfall

"IT'S GOING down," Kryzynski said without preamble. "Tomorrow, sunrise. We've got the house staked out. There seems to be some movement in but no movement out. We're going to have SWAT out here, the DEA—a whole detail. Do you guys want in?"

"I heard that!" Jackson snapped from his spot across the table. "Do you guys want to lose him? Fuck waiting for the detail—go in *now*!"

Ellery tried to shush him, holding his hand up to the phone. "Do you want them to know you're my informant?" he mouthed, and Jackson scowled.

"Don't give a shit," he snarled.

"I thought you wanted out of it!"

"I did until they fucked it up! Give me the damned phone."

"Get your own phone!"

Jackson flipped him off, and Ellery practically crowed.

"Cramer?" Kryzynski prompted. "You there?"

"Are you sure you don't want to go in tonight?" Ellery asked, giving Jackson a significant look.

"We're not sure what we're facing—"

"One man, armed with a bowie knife and possibly police issue," Jackson said in an undertone. "A sniper could get him—two guys in gear could get him. Sending the whole force in is ridiculous."

"One man with a bowie knife and a pistol," Ellery relayed. "He's operated so far with stealth. We think he had a substance abuse problem before Bridger got arrested, and it's gotten out of control in the past couple of weeks."

"Probably because he's surrounded by heroin," Jackson muttered.

"How would you know that?" The suspicion in Kryzynski's voice was evident, and Ellery glowered at Jackson.

"We have an informant," he said with dignity. "Someone who got in and out of the house."

"Is Rivers there?" Oh, hooray—he wasn't stupid. "Look, if it's Rivers, just let me talk to him."

"I have no idea why you'd want to do that," Ellery said blandly. "We're telling you that going in tonight would be your best bet."

"And I'm telling you that it will be safer for our people if we stake out and wait."

"He's going to escape," Jackson muttered. "He's going to make the stakeout vehicle, and he's going to run."

"This man has killed several people, and it's not pretty—"

"We still only have your word for it and—"

"I have an eyewitness who saw him kill a man who is probably still on the premises!" Ellery snarled rashly.

Jackson held out both his hands like "See, was that so hard?"

Yes. Yes, it was hard.

"Is it Rivers?" Kryzynski asked sweetly. "Because if it was Rivers, I would really like to talk to him about now."

Ellery hesitated, and Jackson stood up, leaned over, and snagged the phone from his hand. "Left side of the house, facing," he said quietly. "In the entryway to the crawl space under the house—he was sort of stuffed into the hole and then killed there."

"Really? You saw all this?" Kryzynski snarled. "What the hell were you doing, Rivers, staring through the slats in the fence while a man got murdered?"

"I was trying to get away from the murderer before he shot me full of heroin," Jackson snapped. "I fucking failed. Are you happy to know that?"

Kryzynski sucked in a breath. "Oh God."

"It was worse than you're thinking, so could you maybe use some of that shitty experience and move in on the guy?"

"No—dammit, Rivers, this was the best my lieutenant would give me. It sure would have helped to have an actual eyewitness telling us where to go!"

"I was not exactly in any shape to be running an op. Do you understand me? Do you need me out there now to tell you how to pick your own noses, or can you just run in and get this guy?"

"Not if he's as dangerous as you say! Seven a.m.—first light."

"We'll see you there," Jackson snarled, and Ellery heard the dial tone as Kryzynski hung up on him.

"That went well," he muttered.

"We should call Dakin." Jackson took a couple of pacing steps and yawned. The yawn ended and he fell heavily to his seat. "We should all be there at six thirty."

"No," Ellery snapped. "*I'll* be there—"

"Not on your life." Jackson tried to shove himself up using his bad arm. He yelped and sat down again. "I'll be better in the morning, and even if I'm dragging myself across Meadowview like a slug, you still need to take me with you."

"Augh!" He was right. Ellery hated that he was right, because often it happened using intuition alone.

"I know what the inside of the house looks like," Jackson argued. "I may not remember how many people were in there, but I'll be able to see if anything's changed."

"I didn't want them to know you'd been there," Ellery told him—probably unnecessarily.

"You think I didn't know that? It was sweet and all, but eventually they were going to need evidence—"

"But…." Ellery closed his eyes. "Jackson, they're going to want to know where the DNA came from."

Jackson glared out the back window. "Let 'em," he said, and if Ellery hadn't known him pretty well, he wouldn't have seen that tic in his cheek or the way he was grinding his teeth together.

Or the fact that his ibuprofen had worn off and he was in a lot of pain.

"I just don't want you to have to—"

"You want to protect me. I get it." Jackson met his gaze across the table. "And here, in this house, that's okay. But out there, I gotta do my job. Ellery, there were dead bodies in there—I don't remember how many. These guys, they gotta take that seriously, and they're not going to do it if they're informed by a nameless source. It's got to be a real thing."

"It was a real thing," Ellery whispered. "It was real to *you.*"

"Well, let's make it real to the world." But Jackson let out a sigh and rested his forehead on his fist. "Tomorrow."

Ellery glanced at the clock. "Nine—who wants bed?"

"Not yet," Jackson protested through a yawn, and Ellery wanted to laugh.

"Don't be a macho bastard. Come to bed, we'll turn the TV on in there, and you can fall asleep watching something stupid while I work."

"You'll wake me up in the morning, right?" he asked plaintively.

"Only one of us gets to sneak out of bed to be a fucking hero. Is that right, Jackson?"

Jackson groaned. "That was not supposed to turn out like that."

"But guess what. It did. So now we're going two steps back, and I get to give you shit about it until you are all better."

"Fine." God, he was even attractive when he sulked. "Do I get to do dishes?"

As. If. "No. Not tonight. Tonight you go call Tess Dakin and tell her she needs to be there tomorrow or she doesn't get to whine."

Jackson nodded and yawned again. Ellery could see the lines and shadows of fatigue around his eyes, heard an encroaching cold in his voice.

"What?" Jackson asked as he stood. "You've completely managed my life for the next twelve hours. Why do you have that 'nipple-clamp' expression on your face?"

Ellery didn't even laugh. "I don't understand how you've made it. How did you survive the last eight years since you got shot the first time? It's a mystery. It's a terrifying, heart-stopping mystery."

Jackson shrugged and winked tiredly. "Not such a mystery—I didn't really come close to death until I met you."

"Ha-ha."

Jackson held out his hand, and Ellery put the phone in it. "Try not to get this one stomped on by a drug-addled serial killer."

"We're damned lucky he was drug-addled," Jackson said soberly. "Do you know I had my wallet in my pocket? He grabbed my car keys and my phone and left the wallet."

"Did he grab the dime bag you lifted when you raided heroin family?" That had been bothering him.

Jackson grimaced. "Well, I think I washed that when I threw everything not my sweatshirt and shirt in the washer. It wasn't sealed too tightly. It's probably seeped into the fabric of the jeans."

Ellery sucked in air through his teeth. "Okay. Tomorrow? When Mike is Jackson-sitting? You're going to the duplex, throwing *that* shit away, and moving the rest of your clothes here. It's like you've been trying to do fall and winter in two pairs of jeans and a couple of hoodies. I know you've got more clothes in that garage somewhere."

Jackson gave a half smile, like something amused him. "I do," he said quietly. "You, uh—you're sure." He closed his eyes, and Ellery could see the rise and fall of his chest in a big cleansing breath. "I'm…." He swallowed. "You know… this is a big thing."

"Really?" Ellery's heart was sore, and he found his escape in sarcasm. "It hadn't occurred to me that this could possibly be a big step for you. Because you—not twelve hours ago—were planning to take your cat and go." And ouch, that stung.

"Because the duplex isn't mine anymore," Jackson said softly. "And… and if this place isn't home, I don't have anywhere to go."

Ellery let his sarcasm go in a rush. Very carefully he took a sip of his wine and tried to steady the shaking of his hands. "Come here," he ordered, and Jackson approached his chair slowly. Ellery stood and took his good hand.

"I, Ellery Cramer, promise that any parting of the ways we come to will be arrived at through mutual consent and exhaustion of all other avenues of communication. I will never just kick you out. I will never throw your cat in the carrier and tell you to go. As long as we cohabitate, part of the space here will always be yours. I order groceries and have them delivered—I refuse to let you pay for that. I will accept a small rent stipend after you make arrangements for your half of the duplex and not before. Drive-through and takeout are up for grabs and depend on who's driving."

He took a deep breath and peered at Jackson, who was gnawing his lower lip in a gesture that seemed uncharacteristically young.

"My car payment—"

"Nope. Mine."

He glared. "My cat's vet bills?"

My cat too was almost out of Ellery's mouth before he could censor himself, but he caught it. "Yours. Not a problem. Get two. Pay for them both. We're good."

Jackson raised his eyebrows. "You must like blood," he said. "Billy Bob will fucking kill an interloper."

Ellery narrowed his eyes. "So. Will. I."

And then he could have kicked himself, because Jackson's past was a sore point between them, and Ellery wasn't doing either of them any favors by rubbing on it with sandpaper.

"I promise," Jackson said, surprising him. "I mean, I can't promise I won't get hurt or I won't get mad. I can't even promise I won't disappear again, because I've got to tell you, everything I was doing yesterday made sense to me at the time. But I promise—"

"You've already said it," Ellery told him, the shame biting deep. "More than once. I really only needed once. And I can't promise I won't be bitchy about it. But I can promise I'll never doubt you."

Jackson smiled slightly. "Sometimes it's fun when you're bitchy," he said reassuringly.

Ellery rubbed Jackson's pouty bottom lip with his thumb. "I am insecure because you are…." He laughed, embarrassed. "Really hot."

Jackson ducked his head. "So are you!"

Ellery laughed again, every fiber of his being back in high school where he defined the word "dork" and wore that badge proudly. "I'm paying the vet bills for your fucking cat," he said. He shook his head and stepped back, needing his own space for once. "Go. Go call the sexy woman who tried to hit on you yesterday morning and tell her she can be in on the bust if she plays nice with my guys. When you're done with that, crawl into bed."

Jackson kissed him, quick and dirty. His skin was hot, and his lips were dry under Ellery's, promising a long feverish night ahead for them both. But he kissed Ellery like Ellery was sexy and Jackson wanted him, and then he turned toward the bedroom. He paused at the hallway, though.

"Ellery?"

"Yeah?"

"If we ever get married, I think you need to maybe open a book of poetry or something. That sounded an awful lot like contract law. I'm saying."

Oh God. "Just go!" He made an attempt at laughter, and Jackson must have bought it.

It took him twenty minutes to clean up and set the dishwasher, which was a long time for two people.

His hands were shaking. He walked into the divider between the kitchen and the dining room twice. He almost dropped his favorite wineglass.

If we ever get married…. Jackson had been kidding when he'd said it. He'd been giving Ellery a little bit of shit for drawing up a verbal agreement on the fly, making what should have been a romantic moment dry and reassuring and practical.

But he'd said it. He'd said it like it was a possibility. He'd said it like someday the two of them would wear suits and tell the world they were family.

Who would marry me? Ellery still remembered Jackson's outrage at the thought in August. The idea that anybody would merge his or her future to Jackson's—all the reasons he was a liability, all the shit he couldn't control.

Who would marry me? Ellery would. Ellery would marry him in a heartbeat, whether that meant he got shot tomorrow and Ellery had to live the last four months all over again, or whether that meant he got killed tomorrow and Ellery would cry for the rest of his life.

If we ever get married....

When, Jackson. Not if. When. I'm going to marry you, goddammit. We're going to have kittens.

The kittens part made him laugh, pulled his heart from the dangerous, shaky place of emotional revelation. He dried his hands, grabbed his laptop and his paperwork and the awesome, nonglamorous parts of his job, and sauntered into the bedroom.

Jackson was curled up on his side, the phone next to his head, looking troubled.

"What?"

"You got the number when she gave you her card, right?"

"Yeah?"

"She's not answering—it didn't even go to voice mail."

A cold shiver lanced up Ellery's spine. "Did it just ring and ring and ring?"

Jackson met his eyes. "Why?"

"That's what your phone did."

Jackson tilted back his head and let out a frustrated growl. "Fucking aces! Do you still have her card? Let me call her captain and—"

"I'll call Kryzynski after that."

"And then we'll call Toe-Tag in the morning," Jackson mumbled. "So much for hanging out with Mike and moving some more—"

"The rest of—"

"My shit." Jackson grimaced. "The rest of. Fine. Whatever." He pushed himself up to sitting and held out his hand for Tess's card. Ellery dug it out of the pocket of his briefcase and handed it over before setting up his laptop again and got settled.

He listened to Jackson leave a message on her captain's phone and then look up the desk sergeant and call him.

That phone call didn't go so well, particularly when Jackson gave his own name.

"No, I am not trying to pick up on her. She's fucking missing. Do you even fucking care? Oh, that's awesome that you think she's a great piece of ass. Believe it or not, I was interested in her as a human being. Now call her house, you useless piece of shit, and see if she made it home!"

He hit End Call, and Ellery rescued his phone before Jackson could chuck it across the room.

"We're down to one, cowboy," he said dryly. "Now let me call some police who actually like us and see what I can do."

Kryzynski didn't pick up—but Campbell did.

"A detective?" he asked uncertainly, proving to Ellery at least why he didn't have the chops to be promoted. "She's missing? Wouldn't someone else know about that? Does she work Meadowview?"

"District Three," Ellery said, looking at the card. "So the body that led us to this bust was discovered on her beat. She was a part of this investigation, and we were trying to catch her up in the loop. She's not picking up, and we need you to be on the lookout for her."

"I think I know what she looks like—tall? Blonde? Knockout?"

"Yeah, was that a stretch?"

"Hey—I'm new, remember?"

Ellery took a deep breath and put a damper on his sarcasm. "Yes—I'm sorry. But it's been something of a day. We just thought about her, and she's not picking up anywhere. Given what our PI went through to pinpoint this place you're staking out, we're a bit worried."

"Yeah—no, I get you. Here, let me call some folks. I'll get back to you in an hour."

"Aces." So, there was a promise to wake him up right when he was planning to shut his eyes. This guy wasn't winning any more popularity contests with Ellery.

"Excellent! Talk to you then."

Ellery hung up and looked at Jackson, who was lying on his side again, scowling at him with troubled eyes. With a quick feel of his forehead, Ellery sighed and got out of bed.

"Where're you going?"

"More ibuprofen. And a thermometer."

"You know, I don't think that's really necessary."

Ellery didn't even answer. Just came back with the necessary meds and made him open his mouth.

"Stop scowling like that," he admonished. "You look like Grumpy Cat. And you have a fever. Sit up and swallow."

That Jackson didn't try to make that a dirty joke meant he really *was* feeling like shit. Still, after he was ready to lie down again, he regarded Ellery unhappily through eyes heavy with fatigue.

"You can't leave me tomorrow," he said soberly.

Ellery let out a sigh. "Jackson…." He put his hand on Jackson's forehead and raised his eyes meaningfully.

"No." Scowl. "Irrelevant. If she's missing, it's because of me—"

"Bullshit. It's because she followed you, and *just like you*, I may add, didn't call for backup. Which meant it was either something she wasn't supposed to be doing, or she was trying to be the cowboy and go for the glamour. You going missing was you—with a little help from, you know, a sociopath. Her going missing is the same thing."

"We should be out there now," Jackson rasped, and Ellery heard the rattle in his lungs too.

"Six hours, Jackson," Ellery pleaded, suddenly incredibly weary himself. "Give yourself six more hours. Please."

"Hate this." But he was already mostly asleep.

Ellery waited until his eyes were closed entirely before stroking his hair off his forehead. What would it be like, he wondered. What would it be like to fall in love with another lawyer or a school administrator or a college professor? What would it be like to love someone not damaged, not irreparably hurt by the world before he even walked into Ellery's orbit?

Would the lows be nearly as terrifying?

Would the highs be nearly as good?

The heat of Jackson's skin sweated uncomfortably against his palm. It didn't matter. Ellery wasn't giving him back to the world at large. The world had no idea what it had and refused to take care of him right.

Look at him now, one day out of Ellery's care and he came back broken.

Ellery wasn't going to forgive him for that soon.

It took a moment to go back to work, but he managed to accomplish some documentation of Jackson's day and his whereabouts—enough to satisfy their bosses, hopefully, and to give to Kryzynski so he'd have some proof to back up his call on the stakeout and the op in the morning. He was just packing up when his phone rang.

"Yeah?"

"This is Campbell—your guy was right. Dakin hasn't been seen or heard from since around three this afternoon. But we've had eyes on the place since five. We haven't seen or heard anything that would indicate she's here."

Either she was inside and dead already—or he'd taken off and taken her with him. Either way, Ellery and Jackson weren't in a position to do anything about it, not now.

"We'll be there at six," Ellery said grimly. "Don't expect Jackson to behave if you don't have a fix on her position by then."

He hung up, hating the situation as much as Jackson. Owens could be beating her, torturing her—sexually assaulting her. She could be as lost in her own head as Jackson had been.

But Meadowview was an hour away, and if the cops weren't going in now, nothing either of them could do would make them change their minds.

Next to him, Jackson gave a helpless cough in his sleep.

Ellery had defended scumbags before, and he'd done it to the best of his ability. He'd needed to compartmentalize—he was fine with it.

As he slid into bed and turned out the lights, he realized he was not fine with this. But he'd still pick Jackson's well-being over a stranger's any day.

In fact, he just had.

Still Twitching

MORNING CAME too soon—and not soon enough.

Jackson spent a restless, awful night coughing, battling the fever that he could feel in every breath and bone. When Ellery awakened him at four in the morning, he'd responded by coughing until his chest hurt.

Then he'd swung out of bed, showered, and allowed Ellery to wrap his shoulder in gauze and antibiotics. Then he dressed in clean clothes and brushed his teeth, all while Ellery fumbled for his own shower. By the time Ellery was out and dressed—in a suit since this was official—Jackson had giant thermoses of coffee ready. Ellery prepared another one with hot water that Jackson naively thought was for hot chocolate before they left.

Then Ellery pulled soft knit gloves out of the pocket of his trench coat and a scarf and hat from a drawer, all of which he threw at Jackson as they were leaving the house.

"Thanks?" It hurt to talk—his throat was on fire.

"Yes. You're welcome. By the way, what did you do to the cat? He's acting like we stepped on one of his good legs."

"I don't know. I got up. It was horrible. SPCA is gonna be on my ass next. Those people are vicious."

Ellery laughed sharply as they climbed into the Lexus, and he turned on the car and cranked the heater on. "Seriously. What did you do?"

Jackson grunted, because he'd actually petted the cat to calm him down, but now Billy Bob was apparently another nursemaid who disapproved of Jackson's lifestyle.

"I got up," he repeated. Then he coughed—and coughed and coughed.

Ellery rummaged in the pocket of his trench coat again and this time came up with a bag of cough drops, the heavy-duty kind. He threw them sideways at Jackson.

Jackson totally would have rejected them, if he could only speak.

"Thanks," he said when he could talk again.

The cold dark of November wasn't conducive to idle chitchat anyway, but Jackson was also deep in thought.

"He's got to have another den," he said as Ellery pulled onto the freeway.

"Any ideas?" Didn't sound surprised—this had probably hit him after Jackson had fallen asleep.

"We need to see your transcripts with Bridger," Jackson said, thinking hard. Bridger had been a small-time thug with a badge, really. Owens had freaked him the hell out, even though they were partners. While Bridger had been working for money—and at the bidding of a senator's aid—Owens had been mostly doing it for kicks.

But Jackson had been recovering while Ellery deposed Bridger, and although he'd relayed a lot of the information to Jackson, there was probably a lot more to be gleaned if only one had the time and the motivation and the fine-toothed comb.

"I wasn't at one hundred percent then, but I need to see Bridger's beat again and maybe put some pins on a map."

"We can look that up after this," Ellery said, nodding. "I think the full transcript is at the office. Grab my phone and e-mail Jade. She can have hard copies and a map ready when we get there."

Jackson snagged the phone from the console charger and logged on, texting rapidly even as Ellery swung quickly through what amounted to light traffic that early in the morning. "You don't think Tess'll be at the house, do you?" he asked when he was done.

Ellery didn't risk a glance at him, but Jackson could feel his regard anyway. "Do you?"

"No. Owens made the cops—he could have done it high, he could have done it dead. Whenever, however he took Dakin, he spent part of his time evading the damned police and part of the time in transit."

"And if he's got a problem, like you suspect, part of the time high," Ellery pointed out.

Jackson grunted and rubbed his eyes. They still felt sandy with grit, and the cough drops hadn't cleared the congestion out of his chest any either.

"And he's going to want to play with her," Jackson conceded. Then he shuddered and broke into a coughing fit. When he could talk again, he managed to say, "It's awful—and I hate to think about what she's going through, but he'll probably keep her alive."

"You should still be in bed," Ellery told him. "This isn't your fault."

"Awesome. Let's tell Dakin that after we make sure she's going to live."

But his head pounded, and he couldn't sustain his snark or his sarcasm or even his self-loathing. It was all he could do to lean his head against the window and shiver in the autumn dark, waiting for Ellery's Lexus to bear them back to hell.

THE HOUSING development of Meadowview looked somehow more sinister in the wee hours of the morning. Following Campbell's directions, they pulled into a dead-end courtyard that backed up against the same undeveloped field that sat behind Owens's hideout.

Two cherry tops and an unmarked vehicle sat there, the occupants gathered around the hood of the unmarked, looking at a map under someone's phone light.

Getting out of Ellery's car and venturing into the bone-chilling blackness of the predawn was maybe one of the hardest things he'd done in recent memory. Ellery grabbed the thermos that wasn't coffee and handed it to him as they walked to talk to the officers on duty.

"Drink it," he ordered. "There's Theraflu in there."

Jackson looked suspicious. "It's not hot chocolate? What other reason would you have to make a thermos of just hot water?"

"It's tea, Jackson. And medicine. Deal."

Jackson scowled. "I bet it makes me pee like a racehorse. You watch. Your little cop groupies are gonna be all 'We have to take shit serious!' and I'm gonna have to pee!"

Ellery tried to act bored. "Was that funny? Because from my end, buddy, that wasn't anywhere near funny."

"That was hilarious. That was so hilarious you're thanking your lucky stars I'm here, because I'm the closest thing to comic relief you got in your life."

The gust of his sigh plumed in the dark. "Yeah, Jackson. That's why I keep you. The comic relief. Are you just talking to hear your voice? Because I know it's entertaining that you sound like a whisky-soaked chain-smoker, but you're going to regret talking so much when you open your mouth and nothing comes out."

Jackson opened and closed his mouth like a fish just for entertainment value. His body shook with aches, his chest burned, and his head had exploded about six times in the past ten minutes.

If he couldn't be a festering asshole now, there was never going to be a good time.

They walked up to the huddle around the map, and Jackson defied the custom of personal space and dug his chin into Kryzynski's shoulder.

"Do you have anyone in the back?" he rasped, mostly to watch the blond, blue-eyed young detective flail at him and recoil.

"No! Why would I? There's an eight-foot fence back there!"

Jackson chuckled when he really wanted to throat punch the guy. "Because that's how I got in, with a wounded shoulder and everything."

It ached with fever and possible infection and—more probably—inner muscle tears from the original knife wound. Owens hadn't been wounded at all—it wouldn't have been a problem.

"Fuck!" Kryzynski looked at two of the uniforms and nodded to them. "Go around in back and look," he ordered.

"I tried to tell you this last night," Jackson snapped, suddenly not having fun anymore. "What part of 'I've been here and know the layout' didn't we understand?"

"The part where you were lucid even though you were high as a kite!" Kryzynski snapped back.

"Well, I wasn't high when I climbed the fence, although that might have made it easier," he conceded. "I mean, I *wish* I'd been high when I did that. 'Cause, dude. Also—" And in a breath he stopped screwing around. "—the side gates aren't locked. The far side, the one near the dead end, has the dead guy in it. I don't know if Owens gave enough of a shit to move him, so be aware." Jackson shuddered. "It's not pretty," he said quietly. "The guy didn't deserve to die that way."

Kryzynski nodded and looked around to the rest of the people there. "What about the others—you said there were more?"

"The dead guy was a drug dealer. He was, in fact, a major supplier. Owens took him out to get to me—he had connections to my family. He wasn't trying to take over a business, so he just opened the fucking doors and let people come in and fix." Jackson shuddered. "There were a lot of ODs. Again—not pretty. And he's been there for a week, so not fresh either." Yeah, the more he thought about it, the more he thought Owens must have another base of operations. "We think he's got another den—someplace just his. You know Tess Dakin disappeared last night."

Campbell was there, and he gave Kryzynski a meaningful look. "I told him that," he said righteously.

"And I told you that SWAT doesn't get here for another half an hour, and we don't have permission to go in without them. It was stake the place out with a few of us or give up the op."

Jackson closed his eyes and tilted his head back. "Was it me?" he asked rhetorically. "Was it the fact that we told them months ago this guy was dangerous? Or was it that he was just killing street people? Was that it? He hit junkies and prostitutes so it was all okay?"

Kryzynski had the grace to look away. "I don't know," he said after a miserable moment of not even looking Ellery in the eye. "If what you've told us is accurate, this is going to be a big furry deal, Rivers. I don't know why the brass didn't take it more seriously."

"I do," Ellery said heavily. He grimaced at Jackson in what looked like shame. "The DA's office—not consciously, mind you, but Owens arrested a lot of people. They've spent the last month going over all of Bridger's old cases, making sure none of them were crooked arrests. Do you think they want to do the same thing all over again? If everybody conveniently pretends Owens just went AWOL, we don't have to fix any of the broken."

Jackson let out a grunt, not sure what to do about that line of thought. "Someone is going to have to fix what's in that house." He swallowed against the razor blades in his throat and shivered. "When's your fucking SWAT team getting here, Kryzynski? We need to know whether or not to start looking for Dakin."

Kryzynski looked at Campbell, who shrugged grimly. "You're sure Owens got her?" He sounded sad and desperate.

"Yeah," Jackson told him, relenting on the fuck-you a little. He wanted a chance to look through the house and tell the forensics team what to look for. He had to make nice like a grown-up. "I think she was following me. My car got reported in this area, she checked it out the day after it was wrecked, and he caught her. Her last check-in was three o'clock yesterday. She would have had time to hear about the car by then, probably fit it into her day. He probably got her when she was checking out the house."

"How'd that go?" Kryzynski asked, and Ellery turned away.

"He doped me," Jackson said briefly. "I pretended to be too stoned to move, and when he went to ditch my car, I ran for it."

"He didn't tie you up?"

Jackson shuddered, remembering Owens's scum, his touch, his tongue on Jackson's skin, and how Jackson hadn't moved. "I think it gave him a sense of power to think he didn't have to," he said now, his voice so faint it triggered another coughing fit.

Good. He let that take him out of the conversation for a while so Ellery could move in and ask smart shit.

Jackson's higher reasoning wasn't working so well at this point.

SWAT arrived at a quarter till, and Kryzynski took his little recon operation across the street from Owens's house.

Jackson made Ellery hunker down behind the car while he stood and watched the action over the back.

"What are they doing?" Ellery asked irritably.

"Watching gay porn and getting out condoms."

"*This is the police! Open up!*"

"Jackson!"

"What? They're going in!"

"The people in the house behind us are watching us!"

Jackson looked away from the action—where the SWAT team was swarming into the house like clowns into a car, without resistance or apparent effect—and down to see Ellery pointing at what looked to be a bathroom window.

Jackson risked a glance behind him and saw a middle-aged woman peeking out from the blinds. She saw him looking and dropped the blinds and shut off the light.

"I'd watch too," he said, turning his attention back to the action. "If we're invading the guys across the street, that means we're not coming at them. Besides, do you think they don't know what's been going on across the street?"

"Then why didn't they call the police?" Ellery asked. He sounded a little freaked-out by the sounds of banging going on inside the house.

"Who says they didn't? The cops can only come out and do so many drive-bys. If they don't have enough manpower for the bust, it's not going down. The guys inside have squatters' rights. If nobody's going to serve the eviction notice—and a lot of homeowners and realties can't afford to in a neighborhood like this—there's no way to get rid of the drug dealers. This could be the best thing to happen to these people in a month!"

Or in this neighborhood, it could be another day at the office. Jackson had no idea, but Ellery was taking deeper breaths, and his jitters had worn off, so Jackson considered it a lie well told.

"Wait," he hushed. "They're coming out." The lead officer stepped aside and let one of his men out. The man fell to his knees in the mud in front of the entryway, took off his helmet, and puked. "Oh."

Ellery apparently couldn't stand it anymore and stood up. "Oh what?"

"They found the bodies."

Ellery stood up just in time to watch another member fall to his knees next to his brother-in-arms so they could blow chunks together.

"Oh, Jackson," he whispered. "You were in there."

"I remember." Jackson was simply too sick to get sick. The pounding in his head, the zillion other aches and pains of the cold building in his bones, were plenty enough to distract him from the visceral memory. "I'm going to go in there again." And suddenly this was really important. "But you can't." He darted his eyes to Ellery's. "Please," he said softly. "Please, baby. Don't think of me in there. I couldn't stand it."

Ellery shook his head. "I have to," he said, breaking Jackson's heart a little. "I need to see where you were—and where Tess might have been. It's important. Especially if it goes to trial—I'll be a witness for the prosecution."

Jackson found a chuckle from somewhere. "There should be a law against that."

"Shut up."

His voice was down to rasp and hope by now, so he did. Kryzynski had gone in after the two weak stomachs had given the all clear, and now he showed up at the door, talking on his radio.

"Ambulances?" Ellery queried.

"And coroner buses. He probably had them on speed dial."

"So what you're saying is Owens is gone, and we've got another hour before we can get in there."

Jackson looked at the graying sky around them. "That's what I'm saying."

"No. No we don't."

Ellery shouldered his way around the car and across the street, Jackson in his wake. Jackson recognized the mantle of authority he was wearing, the one that came with the full name of the firm and his own courthouse ID. It was bullshit, of course, because at this point he didn't have a client involved, but Ellery managed to make bullshit look good.

"We won't contaminate your precious crime scene," Ellery said, pulling booties and gloves from his trench coat pocket and giving them to Jackson.

Jackson raised his eyebrows at that level of preparedness. He needed to get him some of these. "I've already been here anyway," he said, voice flat. "We just need to look for proof that he has Tess Dakin so we can get more manpower on the hunt."

"Do you think she's alive?"

Jackson didn't recount their reasoning—just their hope. "Yeah. I really do."

"Don't touch anything," Kryzynski cautioned. Then he shuddered. "You won't want to. Try to stick to the main room. The hallways and back bedrooms are…." He shook his head. "Just really fuckin' awful. Nightmare fodder. Just…."

"Hear you." Jackson nodded, not wanting to see the pity in Kryzynski's eyes when he figured out that, yes, Jackson really had been there.

SWAT had set up floodlights in every room and had gone from body to body, marking the live ones green for the ambulances and the other ones red for the coroner's buses.

There were a surprising number of green markers for such a still mass of bodies.

"The smell is something special," Ellery said tightly as they walked in.

"I've never been so grateful for a head cold in my life," Jackson said truthfully. "It was amazing when I was here before—and even better stoned."

"Well, let's hear it for mucus," Ellery muttered, and Jackson heard the natural sarcasm defense system kicking in. Good.

"Okay—this table wasn't kicked over," Jackson told him, wanting to make the trip brief. He could see Ellery's eyes starting to linger on some of the red-marked bodies, including Jackson's black-tongued friend in the corner. "See the wreckage?" The buckets full of chicken bones had been hurled over the room and all the product that had been slithering off the table scattered with it. The table itself—a cheap laminated wooden one—had shattered up against the wall, and pieces of it still decorated some of the stoned junkies in the corner.

One of whom was looking at Jackson with semilucid eyes.

Jackson walked carefully, disturbing as little as possible. He glanced at the empty spot by the wall across from the couch, the place he'd sprawled, back against the wall, and stared at the dead man in the hall entrance while Owens had defiled him.

Jackson wasn't there anymore.

He wasn't that man, stoned and helpless.

He was sick as a fucking dog, maybe, but he was ambulatory, and he had shit to do.

The guy in the corner was Owens's type, actually—dirty and pretty—his tightly curled hair only slightly grown out from a scalp trim and the soft, faded brown of his skin paled by drugs and malnutrition. He still had a sweet twist to his full lips when he smiled, but the look he sent Jackson from pale brown eyes was frightened.

"Think I'll clean up in jail?" he asked wistfully.

"If you want to," Jackson told him truthfully. "But they've got bigger fish to fry. They may catch and release you after a trip to the doc."

The kid swallowed, and his chin wobbled. He sent a hunted look around the house and shuddered. "This is hell," he whispered. "I don't want to come back."

"Then you need to not use," Jackson said, keeping his voice gentle. "It's as simple as that, buddy. But I know it's not easy."

The kid shook his head and wiped his eyes with the back of a grimy hand. "The guy in here, giving out drugs… he was crazy." He picked at something dried and white on his shirt. "He… he…."

Jackson shuddered. "You're lucky he didn't do more," he said. "If he'd had time, it would have been worse."

Kid nodded. "I saw him do worse. He… he was pissed. Got back from somewhere, had a chick by the arm. Slammed her into the wall and broke up the table. Then…." The kid started to cry harder. "He tore her clothes. Pretty blouse, ripped it. Boobs hanging out. Ripped her pants down." He started to sob. "Was just so glad he left me alone."

Jackson cupped the back of his head tenderly. "It's okay," he whispered. "Can't be a hero when you're stoned."

"I don't want to be stoned no more."

Jackson nodded. “Here—Ellery, give me a card.” He reached out, knowing Ellery wouldn’t ask. “Hold on to this,” he said sternly, and the kid nodded. “They’ll take you to the hospital. Feed you, wash you, clean you out. Ask you questions. When you’re done, call this number. We’ll get you into a program. Give you a job or a place to live when you get out. You got help. Okay, kid?”

“You don’t even know my name,” the kid whispered.

“What’s your name?”

“AJ. AJ Collier.”

“That’s okay, AJ…. Everyone needs a little caring for when they’re down. Call that number. Ellery’ll answer. He sounds like an asshole, but he’s all right.”

The kid smiled a little. “Anything I gotta do for this help?” He looked Jackson up and down suggestively, and Jackson rolled his eyes.

“Kid, I’m at frickin’ death’s door. If I was feeling better, I’d have *him* pinned to the wall. So no. Not that kind of deal. Just call. Ask for help. Sometimes it’s that easy.”

“Oh.” The fact that he looked disappointed was actually sort of good for Jackson’s ego. “Anything I *can* do for you?” he asked wistfully.

“Did he say anything? After he was done with the girl?” Girl. Full-grown woman, rendered helpless, made an object. Jackson wished he could make her day better with a business card and some soft conversation. A rescue and vengeance would have to do.

“Said she’d better not throw up in the car,” the kid said, shivering. “Said he was hungry and wanted some fucking chicken.”

Jackson grunted. “That’s not ordinary chicken,” he said softly, catching Ellery’s eye. The chain wasn’t widespread—only a couple of them existed in the area. “We’ll use that when we look at Bridger’s map.”

Ellery nodded, looking a little green around the gills.

“Kid, you ready to stand up yet?”

AJ shook his head. “No. Sorry, man. Just… just gonna hafta be wheeled out with the other vegetables.”

Jackson closed his fingers tightly over the card. “Call us. You get done giving your statement, going to the hospital, call us.”

He smiled and wiped his face again. “Fucking comedown,” he explained. “Wrecks me every time.”

"Make it your last one," Jackson begged, and Ellery's hand under his arm was maybe the only thing that got him to his feet, pulled him out of that stinking house, saved him from trying to save one last soul.

"There were blond hairs on the corner of the wall," Ellery said as they hit daylight and fresh air. Jackson breathed shallowly through his mouth, trying to get the taint of the house out of his lungs and mucus membranes. "A little bit of blood. Backs up the kid's story."

"You'll be nice to him if he calls?" Jackson knew Ellery was a good person, but you couldn't always hear it in his voice.

"You think he will?" Idle curiosity—nothing more.

"I hope so. Is that wrong?"

Ellery squeezed the back of his arm and let go. "One of the reasons I love you," he said, almost too softly for Jackson to hear.

But Jackson *did* hear, and a corner of his heart warmed, because he was starting to believe it.

"What time is it?" Jackson asked, not able to deal with emotion now.

"Almost eight—Jade should be at the office by the time we get there."

Jackson grunted and spotted the thermos of—ugh—tea left on the hood of the cop car they'd stood behind. "Can we stop for coffee?" he asked pathetically.

"Did you drink all your Theraflu?" Ellery asked, all sweetness.

"Absolutely." Was a blatant lie. You might as well ask Billy Bob if he'd taken his vitamin.

Ellery got to the car first and shook the thermos, then handed it to Jackson. "It's full."

"Some random person stopped and filled it with muck," Jackson said with a straight face. "For all you know, there's more heroin in here than Owens pumped into me two days ago. This could be a trap. I could die."

Ellery's scowl was a thing of epic beauty. "So help me, Jackson, if you end up in the hospital because of your own damned stubbornness, I won't visit you. I won't even text you on the phone. I'll call Kaden and *he'll* come visit you, and Jade will come visit you, and *my mother* will come visit you, and you'll be eyeballs-deep in relatives who want to scream in your face and *nobody to give you a blow job.*"

Jackson grinned at him, knowing his eyes were running and his nose was swollen and not caring. "You'll always want to give me a blow job. Now stop complaining and let's go. We need to search out Popeyes fried chicken. As far as I know, there's only six in Sacramento, and one's damned close to the med center, which could give us a clue."

"One's near Florin Road too," Ellery cautioned, and Jackson cursed his muzzy head. Florin Road was probably where Owens had stopped on his way to the Meadowview house—and there were plenty of places in between.

"We need to check those transcripts," Jackson mumbled. "We've got Popeyes and Bridger's beat—"

"District Three," Ellery supplied.

"Which takes us back to Stockton Boulevard. There's something in there—God, I hope so. He needs someplace private, 'cause if she's still kicking, she's going to be making a helluva lot of noise."

"Lots of those houses have basements," Ellery cautioned. "Easy to muffle a basement."

Jackson groaned, and his head throbbed some more. He couldn't fuckin' think. Dammit.

"Do you think someone tampered with the Theraflu?" he asked, hating himself.

"No," Ellery snapped. "It was as untouched when we got back to it as it was when you were supposed to be drinking it. There was even an undisturbed ring in the dust on the car."

Jackson reached for the untouched thermos, opened the top, and glugged it down.

Tepid, the shit tasted vile.

"Now get me coffee and an ibuprofen," he bitched, knowing he was bitching and not caring. "I need to fucking think."

Ellery, bless him, just nodded and headed for a Starbucks drive-through, while Jackson leaned his head against the window and tried to keep his mouth closed while breathing.

He fell asleep while Ellery was in the drive-through line and didn't wake up until they pulled into the parking lot near the office.

In the cup holder near Jackson's elbow steamed a to-go mug of slippery elm tea.

Jackson took a gulp of it anyway, trying to wake up. Unlike the Theraflu, the mix of anise and grape *wasn't* vile, but it wasn't coffee either. He took another gulp, trying to decide if the anise flavor was pleasant or not, and decided that not having a flaming headache was a bonus.

"Are we going to live?" Ellery asked, acid in his voice.

"Probably not—but I may like you more than anyone else I've ever killed."

Ellery rewarded him with a cackle, and together they managed to get out of the car and walk to the office.

Jade greeted them both with flat, unhappy eyes. "I don't want to hear it."

Jackson grimaced. "I'm sorry. I didn't mean to make you—"

"And you're sick." She dismissed him with a sniff and turned her glare on Ellery. "You said he was home and okay. You did not mention the looking like ass and sick as hell. You're fired."

Ellery scowled. "I said he wasn't dead. That in no way implies 'okay.' That was all you."

Jackson watched her eyes widen, and she shot him a furtive glance. Her voice softened, and her lower lip trembled, and Jackson felt like a complete and total asshole because she was hurt.

"What happened?"

Jackson pulled up a corner of his mouth and tried to not be pathetic and sad. "I'm fine," he said, touching her cheek with a battered knuckle. "There's a cop out there who's not so lucky. We need to find her, Jade. Did you pull out the transcripts Ellery asked for?"

She bit her lip and nodded. "Yeah. In his office."

Jackson reached out his hand, and she smacked his laptop into his grasp just as she said, "Mr. Cramer, can we speak?" without breaking eye contact with Jackson.

He grimaced. They were going to "speak" about him, and there wasn't anything he could do to stop that from happening. Ellery with his functional little psyche and openly communicating family was going to tell Jade all about his night, and Jackson was in no position to argue.

Fine. He rolled his eyes at her and stalked down the hallway without giving Ellery a backward glance.

By the time Ellery walked in, looking almost as tired as Jackson felt, Jackson had the file spread out on his tiny table and a copy of a travel atlas page, heavily red marked, in front of him.

Jackson glanced up from the puzzle he was building with hints from Bridger and his own knowledge of the area and leveled a flat look at him as he nonchalantly hung his coat up and set his briefcase on his desk. Jackson was still wearing the scarf Ellery had draped over his neck, and the gloves were stuffed in his pockets, and knowing that Ellery had given up his own comfort to see to Jackson's ameliorated some of his irritation.

"And…?"

Ellery glanced at him, obviously fighting a look of sheepish apology. "And what?" he asked primly.

"Jade said…."

"She cried," Ellery said shortly.

Jackson grimaced, sucking air in through his teeth. "I'm so sorry."

"I know you are," Ellery muttered, looking away. "That's why I took the meeting."

Jackson blinked, not sure he would have phrased it that way, and Ellery took the conversation out of his hands. "What do you have so far?"

Jackson looked at his map and Post-it Notes and tried to focus his thoughts. "Okay, so here's what we know. Popeyes—so, Stockton Boulevard or Florin Road or off of Auburn. Now, my first thought would be Stockton Boulevard, because Luanne Chisholm was found near here." He circled a vacant field not far from the Shriners Hospital. "But the thing is, that was Bridger and Owens's *beat*. Bridger only *suspected* Owens was a scary fuck—he didn't see him actually kill anybody. So wherever Owens is killing, it's not necessarily where he was working. I went back into your files on Owens and realized that a lot of the people we thought fit the profile were found here." He circled the area between the I-80 split, much of which was occupied with Arcade Creek recreational area and the Haggin Oaks golf course. Many of the bodies had been found in vacant lots, known druggie haunts, tiny parks in the vicinity. They were all close enough to District Three for Luanne Chisholm to throw them off track—but taken on their own, they had a whole different center.

"Okay," Ellery said, pondering. "I get it. He's in a different place, and here's our epicenter." He took a pencil and drew a circle. "Now we know his apartment was not in this place—"

"But that wasn't lived in anyway," Jackson reminded him.

"Yeah—so this place, it's got to have some amenities," Ellery mused, running his finger unconsciously around the lines of the map.

"A place to shower, a place to shit—he probably has furniture here, something personal," Jackson agreed. "But bigger than that. A place to… to work too."

Ellery frowned. "A studio."

"Of course!" Jackson smiled at him and stood up excitedly before the pounding in his head sent him back down. "So, there are warehouses here—" He indicated a section of Watt Avenue near what used to be McClellan Air Force Base. "It's a little bit outside our target area, but if you look here—"

"Lots of thoroughfares," Ellery said, nodding. "And some real prime real estate in that strip." The place had been dodgy when McClellan had been active—lots of X-rated theaters and shoestring businesses. But once the base had been decommissioned, parts of it had been refurbished to create McClellan Aerospace museum, and parts of it had continued to fall apart. Prime real estate for a drug dealer or a serial killer, most definitely. "He could grab a victim, take him to his studio—"

"And work," Jackson said grimly. "He could work."

Ellery met his eyes, and they both shuddered.

"Was that what he was going to do to you?" Ellery asked quietly.

Jackson nodded. "Yeah." Out of nowhere he made a connection, a terrible one that he couldn't escape.

"I bet," he said gruffly, "if we ran him by a profiler, we'd find out that he was raised by a Celia, one who died young."

Ellery sucked in a breath—as well he might. "It could explain his fascination with you," he said, voice raspy.

Jackson frowned at him through bleary eyes. "You're not getting a cold too, are you?"

Ellery shook his head—and then rested a trembling hand in Jackson's hair.

Oh.

"I'm fine," he said, his voice mostly a wish and a prayer.

"No," Ellery stated with simple dignity. "You're not."

Jackson closed his eyes. "I'll be fine," he said after a moment, hoping it was honesty and not bullshit. "I have to be fine."

"Why?"

"Because first we need to have Crystal go over his financials again." He yawned. "Not just see if he's got any outgoing payments to a warehouse space—and I think that's pretty cheap real estate, so it might just be cash withdrawals."

"What else can we look for?" Ellery asked. "And why do you have to do it?"

"We can look for things like gas station receipts and grocery receipts," Jackson said promptly. His voice seemed to come from far away, and he took an experimental sip of his half-empty tea. He'd never had slippery elm before—the anise was okay, but the grape was chemical and gross. Still, he couldn't taste anything that would make the room get smaller, wrapping around him comfortingly. "So, have Crystal run the financials and plot them on this map." He waved generally. "And I need to do it because Dakin was following *me* into my own personal hell, and she didn't need to get sucked into this—"

"This isn't your fau—"

"And because Crystal likes me and responds to me better than you," he finished grumpily. She didn't *dislike* Ellery, but she had a hard time trusting him—said his aura colors were too locked up.

"But you're not okay!"

He pulled some energy out of his socks. "I have to be okay!" he snapped. "Because you and me are all Dakin has, for one—"

"We have the police looking for her too." Ellery folded his arms, looking adamant and unconvinced.

"And because I've apparently moved in with you, for another."

"Jackson." Ellery let out the word on a sigh. "That doesn't make everything better all at once. You know that, right?"

Jackson grabbed Kleenex out of the box on the bookshelf and used it briefly before rolling it into a teeny, tiny, perfectly formed ball. He stared at the ball for a moment, lost in the hypnotic beauty of its roundness.

Ellery called this habit "psychotic," but Jackson had always preferred "antichaotic." The world was a crapshoot, and at any moment, you could get shot all to crap. The one thing Jackson could control at any given time was the teeny-tiny rolled balls of garbage he generated.

With a toss of the Kleenex into the garbage, he decided he was okay with that.

"It's been going on since you met me," he said, smiling faintly. "It's been who I am. Don't tell me after all your bullshit 'I love you' crap yesterday, I'm too much for you."

Ellery inhaled sharply through his nose, and Jackson knew he'd annoyed the man to his last breath.

He was wrong.

Ellery bent down and claimed him, mouth to mouth, germs and slippery elm tea and all, his tongue a powerful presence, his hands framing Jackson's face with the tenderness missing from the kiss.

He pulled back, breathing hard, and Jackson stared at him, appalled. "Oh my God! Get some Airborne—you're going to get—"

"Your sickness is mine, asshole," Ellery snapped. "I don't say 'I love you' to just anyone."

Jackson glared at him. "You will probably talk the germs to death," he muttered in disgust. "Jesus, if anyone could, you could."

Ellery rolled his eyes. "I already took Airborne, by the way. If I don't get sick, you can't blame my mouth."

Jackson grinned, feeling loopy.

"No. Don't say it."

"Heh, heh, heh…."

"God, you are such a child."

"No, seriously, 'cause you've got such a pretty mouth!" Ellery was close enough that Jackson could reach out and touch it too, tracing the lines of it with his knuckle.

"I love you, Jackson, but I'll kill you. No jury on earth would convict me." He dropped a kiss on the top of Jackson's head. "And I do love you. And your sickness is mine. Let's get to work so we can get you in bed and get better."

Jackson allowed himself an unheard-of luxury and relaxed into Ellery's warmth, the protection of his shoulders and his hands on Jackson's upper arms. Suddenly, like nothing he'd had in his life before, Ellery offered home.

"Lots of Airborne," he said gruffly, tilting his head so he was resting it on Ellery's forearm. "I really do feel like shit." Beyond the wall of cotton wool, his head pounded and his throat ached and his chest struggled for air.

"I know." Ellery ran his lips along Jackson's temple. "I think my immune system is in better shape than yours was, but I'll be careful. I promise."

"Thank you." He took a deep breath in anticipation of standing up and going to ask Crystal to run down the financials again, but Ellery put a little more pressure on his shoulders.

"Sh. Just… not yet."

Jackson closed his eyes, feeling weak, knowing—for now—that Ellery would guard him with his strength.

"Okay," he mumbled, closing his eyes. "Just another minute."

The sleep hit him like a sledgehammer. His eyes closed, and he rested his face on his hands before it even hit him that Ellery had dosed his tea with codeine.

Ninja Fish

ELLERY DRAPED his trench coat over Jackson's shoulders before slipping out of the room, the paperwork to request Crystal to run down the financial records already filled out.

Jade was waiting for him as he crossed the office.

"Where's Jackson?" she asked suspiciously. Well, she'd been torn between chewing him out and crying on him. Either one would have been unpleasant, and she probably thought Ellery was trying to save him from making a choice.

Sort of.

Ellery was mostly trying to save Jackson from himself.

"Asleep on his desk," he said, feeling a little smug. That's what heathens got when they'd never tasted tea. "Probably dreaming of purple trees." 'Cause grape-flavored cough syrup and slippery elm—get it?

Jade gave him one of those irritated glances that said not only did she not get it, "it" was not worth her time to get.

"You drugged him?" Just to make sure.

"Hm… how to answer that, how to answer that—"

"Ellery!"

"Yes!" he snapped, done with the game. "Yes, I dosed him, yes, I lulled him to sleep, no, I don't regret it. It will take Crystal an hour, maybe two, to get this done, and by the time we have workable information in our hands, his shoulder might hurt too much to move, and that would be a blessing."

Jade grunted and followed him down the hall. "He was supposed to take it easy today," she muttered.

"Yes, well, there's a kidnapped detective and"—this irritated him because it meant Jackson was right—"a serial killer still on the loose. When that is resolved, I'll bring him in to the hospital myself."

She let out a sigh. "You think the cops ever get tired of him being right?"

"I know they get tired of *me* being right. I don't see why that should change."

To his surprise, Jade let out a startled cackle. "You irritate everyone, Cramer. It's not just the cops."

"Thanks. Thanks a lot."

They'd come to Crystal's office by now, and Ellery paused to try to change gears from the snark and bitch he usually engaged in with Jade to the gentler, more delicate personal demeanor he needed to work with their most proficient computer expert.

"You're going to leave him there, right?" Jade asked, suddenly quiet and sober as well.

Ellery gaped at her.

"I mean, Crystal gives you some info, you and me get in the car and direct the police—Jackson can sleep through the whole thing."

"No," Ellery said, trying to keep his brain from exploding. "Because this isn't that movie. In *that* movie, you and I get our sorry asses shot down and he spends the rest of his life guilty and self-destructing as he enacts his revenge."

Now Jade looked like he'd thrown a bomb in her brain. "What movie are *we* in?"

"The movie where he wakes up by the time we're ready to roll, and hopefully he's breathing and thinking a little better, and he can help save this poor woman who is basically living through hell right now."

Jade pulled her upper lip up just enough to show even white teeth. "That movie does *not* make sure he's okay at the end," she hissed.

"But it *does* make sure he's speaking to the two of us," Ellery snapped. "And it makes sure that Tess Dakin has the best possible chance of making it out alive, and if *that* happens and he *doesn't* have her death on his head, I can deal with an extra day for him in the hospital." He shuddered, a little queasy. "I'm not *happy* about it, but if you love that man, you have to love all of him." As Jackson himself had so eloquently pointed out.

The door to Crystal's office opened, and Crystal herself stuck her head out.

"Are we talking about Jackson?" she asked, peering at Ellery and Jade through her glasses and pushing back her mouse-brown hair. "I'd like to worry about him too."

"How do you know we're worrying?" Jade asked curiously, and Crystal shrugged.

"Jackson is sort of a shiny soul," she said calmly, crossing her arms in front of her. Today she wore a thick chenille sweater, but in the summer she'd be wearing a very thin long-sleeved T-shirt. Crystal had marks on her arms that belied the mild-mannered, casual-psychic, computer-geek first impression, but her heart, Ellery was starting to suspect, had always been a lot purer than the people who surrounded her.

That was more true now than it had been when she'd been a heroin-addicted computer hacker. Jackson had seen it in her first, and Ellery was beginning to trust his judgment.

That boy on the floor of Owens's hideout could call at any time.

"Shiny?" Ellery asked, in spite of himself.

"Shining. He attracts other souls to him," Crystal said softly. "Sometimes the good"—she nodded at Ellery and Jade—"and sometimes the evil." She regarded Ellery levelly.

"He had a run-in with some pure-grade evil," Ellery said.

"I thought so. You and Jade were very worried—the floor felt all wobbly."

Of course it did. "We *were* worried," Ellery admitted. "And now we're *all* worried." He held up the paperwork. "Crystal, a detective who followed Jackson the other day is being held somewhere in this area." He flipped to the map Jackson had so cleverly plotted. "We need you to run Owens's financials again—we need any patterns in this area. We think he lives there—so things like bank withdrawals or where he fills up his car or even where he buys cigarettes or a lottery ticket or—"

"Or distilled water or a lighter or a spoon," she rasped.

Ellery stared at her. "Yes," he said, hating himself for being surprised. "We think he has a drug problem—and it's escalating. And he's got a detective." Ellery swallowed. "And he had Jackson the other day, and his level of crazy is escalating too."

She nodded and patted his arm. "Well, losing Jackson probably set him off. Just like losing Owens is going to set off that cold steel man who was here yesterday." She shuddered. "Make sure he never learns about Jackson. He doesn't know how important Jackson is to us. To bringing down Owens."

She reached out and took all the paperwork from Ellery's hand.

"He is, isn't he?"

Ellery nodded mutely. "Yeah, I'm afraid so."

"Owens isn't the last person in the line," she told him soberly. "This will be done in half an hour."

Ellery grimaced. "Really? The codeine will wear off in about two."

"Did I say half an hour?" Crystal smiled prettily. "I meant an hour and a half."

"What do you want for Christmas?" Jade asked bluntly.

Crystal smiled. "I really love caramel popcorn," she said, and with that, disappeared back into her office.

"Think she wants almonds with that?" Ellery regarded the doorknob to her office like the portkey to hell.

"You will have to ask her." Jade turned on her heel. "I'm going to go pretend that the rest of the office will fall apart without me, and you should probably go brief your police friends and maybe one of your bosses, you think?"

Ellery grunted. Neither prospect was attractive, but…. "Yeah. Sure."

She stalked back down the hallway, which was a good thing, because the rest of the office *would* fall apart without her, and Ellery looked down the corridor at Langdon's office. Jade was right—Langdon would have to be told.

But first he pulled out his phone and hit Kryzynski's number.

"No, we haven't found her," he snarled. "Yes, our captain is shitting bricks. Do you have any ideas?"

Ellery quickly outlined where they thought she was and their reasoning, and Kryzynski swore.

"That sounds awesome—but it's a helluva big area. Don't you have anything more specific?"

"We think he's in a warehouse of some sort—something far away from people—maybe a rental property, but without a For Sale or Rent sign in the front."

"Why no sign?"

Ellery tried not to sound superior. This *was* Jackson's reasoning, after all. "Because he doesn't want to risk someone knocking on his door. It's going to be an isolated place—no in-house neighbors. And it probably has amenities—a shower, a sink, that sort of things. And light," he finished, not wanting to think of why.

"A studio?" Kryzynski asked grimly.

"Exactly. We're running financials now, looking for a way to narrow down the area. There are a lot of properties like that on Watt Avenue—"

"And a lot of secluded spots around Arcade Creek," Kryzynski verified. "Can you send us some victim locations? I know you've been telling us for weeks, but we don't have the info at our fingertips. Some victim locations and—"

"You can use them as an epicenter and work out, looking for overlaps," Ellery said, understanding why the full weight of the department helped. "Sure—I'll start faxing those over to you."

"We should have listened to you," Kryzynski said into the sudden silence. "You and Rivers—you've been this investigation, and it wasn't even your job."

"He's been killing innocent people," Ellery said, some of the fury he'd wanted to spend surfacing in his words now. "How could you not…."

Dirty pretty. How could you not see the pretty for the dirty?

"He picked victims we wouldn't look at," Kryzynski confirmed. Then he sighed. "You know, it wasn't until I saw Rivers talking to that kid today—"

"AJ?"

"See? I didn't even know his name. But he was talking to the kid, calming him down. You forget, when you become a cop, you think about being that cop. Owens may be a serial killer, but I think our system helped make him."

Ellery grunted. "Get in line. I think you had help from the US military to do that. I'll send you victim locations—the ones we're pretty positive about. District Three isn't where he lives—we've pretty much eliminated that, so none of those victims. They may have been his—"

"But they won't lead us there. I hear you. Go do what you gotta, Ellery—and, uh, thank Jackson for us, okay?"

"When he's feeling better," Ellery told him. Because right now, Jackson would probably shoot the entire police department the bird.

"Did he really get—"

"I don't want to talk about it," Ellery said, surprising himself with his own venom. "If you need the evidence and the deposition, it will happen, but not until."

"Oh." Kryzynski sighed. "We found the body on the side of the house—the guy looked wasted. He probably couldn't have lived much longer even without the knife in his throat. How's he handling that?"

"Like all macho bullshit dealers handle pain." Ellery's stomach churned, and he recognized his own hypocrisy. As an attorney, if he had Jackson on the stand, he'd grill him unmercifully, but he wasn't Jackson's attorney. He was Jackson's *lover*, and that made all the difference.

"Shoving it down and torturing himself with it?" Kryzynski muttered. "'Cause that's fun."

Ellery let out a short bark of laughter. "You have no idea."

"Ever dated a firefighter?" The bitterness—oh, dear God, the bitterness.

"I'm fine where I am, thank you," Ellery told him. "And where I am is we're running addresses and he's sleeping off a really shitty couple of days."

"He didn't look too good this morning." Duh.

"He'll look a little better if we can get Dakin back. You guys go hunt and keep me posted."

"Will do. Take care of your guy." Kryzynski sighed, like this was tough to admit. "He really is a good one."

"I just hope I remember that when he wakes up pissed," Ellery told him, and then he rang off.

Langdon wasn't in—which bothered him, mostly because he and Jackson were devoting an awful lot of hours to the opposite of defending people, and the undying gratitude of the police department was not really a lucrative asset for a defense firm to embrace.

But then Jackson had brought in clients when he hadn't even been trying—and heroin family was going to pay well, so maybe Langdon could forgive him a little.

He'd have to, because Crystal was right. After Owens was stopped, Ellery and Jackson were going to have to take a long, deep look at Karl Lacey—because apparently a self-destructing whirlpool of evil like Owens did not just *poof* into life as the invisible henchman of a dirty cop. Owens had been building up to be the perfect storm for a long time, and he'd had some help along the way. Lacey had been a cold bastard, and it seemed to Ellery he held a big enough paddle to fan the flames of Owens's psychosis to a right conflagration.

Ellery went back to his office moodily and took care of the paperwork for cases that actually brought the firm money. His e-mail pinged after about forty-five minutes—Crystal had sent him seven stops that showed up frequently on Owens's finances and a list of properties near the stops. Several of the stops were fairly close together. He got his hair cut near where he bought his cheap scotch, for example, so there were only three lists of properties.

Ellery took Jackson's map out to Jade, along with the lists. "I need this blown up," he said without preamble, "and copies made of these. It's going to take a few of us looking properties up on satellite, pinning locations to the map—it's almost eleven. Owens has had her for eighteen hours."

Jade nodded soberly. "How long's he been asleep?"

Ellery didn't have to ask who "he" was. "About an hour. Let's see if we can get set up before he wakes up. He won't feel like he's lost so much time."

She nodded and took off toward the copy room, and Ellery went back to study the lists of properties.

Some he could eliminate on general proximity to other properties. Some, MapQuest revealed to be already occupied by squatters, or even unregistered businesses. Some were in too poor a shape to be used as a home or a studio of any sort.

Picture by picture, Ellery worked to whittle, refine, and generally guess his way down to three workable lists while Jackson's heavy breaths rattled his chest hard enough for even Ellery to hear it.

That steady, heavy pattern of breathing interrupted itself once, twice, and Ellery looked up from his computer and watched Jackson's eyes open.

For a moment, he obviously didn't know where he was, and Ellery saw stark terror startle him all the way awake. Jackson jerked hard, his hands scattering papers to the floor, and stood abruptly, congestion rattling in his chest. Wildly he looked around, falling to a fighter's defensive crouch before Ellery could calm him into putting two and two together.

"Jackson," Ellery said slowly. "It's good to see you awake."

Jackson closed his eyes and shuddered. "Okay," he said, not moving from his crouch.

"You're in our office." Yeah, no—Jackson was going to work in Ellery's office for as long as he worked at the firm. Ellery was never letting him fall asleep and wake up alone again.

"What—why am I here?"

"You fell asleep because you're sick. You've slept for about two hours. We're just about to start a big mapping project so we can put pins in it and see if we can find Tess Dakin."

Jackson scowled and stood up, stretching more on purpose this time and less on flail.

Then he glared at Ellery. "You *drugged* me!"

Ellery nodded. "I got your cat fixed while you were in surgery, fighting for your life. Why does this surprise you?"

"You Machiavellian *bastard*!"

"And I'll repeat—"

"But Tess Dakin—"

"Would not be any closer to found," Ellery told him truthfully. "Jade is coming in with some maps and some lists. I've just spent an hour eliminating the most obvious ones that don't fit the bill. In an hour we'll have a list we can use to canvass the area. Right now it would just be shooting in the dark."

Jackson let out a grunt, like he was hurt. On automatic, his hand came up and cupped his upper arm.

"Sore?" Ellery asked quietly. Of course it was sore. Ellery was just worried about infection or bleeding.

"Hurts," Jackson slurred. Slowly, like he was afraid the chair would betray him at the last minute, he grabbed the back and sank down. "I can't believe you drugged me."

"I can't believe you thought tea would taste like grape cough syrup."

"And anise," he whined.

"Well, the anise was really the tea," Ellery soothed. "How's your throat?"

"It felt better while I was sleeping," Jackson admitted. He scrubbed at his face. "What do I need to do right now?"

"Take a look. I've got about thirty properties here that will fit the bill for our 'studio.' I just sent the list to Kryzynski, and he's hitting up the Carmichael side. As soon as we plot this shit out on Jade's map, make some probability guesses, we can start working on the North Highlands areas."

"Dandy."

Jackson made to stand up, but Ellery grabbed his laptop and sat down at the table with him. He got a faint smile of appreciation before Jackson took the laptop and squinted at the screen.

"What the—"

"Hush," Ellery commanded, using his proximity to feel his forehead *and* the back of his neck. "God, you're burning up. Jade suggested we leave while you were sleeping. Do you know that?"

The look of hurt Jackson shot him said very plainly Ellery had made the right choice. "Leave me behind?"

Ellery kept it casual. "Hey—that was your ex speaking, not me. I'd prefer someone who knows how to use a firearm, personally."

Jackson groaned. "My fucking weapons were in the fucking car."

"Seriously?" Ellery knew Jackson had two guns—a small gun safe had been installed in his garage when Jackson moved in. He also had a Taser—but he rarely armed himself. "All of them?"

"Yes, all of them. I don't want guns in your house!"

"That's why the safe was in the garage!" Ellery had a horrible thought. "Jesus!" He pulled out his phone and hit speed dial. "Kryzynski, where are you?"

"Carmichael. It's so sweet I want to pick out curtains."

Ellery rolled his eyes. "Not all of Carmichael is that sweet—"

"Yeah, well, there's this apartment on Watt that looks like serial killers live there, but so far we haven't found any warehouses with live detectives or dead bodies. Why are you calling me sounding freaked-out?"

"Because Jackson's car had two guns and a Taser in it when Owens took him. The car was found wrecked last—two nights ago, but I didn't know to check for the weapons."

"Why are you telling me this now?"

"Because Owens has Jackson's guns!" Ellery snapped.

"Oh my God, there is a bad guy in America with a deadly weapon—alert the fucking news!"

Ellery looked at Jackson with flat eyes. "The next time you see this asshole, feel free to kick him in the balls."

Jackson got one of those hooded-eyed grins that Ellery always associated with Billy Bob when he was done licking himself. "Heh, heh, heh, heh…."

Kryzynski exhaled on the other end of the line. "Fine. Why are you telling me this?"

"So if Owens *uses* one of those guns, his lawyer can't get him off by using reasonable doubt and claiming Jackson could have used it." God—it was so obvious!

Kryzynski apparently didn't think so. "Thinking like a defense attorney. Go figure."

"Yeah, go figure. I've almost got a smaller list to send you—try not to get shot with Jackson's gun after I hang up."

"I'll make that a priority."

He hung up, and Ellery scrubbed at his eyes and growled.

"All us dumb cops peeving you off?" Jackson rasped, still smiling.

"If we're going to do hero shit, I would really like a weapon," Ellery told him, but he was unsurprised when Jackson gave a one-armed shrug.

"Says the man who talked our last bad guy into submission. I didn't really like guns even when I was a cop—too easy to use the gun and not your brain."

Ellery grunted. "Can't argue with that." God knows, the evidence had been on social media often enough. Scared cops killing even more frightened citizens, and a government so afraid of its own bias it couldn't admit what was happening. "But this guy is scary dangerous."

Jackson nodded. "Sure—but he's also personal. He's a knife and fist kind of guy. And think about it like this. How much damage could I have done with a gun after I'd been pumped full of heroin? Hm? Bet you're glad I didn't have a gun on me then, right?"

Ellery shuddered, feeling ill. "That doesn't mean—"

Jackson's hand on his knee surprised him. "Don't worry. I'd die before he hurts you."

Ellery squeezed Jackson's hand. "That's actually what I'm worried about." God, he was so sick, his face a wan white, bright spots of color burning on his cheekbones. Ellery closed his eyes and tried to contain his worry.

Jackson's lips—hot and dry—on his temple simultaneously soothed him and worried him further. Ellery savored the brief reassurance, the kindness from a man who didn't know conventional ways to show kindness, before standing up to go get him ibuprofen. The day had hardly begun.

JADE ARRIVED, and in a relatively short time they had a board set up, the victim locations pinned in red, the places Owens had used pinned in blue, and the most likely places for a den or studio in green.

And the list narrowed down some more.

Ellery sent Kryzynski a copy of the refined choices and turned to see Jackson stalking in front of the board.

"What?"

"I know this apartment complex." He traced his finger in a circle around a pin in one of the worst areas of Watt Avenue by McClellan. "It's not that full." He frowned. "In fact…." He turned to Jade, who was manning the computer. "Jade, look this place up, by the community center, okay? The back part—there's a dead-end street behind it."

Jade nodded and started clicking, pulling up Google Earth and playing with the perspective.

"Well, this place looks like shit," she said softly. "I think you're right, Jackson. I'm not sure when they took this shot, but there's tape over all the doors."

"Condemned?" Ellery asked. "How far away is it from other places?"

"Wait a minute, wait a minute…."

Jade switched from Google Earth to Craigslist. "Okay—yeah. This property is for sale, all of it. It's sitting on a two-acre lot—so it goes back bigger than it looks from the front."

"It wouldn't take much to turn the power and water on in there," Jackson said thoughtfully. "And once he got off the street—"

"Nobody would see him."

"Yeah. Jade, is Mike home?"

"Why?"

Jackson pulled out his phone and texted—presumably Mike—and Ellery made eye contact with Jade, trying to figure out what he was doing.

"He'll be here in fifteen minutes," Jackson said. "With his firearm and Kevlar." Jackson shook his head. "Jade, what in the hell is he doing with a Kevlar vest?"

"He practices on the shooting range. You know that!" Her voice pitched defensively, and Ellery wondered if that hadn't been a point *not* in Mike's favor before the two had started dating.

"I did not know about the Kevlar," Jackson muttered. His full mouth quirked. "But then, better safe than sorry. Anyway—he's bringing us a vest and a firearm. Ellery, tell Kryzynski where we're going. He may be able to get there more quickly than we will."

"Why don't you just have Mike meet us there with the equipment?" Jade asked guilelessly, and Ellery shivered at the way Jackson's expression shut down.

"Because you and Mike aren't getting anywhere near that place," he said grimly. Then he let out a moan and leaned his head back, massaging what was probably a sore neck. "But dammit, your SUV might have to be. We can't take Ellery's car there. It'll stick out like a gold thumb."

Jade scowled. "I don't even know what happened to your car. Did *you* wreck it?"

Jackson's panicked look seared Ellery to the bone, but Ellery wasn't going to lie to Jade about this.

"Owens wrecked it," Ellery said softly. "It's how Jackson got away."

Jade stared at both of them, mouth opening and closing.

"You said… you never said any of that." She pulled in a breath and let it out. "Is there… is there something else I need to know?"

Jackson couldn't look at her. "Jade—it was a bad fucking night. You saw the clothes—you've got some idea. Please, honey. Don't make me tell you. Don't. It…. We've got shit to do, and I just don't ever want you to know."

She closed her eyes and inhaled, but her chin wasn't going to stop quivering with just a deep breath. "You sound like shit," she said brutally. "You look worse. The minute Owens is in custody, I'm calling K. He will come out here and yell at you and drag you to the hospital by the fucking ear. And if Ellery already has you in the hospital, he'll make sure you stay."

"Sounds awesome," Jackson returned—and Ellery was sure he meant that. "But first, Ellery, call your guy. I'm going to go get some goddamned coffee, and then we'll go down and meet Mike. He's got a cop, guys. What I went through the night before last was a cakewalk compared to what she's going through. Let's go."

Jackson called break, and Ellery picked up the phone to call backup, but even as he relayed the information to Kryzynski—and lied his ass off about not going in when they got there—he was wondering. Did Jackson really have a plan?

Fish Under the Bridge

EVEN MIKE felt compelled to tell him he looked like hell.

Aces.

"Kid, if you were standing on my kitchen floor, I'd pick you up with tissue and throw you in the crapper. Get your ass to bed."

"Fuck you and give me your gun."

Mike snorted.

"What in the hell do you think you're going to hit with that?"

Jackson took a breath and said something honest. "Celia's killer."

Mike was pulled up alongside their building, idling in a metered spot while Jackson chatted through the window to collect the gun. Behind him he heard Ellery and Jade gasp.

"You looking to do that?" Mike asked soberly. "Because she wasn't worth killing for, kid."

Jackson shivered. "No, she's fucked up my life enough as it is. I'm just saying—the guy is crazy as fuck. And he's got my guns. I've got a permit to carry—maybe not this weapon, but I've got a permit. Protection, Mike. That's all I need."

"Vest is on the seat, gun's in the glove compartment." Mike peered at Ellery, his merry blue eyes as sober as Jackson had ever seen them. "You get around here and drive. I wouldn't trust him with a radio-control car."

Ellery let out a wicked laugh, and Jackson felt just good enough to roll his eyes.

"Thanks, Mike." Jackson clasped Mike's forearm through the window while Ellery scrambled around, dodging traffic, so he could get into the front of Jade's SUV. He must have dropped her off that morning. Shit. "Ellery, give Jade the Lexus keys. We'll switch off when this is over."

"Davis Med Center," Ellery said, clapping Mike on the back as he slid out. "We're going there immediately after."

"Call me."

Jackson slid into the passenger's seat grimly, doing his seat belt as Ellery did his. "I am impressed at how quickly you managed to commandeer my family," he muttered.

"Well, good, because my mother adores you," Ellery told him smoothly. "Now is there any special trick to driving this fucking thing besides remembering it's big?"

"Not hitting anything in the way?" Jackson told him straight-faced. It was a Chevy—how hard could it be?

Ellery grunted and concentrated on getting them out of downtown, and Jackson fumbled with the vest.

Pulling the Velcro on his bad side made his vision swim. God, this fucking shoulder—it had hurt less when he'd been shot. After a particularly nasty wrench, he decided the vest would have to do. In celebration, he leaned his head against the window and concentrated on not throwing up. Ellery had dosed him with more medication, and he was functional, but underneath the adrenaline and the drive to rescue a good woman and a hopefully decent cop was the terrible ticking knowledge of the physical time bomb: He was heading for a crash.

Ellery's voice penetrated the fog as they hit the relative peace of I-80. "Are you?"

"Wgha?" He struggled to sit up.

"Sorry. I should have just let you rest."

Jackson took a moment to look at him as he drove, bony jaw clenched, impressively dark eyebrows furrowed. So earnest. "No worries. What was the question again?"

"Would you shoot him?"

"Mike? No—he's my friend."

"Oh dear God—we're gonna die. I should just turn the car around and take you to the hospital. You're delusional. *Owens*!"

It was cute the way Ellery's eyes got all big when he freaked out, but Jackson needed to keep his attention on the conversation. "Would I shoot him?"

"Yes."

"Well, not in the *back*, but, you know, armed and dangerous, yeah." Because it was pretty much a thing you decided as a police officer—to take someone's life in public service.

Ellery surprised him. "Good."

"Hunh."

"Yeah, not the answer you were expecting." Ellery let out a breath. "I don't want you to have to testify."

Jackson thought about it. “Worse things,” he decided without passion. “Way worse things.”

“Like what?”

Jackson thought about it and shuddered. “Just stay safe while we’re there,” he mumbled, not strong enough to think about the alternative. “Just don’t make me even say it.”

“Yeah.” Ellery let out a breath. “Twelve hours. Twelve hours from the time they found your car to when I found you in our bed. I thought it, Jackson. Ten times a minute, every way you could think it. Just remember that when we’re looking for Dakin, okay?”

Ellery pulled off at Watt and turned north toward some of the more depressing markers of urban neglect—big seventies-era shopping complexes with iced windows and crumbling parking lots, strip malls housing small extremist churches, and miles of liquor stores and cheap fast food with no grocery stores in sight.

On the far end, near Elkhorn, stood an optimistic grammar school, awash in color and desperate hope, next to a newer community center. The apartment complex by the community center hunkered back from the road, wedged between old duplexes with the garage side facing the road and the pleasant green walkway for the center itself.

At Jackson’s direction, Ellery drove through the empty community center parking lot, toward the back. A thicket of oleander separated the center parking lot from the complex, but if you kept walking, down through the vacant field, you could go around the oleander and, hopefully, find a way into the abandoned apartment complex.

“That way.” Jackson pointed to a low place on the curb. “Just floor it—the SUV will take that—we can park on the field.”

“You know, we could have just driven down the cul-de-sac behind the complex—”

“This is better. He can’t see us. I hope. Is your little buddy on his way?”

“He was going to finish the two places he was near when we called.” Ellery scowled in obvious anxiety. “He should be here in ten.”

“Good—he can get credit if we live. Stop here.”

“We’re going in?” Ellery stared at him in surprise. “It’s ten minutes, Jackson!”

"I'm going in. I'm going to look around. Remember, Dakin is the priority. We've been hoping she's got a little bit of time, but if she did, it's running out."

Ellery opened the door and slid out while Jackson was still fumbling for his seat belt. "Dammit, Ellery!" His feet hit the ground with a thump that almost shook him apart, and the icy wind chewed through everything but the Kevlar.

"Twelve hours," Ellery said, coming around to take the scarf off his neck and throw it in the car. Smart move—it would hinder him in a fight. "I'm not watching you go in there sick and shaking to see if you come out."

Jackson didn't have the fight in him for this. "At least take the vest," he snapped.

Ellery folded his arms. "Sure. Take it off."

The sound Jackson made then wasn't entirely sane. "Ellery—"

"Wait for backup!"

Jackson might have, if they hadn't heard the muffled sound of a woman screaming from the other side of the oleander.

Without argument, Jackson took off, knowing Ellery was at his heels. Dammit—*dammit.* He knew this guy couldn't wait. Owens might have been stealthy for the last two years, but he'd been following Bridger around like a lapdog too, trying to fit in, trying to be normal. Bridger got arrested and Owens had spiraled—the drugs had spiraled, the death toll.

Owens imagined some sort of connection between himself and Jackson. If he'd taken Dakin to lure Jackson in, he just didn't have it in him to hold her that long to see if the gambit would work.

Jackson ran like someone else's life depended on it.

He rounded the strip of oleander brush and almost ran dead into a fence. For a moment he geared himself up to climb it, using the faint hope he'd pass out when he got to the top.

Then Ellery tapped his good shoulder and pointed, and he saw the break in the fence.

Slipping through was easy, but in the breathless silence after Dakin's scream, even the slight clink of the wrought iron sounded loud.

They cleared the wrought iron and ducked under the overhang of the upstairs balcony, trying to still their breathing. Jackson took stock of his surroundings.

The complex itself was a big capital *E*. The long bar at the back of the *E* faced Watt Avenue. The bars at the top and the bottom of the *E* framed the quads of the complex, with a double row of apartments making up the middle bar. In better times residents could look over the balcony to the pool on this side or, Jackson imagined, a grassy lawn on the other.

Right now, on this gray November day, the ideal of apartment denizens sharing space peacefully seemed as far away as a warm, comfortable bed and the remote.

Instead the pool in front of him was full of chilly water with some leaves, looking brackish and cold.

But oddly clear.

Jackson squinted at it and then looked at Ellery.

"Does that look clean to you?"

Ellery widened his eyes. "He likes to swim?"

No steam came off the surface, so it wasn't heated, and Jackson was almost afraid to look closer, in case there were bodies weighted to the bottom. Holding the gun out and down, he ventured a little from the protection of the balcony, peered into the water, and came back.

"Only a few leaves—and the filter's on."

Ellery's eyes popped open, and he grimaced. "He washes up."

Oh, gross.

Probably jumped in fully clothed too.

Somehow the macabre image of Owens rinsing off his sins in a giant baptismal pool of dead dreams was almost as disturbing as the blood he was soaking from his skin.

They both shuddered and then held absolutely still.

They could hear it, in the top corner of the complex. "No. No, no, no, no, no…."

A sobbing, whimpering sort of sound, and Jackson wondered if Owens was going to deliver the death blow.

Shit.

"Get her!" he ordered. The pool was oddly shaped—sort of like a big kidney bean, but it didn't run lengthwise to match the shape of the quad. Instead parts of the pool were shaded by the balcony. He had to run to the center of the quad, trapped and in the open, to fire two shots in the air.

The whimpers stopped, and Jackson could hear one of the doors slam against the back wall, but he couldn't see from his position.

"Rivers!"

"Right here, asshole!" Jackson called, projecting past the phlegm and the pain. "You wanna come pick on someone *not* stoned?"

Overhead, Owens's face appeared suddenly as the man himself bent at the waist at the shaky wrought iron rail.

"Jackson!" he said dreamily, that sweet choirboy face lighting up like a supermodel's on carb day. "Jackson—you came to visit!" His knuckles dripped blood—both his and his victim's, Jackson would wager.

"Sure!" Jackson called. "Come on down. We'll have a party!"

"You don't look so good, Jackson. I brought some medicine with me. You want some more?" He winked conspiratorially. "Your mother couldn't get enough."

"Until the end, though, right? You dosed her plenty good at the end!" Jackson had no temper spikes, no painful emotion at the thought of his mother. When everything else in the world felt so fucking dire, it was almost a relief to know that wound was closing, edges meshing together, surface scar not nearly as bad as the divot Jackson would always feel in his soul. But the divot was invisible—only a few people got to see it.

This ass-clown was not one of those people.

"Well, yeah," Owens said, nodding his head like a puppy. "Needed to take my time. You needed to see her, Jackson. Your guy was in your phone—the one I stole. I knew he'd see her, if only she looked alive."

"Mission accomplished." Even better than Owens knew. Heroin family had made themselves obvious because Owens had stepped in and taken over Billy's operation. Jackson might not have been able to track him down if it hadn't been for them. "So, uh, here I am. No need to go back in there, right? Just you and me. Hide and seek. Good times!"

"You'll try to run away, won't you?" Owens said rakishly.

Jackson gave him a death rictus back. "Only if you try to catch me!"

Without warning, Owens bolted, spinning on his heel and heading for the set of stairs that led from his corner of the building down to ground level. Jackson went sprinting for the far corner of the quad, thinking about the fence—and thinking Ellery would go up the stairs as Owens came down, the better to get Tess Dakin.

Ellery was already up the stairs as Jackson passed them, and he spun around for a moment to make sure Owens was following.

He was there, right at Jackson's heels, and instead of heading for the break in the fence, Jackson went for the set of stairs on the other quad of the complex. Ellery would go up to the pool side, getting Dakin. Jackson would run around on this side like a hamster in a Habitrail, hoping Owens didn't notice his victim's escape.

He got to the balcony and heard Owens start the stairs below him. Jackson was blowing like a manatee in a land race, and he hoped Owens was almost as bad. He used the time it took to make the stairs to sprint to the short hallway—the long bar of the *E* had a gap between it and the short middle bar—and Jackson had hopes for a laundry room.

As he lined up to kick the door in, he got a good look at Ellery, emerging from Owens's apartment, Tess Dakin hanging on to him.

For a moment they locked eyes, and then Jackson heard Owens hit the landing, and it was time to kick the door in and hope for a miracle.

Oh God. Even better than a miracle.

An *in-house stair*!

It was like the Winchester Mystery House, a gift to people locked in a life or death chase!

He hit the stairs running, emerging in a downstairs laundry room, small, white, unadorned as the last one—and tiny as the last one too.

It took a few kicks to get the door open here, and by the time he did, Jackson saw Owens's pant leg, crusted with crap at the bottom, emerging from the stairwell.

Time to get a move on.

Jackson emerged into the lower hall, sweating and exhausted, just in time to see Ellery and Dakin running across the balcony and heading for the stairs.

In some desperation, Jackson threw his weight against the door. Anything to keep Owens pinned there, stuck, until Ellery and Dakin slid outside the gate.

Owens's first sally against the door almost threw him back into the wall. He gritted his teeth and held on.

"Give it up, Jackson!" Owens taunted, kicking at the door again. "You'll never escape this place! That's why I chose it!"

"Hell was too warm?" Jackson shouted back. God, Owens was strong. He might have been losing his mental parts, but the rest of him—not degrading yet.

"It's got places to hide. You liked to hide, right? 'Cause I knew all the best places to hide to see the best things!"

"Nothing good to see at my place," Jackson grunted. The door flew back and hit his shoulder, and he let out a bark of pain before running back toward the empty quad. Ellery and Tess were disappearing through the fence as he ran, and he glanced behind him, making sure Owens was following one more time as he sprinted down the hallway.

He got to the end of the hall and realized Owens had stopped at some point and gone back the other way.

Fuck.

Jackson kept going, checking the end with his gun first as he turned the corner, and then again.

What he saw made him freeze.

Ellery had gotten Dakin out, and she was limping down toward the end of the oleander bushes, beyond the fence.

But Owens had grabbed him by the collar as he'd tried to get through.

And now they were face-to-face, a knife in Owens's hand held at gut level as Ellery stared him down.

"Rivers!" Owens called out. "Rivers! You're going to want to face me now! No more rat in a maze, you hear me!"

Jackson raised the gun and aimed, a clear shot at Owens right in front of him.

But his hands were shaking. Every throb of his heart pulled the gun out of alignment. And sweat ran too freely into his eyes, making the shot impossible.

Ellery stood right in his sights at every other heartbeat.

"Put the knife down!" Jackson called out, lowering the gun slowly, grateful he didn't drop it. "Put the knife down and come face me!"

"I did face you," Owens said sweetly. "I looked at your face, dripping with come, and thought you were beautiful."

Jackson's gorge rose. "Well, you know—if you want to see me that way again, you can maybe start by not making me blow your brains out."

"You like this one." Owens cocked his head and peered at Ellery like a cat analyzing a beetle. Using the tip of the knife, he prodded Ellery's chin up, then sideways, checking out his jaw, his ears. Prime horseflesh, ready for market. Do we eat it or do we race it? What suits it better?

"I like all of them." Jackson wasn't sure which would be better or worse for Ellery. Would Owens leave him alone, thinking to please Jackson, or kill him to hurt the most? The image of his mother's body danced in front of his eyes like a macabre puppet. "Let him go."

The knife slid a liquid red line just under Ellery's jaw, and Jackson swallowed his moan. Ellery's teeth were clenched so hard a vein throbbed in his temple, and Jackson wasn't sure what sort of mess he would have made of Owens's body if he had his bare hands on Owens's face.

"You like this one best." Owens looked from Ellery's taut mask to Jackson, smiling luminously. "That's a mistake. They teach you, you know. Don't get attached. Kill your toys, your pets—don't get attached. I looked through your phone, and I thought, 'This one—this one knows. You don't get attached.'"

"But I did," Jackson rasped. Fuck it—he couldn't read Owens. If that knife went deeper, if Owens decided death instead of life, he needed Ellery to hear the truth. "I got attached. That one. That one's mine."

Ellery closed his eyes like he was savoring something bitter, and Owens's smile went wide, turned into a grin. Too quick for Jackson to follow, he whirled, holding Ellery in front of him, walking them both backward to the stairs. "He won't be for long. I'll make him mine. My pet. My toy."

Jackson followed slowly, keeping the weapon midway down, ready but not aiming. He was going to have to walk those stairs without a hand on the rail, and he wouldn't aim at Ellery, not when every muscle in his body shook.

"You don't want him," Jackson said, trying not to pant. The interminable minutes of playing rat bait to Tim Owens's cat had drained his last. "You like young and dirty and pretty. He's not young or dirty—you don't want him."

Owens's eyes lit up, and he caressed Ellery's cheek with the knife again. Another nick, another thin red line. "But you think he's pretty. Nobody else does, but you do."

"He's got a line of fucking cops who want his weenie ass," Jackson muttered with feeling. "And a judge. Don't even fool yourself. He's plenty pretty."

"Awesome," Ellery rasped, rolling his eyes and speaking for the first time. "I'm going to die, and that's the last thing I'm going to hear."

"Shut up and don't argue," Jackson hissed. "I'm working here."

"You're so sweet!" Owens crowed, delighted. "Will you be as sweet to him when I've been inside him with a bowie knife?"

"You just said you don't want him," Jackson baited, sweat breaking out all over his body, running down his wrists, making the gun hard to hold. "Don't you want inside *me*? Don't you want to fuck every hole in my body? You were getting ready for it, remember? If you'd just been able to hold your wad for another minute, you coulda had my pants around my ankles. Go you."

Owens took a deep, shuddering breath and almost dropped the knife. "I wanted you so bad," he breathed. "Would you really give yourself like that?"

"Sure," Jackson tossed, like the thought didn't make him want to run shrieking. "Bend over, blood for lube, go to it. All yours."

Owens cleared the landing and—good soldier that he was—turned his back to the wall, Ellery in front as a shield.

"You are giving him a boner," Ellery muttered, disgust dripping from his voice.

"Yeah," Jackson conceded. "Figured. I mean it." He made it to the landing too and turned his back to the wrought iron—but not before he sighted the pool. Very slowly he began to edge to his left, watching as an enraptured Owens did the same, keeping Ellery between them.

"You do," Owens acknowledged. "See? That's why you don't get attached. If you weren't attached, I'd be dead already."

One more step. One more. There they were. Lined up to where the pool sat under the balcony. Good.

Jackson thought about the day before, how he'd been planning to take his cat and disappear in a corner to die. "If I wasn't attached, *I'd* be dead already," he said, the truth and the irony and the pain all blending into one big ache of body, heart, and soul. He started to crouch, and Owens sliced the knife along Ellery's upper arm. Ellery let out a gasp, and Jackson froze.

"Slowly," Owens ordered, and the dreamy heroin addict disappeared, replaced by the hard-eyed military man. "I can kill him at any time."

Jackson clenched the gun so hard his knuckles turned white. "Let him go," he said, straightening. "And don't hurt him again."

"No, no—put it down. Now." He slid the knife under Ellery's jaw again, red-stained from the wound that saturated his shirt. Ellery's breathing came fast and hard as he tried not to sob.

Jackson would kill Owens for this if he had to gouge his thumbs into Owens's eyes and squish through his rancid brains.

"On three," Jackson ordered, praying for control. He squatted down. "One." Owens took the knife from Ellery's throat. Jackson set the gun on the worn Astroturf that coated the landing. "Two." Owens dropped the arm holding Ellery around the shoulders. Jackson stared at him for a moment, and just as he was relaxing his fingers from around the trigger, he shouted, "Run, Ellery, run!"

Ellery, who never obeyed a fucking order *ever*, sank to one knee and grabbed Owens around one leg as he charged forward. Jackson stood, dropping the gun as he took the brunt of Owens's stumbling tackle. He felt the knife shoving at gut level, slicing through the Kevlar, his clothing, and the top layer of skin and fat on his stomach as Owens threw his weight into the stab. With a terrible creak and a busted rusting bolt, the iron behind Jackson's ass started to give way. Jackson used one foot to pivot while Owens dug for his vitals, trying to find the bottom edge of the vest with the knife.

"You lied!" Owens screamed, pretty face revealed in madness, teeth rotting toward the back, pores black and grimy from malnutrition and abuse.

"I want to live, asshole!" Jackson screamed back and with the last of his strength swung them both around, crashing into the wrought iron again. The extra force broke the section off, dumping them both one story below, into the icy water of the kidney-shaped pool.

The freezing assault on his feverish body shocked him. He managed a hard gasp of air before the cold blue closed overhead, and then he tried to relax, let momentum carry him down so he could push off the bottom.

A terrible pain ripped through his chest just as his feet touched down. His vision blacked, the pain radiating throughout his extremities, and he fought to push off, just a little push and he could inhale, God, take a breath, one burning, searing breath, but it hurt, his shoulders hurt, razor wire carving through his bloodstream with air-deprived red cells. No! As he pitched off the cliff into unconsciousness, the last thing he saw was blood clouding the water and Owens's face, eyes wide and stunned, as his floating body blocked Jackson's escape.

Red Fish

THE RAILING broke, and the two men tumbled down into the pool.

And Ellery's heart stopped.

Cold. Dead. No heartbeat for Ellery.

If I hadn't been attached, I'd *be dead.*

Jackson had meant that. Ellery was his life.

Ellery watched, frozen, as Jackson kicked at Owens in midair, just hard enough for Owens to clip the cement edge of the pool with the back of his head when he landed. Jackson plunged into the water, Owens flopped on top of him, and Ellery didn't remember taking the stairs after that.

Oh God, let Jackson not be dead.

He got to the side of the pool and tried hard not to gag at the spray of gray matter on the far edge. Blood clouded the water, fresh and fountaining from the missing chunk of Tim Owens's skull, but Ellery couldn't see any movement.

Why wasn't Jackson moving?

Ellery stripped off his coat, jacket, shoes, and slacks and dove in.

The cold slammed into his chest, stole his breath, stopped his pulse. Owens's body floated toward him, eyes open and staring, and Ellery shoved at it, not caring, not even repelled by the blood and the brains souping the water.

Jackson!

He was floating toward the bottom, thin ribbons of scarlet flowing from his stomach, arms drawn together to protect his chest.

Oh God, Jackson—so sick, a raging fever, the race through the complex—his body temperature must have been so high when he hit the water.

Ellery swam to a crouch behind him, clasped him around the chest, and shoved up with all the strength he had. He cleared the surface and dragged in air—but Jackson remained terribly still, the Kevlar vest making his weight almost actively leaden.

"Ellery! Here! I've got him! Give him to me!"

Ellery squinted. "Kryzynski?"

"You couldn't have fucking waited?" But Sean Kryzynski, newly minted detective, was reaching for Jackson, taking the weight from Ellery's arms, and Ellery was so grateful he could have cried.

"She was screaming," Ellery gasped. "She was screaming, and he was killing her."

"Yeah." Kryzynski hauled Jackson up onto the patio and stripped off the Kevlar while he lay there, unresponsive. Without another word he started lifting and lowering Jackson's arms, but no water spit out of his lungs.

Ellery pulled himself out, panting, "It's his heart. Water's freezing, and he's burning up."

"Fuck!" Kryzynski pulled his radio off his belt, screaming for backup and for the ambulance to pull around and for the world generally to unfuck itself and come make Jackson Rivers breathe.

Ellery didn't have time for that shit. He fell to his knees, propped his hand behind Jackson's neck, and then pinched Jackson's nose and tilted his chin, giving two quick deep breaths. His skin still raged with fever, because he'd been under less than a minute, but his mouth stayed unresponsive, full lips parted and blue.

Fuck him. *Fuck. Him.* Ellery laced his fingers, found the magic spot above Jackson's sternum, and pushed. And again. And again. And four. And five.

Kryzynski was kneeling by his head by the time he was done, and as Ellery stopped, he gave two quick breaths.

And again.

And again.

Ellery screamed at him as he pushed. "Tell me I'm your life? Move into my house? Saddle me with your fucking cat? And you're going to do *this*? Save my fucking life, motherfucker, and you're going to do *this*? Fuck you! Fuck you! *Fuck you!* Breathe, you fucking asshole, fucking *breathe*!"

"*Ellery*!" Kryzynski panted, shoving at his arm. "Ellery! He's breathing! He's breathing!"

"Oh God." Jackson's chest pushed up under his hands. Ellery shoved under the sodden sweatshirt and T-shirt and flattened his palm over Jackson's left nipple.

He felt the throb of blood under the skin, buried his face in Jackson's neck, and cried.

Wet, cold, trembling fingers massaged through Ellery's hair.

Jackson rasped, "That's my sore shoulder, you prick," and Ellery cried some more.

KRYZYNSKI HAD a patrolman take Jade's SUV to the med center.

Ellery, covered in a thermal blanket and clutching his clothes and shoes to his chest, got loaded in the ambulance next to Jackson. He let the paramedics work on Jackson first, administering adrenaline for his heart and anti-inflammatories with antibiotics for his fever and the infection in his shoulder. When they'd shot pretty much everything they could into the IV in his arm, they let Ellery crouch by his side while they numbed and irrigated Ellery's arm.

Ellery stroked the wet hair back from his brow and looked dismally at his chest. They'd cut off Jackson's sweatshirt, and in the back of his mind, Ellery wondered if he even had another one at the house. God. All his shit was still in the duplex garage.

There was nothing to cover the bruises on his body.

The purple, black, and bleeding mess of his shoulder, the gaping slices through skin and muscle on his stomach from when the knife found its way through. The way his chest labored through the sickness in his lungs.

Jackson fumbled with the O2 mask they'd put on him and gave Ellery what should have been a smile.

"They fix you up?" he asked, his voice barely more than a memory.

The young medic who had worked on him answered Jackson's question. "He's going to need stitches once we get to the hospital, but he'll be able to go home. You, on the other hand, shouldn't have been running around in the first place." He had a shaved head and a handlebar mustache sprinkled with gray. He managed to make that last thing sound severe, like a warning from the gods.

"I'm okay," Jackson said, because God forbid he not.

"I'm not," Ellery admitted—one of them had to say it. "Jade said she watched you die once. That's twice now, Jackson. How many lives do you think you have?"

“One where you and me get a little peace,” Jackson said, closing his eyes. “That one would be nice.”

Ellery helped him put the O2 mask back on and kissed his temple.

“Sounds like he’s learned his lesson,” the medic said mildly, swabbing at Ellery’s wound with deceptively gentle fingers.

“The fact that you think that? That means he’s just saving up the bitching for later,” Ellery told him. He rested his chin on his fist, close enough that every jostle of the ambulance rubbed his knuckles against Jackson’s cheek. “I’ll know he’s okay when he’s whining like a tomcat on a fence.”

The medic chuckled because he thought Ellery was kidding, and the ambulance rolled on.

THEY WHISKED Jackson away as soon as he arrived, and Ellery was taken to an ER cubicle while they worked on his arm. Kryzynski walked in just as they gave him a set of scrubs to wear and his ruined suit in a plastic bag.

The trench coat had a big bloody slice in the sleeve, but it might help keep him warm in the meantime.

“Looks like you’ve got yourself some war wounds,” Kryzynski said, his smile holding nothing of the crush he’d had in August and everything of the tired, dispirited detective.

“How’s Dakin?” Ellery asked. Owens’s “studio” had been as eerily divided as Owens himself. The “living area” had looked like a single man’s apartment—a futon, a dresser, bedding, a kitchen that had been cleaned in the past two days.

The bedroom had been where Owens took his victims, patterned with old blood, featuring hooks and chains dangling from the ceiling, the walls broken and crumbling from abuse. Dakin had been suspended by her wrists from a leather strap hooked to the ceiling and apparently used as a punching bag. She’d been a mess—slices networking her chest, her stomach, her cheeks. Signs of sexual trauma marked her bare body, and bruises, black and terrible, showed the abuse of her flesh.

Ellery cut her down with a knife from the kitchen, then used a piece of rope and a T-shirt he’d found in the “living quarters” of the apartment to bind her arm, which sported the worst wound. He'd helped her drag on the rags of her detective's suit before they'd made their escape.

She'd shown grit then—in pain, terrified, but running as quietly as she could. He'd helped her through the hole in the fence, before shoving his phone and keys into her hand, and telling her where to find the car. He'd turned around to see how he could help Jackson as she'd disappeared around the oleander hedge, and Owens had been right there.

"Dakin is…." Kryzynski pinched the bridge of his nose and tilted his head back. "She'll be lucky if she can work again," he said bluntly. "What happened to her…." He shook his head.

"Jackson was right," Ellery mumbled. "We should have moved faster."

"How?" Kryzynski shrugged. "He didn't know until she was taken. Even if we'd moved on the house the night you called me, how would we have found her? You did your best. Both of you. Told me. Told the department." Kryzynski's eyes grew bright and red rimmed. "He almost died. I remember when you told me to give him a chance, and I thought, 'Yeah, sure. Cramer's got a hard-on for this guy, but he'll see. He'll see Rivers is trouble. He'll see.'"

Ellery let out a gasp of laughter. "Yup. He's trouble."

"He's a good man," Kryzynski said soberly. "That's going down in my report. Which it will take me at least a week to write, by the way, 'cause this has been a big fucking deal."

"Maybe he'll be out of the hospital by then," Ellery sighed. Then, "Hey—did Dakin give you my phone?"

"Nope. It's probably in your ride. We found her hiding in the SUV when we got to the scene. She's the one who said you needed help." Kryzynski reached into his pocket and pulled out the keys. "Please tell me you've got a way to get home."

From outside the curtain, a blessedly familiar, terrified voice cut through all of the bullshit a hospital could throw.

"Do not tell me I don't have the right to see either of them, because I don't even fucking care, do I, Mike?"

"The lady has zero fucks."

"And none to fuckin' give. You heard me—Jackson Quentin Rivers or Ellery Stick-up-his-ass Cramer, Esquire. Where in the hell are they?"

The nurse—poor man—stuttered for an answer, and Ellery put the ER out if its misery. "I'm in here, Jade. Stop terrorizing the health-care professionals."

Jade didn't wait to get to the curtain to start scolding him. "I have seen your mother in action, asshole, and I am not even coming close. What happened? Why didn't you call me? Where in the fuck is Jackson?" She stopped, and her expressive brown eyes grew big and shiny. "You're *hurt*! You've got a bandage, and you look like hell! Jesus, Ellery, if you're hurt, how is he?"

"I'm fine," Ellery said, surprised to recognize concern when he saw it. His voice lowered then, because this was still hard. "He was stable when they took him off the ambulance, but not fully conscious." Ellery let out a snort of pure exasperation. "Probably asleep more than anything else, but…." He bit his lip and met Mike's sympathetic gaze.

Kryzynski cleared his throat and nodded, waving to let Ellery know he'd be back a little later for a statement.

In the meantime, "How bad was he?" Mike asked, letting Ellery finish.

"He and Owens fell into the swimming pool from the second-story landing. Owens hit his head on the way down—"

They both grimaced, and Jade said, "Ick."

Ellery had to close his eyes against the mental picture. "You have no idea," he said, swallowing hard. "But Jackson… the water was so cold, and he was feverish and running his ass off." He swallowed and closed his eyes. "He wasn't breathing, Jade. I pulled him out of the water and we had to do CPR and…."

She threw herself into his arms and hugged him tight. He hugged her back, clinging to one of the handful of people who would recognize the stark terror Ellery had lived through in those moments.

"Scared the hell out of you, right?" she whispered, whole body shaking.

"I don't know how you've done it," he admitted.

She pulled back and wiped her eyes delicately with her thumb. Mike, ever practical, grabbed a tissue from the supply station at the cubicle and handed it to her even as he wrapped his arm around her shoulders for comfort.

"Same way you're going to," she said, a half smile on her face. "One fucking battle at a time." She swallowed visibly and closed her eyes. "But you're going to have to win, Ellery. I couldn't win. He didn't love me like he loves you."

Ellery nodded. Jackson had never said it—not those words. *I got attached. That one. That one is mine.* But the words he'd used—those had been close enough.

"I need to tell Langdon he's out until after Thanksgiving," Ellery said, leaning back against the bed.

"Oh, I will tell him for you. Are you and Jackson coming to the duplex? Kaden and Rhonda will be."

Ellery sighed. He'd made those plans for Jackson just assuming…. Jackson hadn't even yelled at him for it.

"I have tickets to Boston," he said apologetically. "Both of us. My parents."

Jade stroked his temple, like he'd once seen her do with her brother. "I'll have an early one for us," she said generously. "Tell me when you're leaving. We'll do it thc day before."

He smiled, his throat tight. "He'd better be out of the hospital by then."

She rolled her eyes, but they were both so worried the expression didn't carry as much disgust as he once thought. "He'd better. He'll be insufferable if he's not."

AT FIRST Ellery thought Jade was wrong.

Mike ran to Ellery's house to grab them both clothes and pajamas, and Jade and Ellery were eventually allowed into Jackson's room.

He didn't even look *like* hell anymore. He looked like he'd *been through* hell and had come out on the other side looking like shit-bugger-fuck-cock-ass.

Jade's exact words after she'd caught her breath, and Ellery had known them for her attempt to stay strong.

He'd never seen someone with that pallor survive. Jackson's eyes were sunken, and the bags under them practically swallowed his cheekbones. He lay shirtless and bandaged—not just his shoulder, but his ribs and the stitched cuts on his stomach as well.

"I take it I'm not winning any beauty contests," Jackson said dryly. Then he'd grinned, his smile as wicked as it had ever been. "Did Ellery tell you he bruised my fucking ribs?"

"I did not!" Ellery clapped his hand to his mouth in horror and then winced as he stretched his own stitches. "I bruised your ribs?"

Jackson laughed as Ellery pulled up the chair next to the bed. Jade grabbed another one and sat next to Ellery. "You did. I guess you know a guy's nuts about you when he commits assault."

"You were…." Ellery closed his eyes. "You were…."

"Sh…."

"You were dead," Ellery whispered, embarrassed to break down in front of Jade too.

They were on the side with the undamaged shoulder, and Jackson reached out and cupped his cheek. "You fixed that, though," he said. His eyes were closed, but he was smiling faintly.

"I talked to your doctor," Ellery told him, trying to find the irritated place, the sarcastic and angry place, but only finding *this* place, raw and open and tender. "He said you're here for a week—fluids and medicine to keep the fever down and more PT for the shoulder and antibiotics. They're not letting you out of here until you can run five miles again."

Jackson groaned. "Goddammit—did you bribe them or something?"

Ellery snorted. "As. If. They were jumping for an excuse to strap you to the bed and declare you mentally incompetent." He was only exaggerating a little. Dave and Alex, Jackson's nurses from his last two stays in the hospital, had made dire threats about getting bondage equipment from home.

"Well, when are *you* getting out?" Jackson demanded. "You had to get stitches."

"Yeah, ten of them. A little kid gets that when he falls off the swing. I could leave now if I wanted to, but Mike's going to go feed your useless cat."

"You could leave now? Are you *kidding*? You got *stabbed*!"

"Ooooh!" Ellery held up both hands and shook them like he was afraid. "A stab wound! How awful!" He glared. "Your heart stopped, asshole. You're going to be running stress tests until I get you on the fucking plane. We're never traveling anywhere without nitro tabs—you know that, right? You are going to have scar tissue on your heart for the rest of your life!"

"And the ribs are gonna hurt when it rains," Jackson finished, cackling weakly.

Ellery's mouth opened and closed in outrage while he searched for words.

"Hey," Jackson said smugly, "Counselor, come here."

Ellery leaned over the bed then, close enough to see the flecks of darkness in Jackson's crazy-bright green eyes. "What?" he asked, still cross.

Jackson kissed him, softly, with more sweetness than Ellery ever dreamed of.

"I love you."

Ellery shuddered, squeezing his eyes shut and taking the words inside so they could be a part of his heart. "I love you too."

"Now find a way to get me out of here early."

Ellery opened his eyes and showed all his teeth. "Not on your life, Rivers. Not for any sexual favor you could offer. Not even if you threaten to take away your cat."

Jackson glared at him feverishly, weak body struggling to sit up even as it failed him… "But… but… I *love you.*"

"Yup. And if I have my way, you're not getting out of that by driving yourself to an early grave."

Jackson pouted, irritated but not hurt. "I take it back."

"I won't let you."

"Jade, get me an AMA…."

"Get out of bed and do it yourself, asshole. Oh, wait—you're attached to an IV and you're too weak to stand. So never mind. You stay right there."

Jackson opened his mouth to respond—and yawned instead. "Goddammit!"

"Why?" Ellery asked, taking the combativeness out of his voice. "Why do you have to go so bad?"

"I hate hospitals," Jackson told him, eyes bright and shiny with it. "I hate them."

Oh.

"I know you do—"

Jackson shook his head and took a breath to try to calm himself down—but it didn't look like it worked. "I thought it was bad before, but after this summer….” He turned pleading eyes to Ellery. “It feels like the whole building is pressing down on me.”

Ellery sighed and grabbed his hand. “Baby, you are sick. Your heart stopped. You have a raging infection and—apparently—bruised ribs. You can’t come home yet. But don’t worry. You won’t be alone.”

Jackson squeezed his eyes shut tight. “I really am a weenie,” he muttered. “I take it back. I’m fine. Don’t worry. Dave and Alex will come visit, and it will all be okay.”

Ellery couldn’t help it. He smoothed Jackson’s hair back from his brow and just looked at him, even though Jackson was doing his damnedest to look away. “Do me a favor,” he said, closing his eyes against the vulnerable curve of Jackson’s jaw. “Just close your eyes and feel what I’m doing here. Breathe deep and even with me. I’m not going anywhere. If we grabbed a doctor right now and checked you out and took you home—”

“Ellery!” Jade hissed, looking panicked.

“As. If!” he mouthed, and she relaxed too. “You wouldn’t be out of here for an hour. Two, most likely. So we’re not even going to mess with that. We’re just going to sit here and do what you promised in the ambulance.”

“What’s that?” He sounded softer, less manic.

“You promised me peace, remember? Said it was time for you and me to get some peace.”

Jackson let out a tired laugh. “We’re supposed to have peace in the hospital?”

“We’re supposed to have peace at my mother’s house. We’ll do nothing but eat and watch football for a week. You’ll get fat. I’ll laugh at you. My mother will mess with your head. You’ll hide in the kitchen with my father and Rebecca’s husband and complain about how we all try to micromanage your lives.”

Jackson swallowed, and weak tears slid down the corners of his eyes. Ellery suddenly understood. All that noise, that banter, that “Get me out of here!” All because he was afraid of this moment here. This reckoning.

This peace.

“There’s a list of things to do?” he asked, trying to sound cocky. Failing. “I wasn’t great at school—I don’t know if I can deal with a Thanksgiving assignment.”

"You weren't great at school because your school wasn't great," Ellery said, believing this.

"Amen," Jade muttered at his side. "And you only did homework at our house."

Jackson smiled a little. "Your mom… she used to make us do our homework to get dinner."

"Remember when she found out you were failing the whole eighth grade?"

Jackson squeezed his eyes tighter. Didn't stop the thin silver line from escaping. "She stayed up with me doing makeup work for a week," he said, voice choked. Then he stated the obvious: "I really miss her."

"I know you do," Jade whispered. "We all do. Think she'd like Mike?"

Jackson smiled, and Ellery kept pulling his hair back. "Yeah. Mike's from Virginia—"

"I know. They have the same way of saying 'cracker.' You notice that?"

Jackson laughed. "Yeah. But your mom was talking about food." He looked at Ellery as though imploring him to believe this. "She was a lady. She wouldn't actually use it the other way."

"Nope," Jade agreed, her voice thick. "My mom was great. But I'm still sorry about your mom."

"I got nothing else for her," Jackson said, voice hard. Ellery remembered how he'd lost himself in tears for the woman. Yes. Celia Rivers only got that once.

"But you got a chance to go have another one. I mean, she's not *my* favorite person, but that's because she's not my real mom, right?" The warmth in Jade's voice surprised Ellery—all that epic struggle, and it turned out Jade knew exactly what she'd been fighting against.

Ellery caught her eyes as he was smiling, and she winked.

"Lucy Satan's not—" Jackson started. God, they really were children together.

"Yeah, she is." Jade checked her phone restlessly. "You've got a chance, Jackson. A chance to have a mom and a family."

The hurt on his face—unfathomable, and for a moment Ellery was torn between hating Jade for ripping away the people Jackson loved best and thanking her for her blessing.

"You're my family," he said stubbornly.

She laughed. "Of course we are. Baby boy, do you think you can't have both?" She wiped her eyes with the back of her hand. "Do you think I don't want all the family in the world for you? Think about it, Jackson. Someday that woman is going to come here for a holiday. And she's going to sit at your table with me and Mike and Kaden and Rhonda and the whole lot of us—and every person in that room is going to be someone you love and someone who loves you back. It's not yet—I know it. But you, wandering the streets alone, afraid you don't have a soul to turn to—that's never going to happen again."

"You weren't supposed to know," he whispered.

"Oh, honey. I will always know what you are up to." She wiped her face again, then checked her phone. Her expression lightened, some peace stealing across it like Ellery hoped would steal across Jackson's, and she stood up and kissed Jackson's temple. "You are still hot," she sighed. "I'm going to go get you some real pajamas from Mike. Then we'll go home and make you some soup to bring you. Ellery, we'll bring you some too. I'll tell Langdon you won't be there either."

Ellery grunted.

"I have to be—heroin family… I mean… crap—whatsherface with the kid named Jail."

"Langdon will take it," Jade said, surprising him. "Yes, he got back to the firm after you two took off." Her eyes slid to the side, and Ellery wondered what she could have said. "You've been putting this case together on your off hours, and once again you made them look like heroes. I told him you both needed time off, and he agreed." She wrinkled her nose. "It was weird."

Jackson let out a quiet bark of laughter. "Jade, darlin', you are a force to be reckoned with."

"Maybe next time you'll let me come along," she sniffed and then made her way out of the room.

"No," Jackson muttered. "Ellery, tell her no."

He was almost asleep.

"Sure. She can't come with us."

Jackson scowled—but as of yet he hadn't bucked off the feeling of Ellery's hand in his hair. "You're just saying that to humor me."

"Jackson, I don't want anybody we love to see what we saw today. I'm hardly okay with me seeing it."

His eyes completely closed. "Don't leave," he begged, mostly unconscious. "Stay."

Yeah.

ELLERY FELL asleep with his head on the bed next to Jackson's and woke up when Dave, their favorite nurse, walked in with his cell phone and a bag of clothes as well. Ellery stared at the phone blankly.

"I don't… I don't even…."

"Jade Cameron's boyfriend walked it in," Dave said, arching an elegant eyebrow over melty-candy brown eyes. "Said he'd charged it, and your mother has been calling for an hour."

Ellery took the phone, grimacing. "Thanks, Dave."

Dave eyed the telemetry readouts dispassionately. "He's going to be here for a while," he said. "I'll bring you a cot."

Ellery stretched carefully. "Can I use the bathroom and change?" he asked, and Dave shot him a look of pure disbelief.

"You are a grown man! Like you need to ask me permis—"

Ellery held up a hand. "He can't wake up alone," he said simply. "Not for a couple of days. I promised."

Dave's eyes widened, and he tilted his head back. "You are supposed to be keeping him out of here," he said, the recrimination clear.

"I was the one who bruised his ribs, if that helps." Ellery didn't know where to look with that—he couldn't be sorry he'd saved Jackson's life.

Dave apparently thought it was a point in his favor. "Well, not many couples can claim they quite literally saved each other's lives. I mean, he got shot protecting you. You got stabbed and saved his life. It's practically a match made in the med center."

Ellery rolled his eyes. "Sure. I'll be back in a minute."

Dave shrugged and took Ellery's seat. "Take your time—shower. Get pruny. This was my last job of the day. I'll keep the scary monsters gone."

ELLERY GOT back, feeling infinitely better for the hot water.

"Hasn't moved," Dave said without looking up. "He's going to be fine, this time."

"Yeah, I know." Ellery did, although his stomach still knotted with worry.

Dave gave him a brief look, his eyes crinkling in his freckled pale brown face. "Honey, I just keep thinking that if it was Alex, I'd be a mess."

"Yeah, well, it's a weekday and I'm in my pajamas."

A gentle smile flashed. "That is pretty messy for you," he said. "And a bandage too." He stood and stretched. "I'll go ask for that cot now. Me and Alex'll bring you breakfast in the morning. I think you got dinner already."

He was right—when Ellery had grabbed the bag with the clothes in it, he discovered hot soup and crackers in actual Tupperware. Once Dave left, Ellery set about eating about half of the split pea soup. He set aside the rest for Jackson, and then—and only then—did he pick up the phone and call his mother.

"Ellery, I'm at the airport. This had better be good."

"What in the hell—"

"He's missing all night and then he's there and then there's a serial killer found and killed in Sacramento and two men sent to the hospital. What was I supposed to think?"

Ellery frowned. "Well, most mothers wouldn't think her son was involved—"

"*Were* you involved, Ellery?"

"Sort of?"

"That's not an answer. Were you or were you not injured when you helped to capture a serial killer?"

What to say, what to say…. "Well, technically I'm able to leave the hospital," he said, because it was the truth.

"And Jackson?"

Ellery sighed. Whatever. This was never a fun game with Mother anyway. "He's the reason I haven't left yet," he said softly. "He… you wouldn't believe the last couple of days if I wrote them out in a book."

She pulled in a harsh breath. "How is he?"

"They need him here for a week." Ellery's voice wobbled. "He wasn't breathing, Mother. We pulled him from the swimming pool and he wasn't breathing. And I bruised his ribs and he's breathing now, but…." He closed his eyes and tried to pull it together.

"My plane is boarding right now, Ellery. I'll be there in six hours. I still have the key to your house, so don't worry about letting me in."

With that she signed off, and Ellery was left feeling grateful and confused.

But then, that's how he almost always felt about his mother.

Next to him Jackson gave a restless sigh and shifted in bed. Ellery grabbed his hand, and he stilled.

Funny how so much about life—holidays, parents, work—it could all come screeching to a halt when the right person whimpered in his sleep.

Ellery would close down states and freeze transportation systems just to have this quiet moment with Jackson before he woke up and remembered that the world could be a bitter, lonely place.

Quiet Pond

JACKSON HEARD everybody before he actually opened his eyes.

"Mrs. Cramer! How are you doing?"

"Oh, just fine, young Alex. So nice to see you. You too, David. And you brought refreshments—that's kind."

"We promised Ellery—where is he?"

"Getting changed. It was lovely of you to bring the cot out, by the way. You're always so accommodating."

"Well, you know. Anything for…."

There was a silence then, and he felt the prickle of eyes.

"Yes" came Taylor Cramer's voice. "Of course. Anything for him. How is he doing?"

"Awake!" Jackson wanted to snap. "He's awake!"

That's not what came out. What came out was "Fer-fwee-fuk-sake-stop-noise!"

Dave and Alex both cackled, and Jackson actually managed to glare at them through slitted lids.

"Mornin'," he mumbled. "How're you?"

"Better than you," Dave said kindly, bustling up in nurse mode and pulling his blankets up to his chin. "Still sick, Jackson. Fever's down a smidge but not broken completely, and breathing is not happening."

Jackson shivered. "Lungs feel fine."

"That there is a fuckton of painkillers. Enjoy."

Jackson frowned at David's pleasant face. "Food?"

"We've got some oatmeal with fresh fruit for you," he said, patting his cheek soothingly.

"Ignore him," Alex said from Jackson's other side. Tiny, perky as a cheerleader, Alex managed to look like a twinkie in his thirties. "I brought cream-filled éclairs. Everyone needs a reason to live."

Jackson smiled at him, reassured. "If you guys ever quit, I'll start going to Kaiser. You make it worthwhile here."

They looked at each other in that way married couples do. "We'd just as soon you asked us out for drinks and dancing," Dave said shortly.

"Now we've got to go. Don't give Mrs. Cramer too hard a time. She's being awfully nice for a woman who had to come see your sorry ass twice in three months' time."

"Understood," Jackson told him, sober as a judge.

They left, and once again he was in a hospital room with Ellery's mother. "Hello, Taylor," he said, trying to do what Dave had told him to do and be nice.

"I'm much less worried when you call me Lucy Satan." She came to stand by his bed. "How are you, Jackson?" Richly beautiful, dark eyes like Ellery's lined with kohl, her perfectly coiffed chestnut hair put into place by will alone—Ellery's mother would not have been out of place wearing gloves and a pillbox hat. As it was, she was wearing a severe dress suit, and he didn't need to be able to see her feet to know she'd have hose and black leather low-heeled pumps.

Jackson closed his eyes. "Exhausted already."

Her hand on his brow was cool and dry. "I was sorry to hear about your mother."

He swallowed and then wished he hadn't. Not enough painkillers in the world. "Me too." It was only polite, right?

"You know, it seemed silly to fly all the way out here this week when you and Ellery will be out just two weeks later. But seeing you here, I think it was the right thing to do."

"Ellery needs you to take care of him," Jackson said. *I was going to hole up in a hotel and die.*

"Yes," she said without apology. "Yes, he does. That's why it's my job to train you up for the job. For starters, that stab wound on his arm—"

"I'm sorry," he said, voice cracking.

"Oh, don't be. You two are getting a commendation from the police department. It just wouldn't look right if you had all *your* war wounds and he didn't have a scratch. No—I'm saying, you need to encourage him to wear short sleeves as soon as possible. He'll be self-conscious, you see, and it's really very exciting. We want him to look like a badass. Am I right?"

Jackson let out a short laugh. "Yeah. Wouldn't be fair if he didn't look badass."

"No." Her voice fell, and she smoothed the hair back from his face. That's where Ellery had learned it. "It wouldn't. And I think he's going to need to work a bit next week, and you will be chafing at home. You and I have chores to do, and I won't let you shirk them."

"Chores?" Sounded horrifying. "What chores?"

"We need to move your possessions into my son's house—and put up some of your pictures, I think."

"Most of them were destroyed in the shooting," he said. He'd been adrift, neither at Ellery's house nor at his own—he hadn't replaced them.

"Well, we'll fix that, won't we? You can't move into Ellery's home and bring nothing of yourself. Pretty soon you'll be wearing his suits to work and raising your upper lip like you smelled something bad. I mean, *I* like him, and I understand *you* have an attachment, but I don't think we need two of them, yes?"

He couldn't help it. "Wow, Lucy Satan, you just threw your own kid under the bus."

Her level look back told him she'd do the same thing to him in a heartbeat. "I really don't know what you mean. But between that and planning the service—"

"For who? Whom? Who the fuck ever?"

She didn't even arch an eyebrow. "For your mother, of course. You weren't having a service?"

Jackson let out a pained grunt. "No. Why would I?"

Again, that level look. "Because she was a human being, and you could be the only person in the world who will miss her—even if it's missing what she *wasn't*."

Wow. "Fine. We'll bury her ashes, and I'll donate some money to a rehab program in her name." Ellery was apparently paying all his expenses now. Maybe one of the benefits of being a mostly kept man was using that money where it was needed. He thought of Jael and his mother and of AJ, that lost kid in the Meadowview house. "I've got actual people I can give money to," he said after a moment. "Maybe a scholarship to get kids through." He thought of the other half of the duplex and how Mike's acerbic tongue and common fucking sense had gotten him through the eight years before Ellery.

Maybe it could get someone else through some hard times now.

"Or maybe make my half of the duplex a halfway house," he said. "We've got some people who can live there now—"

"Excellent. Very well thought out." She clapped her hands together briskly, making him flinch. "So, you work the idea in your head, I'll take care of the legal end, and that's what we'll do before you come to my corner of the world for the holiday."

Jackson started to sweat. "I, uh, haven't gotten you a gift yet," he said uncomfortably. She'd told him that was one of her expectations of his next visit.

"Well, you and my son shall have to order one," she said, undeterred. "And obviously we have things to do. But first…." She pushed the control for his bed until he was sitting up, then swung the little table over his lap. "Have some oatmeal."

She set up a small Tupperware bowl, still steaming, with chunks of apples and raisins on top.

Jackson stared at it, disappointed. "But Alex said there were éclairs!"

"There are. For good boys who eat their oatmeal and sausage." She set up a sandwich container full of plump breakfast meat, and his mouth started to actually water. He thought that only happened in books.

He thought longingly of sugar, butter, and chocolate, and then the smell of the sausage hit him and he broke. He took one—still warm—and bit it in half. "I'm still eating an éclair," he said when he'd swallowed.

"After your oatmeal."

He stared at her, baffled. "You are diabolical."

For the first time since she'd appeared over his bed, her face softened. "My son is brilliant and stubborn, Jackson, and I managed not to kill him before he reached maturity. Those skills don't go away. Now eat. I need to step outside to use the phone, but Ellery should be back by the time you're done."

The damned woman was never wrong. Jackson had just pushed away the rest of the breakfast, thinking mournfully of éclairs he was too full to eat, when Ellery came back from the shower. Jackson smiled faintly when Ellery paused to kiss his mother's cheek as she spoke on the phone before he came completely into the room.

"Oh wow! Oatmeal!" He grabbed his own Tupperware container from the bag Dave and Alex had left before he pulled up a chair next to Jackson.

"Did you have some of this?" he asked, shoveling it in. "They make their own spice and fruit packets—they're amazing!"

Jackson would have rolled his eyes, but he was, quite suddenly, exhausted. "Sure. Yes. They're awesome." He grimaced. "Your mother is here."

Ellery shrugged. "She's expressed a wish to babysit you when I need to go to work."

"I'm a grown ma—" Ellery slipped the last spoonful of Jackson's own oatmeal into his mouth.

"No," Ellery said, dropping his voice and leaning close.

Jackson swallowed, and that was starting to hurt again. "No what?"

"No. We're not arguing about everything. Not until you're better. My heart hurts with being worried. I know you hate hospitals. I know you hate being at home feeling useless. My mother has come here to help you through these things. You need to be grateful, because I'm still working on that marriage proposal, and I'd rather not strangle you before I'm through."

Jackson closed his eyes and wondered what kind of nightmare these past days had been for Ellery. "I'm sorry," he said, eyes burning, throat tight, everything happening so quickly he realized, like through a curtain, how very weak he'd become, not just physically but emotionally as well. "Fine. I'll get off your back about Lucy Satan and her grand plan."

"You *can* call her Taylor," Ellery said, pained expression making his forehead furrow.

"Oh no, Ellery," Mrs. Cramer said, voice all pleasant as she came back into the room. "That's fine if he calls me Lucy Satan." She bared her teeth at Jackson. "It will give us something to do to pass the time."

"Hunh."

Ellery's eyes widened in alarm. "Hunh what?"

"I *must* be sick. That would have terrified me in real life."

Ellery's strained laugh hurt something that should have been dead or drugged. "Jackson, you know that thing you said to me to get me to let you out of the hospital?"

Augh! Guilt! "That's not the only reason I said that," he muttered.

Something tense in Ellery's jaw released, and he looked younger. "I'm glad to hear it. But if you meant that you loved me, that means this *is* real life. And that you can deal with her. And me. So don't let fear keep you from doing anything important, okay?"

More guilt. "I really do, you know," he said, thinking this was necessary. "Not that I wouldn't like to get out of here, but even if I can't, I still mean it."

A smile curved at Ellery's lean mouth. "I sort of thought you did, but it's nice to hear the words sometime." He gave Jackson an all too familiar level look.

Jackson recoiled. "Uh, sometime when you're looking less like your mother?" he asked, pained.

Ellery's turn to recoil. "Deal!"

Jackson smiled a little, exhausted. "My cat's okay?" You always had to ask.

Ellery looked at his mother. "Billy Bob?"

"Is fine, if—" She sniffed. "—a little rough on hose. And missing you two, of course."

Jackson closed his eyes, ready to rest again. He thought about how welcome Billy Bob's weight would be, his purring steady and even, his shameless bids for affection frequent.

"When can I go home?" he asked plaintively. "I'll do anything, just… I want to go home."

Ellery's kiss on the temple was probably more tenderness than he deserved. "I talked to the doctors," he said. "Your fever needs to break, and your shoulder needs to be clear of infection. They would also like it if you could breathe. So you sleep and practice breathing, and Mother and I will take care of you and the cat. Deal?"

He didn't have an ounce of fight left. "Deal."

He closed his eyes and dreamed of Billy Bob purring on his chest. He dreamed of waking up next to Ellery, sleepy-eyed and sexed out. Sunshine was pouring through the window above Ellery's bed, and they had a rare day off and nothing to do but make love and eat.

He hadn't spent a day like that with any other lover. Had only spent a few with Ellery. But as he immersed himself in the imaginary feel of Ellery's skin against his own and the tiny golden dust motes wandering in the sunlight, he thought he very much wanted to.

He'd have to get better to make that happen.

Old and Fishy Business

ELLERY WAS, in fact, a lot like Jackson. He chafed restlessly at hanging around the hospital when only time would make Jackson better, and Jackson was sleeping through most of the time.

That first afternoon, Jackson had awakened in the throes of a nightmare—something about Billy Bob, but Ellery never asked what. Ellery had been doing paperwork on his laptop, and his mother stood up first, making it to Jackson's bedside.

"Wake up," she'd snapped. "This isn't good for you."

Jackson opened his eyes just enough to focus on her face and then scowled. "Jesus, you're scaring away the monsters."

He went back to sleep after that, and Ellery and his mother took turns over the following days, with Jade and Mike's help, of course.

On day two, Tess Dakin walked into his room under her own power, which irritated Jackson no end. Tess had been grateful to both of them—and bruised, and sore, and shell-shocked.

She'd stood at the doorway of Jackson's small room and told them about grilling heroin family about the house in Meadowview, and how she'd wanted to get a closer look inside.

"My fault," she'd croaked from vocal cords still strained from screaming. "I was more interested in making the bust than doing my job. I knew you were missing. I should have been looking for you, not trying to get the drop on this guy. Letting you wander off like that—not the right thing to do."

Jackson had shrugged it off. "Let's hear it for getting backup," he told her. "Both of us. It should be a New Year's resolution or something."

She'd smiled bitterly. "If I ever go out in the field again," she said softly.

Jackson pinned her with a hard scowl. "I did. I spent a year in the hospital, and I'm active. I was a rookie. You've got more grit than I ever had."

Her smile was delicate, like a wire butterfly. "I think we'll call it a tie. But thank you, thank you both."

She'd left then, probably to go back to her own room and sleep, and maybe cry, and hopefully to talk to a counselor about what she'd undergone.

A kindly looking middle-aged man ventured into Jackson's room about an hour after she'd left and introduced himself as a counselor to crime victims.

Jackson's snarl surprised even Ellery. "I'm nobody's goddamned victim! I'm fucking fine! Go the hell away!"

Ellery's mother discreetly stood up and left, talking smoothly to the poor counselor and asking him to maybe come in later. The man laughed and assured her this wasn't his first barbecue, while Ellery fought the temptation to smack Jackson in the ear.

"Was that necessary?" he asked, fury coming online for the first time since Jackson had agreed to stay and heal.

Jackson's mouth twisted. "So. Necessary."

"Jackson, you were—"

"If you say assaulted, I'm making you leave the room." His jaw was locked stubbornly, and Ellery let out an angry breath.

"Jizzed on? Can I say that? You were helpless—"

Jackson's mouth worked. "No. Not helpless. I got away. I got home. Tess needs him. There's no shame. I'll be okay."

Ellery let out a breath and stalked outside the room to where his mother was talking to the nice man with the prematurely silver hair and neat salt-and-pepper goatee. The counselor nodded and gave Taylor his card, then left.

Ellery shook his head and went to take the card from her.

"No," Taylor said, tucking the card in her wallet. "He's never going to let his guard down around you. He might not even let his guard down around me. This might have to simmer around in his head for a year before he decides to let it out. But it's not going to happen while you're in the room."

Ellery let out a sound of hurt. His arm felt fine—the stitches were coming out in a week—but this thought of being exorcised from Jackson's treatment, that hurt.

"Pride," Taylor said shortly. "I know you have it—just not the same kind. He's tired of you seeing him weak. Leave him alone. Let him be strong. This"—she indicated her chest—"isn't going away." She grunted. "But I am. I need to get the hell out of this hospital, and we need reinforcements."

Ellery smiled grimly. "They're coming." He'd finally given Jade permission to call her brother.

The next day, the fever broke. Jackson was exhausted, of course, and irritable as fuck—so it was a perfect time for Kaden to come down from the foothills and play rummy with him for two days.

Taylor pronounced Kaden a superlative human being, and Ellery wasn't sure what she planned to get him and his family for Christmas, but he warned Kaden: it was going to be big.

Anyone who could deal with Jackson when he was sick, bored, fractious, and trying like hell not to be needy deserved a fucking medal. Those were Taylor Cramer's exact words.

On day six he was discharged.

Taylor stayed at Ellery's, using his console computer and apparently reconnecting with her plans for world domination. Also, Ellery would wager, going through Jackson's pictures with Jade and Kaden, deciding which ones to have reprinted and framed so he could put them up when they got back from Boston after Thanksgiving.

"Are you sure you don't want me to stay here instead?" his mother had asked the day before. Yes, Jackson had improved, but he was gaunt and haggard, and there'd been a reason Ellery had tried to get him to see the counselor. "Traveling is exhausting, you know."

"Not the way he'll do it—he can probably fit four days' worth of clothes in a duffel bag. If he even has them to pack. No. He's lived in Sacramento his whole life. The first time he'd ever been on a plane was when we went to San Diego in September. I want him to see… outside. Other." Ellery shuddered. Maybe if Jackson saw outside the state, he'd remember he was outside the room in Meadowview or, God, please, outside the hospital itself.

He claimed he wasn't a victim.

Ellery didn't understand how he could even see enough of himself to know if it was true.

His mother touched his elbow, hand gentle. "I'll let you call this one. He's got four days at your house with me. If he hasn't killed me by the time I head back for Boston, we'll call it a success."

His pocket buzzed then, and he didn't recognize the name. "Mother—I need to take this—"

She waved him on imperiously, like it was her idea.

"Ellery Cramer, Esquire. How can I help you?"

"Oh God—he's right."

The voice was unfamiliar and quiet, like the person speaking was sick or frightened.

"Who's right about what?"

"The guy… the guy at the house. In Meadowview. He… he said you'd sound scary."

Ellery felt a shaft of hope. "AJ?"

"Yes, sir. You remember me?"

"Jackson said he'd help you. I, uh, I'll be honest. I didn't think we'd hear from you after that."

AJ's half laugh was a weak and broken thing. "I didn't either. But the cops took me to the hospital, and I got through withdrawals. And then… that was it. I was just sort of…." His indrawn breath sounded shaky. "So they let me out in my old clothes, and I realize I can't get into my apartment, and I sold most of my stuff for smack, and I'm not addicted anymore, and this is supposed to be my second chance. I mean, my *body* is over it, but my… my…." He was openly sobbing now. "I had this card in my jacket pocket, Mr. Cramer. It was the only goddamned thing I had."

Ellery frowned. "Which hospital?"

"Med Center. I'm over on Parker now—I just started walking. There's a pay phone here since, you know, cell phone plan gone."

Ellery took a deep breath. "So, uh, if you turn around and walk back to Med Center, I can buy you a meal," he said. "And I can get you into a month-long program." He thought of Jackson's plans for his duplex, which, by all accounts from Mike, was actually close to livable. "I can even get you into a house and pull some strings for a job."

"Will… will I get to see Jackson? You're offering a lot of nice things, Mr. Cramer, but what I really need—"

"Is a friend." Ellery was as gentle as he could be, but he was no match for Jackson. "He's the reason I'm at Med Center. You can come visit before I take you to rehab."

"It's a deal. I'll be there in half an hour. I promise."

"I'll hold you to that," Ellery said grimly. He rang off and turned back into the room. "Jackson, did you put on your human suit yet?"

Jackson had been staring off into space pensively, like he was unhappy with the world. "That depends. Any more shrinks?"

"No—but I do have someone who needs you to be a grown-up. Remember that kid on the floor at Meadowview?"

Jackson straightened up in bed, only wincing a little as he repositioned his shoulder. "AJ?"

"Yeah. He needs an actual stint in rehab and not just medical withdrawal. I'll take him to rehab, but he wants to talk to a friend."

Jackson's eyes—that amazing, clear, and stunning green—brightened for the first time in over a week. "Sure. Yeah. Did you tell him about the duplex?"

"I thought you could," Ellery said. He swallowed and tried not to let his face go gentle. "I figured you could talk to him about other things."

Jackson didn't grimace, and he didn't shudder or roll his eyes. "Yeah," he said softly. "Okay. I can do that."

"Good." And since Ellery was on a roll, something else had happened when he'd gone into work two days before. "And don't forget to tell him he'll be sharing the duplex with heroin family. They'll be out of jail right before Christmas. Claudine will get the guest bedroom, I guess, and the boys can bunk it in the main bedroom and the couch. Just prep him. The Celia Rivers Halfway House is going to be very full."

"I'm not calling it that," Jackson said darkly. "It's going to be the Toni Cameron Halfway House or nothing."

"Sure," Ellery agreed. "That's actually a really nice idea."

Jackson's mouth quirked. "I get them from time to time."

Indeed.

AJ seemed shaky when Ellery took him for food, shaky and desperate. Clean and sober, he was everything Owens had loved to kill—pretty, bright, lost. Ellery told him he'd been lucky—and that taking a second chance proved he was smart.

"I never felt smart before," he said, eating pudding like it was an Olympic sport. "Maybe I'll just keep being smart."

When Ellery took him up to Jackson's room, he asked the obvious. "What's he in for? Did he get shot or something?"

"Pneumonia," Ellery said, because that had been the official diagnosis. "Exhaustion. Heart failure. Infection. All sorts of bad things."

"That's funny. It sounds like real life tried to kill him."

Yeah, that was a laugh riot. "Well, the bad guy helped too."

"Ain't that always the way. I guess it pays to be ahead of real life if you can, so the bad guys have to work harder."

Ellery laughed a little. "That is very wise."

He enjoyed the young man's company, and when he opened the door to Jackson's room and shooed the boy in, Jackson's eyes lit up gently.

Ellery left them to talk while he set up AJ's recovery. When he came back, they were both red-eyed and sober.

But that night and the next morning, as Jackson prepped to leave, Ellery detected a note of peace in him that hadn't been there before.

When they got Jackson home, he went directly to the bedroom. Taylor rolled her eyes, probably thinking he was pouting or faking sleep.

Ellery suspected the truth.

When he walked into the bedroom an hour later, Jackson was lying on his side, still petting his cat. Billy Bob was drooling and sprawled in the middle of the bed, and Jackson was telling him silly things. "You know, like maybe somewhere out there, you've got kittens. You ever think of that? You ever hit any leopardesses? Any bobcats? 'Cause there might be a cat for this kid. I'm just thinking, you no-thumbs motherfucker, if you were going to spread Billy Bobs all throughout the land, this kid could use a cat. Besides, I know you don't think about Albert the German shepherd anymore, but I bet he's pining for you. Another cat might ease his broken heart, you know?"

Billy's response was to purr some more, and Ellery sat down next to Jackson.

"Talking to the cat?"

Jackson gave him a glare with some unexpected heat. "Do you know something?"

"What?"

"Your mother is here."

"I am aware."

Jackson rolled his eyes. "She's going to be here for four more magical days."

Ellery grunted. Yes, yes his mother *was* going to be in his guest room for four more magical days. She was going back to Boston three days before Jackson and Ellery were leaving. They would have a big dinner two nights later at Jade and Mike's with Kaden, Rhonda, and the kids, and get on a plane the next morning. "I am aware."

Jackson shook his head. "No, no, you're not aware. You are most obviously unaware of how much this is not a happy thing."

Ellery frowned. Jackson and his mother had worked on the halfway house idea, they'd come to terms with Jackson's finances—and yet another car, which might have blown Jackson's mind, but Ellery frankly thought it would be his mother's excuse to subsidize a dealership or something.

"I thought you and my mother were getting along," he said, puzzled.

"Yes," Jackson told him, still petting Billy Bob. "We get along swimmingly. Do you know what we *don't* do?"

"Cook?" They'd been living on takeout and Ellery's cooking, mostly, with the occasional pity meal from Jade and Mike.

"No."

"Investigate corrupt military personnel?"

Jackson managed a look over his shoulder. "I thought we were saving him for before Christmas."

Lacey had not sat well with either one of them. But after Jade had driven him to the airport he hadn't followed through on his threats of fiery JAG Corps retribution. On the one hand, that could have been a relief.

On the other hand, Jackson had asked what in the fuck the guy was hiding. Whatever it was, Ellery was still suspicious. Karl Lacey's very coldness had told Ellery something important needed to be flushed out.

"Maybe afterward," Ellery said uneasily. "Let's wait until we can both run five miles without breaking a sweat."

Jackson let out a grunt of acknowledgment. "So that's on the back burner." He pushed himself up on his good elbow and pinned Ellery with a glare, raising his eyebrows. "And that's not what I'm talking about."

Ellery was baffled. "Clarify."

"*Sex*, Ellery. It's been an entire week—don't you miss *sex*?"

Ellery's brain checked out, and his groin held a party without him. When he checked back in, his erection was tight against the placket of his slacks.

"Yes," he said numbly.

Jackson grinned, a little bit of long-buried evil in his eyes. "I could, uh, you know, do something, except…." He pressed against the bulge under Ellery's slacks.

Ellery fought off a moan. "Tonight. Late. When she's asleep."

Jackson dropped his hand. "Three days. Broad daylight. When she's on *a plane*!"

Oh my God. "Seriously?" Because Ellery's erection was *not* going down.

"No, Ellery, there is *no sex* unless your mother is out of the house. I am totally serious."

Goddammit. "We've got to let her stay!" he wailed, sitting down and rubbing Jackson's much-diminished ass through his jeans.

"I know," Jackson said, eyes closing. "Just, you know, wake me up when she's gone."

Ellery wasn't sure if he was joking or not. He'd been pretty active the last two days, but he was looking *very* tired now.

Ellery bent down and kissed his temple. "You go ahead and sleep. Because the minute she's on the plane, you and me are going to be doing the wild thing like lemmings."

Jackson chuckled softly, eyes still closed. "Look forward to it, Counselor. Love you."

Ellery paused, bent over, lips on Jackson's skin.

"I love you too."

Jackson chuckled, still falling asleep. "Surprise!" he laughed.

"Asshole," Ellery accused, but Jackson was out, and he had nobody to complain to but his mother.

THE NEXT three days went surprisingly quickly—and were not as relaxing as Ellery hoped.

He and Jackson had to be exhaustively deposed by the police department for two days, and all the records they'd put together were analyzed ad infinitum. At the end of the second day, Jackson lost his temper.

"I'm done," he announced, standing and walking out of the interrogation room. "Ellery, you with me?"

Ellery startled, shoving papers and files into his briefcase. He'd made copies for the DA's office. Arizona—the lawyer and sometime ally sitting across the table from them this day—knew everything he did.

"Ellery, we're not finished here!" she complained, standing up a beat late.

"Are we being charged?" Jackson demanded, shifting from foot to foot at the doorway.

"No, there are no charges pending." Arizona ran her fingers through her buzz-cut gray hair. "In fact, the department is thinking about giving you a commendation."

"That's lovely," Jackson snarled. "I'd like to live to see it. I'm done with the questions. Ellery gave you all the paperwork. You have nothing to hold us on. It's a beautiful day outside, and I just spent a week in the fucking hospital. I'm. Done. We did the investigative work, and you ignored us. It's *your* job to count the motherfucking bodies. I…." His voice broke. "I saw them up close and personal. I almost *was* one. Twice. Finish your investigation and *then* ask us questions. Jesus Christ, you lazy motherfuckers, do some of your own goddamned work!"

With that he turned and stalked out of the room, and Ellery stood to follow him.

"Ellery!" Arizona cried, sounding a little desperate. "You can't just leave us like this—"

"Sure we can. *We're* not being charged, and *you've* got bodies to count. Remember the last time I sent you evidence that Owens was operating? Remember that?"

She grunted and had the grace to look uncomfortable. "I said you were paranoid and Jackson was delusional."

Well, at least she owned it.

"Well I'm *paranoid* that Jackson's getting sick again, and you're *delusional* if you think I'm staying in this room and arguing with you. He's right. It's pissing down rain—but we're free and clear, and that's a beautiful day."

He stalked out of the law office, furious and frustrated, catching up with Jackson as he strode to the car. "Hey, hey—slow down there! I'm not one of the assholes, remember."

Jackson gave him the side-eye. "Sure you are. I just like your asshole. At least I think I do—it's been a while."

Ellery rolled his eyes. "I am actually so sexually frustrated I almost find that funny." He adjusted the collar of his coat against the rain. "So, what now? Should we go home?"

Jackson grunted. "No. Your mother's there, and *she's* so bored at our house she's going to start baking cookies."

Ellery clapped his hand to his mouth in horror. "And that would be *bad*," he whispered.

Jackson managed a chuckle. “We could always rent a hotel room by the hour,” he joked. “That would be something.”

It was like the entire world spun in a whirling vortex to that moment right there.

“Your HIV test was clear,” he said, and Jackson stumbled on a perfectly even path.

“Uh….” He turned and actually looked at Ellery, green eyes wide, the rain plastering his hair to his head.

“Lube.” Ellery was babbling. “Ten bucks. You can get lube at the grocery store. I’ll get us a nice room. The Hyatt downtown. Upper floor.”

Jackson gaped, wiping water out of his eyes. “And ten-dollar lube?”

Ellery nodded, suddenly desperate for the two of them, naked, without serial killers or sickness or his ever-blessed mother in the way. He held his umbrella over Jackson’s head too so Jackson would know he was serious.

“It’s one in the afternoon. We could be there for hours.”

Jackson turned toward the car lot and walked faster. Ellery’s disappointment hit him in the gut. His feet made leaden splats in the water running on the sidewalk.

“Unless you’re getting sick again—”

He was unprepared for the heat of Jackson’s glare. “Fuck getting sick. Move faster, dammit! You drive. I’ll look up drugstores on the way!”

Fish Flop

JACKSON WAS the one to run into the drugstore.

The premium lube—extra-large bottle—was easy to find, but he threw in a travel pack of wipes, a bottle of Diet Coke and one of Dr Pepper, and a couple of bags of chocolate-covered pretzels (because cravings).

It wasn't until he was standing in line, his basket of incriminating purchases held in his good hand in front of him, that he was attacked by nerves.

We've done this. We've even done this since Meadowview.

We've done this since he said it. The big thing. The scary, irrevocable thing.

Yeah. Sure.

But Jackson had literally died since then. He'd said the words back. He'd had time to grieve, to process, to recognize in himself the vulnerability he'd been fighting all his life.

He'd had a lot of lovers. He'd been careful and considerate with every one of them. He'd never had anyone even remotely like Ellery.

His hands shook as he gripped the basket tighter.

He didn't want gentleness. He didn't want Ellery's kindness and consideration. His heart pounded in his throat, and for a moment he wondered if the scarring he'd been warned about wasn't going to kill him as he stood.

He wanted possession. He wanted it so bad.

Ellery made promises by the porn star's buttload, but oh God—so hard to believe. Even from Ellery. Jackson needed to be taken irrevocably. He needed to belong, inside and out, to the man who'd hauled him from the darkness to the light.

Given how much Ellery probably needed reassurance that Jackson was as committed as he was, getting to play the helpless maiden was a terrible thing to ask.

Jackson paid for his purchases and hurried back to the car, his body wired tight, his previous joy hardened and changed.

He was going to have to be strong—because Ellery needed him.

"Oh my God, you look like you're going into battle!" Ellery laughed as they waited in the valet line in front of the Hyatt.

Jackson craned his head back like a tourist. It wasn't often a native got a look at the Hyatt, and the black-windowed building was pretty classy for someone homegrown like Jackson.

"Making plans to keep you in line," he said, only partially kidding.

He was stunned when Ellery reached over and squeezed his upper thigh. "You keep thinking that. You think that until I have you nailed to the mattress screaming my name."

For a moment Jackson flailed for air. When he finally got a good lungful, Ellery was handing the valet his keys, and Jackson needed to grab his plastic bag of purchases and follow him into the lobby, heart pounding for what he could mean.

Six people were in the elevator as they made their way to their room in the penthouse, and Jackson bounced restlessly on his toes.

I have lubricant in a CVS bag, and we're going to fuck in a top-flight hotel room.

The thought was as unreal as the direction this day had taken. Ellery stood across from him, and through three middle-aged couples chatting about basketball, his eyes caught and trapped Jackson against the back of the elevator.

There was something almost angry in that glare. A delicious half-furious, half-desperate threat.

Jackson stared back. *I'll do for you, Ellery. I'm strong. I can be your lover and a good man.*

That's what he had to prove, right?

But that wasn't what Ellery's eyes were saying, lasering through the genial chatter of people who obviously knew each other.

The car stopped a few floors from theirs, and Ellery and Jackson flattened themselves to opposite sides of the cab to let everybody and their luggage off.

"Are you getting out here?" inquired one of the women—fiftyish, in a sleek velour track suit. She had ash-blonde hair and laugh lines, as well as freckles, and a kindness about her that was almost as surreal as this little excursion.

"No, thank you," Jackson said, charm on automatic.

"I'm on top," Ellery said with a feral smile.

The doors closed slowly, so Jackson had time to register the woman's startled expression even as he and Ellery locked eyes again.

Jackson said, "Oh really?"

And Ellery bared his teeth. "Not another word," he warned, voice low and dangerous. "I like this hotel. Just follow me out of the elevator when it stops."

Jackson's tongue turned to sandpaper. So many things he should shoot back, so many ways he could mock or banter or insinuate, all of them leading to him buried inside Ellery, taking control.

None of them leading to where he really wanted to go.

Still, he found his pride when the doors slid open. No one waited on the landing, and he took a step out of the car. Ellery hauled Jackson back against him and snarled in his ear. "I mean it, Jackson. Just this one goddamned time, follow my lead."

For a moment it was touch and go. He could have whirled Ellery around, ravished him, insisted on his dominance. Dammit, he *was* that guy!

But Ellery's arm had moved, was crushing his chest, holding him so firmly, so mercilessly.

So safely.

Of all the things in his life he'd never had, safety was primary among them.

"I—"

"Please," Ellery whispered, breaking him. "I need this from you, Jackson. You will never know."

"Yeah."

Ellery slid past him, taking the lead to their room. Jackson followed on his toes, all their other sex somehow falling away from this moment, from this reckoning.

The place smelled rich, but the bright details of the carpeting and the view of the city from the end of the hall faded. Jackson was left with an impression of the Sacramento skyline under the deep shadows of a rainy afternoon and the sound of the crinkling plastic bag in his fist.

Ellery turned in to their hotel room, and Jackson went after him meekly, not sure how this had gone from spontaneous to serious quite so quick.

"Nice digs," he said, voice bright as they passed the short hallway that opened into the suite. "Do we really need all this for—"

Ellery shoved him against the wall without warning, taking his mouth savagely.

Jackson, who had been afraid of feeling weak, afraid of failing in this, the one thing he knew he could do, found himself relishing the force between them. He returned, hard, nipping, cupping Ellery's scalp in his spread fingers and holding him there.

Right where Jackson needed him.

Ellery tore his mouth away and started ripping at his clothing. Jackson's hands went to the hem of his own sweatshirt, but Ellery stopped him, suit jacket puddling on the floor, tie askew, shoes already toed off.

"You will stay right there," he panted. "I'll undress you."

Jackson managed to cock his hip and roll his eyes in spite of the way his heart beat so hard he could feel the throbbing in his balls. "Bossy much?"

Ellery kissed him again, hard, mouth-to-mouth contact only while he continued to drop his clothes. Jackson forgot about his own skin, greedy and starving for Ellery's under his palms.

Jackson rubbed his chest, his upper arms, and, as Ellery shoved his slacks and boxers down, grabbed handfuls of taut backside. He needed so badly, he pushed off from the wall and tried to turn the kiss. He wanted his lips on all of Ellery, every pale, exasperating inch.

Ellery's response was to push at Jackson's chest, near his throat, his thumb and forefinger spread so Jackson's swallow bobbed in the vee of his hand.

"I will bind you in place with my necktie if I have to," Ellery promised. "Don't test me."

Jackson's knees almost gave way, and his eyes rolled back in his head.

Ellery nodded fiercely. "I need you where I need you," he said—maybe irrationally, but Jackson understood. He reached for Jackson's hands and lifted them up, pressing them against the wall by the wrists. "You can lower them if you get tired," he said, all consideration. "But just… just… I *need* you like this."

Jackson swallowed, out of words. He nodded briefly and pressed his hands back against the cool plaster while Ellery, naked and glorious, yanked on Jackson's sweatshirt and shirt, hauling them over his head.

Jackson ducked and helped that way, but after Ellery dropped the clothes on the floor, he glared meaningfully, and Jackson, obedient and needy, braced his shoulders against the wall again and raised his hands, wincing a little, because, dammit—

Ellery took his weak hand from over his head and lowered it slowly. Turning the palm down, he pressed it against the plaster at Jackson's thighs. "No pain," he whispered.

Jackson nodded, feeling his eyes burn. "Okay."

Ellery's mouth on his was still urgent but less violent, and Jackson opened, undone by his gentleness. Ellery pulled away again, nibbling down his jaw when Jackson tried to follow. He kept nibbling, down his throat and across his chest.

He gave Jackson's shoulder—barely out of bandages, still bruised—excruciatingly gentle touches of his lips, and when he reached the nipple on that side, he rubbed his lips and then licked. And then rubbed his lips and licked.

Jackson moaned, all breath, and arched his engorged and aching erection against Ellery's. They flopped together, bouncing off each other but not touching with any friction.

"Harder," he begged.

Ellery straightened and buried his face in the hollow of Jackson's neck and shoulder. "No."

Jackson half laughed. "*Ellery*!"

Ellery nipped his earlobe and then said it again. "No."

Jackson's skin ached. "But—"

"But no pain." Ellery's voice grew thick. "I'm not going to hurt you."

"Blue balls will hurt," Jackson grated, frantic.

"That's not going to happen either."

His skin slid over Jackson's like rough satin, and he kissed another path, this one tugging on the other nipple and then moving down, and down. When he got to the taped gauze on his stomach, Jackson tried to stop him with fingers in his hair, but Ellery stopped and pressed both his hands against the wall again.

"My necktie, Jackson," he warned gruffly. Then he sank to his knees and slid his palms up Jackson's thighs.

His breath puffed against the dripping end of Jackson's cock, and Jackson grunted, because it was not enough and way too much.

"No," he protested. He knew what Ellery wanted. "Ellery—"

Ellery licked his head slowly, and Jackson pounded at the wall. He wanted… needed… so hard, so fast, pain be damned!

But Ellery did it again, this time adding his hand and squeezing from base to tip. Jackson's shoulders sagged against the wall in relief. "Yes. Please, Ellery—please."

Begging for it felt raw and honest, and Ellery didn't make him wait long. The heat of his mouth seared Jackson's nerve endings, and the wet silk of his tongue soothed the fire. His hand squeezed firmly around Jackson's shaft, and he wasn't tentative or gentle on the stroke.

Jackson gibbered, propping himself on the wall, wanting to tangle his hands in Ellery's hair, wanting to hold him, anything. But Ellery kept sucking, stroking, a delirious pressure that melted Jackson's brain, his needs, his best intentions.

Jackson didn't even notice the hand switch off until two fingers, slick with spit, groped and then breached him, not rough enough to hurt, just rough enough to get his attention.

Ellery pulled away from Jackson's cock, sucking hard enough to make a popping sound, thrust those two fingers, stroked Jackson's shaft, licked the end—and closed his eyes.

Jackson would have protested—no. God. No. But the cool air hit his sensitized head, and Ellery scissored his fingers.

Climax rushed him, a scalding volcano from his thighs, his spine—he came, knees giving, pleasure and shame exploding behind his eyes.

With a little groan he sank to the carpet, falling into Ellery's arms.

Ellery tugged his hair until he leaned back. "Look at me," he commanded. Jackson closed his eyes, and Ellery tugged again. Ellery's brown eyes bored into his own, intensity squared. Semen striped across Ellery's cheeks and dripped off his chin, sliding from the long bridge of his nose. "What do you see?"

"I want you," Jackson told him, asshole aching for possession, cock tingling and ready to go again. "You're beautiful."

Ellery's eyes darkened, and he pulled Jackson into a sloppy, bitter kiss. Jackson licked the come off his lips, his cheeks, then suckled the point of his chin. Ellery whispered, "You're beautiful, Jackson Rivers. I want you. I want you so bad. I love you."

Jackson moaned faintly, the word abrading the skin he'd been trying to grow back over his emotions. His heart was still so raw. *Here* was the pain Ellery should have been worried about.

"I love you too," he breathed as Ellery nipped at his throat. Not saying it would have hurt worse.

"On your back, legs spread. I need inside you. Like breathing."

Oh God *yes.* Even the best rugs were rough on the skin, but Jackson didn't care. He wriggled out from the wall enough so his head didn't hit, then spread his thighs and bent his knees, biting his lip as he watched Ellery spread lubricant on his fine cock. Jackson reached out, whimpering a little, because *he* wanted to touch, but Ellery shook his head.

"I'll come," he admitted hoarsely. "Just a touch. Just a breath. Wait!"

"What in the hell—"

Ellery stood and gave Jackson a hand. "Bed," he told him unequivocally. "Ribs, Jackson."

"Fuck the—"

Ellery started kissing him again, and he came to on the bed, knees spread, with a pillow shoved under his ass and Ellery's tongue rimming his asshole while his fingers stretched him again.

Jackson closed his eyes, his identity slipping away in the dreamy pleasure. He knotted his fingers in Ellery's hair and tried not to shake off the bed, abandoning any attempt to control the sounds he made, the words or half words, the things he might say.

He'd agreed to submit. He'd agreed to trust. Trusting meant letting Ellery choose the time, choose the position.

Ellery was the one person in his bed who had never let him down, never hurt him, never used him.

Jackson was only peripherally aware of Ellery moving, of Ellery's cock at his stretched and sloppy entrance. He was deep under, in the world where he would do anything, say anything, endure anything to just know Ellery would be there, that Jackson could cling to his hand when he was lost.

Ellery breached his asshole, and Jackson was abruptly present, in his body, where the immediate pleasure threatened to overwhelm him. His body and skin were real again, and Ellery thrust inside him, hard and committed. They were a part of each other, and Jackson couldn't breathe.

"Ellery!"

Ellery cupped his cheek, shoved a thumb into his mouth as he bore forward, and Jackson sucked hard, the dreaminess replaced by nerve centers exploding outward. "Mmm!"

Ellery passed the first tight barrier and then threw his hips forward, filling Jackson to the point of delirium, to the point where words didn't exist anymore.

Heedless of his ribs, Jackson grabbed his thighs and invited him closer, harder, deeper, and was rewarded by another merciless thrust.

Augh! Yes!

Ellery fucked him with purpose—this act was everything. It was their bodies meshed together, their pleasure releasing endorphins, their climax rendering them weak and vulnerable before each other. It was trust, it was promises, it was fulfillment of every hope Jackson had ever had for letting another human being close to his heart.

It was the most terrifying, most exhilarating thing Jackson had ever done, and he watched in wonder as Ellery closed his eyes and pumped his hips, finally turning inward where he could chase his own orgasm, while Jackson's threatened to obliterate everything he'd ever believed himself to be.

Hold on. Hold on to who you are.

Ellery opened his eyes and glared. "Don't you dare," he panted. "Nothing back, Jackson. Come for me. Goddammit, *come*!"

And Jackson lost who he was, lost the reasons he didn't trust, the reasons he should have been too scarred to love, the fears that came with baring his soul in front of another human being.

This climax was a slow, rocking wave that started at his asshole and rippled out, taking his taint, his balls, his thighs, his heart, his breath with it, leaving him a screaming, sobbing, sated naked man where a posturing frightened boy had been.

Ellery groaned above him, and at first Jackson thought the hot drops of salt on his stomach and chest were sweat.

But as Ellery came, his eyes were screwed shut, and he fell forward with a terrible cry, burying his face against Jackson's chest and trembling in the aftermath.

Jackson felt Ellery's spend fill him, leaking hotly onto Jackson's thighs before Ellery was even done pumping into Jackson's body.

Not sweat—not sweat. Tears. Ellery was weeping openly on Jackson's chest, and Jackson held him tight, whispering to him, nonsense words about how he fucked like a god and they were going to be all right.

He thought he was flattering, lying outrageously, when his own body gave one last shudder and his brain and words shorted out.

For a moment he and Ellery just breathed, one after the other, their great chest heaves swallowing the whole of the oxygen in the room.

And in that insidious quiet, *that's* when he realized the words weren't bullshit.

By all that was holy, Ellery fucked like a god. He'd nailed Jackson to the mattress until all Jackson's painful self-doubt was fucked away.

And maybe—with some work, with some patience, with some kept promises on both their parts, it was all going to be okay.

Jackson grinned and kept stroking the back of Ellery's neck. He spied the clock on the side of the bed and let out a short laugh. "Well, that was half an hour. What are we going to do until ten o'clock at night? Watch TV and order room service?"

Ellery grunted and rocked his hips. His cock, which had been softening like a good sexual organ after intercourse, began to grow again.

"You. Wish."

Jackson caught his mouth in another kiss, and Ellery kept rocking. Suddenly they were in the middle of round three, and it should have been slower, softer, with tenderness and sweet words.

They *might* get to those in round four.

Round three was a long-thrusting, brutally hard powerfuck that left them both breathless and dripping with sweat and with come. At the end of it, when Jackson's cock had spurted again, an agonizing stripe of semen that coated both his stomach and Ellery's chest, Ellery gave a moan and rolled off him. They both sprawled under the ceiling fan, looking out at the city in the dark through the window.

"Don't take this the wrong way," Jackson panted, too weak to move for the moment, "but I almost think you have something to prove."

Ellery rolled to his side, his hair hanging across his brow in long strips. "Do you love me?" he asked, not even smiling.

Jackson was helpless against the full-body flush that replaced his fuck-flush.

"Yes," he replied, because he'd said it and because the words *couldn't* scare him anymore or he'd sabotage the two of them with his doubt. "Yes, I love you. Do you love me?"

Ellery nodded, his throat working, and he reached out to drag a knuckle down Jackson's cheek. "I watched you in the hospital for a week," he croaked. "And some days, it felt like you got thin."

"I got *scrawny*," Jackson complained, because it was true. You could see his ribs now, and his collarbones stood out in stark lines from his chest.

"Not like that," Ellery whispered, rubbing Jackson's lip with his thumb now. "Like… like you were fading from us, transparent. Like you had given up your body, your life with me, because it was just too damned hard."

"It was hard," Jackson admitted. He gave a tentative smile. "But I wouldn't just give you up. Not without a fight. You know that."

Ellery closed his eyes and bit his lip. "I hoped," he said. "I needed this. Your body, mine. So I could know the hope was real."

Jackson could understand that. He bit his lip and looked away. "I needed you," he admitted. "Needed to know it was real."

They lay there in quiet for a moment, and then Ellery swore.

Jackson's eyes popped open. "What? What's wrong? What did we forget?"

With a sigh Ellery shoved up to sit with his back against the pillows. Jackson did the same thing and then pulled the comforter up against the chill in the air.

Ellery grunted. "Okay, if I start going to temple every Saturday, will you think I'm crazy?"

"What in the fuck?" Jackson's eyes crossed in an effort to make *that* happen.

"I just… it's just that I sort of promised God that I'd do that for a year, if only he'd bring you back."

Jackson started laughing, every pump of his diaphragm reminding him that he'd just abused his recovering body, every burst of laughter reminding him that he didn't care.

Ellery tagged him on the arm irritably. "It's not funny. I was desperate, and… and… it was like God brought you back to me."

Okay. He nodded. "Ellery?" he said, deadly serious. He leaned forward and kissed his lover tenderly, with sweetness and respect.

"What?" Ellery the Dominator was gone now, and in his place was the man Jackson found persnickety and irritating—and so very, very dear.

"That kiss? Our bodies here, together? The fucking miracle that I can tell you I love you?"

Ellery nodded seriously.

"That feels like church to me."

His lean mouth curved into a smile. "That's cheating," he sang softly.

Jackson nodded and leaned his head against Ellery's shoulder. "Yeah. Let's have some snacks and cheat some more."

New Currents to Explore

ROUND FOUR—SWEET. So very, very sweet.

Ellery—never ashamed to bottom—straddled Jackson for round four, rocking back and forth slowly, listening to Jackson's every whisper, every held-back cry.

He'd said their lovemaking was holy.

That thought echoed in Ellery's bones, in his sinews and the chambers of his heart. When Jackson tilted his head back and moaned in climax, Ellery heard a prayer.

Ellery's climax rolled through him, powerful in his body, yes—but secondary to the thing that was happening in his soul.

He slumped forward against Jackson's chest, thinking *How am I going to put that into a marriage proposal?*

Jackson smiled at him, his mouth quirking up on one side, and then yawned. Ellery grinned and threaded his fingers through that thick dark blond hair before leaning forward on his elbows and kissing him briefly. "Here. You nap. I'll order room service and…." He grimaced. Jackson was still *inside him*. "Uh, call—"

Jackson laughed softly and rolled away. He grabbed one of the wipes he'd brought, and then handed one to Ellery. He used to be fastidious about this—to the point that Ellery felt hurt—but this was just so they could put their boxers on and not rip their pubic hair out when they took them off.

"If we put on our shorts, can you call your mother?" he asked, finding both pairs in the puddle of clothes near the entryway.

"Yeah, smartass." Ellery found his boxers and watched as Jackson slid his on and snuggled back down into bed. He looked tired again, dark circles showing harshly against his still-pale face. Ellery sat down next to him and smoothed back his hair. "Nap. I'll call Mother and do some work. Would you rather go home later or get up super early?"

Jackson chuckled, the sound still filthy for all he looked like the cat's breakfast. "I'm a fan of the early morning walk of shame myself." His smile up at Ellery was almost impish.

"Okay. Good. Hamburgers for dinner?"

"Whatever." Jackson yawned. "Not picky."

Yeah, and not hungry either, given how much Ellery had been able to get him to eat. "Steak," Ellery decided, but Jackson's next breath was even and deep. Well, one thing at a time.

Ellery took his time, putting on a bathrobe before hanging his suit up. He'd just set up his laptop at the desk when his phone buzzed.

"Mother?"

"You sound guilty. What are you doing?"

Oh God. "Well, Jackson and I got out of deposition a little early. We thought we'd take some time to ourselves—"

"You rented a room and did unmentionable things," she said. "It happens. Will you be home in the morning?"

"Yes—I need to drop Jackson off before work."

She lowered her voice. "Is he sleeping now?"

"Yeah."

"Good." They shared a moment of worry, and Ellery thought it might always be this way, worrying about Jackson. "There's something I need to talk to you about, and you need to share with him, I think."

Apprehension shot an ice dart up his spine. "Shoot."

"You know Harold Knudsen, my client who contracts for the military?"

Ellery frowned. "I guess. I mean, I know his firm. I never really thought about him personally."

His mother's sigh on the other end was painfully familiar. "Yes, Ellery, there are real people behind the corporations. I believe us liberals have even made it a slogan."

"That was the conservatives, Mother. John Oliver did a thing about it. But anyway, Knut Harold—"

"Harold Knudsen—don't be a child. He got an ultimatum from an obscure branch of the military he'd never heard from before today."

That dart spread its icy poison to Ellery's lungs. "Behavioral engineering?"

"Close. Soldier Modification."

Ellery frowned. "That can't be real."

"Oh, I assure you it was real—as in they *really* threatened to pull all of their contracts from Harold's company if he didn't change his counsel."

"Mother?" His voice was saturated with worry. This was his parents' income, and Ellery was *not* going to be the reason they lost money.

"Darling, you do know your father is independently wealthy. Money in six banks—that sort of thing. And I have ten clients bigger than Knudsen. I told him to go ahead and hire my old protégé, the one who started her own firm. She squeezed him in, but I needed you to know, somebody in the military is putting the squeeze on *me.*"

Ellery's breath grew shallow. "And on me."

"By proxy, I would imagine. Yes." She chuckled. "I do believe they thought I would try to control you. I find that highly amusing."

But he couldn't smile. "I think we're going to have to look into that," he said slowly, thinking of Karl Lacey and some hellhole in Nevada that nobody was supposed to know about.

And two mechanics in a dust-speck town who would need to be—very carefully—disturbed.

"Not now," his mother said, showing no indication whatsoever that Ellery was not the sort of son who would be controlled. Her voice softened. "You and Jackson need a break. We're spending tomorrow together before I leave, and then I believe you have your first Thanksgiving before you come back to Boston. Am I correct?"

She damned well knew she was. She and Jade had walked a careful line around her presence. Jade had politely asked and Taylor had politely declined and then moved her flight forward as a reason. She'd told Ellery quietly that someday she hoped to be welcome at the Cameron table—but this Thanksgiving they were going to be thankful about Jackson, and she wanted to give them room to do that in their own way.

"I told Jade I'd make German cabbage," Ellery told Taylor, although he was pretty sure she knew. "She seems to think it's a myth and nobody really eats that crap."

His mother laughed. Ellery had loathed German cabbage as a child, but as he'd grown, it had become one of his favorite things. "Make sure you use at least a pound of bacon and the good vinegar." Because God forbid he be allowed to remember the recipe on his own.

"And the dark brown sugar," he finished. "I remember."

"Good. Then I'll see Jackson early tomorrow, and you have a half day before we go out to lunch. Our schedule is all set, then."

"Don't forget to feed—"

"This enormously inappropriate cat. Yes. I understand. He has made it known that his bowl is half-full—I take it that is wrong."

Ellery had to laugh. "Yes, it is wrong."

"What about his place *on the table*?"

"Well, it's wrong, and sick, but sadly not unusual."

Her voice darkened. "We shall just see about that." Then, "Take care of him tonight. Let him heal over the holidays. This other thing—you two can't go after it guns blazing if he's not strong."

"I understand," Ellery said. In bed, Jackson was curled in on himself, the covers over his eyes to block out the light. The back of his hand still bore faint bruises from the IV, and he had an appointment in two days to get the last of the stitches out of his stomach. Ellery wondered how long he would nap before the nightmares began. "We'll get him healthy. See you tomorrow, Mother."

"See you tomorrow."

She hung up, and he ordered room service like he'd promised and then spent an hour answering routine e-mails. After he sent the last one, he closed his laptop with finality and turned his chair to watch Jackson sleep.

"Food coming?" Jackson mumbled, not surprising him. A true sleep would be too much to ask for.

"Yes—a couple of minutes, I think. Hungry?"

Jackson sat up in bed a little. "Cold," he said, voice husky. "Want to join me in bed?"

Ellery laughed shortly. "Not until food comes. I see what you're trying to do here, and I will *not* be caught bare-assed naked in front of the bellhop."

Jackson gave him a choirboy's smile, and Ellery rolled his eyes. "Our case—it's not over yet." He told Jackson about Harold Knudsen and the reason Karl Lacey really had to be investigated.

Now Jackson nodded thoughtfully. "You want to look into them after Thanksgiving?"

Ellery shook his head. "After Christmas," he said softly. "I still need to go to temple a couple of times, just to make sure."

Jackson frowned. "I thought we were holy and shit."

God. He was so beautiful, and Ellery had just gotten him back. "No, love. He gave you back to me. I need to make sure you're going to stay a while before we go back into the wilderness, okay?"

Jackson didn't seem to know where to look, but that was okay. Ellery was on the verge of embarrassing himself anyway. Room service knocked, and he felt like God had, once again, intervened.

They ate—Jackson not enough—and made love again and showered. They bantered and touched and fell asleep in front of the television while a rom-com played in the background.

And the thought wouldn't leave him that they weren't done yet.

God had given Jackson back to him—had given Jackson more lives than any normal cat could claim.

That usually only happened when the big guy had work for you to do.

Jackson and Ellery—they had more work to do.

Accompanying Stories

SOME OF the action previous to *Red Fish, Dead Fish* happened outside *Fish Out of Water.* Following are four stories that were posted on various blogs before I started writing *Red Fish, Dead Fish.*

Two of these stories involve Ace and Sonny from *Racing for the Sun*, and the action from these stories *is* discussed in *Red Fish, Dead Fish.*

No Day at the Beach

JACKSON SHIFTED in the front seat of the car, *willing* himself not to take another pain med, although the last one had worn off hours ago.

He was not going to be an addict.

And he was done living off Ellery's charity and the firm's paid sick leave. Yeah, sure—they promised they'd hold his job for him as long as he needed it, but there were always cops retiring who thought PI'ing for a defense firm was a cushy way to beef up their social security.

Jackson was there first, dammit.

He shifted again and grunted, pulling out his binoculars to see if the prosecution's star witness had emerged from the bar yet. Nope. This guy was getting good and plastered before he got behind the wheel.

Jackson checked his phone to make sure it was charged up and ready to take pictures that would blow the witness out of the water. The phone started to ring, and he almost dropped it, straining his healing shoulder in an effort to get the phone back.

"God*dammit*!" he snarled, just as he pushed the button.

"Nice to hear from you too. Why aren't you home?"

"Because home is still being repaired," he said sulkily. He had another month before the AC unit came in, and the structural damage still had not been repaired. He was starting to suspect his tenant was bribing the construction crews to go slow in the hopes that he and Ellery stuck and Jackson wouldn't need to move back in.

The idea *was* tempting.

Apparently Ellery thought so too.

"Bullshit. Home is where your cat is throwing up on my loafers. Right now that's here on American River, which is where I am, which is how I know you're *not*. What are you doing?"

A guy came out of the bar, and Jackson stiffened and then relaxed. Nope. Not his scumbag.

"Waiting for the star witness of the prosecution for the Stanley case to drive intoxicated."

"Are you kidding me?" Ellery's voice broke, which was adorable.

"Well, you said he was usually unflappable."

"I know what I said."

"You said he was a perfect witness, and you wish you had something on him."

"I know what I said!"

"You said that if only you could puncture this guy's credibility, you could give poor Gilbert Stanley a chance to stay out of jail because just this once, he wasn't doing anything wrong, and he really does take care of his saintly old mother in San Di—"

"*I know what I said!*" Ellery roared. "I did *not* mean for you to go back on stakeout so soon after you got out of the hospital!"

"Well, what did you expect me to do? Spend my days down at the river, cooking on the beach?"

"You have three months of paid leave and the most luxurious you can possibly get is the river?"

"Where do you expect me to go? San Diego? Those beaches are dangerous—haven't you read the headlines?"

Ellery's long-suffering sigh indicated that yes, he had read the headline Jackson had sent him as a joke. "An Epic Lego Shipwreck Has Been Washing Thousands of Legos Onto Beaches," he intoned dryly. "It's hardly life-threatening, Jackson. It might even give you something to play with while you're there."

"Don't I get to play with you?" Jackson mock pouted. "You're going to send me down to a bustling seaside town to get maimed by Legos, and I don't even get to play with that thing you don't want me to le-go?" He chuckled, because puns! They beat recrimination and guilt.

Apparently Ellery wasn't a fan. "If I take two weeks off and come with you, will you for fuck's sake stop working and heal?"

Jackson grunted and put the phone on speaker. This guy who couldn't walk straight—this was his scumbag. "I am *trying* to help you wrap up your case," he pouted. "Hold on a second." *Click.* And there was the guy emerging from the bar. And *click.* There was the guy obviously staggering. And *click*, there he was on his knees, throwing up. Goddammit.

"Ellery, here, I need to move the car and call the cops, okay?"

"Dammit, Jackson, you'd better not wreck the fucking car!"

Yeah, sure. Whatever. Jackson hit speed dial for his one friend left in highway patrol.

"Davis?"

"Rivers? What in the hell—this is my work line!"

"I know. But I'm at a dive bar on F Street, taking pictures of a guy who's about to get behind the wheel after throwing up in the gutter. I don't want that on my conscience. Do you?"

"Oh Jesus. No. Can you stop him?"

"I'm on it," Jackson muttered, easing his new Honda CR-V into traffic. The guy was parallel parked, so blocking him was easy. But it wasn't going to make Jackson a whole lot of friends.

He cruised forward and stopped next to the drunk guy's vehicle, pulling just forward enough that for the guy to get out would mean using his passenger door. Then he put the car in Park, turned on his hazard lights, and pulled out his Sudoku so he could settle in for the wait.

Then Emile Dellacorte staggered to his feet and hauled his puke-ridden carcass to the driver's side of his old Mercedes, swearing at Jackson as he wobbled.

"Get out of my way, asshole!"

"Sorry! Car broke down! Won't get out of Park!"

Emile started swearing at him, and Jackson rolled his eyes and feigned deafness while rolling up the window.

It was probably a dick move to antagonize a drunk guy—at least Jackson thought so in retrospect.

That was *not* what he was thinking when Emile got into his car, revved his engine, and took off the brakes.

GOD, THOSE highway patrol guys could *talk*.

Two hours later, Jackson dragged his sorry ass into Ellery's lovely, air-conditioned, comfortable home and limped to the couch. He collapsed there, wondering if he could convince Billy Bob, his cat, to go get him his pain meds, the rockin' ones in the bathroom cabinet that he didn't carry with him because they didn't let him drive, and tried not to take anyway because reasons.

"Jackson?" Ellery came out of the kitchen smelling like herbs and vegetables and some sort of chicken. He could cook. It shouldn't have endeared him to Jackson, but it did. "Jackson, are you okay? Oh my God! Your face! Is that—did your airbag deploy?"

"Sorry about my face," Jackson mumbled, "And yes. Yes, the airbag *did* deploy. Davis had the Honda towed to the shop and dropped me off."

Davis, one of Jackson's few friends from his academy days, had almost shit himself laughing too. Jackson Rivers? *Here?* Well, it was a mystery to Jackson as well.

"Oh my God! Jackson! Did you even go to the doctor?" Ellery's hands on his cheeks, checking his bruises and the bag burn on his forehead, felt absurdly wonderful. "Why didn't you call me?"

"No doctor," Jackson said, stubborn. "Had enough of that noise for a long time." He'd spent over a month healing from a gunshot wound. God, what a waste of time.

"Fine—can I get you something?"

"Pain meds?" he almost whimpered, hating himself. "Please?"

"On one condition." Ellery folded his arms, glaring, his dark brown eyes snapping and serious and his long jaw set just as stubbornly as Jackson's.

"Will it get me a giant ibuprofen?"

"Sure. In fact, we'll go for the Vicodin. I'm going to call Arizona and tell her that her witness is fucked, and she's going to ask the judge for a continuance. It won't do her any good, but it will give me two weeks between shit I absolutely must do."

"Oh God," Jackson moaned, knowing where this was going.

"I want to hear that some from you," Ellery told him sweetly. "When you're naked, in bed, and on the bottom. But right now—"

"Oh God!"

"Yes. All I want to hear from you is that you and me are going to fly down to San Diego, and you are going to spend a week on the beach while you recover!"

"My cat—"

"Can live with Jade. She'll agree with me on this, Jackson. She thinks you're overdoing it too."

"Oh God!" Couldn't he even—

"Jackson?" Ellery had drawn even with him and was staring at him from about six inches away.

"Yes?" he gasped, his arousal stirring in spite of his pain.

"We're going to San Diego—"

"Do you want me to maim myself on giant Legos?"

"Sure. Knock yourself out. I also want you to fuck me blind. Several times. And then sleep in the sun to recover."

Jackson slow-blinked and tried to wipe the picture of a giant Lego guy supine in the sand right out of his catalog of mental images.

He replaced it with Ellery, supine in bed, legs spread, pale, patrician features blotchy and flushed with lovemaking, Jackson's come running from his mouth and backside, too stoned with sex to move.

"Okay," he said helplessly. "Fine. You want to take me to the beach, I don't mind."

Ellery's shark smile showed that Jackson had caved easy, but Jackson couldn't hate himself for *that*. "That's a good boyfriend. Let me go get you some drugs."

Abruptly Jackson's aches fell back on his body with a vengeance, and he accepted the meds gratefully.

Not even Vicodin could obliterate that image of Ellery in bed, though. It was totally worth going to the beach if he and Ellery could make that come true.

Redirecting the Blast—
A few words from Ace

THERE'S THINGS you have to remember about living with a ticking time bomb.

Thing the first—just 'cause you can't hear it ticking doesn't mean the mechanism ain't a "go."

Thing the second—just 'cause the bomb will probably not go off when you're in the room don't mean you won't get hurt.

Thing the third—it's possible to control the blast.

Or so I hoped. 'Cause the kid holding the gun at Alba's head was looking scared and shaky—and Sonny was looking like a dirty bomb.

The day had started out okay. Since them doings in Bakersfield a year ago, Sonny and I been lying low. As soon as he got out of the hospital, we came back to our little gas station in Victoriana and continued doing what we'd been doing before—making a life. I still drove the souped-up Ford, but we only topped 150 out in the desert, Sonny by my side, as the purple shadows lowered. No more racing, like I promised him, and the money from my last… adventure… had kept us going until we made enough business to keep us in the black.

It also provided enough money for a college fund for Alba, our part-time help. Since she'd stopped wearing tight titty blouses and a truckload of makeup, she'd decided she was gonna be a good girl. I was looking for words to tell her that someday, right time, right people, she could wear whatever she goddamned pleased, but for right now, "good girl" meant schooling, and Sonny and me were all for that. So was Jai, our giant gay Russian enforcer, who would have stayed with us for minimum wage but was now fiercely loyal since we paid him enough to drive to Vegas once in a while to get laid.

Jai was very protective of Sonny and Alba. Once he figured out that I killed the guy who hurt Sonny, I had the feeling he would have blown me every day and polished my rim to boot, except that would have meant me cheating on Sonny, and, well, that left him in something of a quandary. Let's just say Jai woulda done unspeakable things for the three of us and leave it at that.

Well, I wished I coulda left it at that.

Sonny and Jai were under a Ford F-150 in the auto bay, dicking around with a transmission that should have been shot, burned, and buried about ten years before, and I was going over the ordering with Alba.

She squinted through the small service window at their feet sticking out under the truck and listened to their bickering. Sonny spoke redneck, and Jai spoke redneck with a thick Russian accent, and they were both talking about car parts using pet names developed over nearly a year and a half of working together.

"That don't sound like English," Alba said after a moment or two of us just staring at them and listening.

"They're gonna ship one of those guys who invent space languages out here to figure out what the fuck that is," I agreed. "Think they'll give us money?"

Alba rolled her eyes. "They don't pay dumbshits for being stupid," she said. "But I need my mommy not to come hear them. She'll think that stuff I do at school, I'm doing it wrong."

At that moment a dying Kia Sportage came chugging into the lot, blowing black smoke and rattling loud enough to echo off the distant mountains. As Alba and I stared and Sonny and Jai shoved out from under the truck in the bay, a thin kid got out wearing a black hoodie, black track pants, and black tennis shoes in the 110-degree heat.

I stared. The last time I'd worn an outfit like that, I'd killed a man.

The kid was holding a hand to his side, and blood was dripping down to the white foam tread of his trainer, and I figured this kid was not that far off from that level of desperate.

"Get down," I said to Alba.

"But—"

"Just get down under the counter. I don't want him seeing you!" Because she was a girl, and desperate men preyed on the weak. She wasn't weak, but he didn't know that.

"I need someone out here!" the kid shouted. "Someone get out here and fix my fuckin' car!"

I shot a look behind me to the auto bay and shook my head at Jai and Sonny to let me take care of this. Sad, yes, but true—I really am their best bet in a crisis. My hands at my sides, palms out, my eyes level, movements steady, I took a few steps out of the cashier's cubicle and then out into the searing desert sun.

"I see you," I said calmly. "And I see your car. And you're both banged up some. Honestly, I think some bandages and antiseptic, you got a better chance than the car."

The kid swallowed and looked behind him, like he was expecting retribution to be riding down his ass with cherry lights on top. "I… I can't do hospitals," he said, voice weepy. "And… and I gotta get this money to a friend…." His voice cracked. "She's…." He reached behind him and pulled out the gun I'd just known had been tucked in the back of his pants. "It doesn't matter, man. Just fix the goddamned car!"

"Okay," I said, hands still out. "But I'm going to have to drive it into the bay. Do you want to sit next to me while I do that or—"

"Wait—who was that?"

I didn't look. "Who was what?"

"That girl—yeah, you go ahead and drive the car into the bay. I'll be right there with the gun pointed at that girl!"

"There is no girl," I said in my strongest voice, because maybe Alba would get the fuck back down and I could drive the car to San Diego and crash it into the police station, which was my plan.

The shot went wide—as he'd meant it to—but still. The weapon discharged into the desert to my left, and it doesn't matter how many times you hear them or how many times you fire them, a gun report should do something to a man, or he's forgotten why he's alive.

"Move the fuckin' car!" he yelled, and then, never turning his back to me with that gun, he edged himself alongside the cashier's cubicle and into the door I'd just come out of. Alba was standing by that time, her hands up, mouthing "I'm sorry, Ace" at me like that was gonna help if she got her brains blown to kingdom come.

I moved the car, making the assessment as it rattled into the bay. Blown gasket, blown pistons, hole in the radiator, transmission fluid a fuckin' memory. This thing should not have been running.

It gave its last gasp as I pulled up to the bay, and I coasted it in next to the truck and waited for Sonny and Jai to poke themselves back from under the truck. Smart boys.

"He's got a gun," Sonny muttered. "In there with Alba!"

"Jai, go fetch Sonny's car, okay?"

"What?"

"What in the—"

I held up my hand. "He's hurt and he's desperate," I said levelly. "We're going to give him transportation and let him get the fuck out of here. Odds are good he's going to pass out in twenty minutes anyway, and if he's not here, he can't hurt us."

"But someone on the road—" Sonny said, and my heart warmed. These last two years, he'd grown a little. Part of that growing meant he didn't just look at me, or even just Alba and Jai. He looked a little bigger now.

But we couldn't.

"Look—just get him the car. Maybe I can get rid of the gun and we can get him to the hospital or something, but first, let's get him out of there with Alba!"

Bam!

If I hadn't just taken my morning constitutional, I swear it would have been in my shorts. But I saw the sun shining through the hole in the auto bay and realized he'd fired over our heads.

"What're you doing?" he screamed, and I glared at Jai to go do what I said, then turned and approached the cashier's cubicle, palms out.

"Your car's done for," I told him. "We're getting you one that runs."

"What?"

I took a few more steps so I could see them. He had his arm around Alba's shoulders, and she was holding on to his wrist and glaring at him. I suspected that if he pointed the gun anywhere but her one more time, he was going to be bleeding a damned sight more than he already was.

"Your car—last time I saw something like that, it took us a month and special parts flown in. It's fuckin' toast. We're getting you my boyfriend's car so you can get the fuck out of our lives."

His face crumpled. "But that would be stealing," he said nakedly. "I'm no thief."

"What in the fuck did he just say?"

Oh God—Sonny was behind me, and I stepped to the right in an attempt to block him.

"Who's that?" the kid asked in tears. "What does he want?"

"You're not a thief? You come in here and hold a gun on a sixteen-year-old kid, and you think you're some kind of a hero?"

Oh God.

"That," I said distinctly, "is my boyfriend, who's about to give up his car so you can get your gun away from our friend."

"I just need a fuckin' car!" the kid cried. "Man, they got my sister, and I had to run the drugs to Vegas and then get back with the money, but the guys in Vegas had guns, and they started shooting before I could even hand off the drugs, and the guys in Chula Vista got my sister and—" He let out a little whimper then, and the arm with the gun fell.

Alba put one fist in the other and elbowed him right in the chest, and that was when the gun went off. I felt a ripping pain through my leg, but that didn't stop me from grabbing Sonny as he went hauling into the tiny cubicle with nothing but a tire iron in his hand. He caught me in the head with his upward swing, and that did it. I went down and didn't wake up for twenty minutes.

"Ace?"

I was lying on my back in our little house, with a familiar weight on my chest and a small tongue licking my cheek. "Duke?" I said, confused. The Chihuahua didn't usually talk.

"No, dammit, it's me."

I looked up at Sonny, who was sitting, red-eyed and repentant, on the floor next to the couch.

"Where's Alba?"

"She's fine. We closed up shop, and her mom came and got her. She'll be back in tomorrow."

My head ached fiercely, and I stared at him. "She'll be what?"

"Was really sweet. Kept thanking us for trying to save her. Said it was real nice how we gave up my car to make sure she was okay."

I was not tracking. "The kid…?" God. Poor kid. Desperation did not make people do nice things—but he'd been appalled by the realization that he was holding a gun on a young girl. Probably hadn't thought of her as a person before that. Of course, if he'd hurt Alba or Sonny, I would have beaten his brains to powder and not given a shit.

"Jai wrapped his side—through and through, so he should be fine if he gets antibiotics. Then he put the kid and the drugs into my car and took off."

I tried to process this. "Took… off? In your car?"

Sonny nodded soberly. "I think…. Ace, I think as long as the kid and his sister are okay, we'd better not ask too much about what happens after that, okay?"

Oh Lord. This wrong side of the law thing got murky. "The kid's going to be okay?"

"Yeah. You went down, and he thought he'd shot you, and he just fell apart. Dropped the gun, cried. I got you into the house and checked your leg—it was a graze, by the way." As he said it, I could feel the stinging pain of it. Hurt like a sumbitch too—but not as much as my head.

"Jesus, you really clocked me," I mumbled.

Sonny nodded. "I did." He put a bag of ice on my temple where the tire iron had caught me hardest, and the cold woke me up. "You need to stay awake, now that you're up. I looked shit up on the computer—we've got some Tylenol with codeine, and you can have that as soon as you sit up."

I struggled up, holding the ice compress to my head with one hand and moving Duke to my lap with the other. "Oh dear God," I muttered. "This hurts. I remember this—this is no good."

"Yeah." Sonny let out a breath and thrust two tablets into my hand and followed it up with water. I felt better after I drank the water, even, and figured once the painkillers kicked in, I might be okay. For a moment I was quiet, and the only sounds in our little house were my breathing and Duke's little dog whimpers as he relocated.

"I'm sorry," Sonny said quietly. He'd climbed up on the couch when I hadn't been paying attention, and I lifted my arm so he could put his head on my shoulder. His blond hair had grown shaggy in recent months, and I liked it that way. He didn't look vulnerable or naked like he had when it had been shaved down to his scalp.

"Was an accident," I said.

"Yeah, but the coming unglued part wasn't. That was me just being me," he said bitterly. "You had that kid calming down, and I just… you and Alba and the fucking gun and I lost it."

I laughed a little. "Yeah, but you've lost it worse." He had. He wasn't great with people—never would be. "And you were afraid for Alba, and you didn't used to give a shit."

"But not for a long time," he reminded me soberly.

"Yeah. I know. But makes me proud still. You were doing what I was doing, Sonny. Your best for your people."

He sighed again. "I… I just gotta think better, you know?"

"Well, I put myself in the damned booth. I just thought… you know…."

"If we gave him the car he'd go the fuck away?"

"Well, yeah." Because cause and effect, right?

"Well, it worked. He went the fuck away." And right before I was going to ask about Jai, his phone buzzed. He reached into his pocket and pulled it out and grunted. "Jai's fine," he said. "Took the kid to the hospital." The phone pinged. "And I need to call the police and report my car stolen."

My eyes widened, sore head or not. "Here," I said, flailing for my coveralls on the floor next to the couch. "Let me use my phone."

I spun a story, oh yes I did. How the thief shot at me and missed, then whacked me on the head, and how we'd had the keys in Sonny's little beater Corolla so we could move it around easy, and Sonny found me after he got back from the *ampm* across the street with sodas and took me inside to treat me.

The cops took it down, every word, the wound on my head and my leg to verify, and the car was registered all legal-like. The local cops took down the info and grunted and asked me if I wanted to go to the doctor's, but I wasn't excited about that, so they left me alone.

As soon as they were gone, I collapsed on the couch and called Alba.

"Alba?"

"Mr. Ace?"

"You didn't work today."

"I'll tell Mommy. Do I work tomorrow?"

"Do you still want to?" Because Jesus.

"You gave up your car for me. I think Jai's killing people. I'm safe there. It's good."

She hung up, and I had to give the girl credit for practicality. I was a two-term veteran, and I didn't think I could have been so casual.

Sonny had kicked up the air-conditioning in the house, and the sun was starting to go down by the time it was all done, and I was fine with sitting around in my boxers and letting television wash over me like the sea. Sonny was fine with feeding me and making sure I didn't puke and petting me every now and then too.

Into that quiet, Sonny said, "So, where do you think Jai's gonna hide the bodies?"

I grunted. "Sonny, that has got to be a question we never, ever ask him, okay?"

Sonny nodded soberly, but his lips were twisted up. "He said he got the girl away from the bad guys. Think he's like a superhero?"

"Deadpool or the Punisher?" Because hadn't those guys been sort of dark and below the law?

"Yeah!" Sonny said, eyes big. "We know Deadpool!"

I didn't remind him that I'd been the Punisher a year and a half ago and that it wasn't that glamorous. Then he said, "But I don't care how many bodies he's buried, he's still not half the hero you are, for trying not to let things go south." He kissed my cheek then, and I closed my eyes tiredly. So, okay. There was still blood and still crime and still shit we did not plan on, but at least Sonny appreciated trying not to kill people. And hey—I'd been out for twenty minutes, and he'd apparently kept his cool.

I was calling it a win.

But I was going to have to be really careful about not dying until I was sure he'd take that as well as he'd take knocking me on my ass for twenty minutes. You just never knew.

Fish in the Desert

ELLERY'S BLUE-BLOODED roots were never so apparent.

He stood in the auto bay of the tiny garage in the middle of Victoriana, California, and looked like a sweaty guy in a pricey suit. His normally slicked-back mahogany-brown hair hung straight and lank in his eyes, and his once-white shirt showed dust creases where he'd pushed it up around his elbows in the ungodly September heat. His suit—which would have been perfectly fine in Sacramento, where things were, thank God, in the eighties at the moment—was a prison down here in San Diego, and he kept doing a little shimmy like it was sticking to his creases.

Well, it was tight enough.

But still, he was trying to maintain professionalism, and Jackson tried to keep his eyes from rolling out of his head.

This interview was not going well.

Ace Atchison seemed like a decent enough guy. Although he sported a healing wound on his forehead that looked like it could have used stitches, and walked with a limp, that didn't detract from a handsome young serviceman with dark brown hair, gold-brown eyes, square jaw, and a way of gritting his teeth, lowering his head, and glaring at the world straight. Between that and biceps the size of softballs—and as soft as hardballs—the guy was damned easy on the eyes. And amiable too, in a good old boy sort of way.

He'd been helpful in the extreme—lots of "Yes, sir," and "I'm sorry sir," and "Well, sir, Sonny and me, we woulda seen that, sir," and not a drop of goddamned truth.

"Look, Mr. Atchison," Ellery said for maybe the fourteenth time.

"Ace is fine," he said, nodding and winking. "Now, I can see you're getting upset, but I'm not sure what I can help you with here. Your guy, the one you're trying to defend, says that he could not possibly have killed anybody in Sacramento because he was down here shooting a kid in Las Vegas. And that we would know that, because he heard the kid came by our little flea-shit shop to fix his broke car."

Ellery nodded definitely. “That would be correct,” he rasped, wiping sweat from his eyes with a handkerchief that used to match his shirt.

Jackson had two bottles of water in the pocket of his cargo shorts, and he pulled one out, cracked it, and handed it over. Ellery took it without looking at him or even nodding thanks. Jackson rolled his eyes—and kicked Ellery in the ankle.

Ellery glared at him, but Ace kept talking. “Now, see, I don’t remember that. And I’da remembered that, ’cause you say the car was shot, and it’s hard to fix a shot-up car, sir, so I think maybe this kid stopped by another gas station.” He paused and raised his voice so it could carry over the knocking of wrenches coming from under a Dodge Caravan on the rails in the bay proper. “Sonny, do you remember a kid coming by here with a shot-up car?”

“No, Ace, I do not.” The words were staccato and wooden—and rehearsed.

“Jai, do you remember anything like that?”

“Nyet.” The Russian accent sounded wholly authentic. And deep and resonant enough for a big, big man.

Ace looked up at both of them and smiled a knee-melter of a lie. “Well, sir, you heard ’em. Sonny and Jai don’t remember, so it must not have happened.”

“But the police said you got shot and coldcocked by a thief—we have that on record!” Ellery’s voice cracked, and Jackson wasn’t sure he’d ever seen the man so discombobulated by a lie.

“Well, yeah. But, you know, I was coldcocked. I can’t remember much more than waking up. Alba wasn’t here. Jai and Sonny were out. The guy stole our money and Sonny’s car. Isn’t that right, guys?”

The two men in the auto bay both said “Yup!” and “Da!” at the same time.

Ace turned and smiled gamely. “And that’s what we told the police, and that’s the God’s honest truth.”

The sound Jackson made was a cross between a snort and a “bullshit” and a cough, and Ellery glared at him again—but this time with his mouth open, and Jackson thought it was time to change tactics.

“I’m sorry,” he said with a smile. “My friend here has some other questions to ask you about that day, but I’m telling you, I gotta piss like a racehorse. Do you folks have a restroom here?”

ACE'S LOOK in Jackson's direction had a smirk in it. Ace knew what Jackson was doing, Jackson knew that Ace knew, but Ace was pretty damned sure there was nothing to find. "That's fine. Alba over there has the key to the john around the corner. Let us know if it's not stocked or gross or anything. She prides herself in keeping that thing clean."

"Thank you, sir. Ellery, be nice to Mr. Atchison. I have the feeling that's about all he knows." But he kept eye contact with Ace as he said it, so Ace would know that he knew that every word of his story was grade AAA bullshit.

The teenager behind the counter wore a bright turquoise T-shirt—a little tight but not uncomfortable—and a bright flowered comb in her glossy raven's-wing hair. She had a schoolbook in front of her, but her eyes were all for Ellery and Ace in the center of the auto bay—and for the two sets of feet sticking out from under the Dodge Caravan.

"Heya," he said, flashing his sweetest smile at her. "I understand you can give me the key to the bathroom."

Her wide, expressive brown eyes went narrow and flat. "Did Ace tell you yes? I'm not doin' nothin' Ace didn't say."

"Yeah." Jackson nodded sincerely. "Ace said it was fine. Told me to let you know if the paper wasn't stocked."

The girl—Alba—swore at him in Spanish. Jackson kept his face impassive, and she told him that if he said one goddamned word about the state of her pristine bathroom with the potpourri she picked out just for Ace, she would tell her gay cousin who lived in Twain Harte to come out of retirement as a brujo and curse off Jackson's balls.

Jackson endured it all with a straight face until she got to the part about his balls—he was still a little sore from the thought of his poor cat.

"Your cousin can leave my balls out of it," he said blandly in English. "Sweetheart, I just want to use the head."

She made a face at him and gave him the key before she buried her nose back in her book, but Jackson wasn't done yet.

"Chemistry?" he asked—in Spanish. "That's good. You look like a smart girl."

Alba looked up warily. She was a beautiful girl—but she probably heard that a lot. A girl who prided herself on her brains didn't hear praise for it nearly often enough. “Ace, he’s going to send me to college,” she said in English. “He and Sonny, they’re good men.”

And then, as though she’d revealed too much of herself, she went back to Chemistry, and Jackson took the hint. As he walked away from the cashier’s window, he noticed that to the side of the garage sat a small white house. Someone was trying to grow grass and was growing algae instead, and a yapping dog was losing his shit from inside. But the swamp cooler was on, probably to keep the dog comfy, and there were curtains in what looked to be the kitchen window by the porch stairs. Who lived here, he wondered. Ace? Sonny? Jai?

Probably Ace. By himself?

He rounded the corner just in time to see a black-bearded, bald man-mountain in blue coveralls escape from the restroom, wiping his hands hurriedly on his ass. He was pretty sure this one wasn’t Sonny.

“Heya there,” he said with a smile, running to catch the door before it slammed shut.

Man-mountain slammed it shut and eyed Jackson impassively as he approached.

“Well, that was unfriendly,” he said.

“You walk stiffly,” the man said, his voice thick with accent. “You are either horny or injured.”

Jackson choked on a laugh. “Oddly enough, injured and not horny.”

Man-mountain nodded thoughtfully. “The silly man in the suit is not bad-looking. Is he yours?”

Jackson swallowed past the relationship panic he’d been fighting since he’d been forced to move in with Ellery while his house was being fixed. “For the time being.”

To his surprise, Man-mountain—Jai?—slumped a little, looking defeated. “I would fuck you until you sobbed. I like the yellow hair.”

Jackson’s eyeballs were going to pop out of his head. “That’s, uh, flattering. And terrifying. And flattering. But I really do need to use the john.”

Jai waved his hand expansively behind him. “Do you? There is much desert that needs water.” He smiled, and his white teeth looked as big as roof tiles. “It is even the same color.”

Oh God—he couldn’t even stop it from coming out of his mouth. “Piss yellow is a coward’s color,” he said, lowering his head and getting ready to get beaten back into the ground.

But the giant just cocked his head. "Which is why it is a good place for burying cowards," he said, flashing more roof tiles at him. Then he stepped sideways out of the way. "Enjoy your piss, yellow-haired man."

Of course, after that conversation, Jackson really did need to pee. He finished, sweltering in the little bathroom attachment, and exited quickly after splashing water on his neck and forehead.

He ran straight into the slighter, shorter man in the blue coveralls. He had blond hair over his collar, blue-gray eyes, and a thin face. Pretty, in a faded sort of way, like he had to rub off layers of scared to find himself. He was stringy strong, not bulky at all, and would probably be tough as tree roots until he lived to be ninety.

This must be Sonny.

Jackson tried a smile again and wondered how Ellery was faring, banging his head against the brick wall in the auto bay.

"Hello there. Should I give you the key or get it back to Alba?"

"Ace didn't do anything," he said flatly.

"Uh, we didn't say he did." Sonny's eyes were cutting to the desert and back in hard little darts, like he was having trouble focusing on the goal. "We just—we just want to know if a kid came in here shot."

"Kid didn't do anything either. I mean, if one did. 'Cause he's the one that was shot, right? Kid that's shot, he's not going to be the bad guy. Just running from the bad guys."

Well, couldn't argue with that. "Yeah, well, the guy we're defending isn't great."

"Ace is," Sonny said, and Jackson thought that, should he have to fight one of them, the man-mountain or this rabid rat terrier here, he'd take the man-mountain. Sonny would sink needle teeth into Jackson's jugular and not let go.

"Is he, now? How'd he get hurt?"

Sonny looked down. "I did it. Swung my wrench wrong, nailed him in the head. Not his fault. None of it is his fault. He's a good guy." He fixed his eyes on Jackson's face again. "He's the best guy. Mine. You don't go fooling with Ace now, you hear?"

Oh hell. This was a surprise. "Well, as long as he doesn't go fooling with Ellery, I'm fine with that."

Sonny shook his head. "Ace takes care of people. Alba, Jai…." His voice trailed off. "Me. He takes care of me when shit goes south. You can't be yelling at Ace."

Oh hell. Sonny lived in the house too.

Jackson heard Ellery's voice raised loud enough to be heard over the small garage.

"I'll go fix that," he said calmly. "But look—I need you to tell me one thing, and then you'll never see us again."

"We'll see what the thing is," Sonny said cagily.

"If, say, a kid came by this garage, bleeding, what would you do?"

"That depends," Sonny said softly.

"On what?"

"On whether he was a bad kid or a good kid. If he was a good kid, just trying to get his sister back from bad guys, well then, we'd help him. If he was a bad kid and he held a gun on one of us, we'd hurt him."

That was oddly specific. "And if he was both?"

For the first time, Sonny met his eyes. "We'd do both."

Jackson nodded. "Well then. We'll be on our way."

"Will you be coming back?" Sonny asked, his voice hard and vulnerable at the same time.

"Not on your life," Jackson said grimly. Or his life. Or Ellery's life. Because Jackson had no idea that coming back to this place might not end in death or blood or terrifying sociopaths holding tightly on to their one true person by killing the whole world.

But it might.

He rounded the corner, and Ace hadn't broken a sweat—but Ellery had.

"Won't you even check the calendar?" he yelled.

Ace Atchison just smiled. "Well, sir, I could, but we're simple folk. If Alba didn't have to go to school, we might not even know where summer stopped and winter began. I mean, this is the desert, after all. Unless the rains come or it gets hot enough to cook a dog in the road, we don't always know."

"You know what month it is!"

"No you don't," Jackson said, grabbing Ellery's bicep and hauling him toward the Lexus.

"Jacks—"

"Sorry to bother you, Mr. Atchison!" Jackson called over his shoulder. "I promise you if you ever see us again, it's 'cause we're having car trouble on the way to Vegas and for no other reason!"

Ellery was literally digging in his heels, and Jackson just kept going, letting the hard soles of Ellery's shoes stir up little dust devils around his legs. "Jackson, he was just going to—"

"Not tell you a fucking thing," Jackson muttered, throwing Ellery into the car—passenger's side—and getting into the driver's side before Ellery could even scramble to the other side.

"Got your keys?" Jackson asked, and as Ellery was patting his pockets, Jackson used the push-button ignition and started the car. He didn't rip out of the dusty parking lot, because that would have resulted in a giant donut and Ellery's first aneurism. He accelerated at a leisurely pace and turned the car west, toward San Diego.

"Jackson—what in the hell?"

Jackson glanced at him and thought he looked rumpled and pissed and… oddly dear. Innocent. He hoped Ellery was innocent enough for what Jackson had to say next to appeal to him.

"Ellery, I want you to tell me Gordie Ripkin's story one more time."

Ellery huffed, put his seat belt on, and crossed his arms in front of him. "Gordon Ripkin, small-time thug, mob muscle, drug dealer, petty thief, conman. Pulled in for questioning literally two-dozen times, arrested once. Our time. Someone paid his bail and hired us to defend him."

"Awesome. So we're defending a scumbag. Go us. Now tell me his story."

"He is accused of shooting a store owner in Sacramento in June. He claims he couldn't have been, because he was involved in a drug throwdown in Vegas. He and another small-timer were hired for the moment, and some kid was supposed to deliver drugs in Vegas or his sister would eat it in San Diego. It was a double cross—the two bosses in charge had no intention of either giving up drugs or giving up money, and the kid and his sister were sacrifices in some big fucking game. Gordon and his buddy shot at the kid, but the kid drove off. He left a blood trail, and his car was leaking oil, so they followed him to the little shithole we just left."

"Victoriana," Jackson said, but seriously. How many shitholes were there on that road with a Carl's Jr./ampm, a service station, and a garage. And nothing else.

"Victoriana," Ellery confirmed. "Anyway—that's when things get fuzzy. Gordie and his buddy didn't see anything at the garage, so they took off toward San Diego to see if the kid made it back for his sister. They found no girl—but no buddies either, and a fuckton of blood."

"And then…." Jackson needed him to see it.

"And then they drove back to the people who hired them in Vegas and…."

"And some Russian mob—these guys were working Italian—but some Russian mob guy tells them that the shop is closed and they shouldn't be seen any farther south than Bakersfield. And that's when they drove to Sacramento, that day."

"Mm-hm…."

Ellery grunted. "I mean, it's an unlikely story."

"It is."

"If we can't find some corroboration, I'm going to tell him to plead out."

"It sounds poetic."

"But that doesn't change that we don't know what happened, and there might be a murderer out there."

Jackson sighed and edged up the speed in the rental. His own car was in the shop—he'd promised Ellery a trip down to San Diego, and Ellery asked if he could take care of some business before they parked themselves at the San Diego Marriott and spent most of their time naked in the hotel room when they weren't looking out over the harbor.

"Ellery, do you know why we discourage the hunting of rattlesnakes in California?"

Ellery frowned. "Because there's no reason to. They fulfill a vital part of the ecosystem, and they don't seek people out to kill them. If you introduce a pot-bellied pig or a natural predator to their environment, they don't overpopulate to the point that they seek out animals or humans. Mostly, you don't bother them, they don't come bother you."

"So I want you to keep this in mind. Imagine you are holding a small garage together by the seat of your pants—"

"And suspected illegal street racing," Ellery said dryly, because that had been in Ace Atchison's docket too.

"Still—not pulling in buckets of cash. And suppose, there you are one day when a kid in a broken car pulls into the service station and holds a gun on you—or one of your people."

"Then that kid would be dead," Ellery said seriously.

"Well, if it was me, yeah. But suppose you're the one used to talking people down, and you do this on a regular basis because your boyfriend is a borderline psychopath and you need to keep him together."

"You got all that from running into the little blond guy at the bathroom?"

Jackson remembered Sonny's eyes and shuddered. "Yup. So you talk the kid down, and your boyfriend comes unglued and accidentally nails you in the head with a wrench and the kid accidentally shoots you, and you wake up going, what the fuck?"

"You call the police?" Ellery asked, like it was obvious.

"Unless your trusted employee, and the other person you depended upon to keep your boyfriend from collecting scalps like beads, disappears with the kid to help him get his sister back. Your trusted employee is a big Russian guy with mob connections and a soft spot for young girls—not the pervy kind, just… you know…."

"Sisters," Ellery said softly. Well, yeah. Jackson had a soft spot for his own sister. That was the kind of person that would give a young girl a flowered comb that she'd wear with pride, even though it was hopelessly out of fashion.

"So the Russian guy disappears and comes back and tells you it's taken care of. And you don't ask another question."

"Because Russian mob?" Ellery asked, sounding appalled.

"Because family," Jackson insisted. "Because you were making your family safe and trying not to bite the unwary traveler. And your family closed ranks to take care of you."

"But…." Ellery flailed. "My client!"

"I'd hazard a guess that your client is more dangerous unprovoked than those people are if you walk into their place of business with a gun and insist that they help you so your sister doesn't die."

Ellery let out a groan of frustration. "We don't have any proof of any of this!"

"Nope," Jackson said smugly.

"But our client is going to be convicted!"

"And that's bad because…."

Ellery's voice dropped with embarrassment. "It will fuck up my record."

Jackson laughed, because Ellery didn't like to admit he was vain, which meant Jackson had him.

"Rattlesnakes, Ellery."

"A helpful part of the ecosystem."

"But don't step on them by accident." Ellery nodded, understanding, and Jackson smiled. "So, San Diego Marriott?"

"You owe me!" Ellery demanded.

"I owe you nothing but a dick up your ass. And you'll like it!"

"This is going to haunt me," Ellery muttered.

"Legally you are under no obligations here. This is purely speculation. The official record stands and backs us up. And all of the evidence is, more than likely, rotting in the desert. And I don't see it coming back."

Ellery grunted. "I'm not… this isn't…."

"I'll top all week, Ellery. All week."

"I like topping!"

Jackson laughed, low and dirty, and imagined Ellery on his stomach, thighs spread, body despoiled, monosyllabic with satiated lust.

"So do I."

"What if I think of a reason—oohhh…."

Jackson squeezed his thigh, then higher, then higher, steering with one hand. "All week."

"You are still injured."

"We shall find ways."

"I want to top," Ellery said petulantly, and Jackson found him, swelling under his boxers. He swallowed audibly. "Eventually."

"Are we going to tell the police about that little service station in Victoriana?" Jackson asked silkily.

Ellery melted into the leather upholstery, thighs spread. Yeah, it had been a long time since Jackson had been able to top. "Nothing to tell," Ellery mumbled. "You know I'd do it if we had even one scrap of proof…."

"Sure. Sure you would."

"Can we stop on the way and nail each other?"

"A shower, Ellery?"

"Oh God. You suck."

"I do—I suck a lot. I suck, I rim, I swallow…."

"Hurry, Jackson. We've wasted enough of our vacation already."

"Sayin'."

Birthday Fish

JACKSON FROWNED at the mail on the table. His was still being sent to his duplex, and he was starting to wonder when he should fix that.

If. If he should fix that.

If he should fix that by moving out, right?

"Mother sent you a birthday card," Ellery said, handing a mauve envelope to Jackson as he walked by.

Jackson reached out with his weak arm, determined to rehabilitate his recently repaired shoulder. *Twinge!* He hissed in a breath, and Ellery glared at him. A few months before, Jackson would have said that look in his eyes was cold disapproval, but now he knew better.

That particular look was hot irritation.

"A week, Jackson. Give it a week."

"Your mother sent me a card?" he asked, not taking the bait. Yeah, sure, Ellery wanted him to take it easy. Ellery wanted him to move in too, but Jackson was… well, it would be easy. He'd love to move in. Ellery's house was wonderful, Jackson's cat loved it here, and Jackson didn't mind either—but he didn't want to impose.

Didn't want to get too comfy.

Who knew when he'd drop the last straw of irritation on Ellery's back and Ellery would ask him to leave?

Yeah, just as well Jackson's duplex would be repaired in a month or two, right?

"Did you hear me about the shoulder?"

Jackson glared back. "Why is your Lucy Satan sending me birthday cards? My birthday was last month. How did she even know?"

"Did you tell her?"

Jackson frowned. "Jade or Kaden might have—I was in the hospital. A lot of people were talking about me."

"There you go," Ellery said.

Did *you* know it was my birthday?" He couldn't remember ever discussing it with Ellery. They'd worked at the same law firm for years—

Ellery as a defense attorney and Jackson as a PI—before they'd bonded over a case defending Jackson's best friend.

They'd just been getting used to the idea of being lovers when Jackson had gotten shot and his house destroyed.

"No, I didn't know I missed your birthday," Ellery said, annoyed. "My mother had to tell me. If you can avoid wrecking the car or bleeding between now and when I get home tomorrow night, I was going to take you out."

Jackson blinked. "Why?"

"For your birthday, asshole! Oh my God. I *know* Jade and Kaden had to celebrate your birthday. They seem like perfectly normal people, and somebody had to have baked you a cake at some point, Jackson. Why are you being dense?"

"Because it was last month!"

"But you missed it! C'mon, Jackson—making up for someone's birthday is standard operating procedure—I know you know this!"

Yes, Toni Cameron had made him birthday cakes after she'd taken him under her wing. Yes, Jade and Kaden remembered his birthday—he'd gotten a kiss on the cheek from his hospital bed this year. Next year he was expecting a phone call and probably a gift certificate from both of them because that's as elaborate as they got. He returned the favor for them and for Kaden's wife, Rhonda, and their kids, River and Diamond.

But he'd never had a lover, male or female—with the exception of Jade, but she mostly didn't count that way—make him a birthday celebration.

As promiscuous as he'd been before Ellery, he'd usually made it a point to sleep alone on his birthday.

"I don't…. It's not a thing," he said with dignity. Then, almost accusingly, "When's *your* birthday? For all I know, it happened already too, and you're just waiting to hold it over me that I didn't know when your birthday is!"

Ellery blinked at him, mouth gaping open. Billy Bob jumped on the lovely oak kitchen table and curled up on the embroidered satin runner, and Ellery ignored him, which was unheard-of. He was clearly still in shock.

"I'll be in the backyard," Jackson muttered. "I've got some work to do."

Ellery let him go, and Jackson took his laptop—and his birthday card. The backyard was well kept—thick grass, mown to a good length for a toddler to play on, and pruned jasmine around the wooden fence. Ellery's backyard was the sort of place family movies were set in. Jackson couldn't stop spending time there, now that the weather was nice. He sat on the porch, under the overhang, kicking back on a lounge chair to work. He was in the middle of running down leads on Ellery's latest case to see what he could dig up on the witnesses who seemed to be coming after Ellery's guy for plain meanness. Once he'd set the computer to run searches, he opened the card.

"Cute," he muttered. She'd sent him a kid's birthday card, with a brightly colored lion and a cat counterpart and a goofy little rhyme. It was the expensive kind, the kind that cost three dollars at the grocery store. He'd never gotten one of these, really. Jade and Kaden had made him cards—and he'd been thrilled beyond words to get them, because his own mother was usually too high to remember his birthday.

But this—this little kid's birthday card with the gift certificate to Baskin-Robbins— this was….

Painful and thoughtful at once.

Ellery's mother was a scary fucking woman.

He stared at the card, absurdly touched. When Ellery came out to sit in the lounge chair next to him, he wasn't sure enough of his own composure to look up. He patted Ellery's hand on his shoulder when he squeezed, though.

"January 12," Ellery said quietly. "Capricorn."

"August 22," Jackson said back. "Drunken high school Thanksgiving orgy."

"A Leo," Ellery told him. He'd heard that before—didn't everybody want to know what their sign was? "We shouldn't get along at all."

Jackson let out a halfhearted bark of laughter. "We don't."

"We seem to be doing okay."

Jackson thought about it. He'd been out of the hospital for almost a month, and Ellery hadn't irritated the fuck out of him yet—that was promising. Ellery seemed to tolerate him… care about him.

Ellery seemed to care about him.

"Your mother gave me ice cream for my birthday," he said, the absurd emotional response not leaving him. "That was… I mean, I didn't think Lucy Satan could be sweet."

Ellery snorted. "Mother? She's manipulative as fuck. If she gave you ice cream, she wanted you to know you're her child. Fucking subtle, right?"

Jackson almost dropped the birthday card. "Why? Why would she do that? I tried to tell her, Ellery. I tried to tell her in the hospital room. I asked for money to leave you alone—remember that?"

"Yeah, Jackson—I remember telling you it wouldn't work." He sighed and leaned forward on his elbows, slapping at a mosquito. Seven o'clock—the sun was waning in the sky, and the shadows were long. "Maybe she wants the same thing I do. She wants you to be permanent in my life."

"Ice cream is going to do that?" He hated this feeling. Ellery's entire life was different than his. His family was different. And Jackson, who had been taking care of himself since… since he was a baby, was suddenly being very personally, very meticulously cared for.

All he'd done to deserve it—as far as he could see—was take advantage of Ellery Cramer's fascination for him and be a human target.

"Ice cream makes everything better," Ellery said with dignity. He sighed and stood before crouching in front of Jackson and gently shutting his computer. "C'mon, Jackson—what's it gonna hurt if a couple more people celebrate your birthday?"

Ellery's eyes were really exceptional. Big, almond-shaped, deep nut-brown—much like his hair. There were times when Jackson was just caught by them, fascinated like a cat with a laser pointer. "Ice cream?" And right there, his inner five-year-old, asking plaintively for his friend to go get ice cream with him. Like he was a real boy. He couldn't decide whether to be humiliated or proud of himself.

"Sure," Ellery whispered, reaching up to cup Jackson's cheek. He rose slowly, captured Jackson's mouth with his own, and very carefully moved the laptop to the table.

Jackson opened his mouth and allowed Ellery to sink into the kiss, sink into *him*. Their kisses always seemed to fit perfectly, and what started slowly, kindly, Ellery's attempt to comfort him for something that should not have been a wound, quickly became passionate, needy, and urgent.

Jackson shoved his hands down the back of Ellery's slacks, kneading his backside, wanting *in* his bony, stringy body, wanting that odd power he had over Jackson to keep working, to keep dragging Jackson into his little world of "normal." Ellery took care of Jackson in "normal." Mothers gave ice cream for your birthday in "normal."

Jackson could provide for his lover, give him what he needed in "normal."

"Bed," Ellery groaned into his mouth. "Bed, now."

"Bossy fucker," Jackson mumbled, but Ellery kissed the objections right out of him. When Jackson came to, Ellery was dragging him to the bedroom.

When they got there, Ellery took everything off—button-up shirt, slacks, T-shirt, underwear—and draped it gracefully over the chair in the corner. Jackson dropped his T-shirt and cargo shorts in the corner by the hamper and joined Ellery on the bed, suddenly needing more than normal. He needed *Ellery*.

"All those clothes," Jackson muttered hoarsely between kisses. "All those clothes, and I just want you naked!" He moved down Ellery's body—awkwardly, yes, because he hurt—and sucked on a tan nipple. Ellery gasped and wrapped his legs around Jackson's hips, bucking against him.

"You," Ellery gasped. "Inside me! Now!"

"Did I mention the bossy?" Jackson thought Ellery's cock looked like an ice cream cone—he wanted to lick it.

He did, from base to tip, teasing, mouthing, *enjoying*—no discomfort, no doubt existed, here in their bed. Jackson was an equal here. Jackson could *dominate* here, and Ellery, most of the time, just yielded, all his planes and angles and his sharp, shrewd mind becoming soft and pliant, open to Jackson's plunder.

"*Please*, Jackson," Ellery begged, arching into his mouth. Jackson could stroke the blond, almost invisible hair on his calves and thighs forever, but he was too busy playing with Ellery's testicles. And, oh yes, spit-slick, slippery, clenching for Jackson's attention, his entrance. He wanted Jackson there, wanted him badly, and Jackson was hungry to be part of him.

"I love it when you beg," Jackson admitted. "Beg me some more!"

Ellery fumbled over his head, finding the lubricant they kept under the pillow. "I'm begging you to put this in my asshole and nail me to the bed, dammit!"

Jackson laughed. "Counselor, I have no objection to that." He fumbled with the bottle just as Ellery wailed, "Aw, c'mon, Jackson, *fuck me*!"

Jackson breached him with two lubed fingers just to watch Ellery flail his hands and to feel him, broad and long, hitting the back of Jackson's throat. Oops! He spurted a little there. Jackson was going to have to stop playing with his toy.

He sucked one more time and pushed up, rolling off the bed. "Hands and knees," he said gruffly. There were only so many positions he could manage with his injury, and Ellery, eschewing the romantic notion that they had to be gazing into each other's eyes the whole time, preferred his hands and knees.

Except this time he didn't. This time he put his ass at the edge of the bed and grabbed his thighs.

Jackson stared at him, dismayed, and Ellery stared back. "C'mon," he dared. "Take me."

"Fine."

He wanted to be rough—but he couldn't. He never had been. And Ellery, staring at him, begging him for his heart, for his body, for his commitment and his soul, knew it.

Jackson thrust inside slowly, waiting for Ellery to stretch for him. Ellery tilted his head back, enjoying their coupling unashamedly.

Jackson loved—liked—admired that about him.

He loved sex. He never minded wanting more. He was proud of the things their bodies did, excited that climax for the two of them was never soft, never easy. It was a rolling, thrashing struggle that ended with a torrent of brilliant release.

"*Now!*" he commanded, and Jackson felt freed. He thrust his hips hard and fast, and again, the sound of their flesh slapping loud in the September twilight.

Ellery's sounds changed, became frantic, and he begged, pleaded, "Please… please… yes… harder! Harder! God, thank you! Fuck me more! Right… right… right *there*!"

His climax ripped through him, without even a hand on his cock, and the wash of bliss on his face was almost as arousing as his grip on Jackson's erection.

Jackson closed his eyes because he had to and poured his heart, his soul, his come into his lover, his one lover, who would give enough of a damn to celebrate his birthday.

Ellery groaned and wrapped his legs around Jackson's hips, while Jackson collapsed on his good arm and then rolled to the side, trying to catch his breath.

"That was—" Pant. "—unexpected."

"Yeah, you're telling me!" Ellery's chuckle sounded like pure joy.

"Is this why you wanted to celebrate my birthday?" Jackson asked, feeling playful now instead of defensive.

"Sure. But what I really wanted was ice cream after dinner."

Sure that's what he wanted. Jackson laughed anyway and kissed him, glorying when Ellery opened up for him and let him in. Jackson couldn't stop kissing him, his gift, his unexpected lover, someone who wanted him and didn't hesitate to let him know that his life on the planet was a good thing.

"We can go for ice cream afterward," he promised, kissing Ellery's neck. Ellery tilted his head back hedonistically and accepted Jackson's nibbles.

"After what?" he panted. But he was already starting to harden again, and Jackson could take him one more time or five more times or again and again and again until their hearts burst.

"After I have what I really want for my birthday," Jackson whispered, and Ellery laughed, because it was playful and pillow talk and fun.

But as they threw themselves slowly and wholeheartedly into round two, Jackson knew the truth.

Right now, making love in the evening, thinking about ice cream they'd have the *next* day after dinner—*this* was the best birthday he'd ever had.

AMY LANE is a mother of two grown kids, two half-grown kids, two small dogs, and half-a-clowder of cats. A compulsive knitter who writes because she can't silence the voices in her head, she adores fur-babies, knitting socks, and hawt menz, and she dislikes moths, cat boxes, and knuckleheaded macspazzmatrons. She is rarely found cooking, cleaning, or doing domestic chores, but she has been known to knit up an emergency hat/blanket/pair of socks for any occasion whatsoever or sometimes for no reason at all. Her award-winning writing has three flavors: twisty-purple alternative universe, angsty-orange contemporary, and sunshine-yellow happy. By necessity, she has learned to type like the wind. She's been married for twenty-five-plus years to her beloved Mate and still believes in Twu Wuv, with a capital Twu and a capital Wuv, and she doesn't see any reason at all for that to change.

Website: www.greenshill.com
Blog: www.writerslane.blogspot.com
Email: amylane@greenshill.com
Facebook: www.facebook.com/amy.lane.167
Twitter: @amymaclane

Choose your Lane to love!

Orange

Amy's

Dark Contemporary Romance

Guess who's swimming in the same pond...
FISH OUT OF WATER
Amy Lane

Fish Out of Water: Book One

PI Jackson Rivers grew up on the mean streets of Del Paso Heights—and he doesn't trust cops, even though he was one. When the man he thinks of as his brother is accused of killing a police officer in an obviously doctored crime, Jackson will move heaven and earth to keep Kaden and his family safe.

Defense attorney Ellery Cramer grew up with the proverbial silver spoon in his mouth, but that hasn't stopped him from crushing on street-smart, swaggering Jackson Rivers for the past six years. But when Jackson asks for his help defending Kaden Cameron, Ellery is out of his depth—and not just with guarded, prickly Jackson. Kaden wasn't just framed, he was framed by crooked cops, and the conspiracy goes higher than Ellery dares reach—and deep into Jackson's troubled past.

Both men are soon enmeshed in the mystery of who killed the cop in the minimart, and engaged in a race against time to clear Kaden's name. But when the mystery is solved and the bullets stop flying, they'll have to deal with their personal complications… and an attraction that's spiraled out of control.

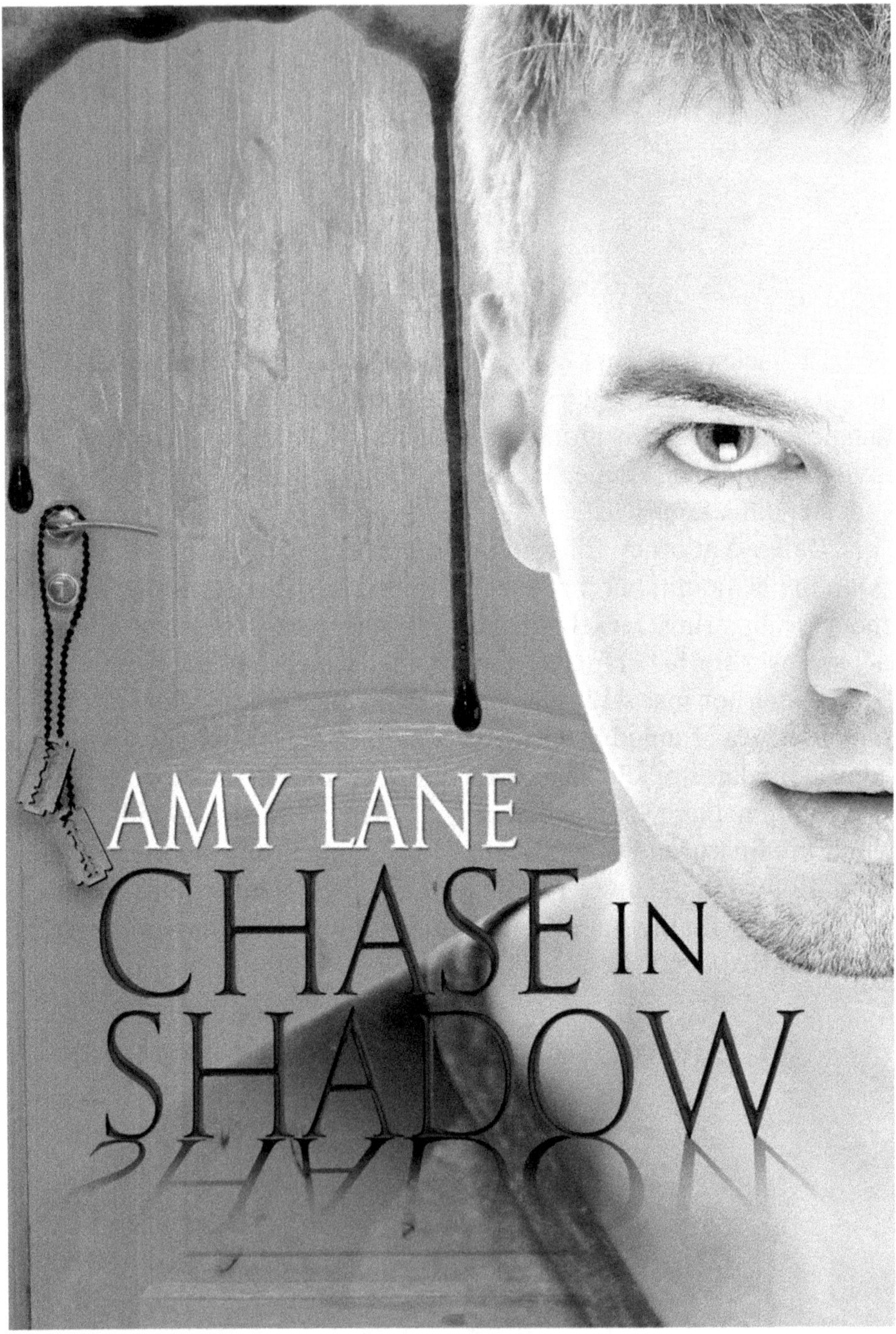

AMY LANE

CHASE IN SHADOW

Johnnies: Book One

Chase Summers: Golden boy. Beautiful girlfriend, good friends, and a promising future.

Nobody knows the real Chase.

Chase Summers has a razor blade to his wrist and the smell of his lover's goodbye clinging to his skin. He has a door in his heart so frightening he'd rather die than open it, and the lies he's used to block it shut are thinning with every forbidden touch. Chase has spent his entire life unraveling, and his decision to set his sexuality free in secret has only torn his mind apart faster.

Chase has one chance for true love and salvation. He may have met Tommy Halloran in the world of gay-for-pay—where the number of lovers doesn't matter as long as the come-shot's good—but if he wants the healing that Tommy's love has to offer, he'll need the courage to leave the shadows for the sunlight. That may be too much to ask from a man who's spent his entire life hiding his true self. Chase knows all too well that the only things thriving in a heart's darkness are the bitter personal demons that love to watch us bleed.

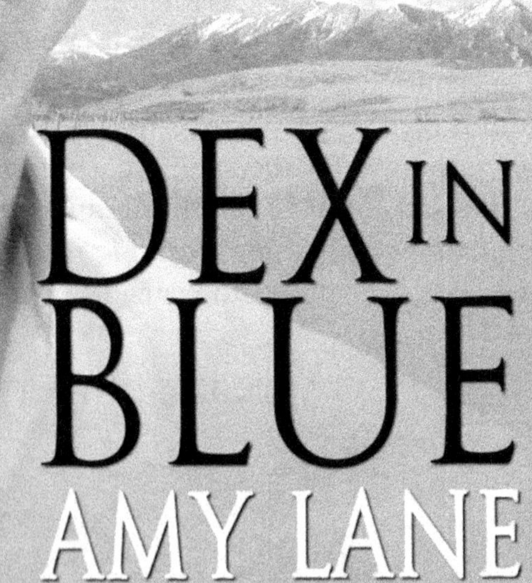
DEX IN
BLUE
AMY LANE

Johnnies: Book Two

Ten years ago David Worral had plans to go to college and the potential for a beautiful future in front of him. One tragic accident later, he fled to California and reinvented himself as Dex, top porn model of Johnnies.

Dex's life is a tangled mess now, but the guys he works with only see the man who makes them believe even porn stars can lead normal lives. When Kane, one of Dex's coworkers, gets kicked out of his house, the least Dex can do is give him a place to stay. Kane may be a hyperactive muscle-bound psycho, but he's also a really nice guy. What could be the harm?

Except nothing is simple—not sex, not love, and not the goofy kid with the big dick and bigger heart who moves his life into Dex's guest room. When they start negotiating fractured pasts and broken friends, Dex wonders if Kane's honest nature can untangle the sadness that stalled his once-promising future. With Kane by his side, Dex just might be able to reclaim the boy he once was—and if he can do that, he can give Kane the home and the family he deserves.

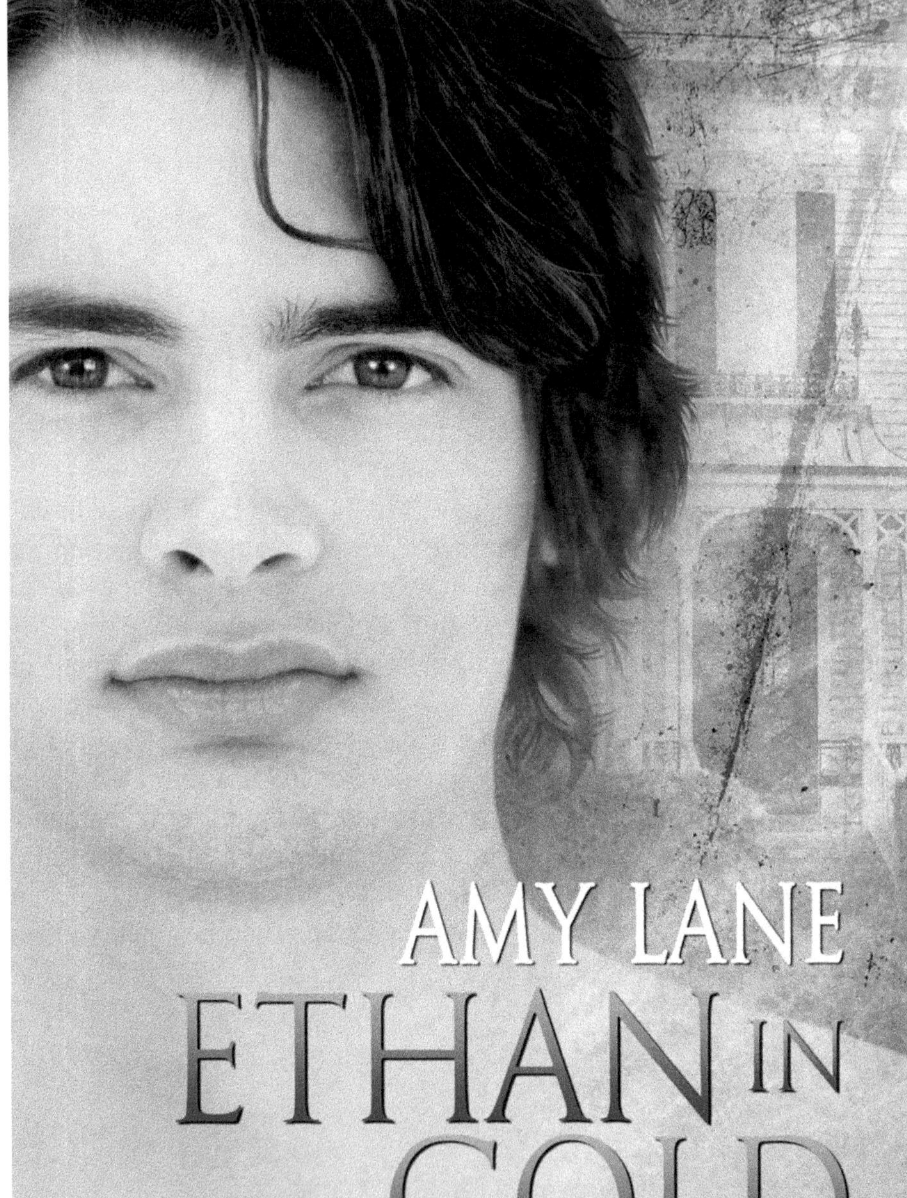
AMY LANE
ETHAN IN
GOLD

Johnnies: Book Three

Evan Costa learned from a very early age that there was no such thing as unconditional love and that it was better to settle for what you could get instead of expecting the world to give you what you need. As Ethan, porn model for Johnnies, he gets exactly what he wants—comradeship and physical contact on trade—and he is perfectly satisfied with that. He's sure of it.

Jonah Stevens has spent most of his adult life helping to care for his sister and trying to keep his beleaguered family from fraying at the edges. He's had very little time to work on his confidence or his body for that matter. When Jonah meets Ethan, he doesn't see the hurt child or the shamelessly slutty porn star. He sees a funny, sexy, confident man who—against the odds—seems to like Jonah in spite of his very ordinary, but difficult, life.

Sensing a kindred spirit and a common interest, Ethan thinks a platonic friendship with Jonah won't violate his fair trade rules of sex and touch, but Jonah has different ideas. Ethan's pretty sure his choice of jobs has stripped away all hope of a real relationship, but Jonah wants the whole package—the sexy man, the vulnerable boy, the charming companion who works so hard to make other people happy. Jonah wants to prove that underneath the damage Ethan has lived with all his life, he's still gold with promise and the ability to love.

www.dreamspinnerpress.com

www.ingramcontent.com/pod-product-compliance
Lightning Source LLC
LaVergne TN
LVHW020531100826
845148LV00010B/1423